# WHERE'S SAILOR JACK?

John Uttley was born in Lancashire just as the war was ending. Grammar school educated there, he read Physics at Oxford before embarking on a long career with the CEGB and National Grid Group. He was Finance Director at the time of the miners' strike, the Sizewell Inquiry and privatisation, receiving an OBE in 1991. Shortly afterwards, he suffered his fifteen minutes of fame when he publicly gave a dividend to charity in the middle of the fat cat furore. More recently, he has taken an external London degree in Divinity while acting as chairman of numerous smaller companies, both UK and US based. This is his first novel. He is married to Janet, living just north of London with three grown children and dog.

# WHERE'S SAILOR JACK?

John Uttley

First Published in Great Britain
by John Uttley

ISBN 978-1508966241

Cover Design by Gracie Carver
Typeset by Green Door Design for Publishing

To my family

# PROCESSIONAL

Family history only makes sense looking backwards. Yet hindsight creates illusions that defy contradiction. With a few peeks in the rear view mirror, this story must go onward and forward. But from when? The end of 1944, with the Christmas leave Petty Officer Jack Swarbrick, from St Chad's near Blackpool, and Sergeant Michael Shackleton, from Bolton, separately managed to wangle? These two guys never knew each other. The famous cup final between their two towns in Queen Elizabeth's coronation year, when Bob Swarbrick at the age of seven and a half first watched television and Richard Shackleton, two days younger, made the trip to Wembley? At that young age their illusions were of the future.

The two boys weren't to meet until forty years later, Lancastrian red roses cresting their caps, when their career paths crossed in the privatisation of Atomic Futures. Engineer Bob was Chief Executive of the company and Investment Banker Richard led the multi-billion flotation for Grindleton's. A decade further on again, the roses were beginning to wilt. Richard was struggling to keep his job after a row with his Chairman, Sir Charles Norman, coincidentally Bob's nemesis a few years previously. Their time of being in the thick of it was up. Their catch-up lunch in a dark cubicle of a dingy steak restaurant in Smithfield was subdued. That's where to begin, well through their story of life, with their dreams in the past, the back fold of the dust jacket the more practical bookmark.

Following over-generous alcohol intake in his thirties, which fortunately had left no lasting damage, Richard was teetotal. His companion had to order by the glass. Bob was morosely finishing his second. The cricket season had just finished with Lancashire again finishing runners-up. For this, Richard blamed his Dad, who'd begun the affair that wrecked his marriage back in 1950. "That's when we cocked the last game up and only shared the damn thing with Surrey. The Almighty's had it in for us ever since."

"The sins of your father shouldn't be visited on me too," felt Bob. "My Mum and Dad were happily married. Mind you, I've not been entirely blameless since Jane divorced me."

Richard confessed to transgressions in the years between, before he met his wife Helen. "It's the three of us in series that's stopped us winning it."

"Plus the fact that Manchester's monsoon season is August," Bob grouched, proud of the Fylde coast's better rainfall record than most of the county.

"And the rest of the year," added Richard, in tune with West Pennines persistent precipitation. "Any new woman in your life?"

The drab surroundings led Bob to be more downbeat than his cheerfulness usually allowed. "Not recently," he said lugubriously. "You've had it the better way round, single when young, married when knackered."

"I don't know about that. At forty, the weekend before I met Helen, I was still on my own, putting up the Christmas tree with lights, baubles, tinsel, angels and a Father Christmas."

Bob was unimpressed: "Bloody hell, you'll be telling me there was a fairy on top next."

"It was a star. Try to feel the pathos."

"No dangling chocolates?" Bob asked. "You must have been

hungry after all that emoting."

"No, I'd already eaten them."

Bob gave a wry grin. He asked Richard how he'd managed to get that far through his life without being snared. Richard admitted to being burnt by an early girlfriend, the first girl he'd made love to, who'd had him on a string for too damn long.

Bob hid well any empathy he might have felt. "I was incinerated by my first shag as well. I got her pregnant with our Ruth and married her." His eyes gazed soulfully into the distance. "Jane's still the same girl, and she sure wasn't the right one. She buggered off to live with a bloody weasel." He slowly skewered the air with his fork as he searched for the right words. "I don't think it was because either of us changed that much. The person we become in life is already in us in the womb."

"In which case, I'm going to be hanged. I was nearly strangled by the umbilical cord," Richard revealed.

"You'll be kept in suspense to the end then. Our first days were filled with utility furniture and rationing so we'll have a gloomy death," prophesied Bob, who enjoyed playing the Jeremiah. Both were deep-voiced, with Bob's rasping lead harmonising well with Richard's gravelly reflections. They'd moved about too much to retain their youthful best friends and, on an occasional basis, they'd become the brothers they'd never had to each other. Together they ran through their memories of queuing for rationed bananas in the forties, and fifties' family Christmases when the fates allowed. They reached Larkin's 1963, the de facto standard dating for the end of the old order. Bob was the rocker of the two and didn't like Elvis being from the old world. He played older brother. Richard sang the first two lines of 'Girl of my Best Friend' while he contemplated this, causing Bob to scowl. The two days age gap between them had made a difference. Bob would have sung 'Heartbreak Hotel', agreeing with John Lennon that Elvis died when he joined the army. Richard rejected Bob's earlier dating, mainly because Freewheelin' had been released not that long after the Beatles first LP, and Dylan became their main man right the way through

Bob had to agree with this. "Us darling young ones really got going then. Sex wasn't discovered that early though, whatever Larkin thought."

"Too right. Apart from reading Lady Chatterley, my hand stroking the bit of flesh at the top of Susan Harwood's stockings was about as far as I got."

You couldn't be a baby boomer, according to either of these founder members (despite statisticians making the start birth date for the category three months after they were born), unless you listened nostalgically to Buddy Holly to remember when you were learning the game.

"One way or another, we learnt it, kid," Bob was brave enough to say. Richard wasn't that cocky, not having been able to roller-skate. Bob had fewer doubts about his competence. "I never could jive. What the hell! I can do simultaneous equations."

"Did that pull the girls?" Richard enquired, eyebrows ironically raised in the middle, one of his winsome tricks. "Not in an all-boys school," Bob had to reply. Richard recalled his teenage years, when the smell of floor polish at the Church youth club, blended with a hint of disinfectant from the lavatories, competed for supremacy with the aroma of the generously-scented soap the girls had used, if sparingly, at bath time. Bob had similar memories and suggested that they both could have done with something more earthy, losing their virginity earlier.

"It's who we are," Richard propounded. "We've invented our own hinterland, a bit like Graham Greene did. Ours has never become fashionable with society girls though. It's Anglican innocence rather than Catholic guilt."

They looked up as an immaculately feather-cut blonde head giggled at what she heard as she was passing with her partner, a guy who had public school banker swagger sewn into the seams of his suit. As he chivvied her along, she planted her feet firmly down alongside the table and asked, "Still too mean for the Waterside Inn, Bob?"

The head belonged to Rebecca Moore, the very svelte, delightfully cool, former PR Director of Atomic Futures. The swaggerer was her husband rather than a business acquaintance. Despite its unpretentious name, the Inn in question is the great Roux confection on the Thames at Bray. Bob explained to Richard that Rebecca's dig was caused by a claim for a meal for two she'd put in on her expenses. Richard had eaten there too, and he said the black pudding had been nearly as good as the ones of his youth at the Art Deco UCP restaurant in Bradshawgate.

Rebecca's shining eyes tilted at his inverse snobbery. "You'd have had no idea what Art Deco was when you lived in whatever one-horse northern town that's in. You're worse than Bob. He summoned me up to his office to ask if the local Little Chef had been shut. I enjoyed telling him the Chairman had insisted that's where we were going."

Smoothie-chops husband frogmarched her to their cubicle. Bob's eyes too often looked that way over the rest of the meal. Richard had also detected that Rebecca's eyes had glowed too much while she'd been looking at Bob. He couldn't resist finding out more about the rumour that the two of them had been walking out together during the flotation. "Well, maybe," was Bob's response. Richard asked why it didn't work out seeing that they'd looked like great chums.

"She finished it," admitted Bob. "We were chatting about all this postmodern, structural stuff you intellectuals are into and she gave me a book to read. I quite liked it."

Richard was sceptical. "No, you didn't. You wanted to impress your way into her knickers."

"Don't judge me by your standards with Susan Harwood," Bob retorted. "Having offered up my innocence I got repaid with scorn, as our main man found out. I said something too concrete by way of interpretation. The look on her face came from the same pattern in her brain as when she wanted to be sick."

"Helen specialises in that look. It's generational, not personal," Richard confided unconvincingly.

Bob wasn't persuaded either. "I tried to recover by suggesting that we do have a bit of free will in the scheme of things, the way characters in a novel pull on the author. She argued that there was no author of a book at all and finished with me that evening. She married that master-of-the-universe banker she's with, who designs derivatives of derivatives, and has an even more tenuous grasp of reality than she does."

Richard guessed that the offending book was Mythologies, which he said should also be the description for derivatives on bank balance sheets. "It was a bit paradoxical if her thinking she had no agency was her reason for dumping you." He looked across towards Rebecca before carrying on with his musings. "Not that I'm sure we've any either, as you know. We can enjoy the roller coaster but have no choice where it goes. What we can do is think whatever we want to afterwards. I guess that's better than nowt."

At their age, making sense of life was mugging up for finals. Only their children and finding comfort in the love of a good woman (or failing that, in Bob's case, a bad one) mattered more. Their kids weren't in the restaurant and Rebecca was taken. Richard was about to add that you were only free when you'd nothing left to lose. He changed tack when he saw Bob again gazing in Rebecca's direction. Richard's latter-day problem was having nothing left to win. He believed that ideas didn't follow any laws but actions were dictated by them. "It's clearly a law that every ten seconds you look Rebecca's way," was the proof of his theory.

Bob guiltily shuffled around in his chair so that he couldn't see her. "You're probably right. The non-existent God plays dice and we're clutching at straws."

Richard said that conscience was the straw he grabbed at, the bit of him that didn't come either from carnal desire or the wish to conform. "If there's anything left after taking those out," he continued, "it's always too slow to change anything, and just adds to your regrets further down the line."

"Perhaps as well," said Bob. "Wasn't it free will that turned Satan to rebellion?"

Both of them were cradle Anglicans, who still honoured their faith as middle-of-the-road Churchmen. Richard needed a curator to draw, tend and nurture his spiritual world, his reality. For Bob, God had to have created the cosmos from nothing with an act of willpower or nothing could ever be changed by creator or created. Like St Paul, they'd both been untimely born. Things before Elvis had been staid, and after Sergeant Pepper they'd been stale, apart from their main man and just a few others. The rot set in according to Bob with John Lennon spending days on end in bed with Yoko. A few years later, his then wife Jane had made him listen to a Yes album. His growled view of Prog Rock that he'd rather listen to bloody Mantovani anticipated what punk rockers were also to think. Richard had tried to join in the seventies by growing a Jason King moustache, which he'd never quite managed to get the same length either side. He'd worn the polyester suits too, but they'd made his underpants stick to his bollocks. When the women's movement and disco music came along, white, non-jiving, northern males were what they replaced first. The grammar schools coming and going had cut the two of them adrift permanently from the previous and following generations, by first educating them and then having them think it meant something.

The waiter came and took orders for two tarte Tatins and coffees. Neither cared that much for tatty tart, and wouldn't pretend they preferred rock-hard fruit in puff pastry to sweet, mashed-up Bramleys in a shortcrust. When the bill arrived, Richard put down his company credit card. Bob threw it back to him, saying it was his turn to pay. Richard insisted: "Take it. You've earned enough money for Grindleton's in your time."

"It doesn't sound from what you've said that you'll be there much longer. Once the press have got hold of a Board Room row, someone has to go. As Charlie's the other guy involved, that's you."

Richard had recently refused a bonus, saying it was too generous, and the incident had reached the FT Diary Column. So when the waiter eventually came, Bob didn't mind that Grindleton's paid. Outside the restaurant, a dense black cloud was approaching from the north-west.

"That sky looks ominous," warned Richard as he checked that his umbrella was in his briefcase. Bob raised his collar. "Aye, it'll rain, snow or go dark before morning. Good seeing you again, pal. Maybe one day the Lord will forgive and Lancashire can win it."

"Next year in Jerusalem," Richard hoped, expecting the wait to be another two millennia. "You're looking a bit flushed. Are you OK health-wise, cocker?"

"It's just the red wine. I'm fit as a fiddle. I need a change of scenery and I'm looking at houses back up in St Chad's. I'll be right as rain once I've moved back."

Richard left Grindleton's within a month of the lunch. He and Helen were comfortably off with substantial savings tied up in investments. He couldn't be bothered to sort all that out, and there were mouths to feed, human, canine and feline, so he'd lined up a role with Divinity Partners before resigning. He refused a generous termination pay-off on principle.

In the next spring, 2007, Bob moved his main home to a solid Edwardian semi-detached house about a quarter of a mile from St Chad's square, keeping his London flat for business needs. He and his sister had grown up in the square, along with their dog Rover, above the ironmonger's store his parents had owned. It had become an off licence. Even so, his return gave him the air he needed, the soft rustle of trees, the cool smell of the dark evening, and the warm afternoon dampness of Fylde fields gently blowing in from the River Wyre. He couldn't pin down who he was but he did know where he was from.

# CHAPTER ONE

On a Sunday soon after his move north-west, Bob was flying high on Virgin, to LAX, as everyone but he knew Los Angeles airport was called. His last long-haul flight had been on Atomic Futures' business in the bulkhead with British Airways. At over six foot and heavily built, he could make good use of the leg room. In an unflattering lavatory mirror, he saw receding, greying hair and many wrinkles above a jaw line a boxer could break a fist on. He'd never quite understood how his rugged looks had charmed the several-to-many women along the way. The seating arrangement in Virgin's best seats made the cabin look like a beauty salon, but he'd played safe and eschewed the offer of an on-board facial. The Journey Information on the monitor told him there was about an hour of the flight to go, confirmed by something looking like the Grand Canyon out of the window, though it looked bleak enough to have been the surface of another planet.

He was trying not to sleep on the way out, nor to go to bed until at least ten o'clock Pacific Standard Time. He'd flicked between the films on the in-flight entertainment system, and found nothing he'd wanted. He'd then settled down to listen to some music, first Elvis, then Ray Charles and finally Abba, who'd bounced along merrily at first until a cold sweat told him that he was the loser standing small alongside seventies woman. He switched Agnetha off to pick up the book he'd brought, Ian McEwan's Saturday, which he immediately put down again. His eyes were tired.

He reclined the chair to be alone with his musings on his return to Lancashire. Blackpool was making a good fist of doing itself up, despite New Labour lousing up the Las Vegas style casino scheme, not that he'd ever really wanted it. In the evenings, the place was alive with young ladies joyfully, sometimes even decorously, celebrating their hen nights with like-minded friends. The folk who lived in St Chad's hadn't changed that much. The young people at church had the same freshness that he'd once had, full of their multimedia world and excited about their opportunities, though the ladder had been pulled up since his day, leaving cows from the Fylde fields with more chance of going through the eye of a needle than any ordinary kid entering the kingdom of riches he'd inherited. Lancashire wasn't at the centre of things the way it had been back then, with Blackpool the Mecca for comedians, Liverpool the capital of music, the mighty Granada television like a second BBC, and the Manchester Guardian thinking about what the world would do tomorrow. He saw The Guardian moving to London as an even bigger betrayal than John Lennon's sleep-in.

The summer of 1963 with Freewheelin' on his turntable and the Mersey sound on every radio was forever to remain his Archimedean point. Martin Luther King was dreaming his dream accompanied vibrato by Joan Baez and civil rights were coming. Bras weren't being burnt though. Much later Jane challenged him with why not. He'd answered that women's liberation hadn't come out of nowhere. She'd generously agreed that it was only fair for apes like him to have had their day in the sun before the real business got done.

He'd had a vacation job in Stanley Park and that had given him an affinity with the old codgers from the Great War who came for the brass band concerts. Though they were sitting in God's waiting room, they were cheerful, talking for hours about space travel and the like but not of course about their health problems or the trenches. He thought of his never-liberated Grannie who died at the start of the pivotal year. She'd make him green jelly with bananas whenever he went round as a kid and had knitted most of the jumpers he was still wearing through university after her death. His sister had in her kitchen the old milking stool from Grannie's farm-girl days, with more than a thousand years of history stored in its battered wood. Like the religion his ancestors had shared, its purpose had been endorsed by the long passage of time. To lose either would be to lose his soul. He didn't want to live so long that his memory of Grannie dimmed.

He was off to LA to discuss the possibility of him chairing a solar technology company, The Northern Solstice Inc., looking to be floated on AIM, the small companies' part of the London Stock Exchange. He'd created a portfolio of non-executive chairmanships since his nuclear demise; nice work if you can get it, he'd say. He'd had surprising success given that he was temperamentally stuck somewhere between public and private sector. On one venture, he'd helped rescue a telecoms company after the dotcom bubble burst, which he'd then sold to a trade buyer, a conglomerate chaired by Sir Charles, for a huge profit, a month before the market fell again. He'd found that the private sector was about living on your wits rather than on solid ground.

He hadn't much knowledge of solar economics or if it was such a good environmental thing. He hoped that this opportunity could provide some atonement for his past environmental sins. As a nuclear man, he'd never been a denier of the greenhouse effect. He knew how expensive nuclear had been but could see no better option despite his lingering doubts on waste disposal, weapons proliferation and operational balls-up issues. He was as antagonistic towards wind power as most power engineers and ornithologists were.

The invitation to LA had come from a woman he'd got to know at Black and Robertshaw, an accounting firm working out of Bristol whose corporate finance arm had handled the telecoms sale. They were advising on the Northern Solstice flotation, acting as Nomad – shorthand for nominated adviser. Wendy Ballinger was already in LA and he was to meet her the next day with the acting Chairman and the CEO.

In the arrivals hall, the driver arranged by Virgin was holding up his name. All upper class passengers could have a limo for up to an hour's journey. Anaheim was in the band. He was stopping at the Stonehaven there, near to the Northern Solstice factory in Yorba Linda as well as close to Disney. Wendy was upmarket and uptown, staying at the Westin. His mobile beeped a message as he reached his room. Wendy wanted a word. He was desperate for the lavatory, but couldn't prevent himself from ringing her first. As he waited for her to answer, her face appeared in front of him on the screen in his brain (not on his phone, that was an early, basic model), almost elegant, with a distinguished nose. Her blonde hair looked natural enough but did owe something to a bottle. He found her both friendly and competent, a pleasure to do business with. She was a while answering and his internal camera panned slowly downwards. In her early forties, married without children to an older man, her bosom was worthy of the name; her long legs went all the way to her not insubstantial bum. And she was intelligent. He should have thought of that first.

She had bad news, disclosed in pure, gentle, Gloucestershire tones that could have belonged to a sixth former. She'd been at a pre-meeting with the acting Chairman, a guy called Peter Forster, along with the CEO, Emil Fares. Forster was a hard-nosed South African who owned Forster Capital, the largest shareholder. He'd told Wendy that they didn't want her to handle the listing as Black and Robertshaw had no market strength.

Bob wanted to ask if that meant he'd wasted his time coming out, and if somebody would be reimbursing his expenses, but realised he'd better sympathise first. She didn't need that, believing that her firm, although not a strong broking house, had done a pretty good job. "No first division broker would handle such a small transaction," she asserted. "And there's so little time before the date they want to float that they'd like to take a look at you. They'll also want to know if you've any other ideas as to who else could act as Nomad."

"I'd have no idea. I wouldn't want the job now anyway," he said, honestly enough as Wendy was a big part of the attraction.

"That's up to you, but I'd be grateful for my reputation if you could hear them out. Perhaps Divinity might do it. They're pitching hard into renewables."

Bob became more interested. "Fancy that. An old friend of mine from my nuclear days, Richard Shackleton, told me over a round of golf that he'd just joined Divinity Partners. He said it was about time the Godhead had some new blood. Do you know him?"

Wendy did know Richard, who she called a terrific bloke. "Hey, thee, me and him could make a great team if they'd have us," Bob reckoned. "Can't we get him to do the broking and you to be the Nomad?" Wendy doubted Forster would agree to that idea but was happy for Bob to try it on.

Bob was already looking forward to Richard joining them and started to tell Wendy about his daft ideas. "Like me, he doesn't think metaphysics should be a dry study of what can and can't be said, but a licence to think insanely. According to him, we can't actually change anything physical and all events rigidly follow the laws of nature. But we are free to make whatever we want of what happens. I remember a flotation meeting with loads of advisers. We took time out to discuss Schrödinger's cat, as you do. Richard..."

"As you and Richard do, you mean. Tell me about that some other

20

time," she interrupted. "George Coulson, the CFO, will be in the hotel lobby at nine o'clock to collect you. We're meeting in Emil's office at nine thirty."

Having at last managed to have a pee, he unpacked his case, lining up one shirt and tie, his suit, a pair of socks and shoes for the morning. He put pyjamas on the pillow, soap bag and razor in the bathroom, Saturday and the alarm clock by his bed, before he had had a quick shower, drenching the bathroom floor. At a quarter past nine PST, twenty two hours since leaving his London flat, he went to bed.

He quickly went to sleep, only to wake with a start at about two o'clock, gasping for breath. The heavy quilt was over his head. He pulled the quilt halfway down the bed and managed to sleep again. An hour later he woke again. This time he turned the air conditioning off. Sleep wouldn't come. He tried to read for a while, propped up against the pillows. In the big mirror on the opposite wall, he caught sight of his gaunt face drained of colour. With a shock, he realised he was looking at his Dad, Jack Swarbrick, laid out at the funeral parlour. That Swarbrick big conk was a matter of pride.

Of course it wasn't his Dad, but the embodiment of hard-wired genetics. Wendy's face, and much prettier conk, had frozen on his internal screen. He slept through till 6.30am with her in view.

## CHAPTER TWO

J ane still shared with Andrew the house in Mossley Hill she'd moved to some twenty-five years before. She hadn't been blessed with further offspring, which wasn't altogether surprising to Bob, given that polecats and weasels can't breed together. Andrew had recently retired as head teacher of a community comprehensive school. Jane, eight years younger, was professor of sociolinguistics at Mount Vernon University, the study of the relationship between language and society. Jane specialised in research on gender differences in workplace speech. Bob's definition of her expertise was the humiliation of males without anaesthetic or the right of appeal. But to be fair, Jane had a carrycot beside her on a Saturday as she read The Female Eunuch while studying for her degree. Bob was out playing cricket.

As he was talking to Wendy on the phone in LA, Monday started in Liverpool with Jane late out of the bathroom after problems with the soap holder in the shower. This was meant to be held in place by suction pads, but they sucked insufficiently and an almost full shampoo bottle was deposited onto her toes. She wrote mocking comments in her diary about how Bob had once carefully drilled a screw hole for a similar holder, through sellotape to prevent any crack in the tile, before dropping his drill and chipping the enamel tray. But her final words on the subject were, "At least he tried."

While she ate her breakfast, Andrew stared out of the window at the birds rather than reading The Guardian he was holding. This was worthy of diary comment as his utopia had never needed a bird table, nut feeder or tits. When the kids were young, Bob had spent hours on elaborate schemes to stop squirrel raids. Unsuccessfully, according to Jane, as she sided with Andrew in this entry, complaining of how the dawn chorus kept her awake, and pondering if the damned things stopped singing once they'd found a mate. She finished with the unkind thought of Bob chirping into the evening right the way through to autumn.

She'd then heard a loud crash from the kitchen, a bang followed by a series of clatters, each seeming an echo of the last. As far as she could tell, it wasn't a poltergeist. The metal tea caddy had fallen off a top shelf because, struggling to reach, she'd left it too near the edge. The caddy had slid through the open cupboard door, knocked into the kitchen roll holder on the work surface below which had then banged into the china biscuit barrel. This had acquired enough momentum to crash to the floor, finding its state of lowest potential energy (as she could hear a 'Bob' in her head saying) after it had shattered into many pieces. She'd had to apologise to Andrew as the barrel had been a wedding present from his sister. He'd reacted with his customary eye-rolling routine. She'd found the dustpan herself, hearing 'Bob' yet again philosophising about the direction of time being that of increasing entropy. She disagreed with that. She could bring order from chaos. Or, as the real Bob had said in one of their many rows, stamp her pre-conceived notions on the world. She did like to think that language could change society as much as society changed language.

She quickly made a cheese and coleslaw sandwich and dashed to her car parked in the drive, a beaten-up MX5. Through the window, she saw Andrew get out of his chair to go to a similar room to the one that, thousands of miles away, Bob was also trying to reach. She didn't know until later that Andrew's problem wasn't with the Guardian editorial or birds singing. There was blood in his stools not caused by piles. He was muttering a resigned, "Heigh-ho."

Jane was giving a lecture to a feminist summer school, followed by a class with some of her post graduate students. In the previous day's diary, she'd castigated Andrew for loafing about the house in his slippers and suave dressing gown. She'd written that, for all the good he'd done, he might just as well have been Noel Coward presenting crazy reactionary views to his confused pupils rather than teaching his preposterous revisionist crap. They'd met as she'd been about to cross a picket line during the winter of discontent. Fatefully, she'd turned and stopped to talk. Under her influence, he'd wholeheartedly embraced child-centred approaches to teaching. In later years he'd adopted soothing, caring tones so that 'patronising' was her adjective of choice for him. She preferred the self-sufficient arrogance of the tall, wiry picket, except when he tried and failed to be like his heroes, intellectuals from the beat generation. Existence precedes essence, we're self-made, he'd argued in an early dispute between them, adding snidely that she hadn't made much progress to date.

Neither's working-class credentials were legitimate anyway as far as Bob was concerned. Andrew was from Southport, the smartest town in Lancashire until placed in the newly created Merseyside as part of Edward Heath's eccentric reforms. Andrew had been one of the few daft enough to welcome that change. Jane was from similarly affluent Knutsford in Cheshire, which sensibly stayed out of the clutches of Manchester.

As she pulled up in the departmental car park, Pratap Dongre, one of her older post grads, greeted her. He was a handsome guy and a good student, if a bit over-literal, keen to please, with white flashing eyes and impeccable manners. If she'd said he'd got the wrong end of the stick, he'd ask where the stick was. He wanted advice on the direction of his research and they arranged to meet in her office at lunch. In her class, she was less on her high feminist horse than usual, hedging her assertions. She didn't know why. Even Bob wouldn't have her abandon her feminism, though asking his advice would be similar to asking Dawkins for his views on Anglican liturgy. He'd have some interesting ideas without being quite the one to chair the working party.

Pratap was waiting outside her office. Feeling hungry, she ate her sandwich as discreetly as possible while letting him talk, wishing she'd brought some cake too. 'Bob' was saying that he could eat a scabby donkey. She learnt that Pratap lived with a younger girl from Australia who was too possessive and hit him quite regularly. He wouldn't retaliate. She moved on to the problem with his research.

"It's the data collection, Professor," he told her. "We're too far from India to have insight into the language used by the different castes. I've tried with Hindus here but they become westernised quickly. It would be better if I could go home to Kolkata for a few months."

Jane agreed that he would benefit from real Indian fieldwork and promised to see if the department could find the necessary funds for him to go back in the holidays. She thought that he needed a break from his aggressive partner anyway. Most post-grads called her Jane without asking and she suggested he do likewise.

"They do not give you the respect that you deserve," he replied in all seriousness. "I shall only call you Jane if you do me the honour of signing my copy of your magnificent text book." He carefully stressed each word as though reading from a sacred text. She realised that Pratap had taken more than a shine to her. He produced a well-thumbed tome from his briefcase. She wrote, 'To Pratap, with best wishes, Jane Burrows,' in her best handwriting. She used her maiden name at work, and for her publications. Suspecting he was lonely, she asked what other friends and interests he had in Liverpool. She was partly right, though he did play squash and he'd found a meditation centre.

"How interesting! I've always intended to give meditation a go, but never got round to it," she lied.

"You're one of the few lecturers here who isn't prejudiced against religious discourse. Are you a practising Christian?"

"Not now, I'm afraid, Pratap. The church is against too many things, feminism, homosexuality and the like, and I've found it easier to drop the whole idea of God."

Pratap accepted that Hinduism could also get too theistic and too noisy. Buddhism could take the Gods out of the narrative, replacing them with a deep silence, he said. He was looking at her too intently to suggest he'd found an inner peace. She asked why he put up with his girlfriend's violence.

He grinned sheepishly, shrugging his shoulders. "She's a lovely girl when she's nice."

So the girl was a good lay at least, guessed Jane. "But when she is bad she is horrid," was what she said. She decided to tease him no longer, at least for the time being. "I'd better be going, Pratap. I've a mound of ironing to do at home and we've a reception with the Vice Chancellor this evening. I don't like to advise people on their personal affairs, but if you were a woman telling me this tale, I'd be advising you to leave."

Promising to email Pratap about the funds, she made for the car. The Head of Psychology, Geoffrey Parkinson, was leaving at the same time. "You look lovelier every day," he simpered "Does Andrew know how lucky he is?" Soon after marrying Andrew, she'd had a brief affair with Geoff. She agreed to postpone the delights of ironing for those of the pub. Once the drinks were on the table, Geoff carried on where he'd left off. "Did your first husband not appreciate you either?"

She hoped 'Bob' hadn't got into Geoff's head as well. "Mainly it was me not appreciating him, Bob Swarbrick. He became CEO of Atomic Futures. He wasn't a bone-headed engineer and was very open to ideas. But there are the two cultures, the scientists and the humanities. He was with the losers."

"I'm on both sides of that debate. Your side may have exposed the emptiness at the heart of theory, but you've, we've, replaced it with nothing," he humbly observed.

"We've had a good time. Andrew has his left-wing views but I can humour those."

Geoff didn't like Andrew too much. "That can't be easy. Whenever I meet him, he has this turgid need to fulfil some clanking metaphor of having iron in his self-created soul."

Jane smiled. "Yeah, he reviews his progress on that every day in the mirror as he shaves. But Bob refused to join the zeitgeist. When my sister Mary enlisted into the burgeoning ranks of social workers in the early seventies, he said to her face that they'd do more harm than good. 'Grammar school snots patronising sec mod kids who can manage on their own,' were his actual words."

Bob's views on that didn't change much with the years. As Geoff went for more drinks, in her head she was viewing Bob's real face, his defeated face, outside the divorce court. The last time they'd met he'd told her how his old friends all seemed to have retired and moved to Kendal with their first wife and second dog, a Wainwright's World theme park with laconic text and lovely drawings. He could see through what he'd preferred to stay with, but stay with them he had. Geoff returned, slopping the drinks on the beer mats, finding her deep in thought. He asked if she was thinking of Andrew or Bob.

"Bob. I do more nowadays. He wasn't a bad guy and he was the father of my kids," she admitted, more to herself than to Geoff.

"You see yourself hip and him a hick. Probably that's how you see me too."

Jane was gratified that Geoff was still carrying a torch, but wanted to keep him at a distance, for the time being at least. "You've never played in the same league as my previous or present husband, sweetheart. I did love Bob, while resenting that I had to marry him because I was pregnant."

Geoffrey bravely continued with his enquiries. "How soon before you were unfaithful? I know from personal experience that it didn't take that long after you married Andrew."

"Get it, will you? You were never any big deal. Bob was the only man I'd ever made love to until I met Andrew," she snapped.

"I remember you being very familiar with a young man at a student party in Tue Brook," Geoff persisted.

Jane was disturbed as well as annoyed. "Were you there that night? Are you some weird kind of stalker? You were a lecturer by then, for God's sake. I'd found a baby sitter for once. I smoked some pot, drank too much and then snogged John Westwood. In the nick of time, I made an excuse and left."

"I know. I opened the front door for you. The party was at my house."

Jane grinned ruefully. "I'd forgotten that, my plumpish little guardian angel. Maybe someday I'll need you again. Do you still know John? He's a sociobiologist in the US now. I meet him occasionally at conferences and it's still unconsummated."

"I've met him once or twice. Was Bob resentful of your academic success?"

Jane still didn't know. "I can remember the shock on his face when I snook a first. But he switched to delight almost immediately."

When she'd left Bob, he'd accused her in his rage of not existing, because she couldn't be constant about anything. That sounded worse than jealousy. Not only did she not have an essence according to Andrew, but Bob didn't even think she existed. She'd always thought that he confused existence with free will. She had no such problems. Humans had coined the word 'exist', and whatever they used it for was what 'existence' was. Bob had unsuccessfully argued that not to work for a dog.

She'd had enough of Geoff's questions and told him he'd be a terrible practising psychiatrist. "You're not always that likeable, you know, Jane, much as I adore you," was his frustrated parting shot. Her diary was reflective of why Geoff had said that. However hard she tried, she divided people. People liked or loathed her.

Andrew was still with The Guardian, working on the crossword when she arrived home. He turned away as she tried to kiss him. She told him about this Indian student whose Aussie girlfriend was beating him up, and who wouldn't retaliate. She noticed that he was trembling as he discussed the issue in terms of their behaviour echoing the two country's post-colonial legacies before returning to his crossword.

She assumed wrongly his tremble had come from self-righteous anger. She did half an hour's ironing before going upstairs to Skype Ruth, her first child with Bob, and to watch baby Ben gurgle, She asked Ruth if she'd seen her Dad recently. After Ruth's snide remark that if she really cared she'd phone him herself, she gleaned that he'd dropped in on his way down to London a couple of days before. He was off to Los Angeles for some business. She'd asked if he was wanted in the movies; a remake of The Misfits maybe?

Jane and Bob had swapped phone details at Ben's christening. Over the last few hours he'd been in her head like a maggot in an apple. She had an impulse to talk to him, whatever the cost of ringing a mobile in LA. Once she'd worked out that it would be about eight o'clock in the morning in California, she hit the call button. There was a gruff,

"Hello," after the transatlantic pause. Bob usually spoke in an unhurried voice formed from the straightforward vowels of the Fylde, but the surprise call in his hotel room had him worried that something was up. Jane reassured him quickly with a lie. "No, I was ringing up to have family talk with you. Ruth tells me you're flying to Los Angeles next week. What's that all about?"

"I'm there now. Do you want me to ring you back?" he volunteered.

Jane wasn't a cheapskate. She refused his offer. She did discuss children and grandchildren first while she tried to understand why she'd rung him. Bob was fond of his grandchildren too. "Tom's been in the Under 11 cricket team, did you hear? And what about young Rachel? She's a talkative one. I wonder which grandmother she takes after."

"Watch it, buster. I've got an old friend who's a sociobiologist in LA. I wish I was there with you."

This last bit was true but Bob was the one on her mind. He didn't realise this and even if he had he would have thought it safer to focus on the other guy. He asked, "What on earth is sociobiology?"

"If you need to ask the question, you wouldn't understand the answer."

That was Jane through and through, followed by Bob at his best. "You mean you don't know either. Is he an international conference acquaintance, David Lodge style?"

She changed the subject quickly, moving to another potential trouble spot, the Indian student who was being beaten up by his girlfriend. "I somehow can't see anyone ever having done that to you," she sniggered.

"You might be right there. I guess it's the pacifist ideas, it would be wrong to retaliate. One Indian guy I knew said it was the vegetarian thing in Hindus; they don't eat much meat. That's why the Pakistanis have the better fast bowlers."

She remembered how her mother had found him coarse. "So you'd advise him to eat cold steak and kidney pies for breakfast like you used to do when I met you."

"Yeah. And then next time she does it, to pull her knickers down and smack her arse."

Jane surprisingly didn't choose to view this as an act of male aggression. As if she'd missed out, she murmured, "You never did that to me."

"I should've done; anyway you never hit me."

"I should've done. You always left me to do the telling off with the children."

Bob couldn't resist the remark he knew he could soon be regretting, "You were so much better at it than me."

But Jane pulled her punches after setting up the attack. "Half the time you were missing at one or other power station, or playing cricket somewhere. At least that's what I used to think. But I can remember how much help you gave with my first book."

"Not that you took much notice. You always wrote the opposite of what I suggested," he recalled.

She gave him a compliment. "No, I didn't. We were a near miss, but a miss is as good as a mile. I'll concede you did have a certain je ne sais quoi."

"Je ne sais what?"

She even had the grace to laugh at being slightly bested. "Now this Indian guy meditates, he contemplates the nothingness at the heart of his existence. Is that perfection?"

"Before all this stuff about string theory, which I never can quite get, a guy at Atomic Futures would tell me about particles and antiparticles springing in and out of existence from nothing. There's always summat and nowt there."

"I could have told them all that but I'm clever enough to get string theory. I bet you don't know how long the piece of string is," said Jane, knowing why she'd rung. She'd been missing any decent verbal sport recently.

"About the Planck length, I guess," he tentatively ventured.

He'd left himself wide open. There were three rules to word games with Jane which mirrored thermodynamics. You can't win. You can't break even. You can't leave the game. He'd walked straight into her haymaker. Jane was exultant that he'd admitted he was as thick as one short plank, if not two, condemned from his own mouth. He tried to recover by stating that he wasn't that daft as the string had no thickness at all but oscillated in ten spatial dimensions, reckoning her backside also wiggled in the other seven as well as the normal three. He paid full attention to a posteriori views of his women. Jane was flattered, but she'd counted him out before the cheeky remarks. She remembered how he'd used to think that a photon of quantum uncertainty could be sent from the spirit to the brain by human will. She told him that was old hat. The science guys at her university didn't believe all that uncertainty poppycock and thought that every possibility that could happen did do in parallel multiverses.

Bob hated these ideas but wanted though to show Jane how broad-minded he was.

"Maybe somewhere out there you and I are living together in married bliss," he mused. She excluded this on a priori grounds, not believing they'd made the grade in any universe. She then wanted to know if there was anything new in his life, clearly meaning a new woman. He answered that there wasn't, but not for the want of trying. She liked this answer and reverted to sweetness. "Come on, most women would have you like a shot. You're too picky,"

"Only the unsuitable ones. I embarrass myself when I remember some of them."

She genuinely wondered if that included her. He said she was top of every list, including that one. Their goodbyes were friendly.

While she was upstairs on the phone, Andrew was wishing that he could be easier in conversation with her, thinking how his superior attitude didn't wash. His stomach churned at the thought of the greatest humiliation in life. A couple of years after Jane and children had moved in, they'd banned Ruth from going to church and youth club on Sunday evening after she'd returned home late too often. Bob happened to be in Lancashire that next Sunday after visiting his parents and dropped in to go to church with her.

After the initial glacial politeness, Andrew had slipped his leash first, calling Bob a coward for clinging to his religion when he must know it was incoherent. Bob in reply had accused Andrew of treachery towards his roots, saying that religion was at least interesting, whereas socialism made everyone bloody miserable. Andrew hadn't been able to stop himself saying that Bob was the miserable one, unable to adjust to human realities like losing his wife. Bob, displaying a yobbish side to his character he only very occasionally found a need for, had grabbed Andrew by the collar and smashed him into the wall. Andrew had been rescued, if that was the right word, by Ruth shouting, "Don't hit him, Dad, he's not worth it." Jane had been struck motionless by Bob's aggression, their younger child Robert spellbound.

Andrew shivered at the memory of their insolent swagger as they'd walked off to church. He thought of the incident often, each successive time a further hammer blow nailing down the coffin lid on this marriage. A few months later, there'd been a triumphal, ugly victory roll. Robert had his BMX stolen after foolishly leaving it outside the park unlocked. He'd been told he couldn't have a new one until his birthday. The next weekend Bob had knocked at the door with the latest model.

Andrew hadn't been reading The Guardian all morning. He'd been to the doctor's surgery about his problem. That's why he'd been shivering. He said nothing about it to Jane and bravely managed the VC's reception. He looked like death on the journey home, and went straight to bed. Jane wrote up her diary first. Her diaries were meticulous all the way back to her sixth form days. As she joined him in bed, his eyes were open wide as if he'd seen a ghost.

"Jane, I might have some bad news. I've been to Dr Duncan today and he's referred me to the Royal. It may be nothing but he wants me to have some blood tests."

Jane found it difficult to sleep that evening. She couldn't understand why she felt so excited.

# CHAPTER THREE

The slow passage of time that Monday was marked by the ticking of Richard's antique clocks at the Shackletons' house. They'd lived in this rambling, sixteenth century cottage in the Hertfordshire village of Monkey Mead since they'd married some twenty years previously. The village like so many close to London had expanded in an asymmetric bubble, with shiny, unhappy people in top City jobs driving out the older middle class unused to moisturising products from the best houses. Back office staff occupied the new estate. At the church, a trainee minister, not having much luck with his attempts to engage, noted that the people were very arrived. "Arriviste more like," Richard had replied.

Hummills was bathed in sunshine that afternoon. Both parents had taken the afternoon off for Amy's birthday tea. Helen was supervising Amy while reading a magazine. Amy, the result of a delightful mistake and six this day, was tirelessly climbing up and sliding down the 'water chute', a construction in which the bottom end of a plastic slide had been placed into a paddling pool. On the other side of the garden, a ferocious game of cricket was being played. Matthew, aged twenty, Laura, sixteen, and James, twelve, were in action, as well as Trotter the Border Collie, who was fielding at mid-off. Matthew had recently come back for the summer from Leeds where he was studying Civil Engineering. Laura and James had arrived home half an hour before, day pupils from the independent school that Matthew had previously attended. Amy went to the local state primary. Helen and Richard had considered state secondary education, but not for long. She'd been privately educated anyway. He'd agonised for a bit. Then they'd trooped round the open evening at the designated concrete comprehensive. The open day at the independent school was like going back to his direct-grant grammar – an academic ethos, school chapel and, better still, football rather than rugby. His social justice scruples had been set aside, to resurface whenever he encountered plummy arrogance, when he would worry that his children might also not appreciate that they weren't worth what they'd got. He knew that it was only his own innate ability to blag that had made him rich.

The garden was looking pretty good. When they'd first moved in, Richard had planted magnolias, camellias and a wisteria over an old arbour as he went for a mansion-look commensurate with his inflated salary. He'd since changed tack to covering every bit of bare soil with traditional plants, cottage-style, matching his choice of dog. Keeping the proportion of plants to weeds by surface area at greater than one was the fresh challenge, so he was weeding while everyone else played. He'd a hoe and trowel by the wheelbarrow but was using his bare hands. Gardening with gloves on was like making love with a condom, he'd say, justifying his carelessness of six years, nine months ago. Chloe the cat was skulking in the bushes, and he was also keeping look-out on behalf of the robin helping him weed.

The more prosaic Helen had taken it on herself to re-design the front garden, including a carriage drive and the inevitable block paving, with his silence deemed as acquiescence. "Alleluia, what a paviour," had been his comment as he surveyed the desecration. He'd wanted cobbles but then he'd have preferred the M61 cobbled through Bolton. Inside the house was an eclectic mix of styles or a hotchpotch, depending on whether Richard was talking to a guest or to Helen. There were antiques from his single days and traditional furnishings reflecting her tastes.

Richard was of average height and build. He still retained the round, handsome features which had a fair number of women eating out of his hand throughout his life too. He'd looked like a pop star in his youth, blond with big blue eyes. His hair, by this stage silver, was in the same style as forty years ago. He believed it theologically unsound to use hair dye. His Bolton accent with its homely, complex vowels was still strong. His bass tones were used to full effect with a, "Hello, I'm Johnny Cash," whenever one of the great man's songs was played. Helen, who hadn't done time at Folsom Prison, was bemused by this, although when in vino she'd shoot his sacred cows just to watch them die.

She was a vet, blessed with great beauty. Her soul wasn't a perfect form of the body but wasn't that far off. Her firm face, more triangular than oval, was animated by pale blue eyes and lush eyebrows capable of displaying pleasure or irritation from a minimum of movement. Whereas Richard was an endomorph, she was a mesomorph, and a fit one at that. Her hair was a natural silver blonde and, unlike Richard's, not courtesy of advancing years. When still, she looked cool and calm; animated, her facial lines were welcoming and warm. She's still like that. There were and are exceptions. If she loses her temper, not an infrequent occurrence, she's simultaneously a mix of ice and fire, a battle-maiden on the way to Valhalla.

Nearly fifteen years younger than Richard, she'd been brought up in a Sussex village. Her adoptive parents, Bernard and Elizabeth Durell, had slowly slid down the wealth league table during her life. Her father was a gentle soul who toiled to little effect as an artist, mainly in watercolours. Her mother had never worked. Down there was another world to Richard. Subtleties existed in manners he'd not encountered even at Oxford. He complained when he first visited that he'd had to ask at the baker's for a croque monsieur and a millefeuille rather than a ham sandwich and a vanilla slice.

He purposefully pushed his full wheelbarrow over to the compost. On the way back, as he glanced at a haunted looking curly willow, he shuddered at the thought of Hummills falling apart the way his Bolton home had. Far from the twisted reach of crazy sorrow, or so he hoped, he was deliberately reliving the fifties here, a golden age before Catharine and Michael, his parents, split up, his older sister Carol left home and Nell, the family dog, died. Michael made the first switch from working-class, reaching management ranks in Bolton Town Hall. They'd moved to Bromley Cross when Richard was eight, the year after that Cup Final. "Them's gentry houses," was what his Grandma had said. Carol and Nell loved the extra space. But his bedroom Wonderwall of two items from the old terraced house, his signed photograph of Nat Lofthouse, the Lion of Vienna, and his scroll of the Lord's Prayer, went missing in transit.

His world didn't collapse all at once. He'd ride on a little seat on his Dad's bike crossbar to watch him play cricket in the Bolton League. Michael would tell him of the great Lancashire cricketers who'd knocked the Yorkies off their perch in the twenties, glory days for the Wanderers too, with three FA Cup trophies. They were real chums.

But slowly, the curse of affluence produced fresh choices. After the Great War Michael's father, Richard's grandfather, turned to gardening rather than return to mining. His brother had been killed just before the war started in a pit disaster. In time, he became Head Gardener of a stately home on the edge of Bolton, owned by a self-made mill owner knighted for his paternalism. Michael had been brought up alongside the sons of the big house. The Good Knight had wanted

Michael to pick himself up by his own bootstraps as he had himself. It was a legacy from this benefactor that had helped pay for Bromley Cross. A decent job at the Town Hall was the best Michael managed, leaving him wanting more than was on offer. When Catharine had said bitterly to him as he left that he hadn't any morals, Richard wanted to shout out that he had, that he was the best guy in the world, but he'd stayed silent. He'd prayed every night that his parents would get together again. They hadn't. After the separation Richard would say that he didn't see much of Michael, who'd moved down to Essex for a Borough Treasurer's job. He'd re-married, something Catharine never did. A few years later Richard transferred to London. When Lancashire played Surrey at the Oval, the rain was so incessant that the gates to the ground weren't opened. Two bedraggled figures a generation apart walked round outside in opposite directions and bumped into each other by the gas holder. They never lost touch again. The day before Michael finally took to bed, he told Richard that he was sorry for letting him down. The sentence took him five minutes, riven with cancer as he was. His last words were that he was jiggered.

Richard internalised memories into idealised short passages of almost religious intensity. He wanted the story to be perfect. He couldn't have ideas without trying to improve on them. He actually saw more of Michael before the gas holder meeting than he cracked on. The deathbed recollection was authentic. He claimed his first memory to be Nell arriving as a puppy when he was three, but that was also a much-told family tale. His recollection of the look on her beautiful face, cocked to one side after a stroke she'd survived, as he left home for his second term at Oxford, both of them knowing that they'd never see one another again, was searingly honest. The person he made of himself worked well enough.

Catharine had moved to Norfolk after the separation to be close to

Carol, and nearly fifty years later was still there, recently placed in some confusion into a nursing home. Richard would visit every weekend. His last visit had brought distress as she'd thought him to be Michael and had blamed him for all that had happened. He'd spent the next two hours failing to convince her otherwise.

At Oxford, after good days at Oriel reading theology, Richard had switched half a mile north to Lollard theological college. He'd jacked in the thought of becoming a clergyman within a few months when he'd found it impossible to believe in fire and brimstone, thinking either that nobody would be saved, or everyone would, Satan included. Near strangulation at birth and other disappointments in his early life had made him more rueful than cynical. When he'd given up on being a clergyman, he'd become an accountant, interesting Rouse Cromarty on the milk round. He'd moved to their financial advisory division after several years in audit. He'd shown a real flair in the advisory role as he waited for his redemption day. This didn't come until he was forty, when Helen gate-crashed a Christmas party given by Rouse at the Savoy. Family life and career then had their inflationary epoch; children were born at a rate of knots and Grindleton's head-hunted him to be an investment banker. He was in some respects doubly happy, first from learning to ignore the bad times and then from appreciating the good.

His back was hurting badly from weeding and he put his trowel down in time to prevent Chloe going for the kill with the robin. He blamed his back for not joining the cricket game. Helen explained to the children that their Dad was an old man and they had to be kind to him.

That evening, he had a Parochial Church Council meeting. He tried to cuddle up to her for a kiss before he left. She rejected his overtures in favour of the television programme she was watching.

"We'd sit either end of my old Chesterfield like bookends

massaging each other's feet when we first married, or you'd sit on my knee with your arms around my neck while we snogged during every programme break," he reminisced fondly.

"I've had my lifetime's quota of foot massages. I'd miss half the programme as you'd carry on after the adverts."

He'd have been a lot more offended if he'd known of the turmoil behind those unrevealing eyes. A good-looking French vet had joined the practice a few months before and his cool demeanour was proving an attraction to parts of her that Richard's earnestness couldn't reach. She was ashamed of herself, as she did love Richard and liked the lifestyle they'd created at Hummills, but the place was beginning to feel like a gilded cage housing the dove she'd become. Scared that Richard was reading her thoughts, she tried to be nice to him. "Sorry for that crack about you being an old man in the garden. You're ageing pretty well, still handsome enough for you to have a fan club in the playground."

"It's Trotter who has the fan club. Are you sickening for something? I've never known you apologise before," he said perceptively.

She revealed the only bit of what she'd been thinking that she could. "I know I've been lucky with you. You're generous and couldn't be more kind-hearted. I like you that way, but it's not the way I am."

"You're far nicer than you think you are; only you won't admit it. You're too damned determined to be independent," was his further insight.

"I've not been independent enough. When I chose you, you not being a paid-up member of the home-counties' middle classes was part of it. I don't want you to join. You'll not quite pull it off. You're interesting and funny the way you are, apart from when you tell jokes. So don't blow it."

He hoped he wouldn't, but couldn't be sure.

# CHAPTER FOUR

Bob had finished the phone call with Jane at half past eight. He'd already eaten a big buffet breakfast and had returned to his room a couple of minutes before she'd rung. He went down to Reception to look for someone who could be called George Coulson. Almost immediately, a large Chrysler car was slowly driven up the drive and carefully parked. A distinguished occupant walked into the lobby. Bob stood up as he could see the guy was either a five star General or a Chief Financial Officer. A crisp voice asked him if he were Bob Swarbrick from ten yards away. George was cheating though; he had Bob's mugshot, from his CV, taken in his last days at Atomic Futures. When his daughter Ruth had first seen that photo, she'd said that he looked like an undertaker, stressed out as he was then.

As they arrived at the Northern Solstice building, a limo pulled up. Bob could see Wendy Ballinger fiddle with her handbag in the back seat. He preferred to ride shotgun if he could. Wendy revealed more than she'd intended as she struggled from the car into the vertical position and on to her killer heels.

He shouted over to her: "Heck, Wendy, are they shoes or stilts? Good to see you though. You're looking well."

"Did you get that suit from Oxfam? You're not looking that bad though, considering," she answered.

He wasn't sure if a charity shop was an improvement over robbing corpses for his source of clothes. Wendy thrust her suitcase into his hand. They walked upstairs into a conference room which doubled up as the Board Room. Peter was sitting in the centre of a large table with a cup of coffee in front of him and a pastry halfway into his jowls. Emil, a purposeful, stocky man, walked in. As Wendy hovered in the background, Peter focused malevolent eyes on her.

"Have you done anything yet about finding more potential investors?" he barked, not something a dog would ever attempt with a full mouth.

Despite the shower, Wendy didn't blench as she replied: "The appetite for AIM stocks is weaker than this time last year, as I've said. You need someone with stronger placing power."

Peter finished masticating before turning to Bob. "I've already found two million dollars of private investors in South Africa. Wendy's guy was clueless when I rang him. Who would you suggest we get?"

Bob tried to look as if he was reviewing the worldwide population of potential advisers before saying: "I'd like to find out a bit more about the company first. I think firms who are brokers first and foremost will have contacts Black and Robertshaw haven't cultivated yet. They're recruiting but I guess we can't wait for that."

Neat use of 'we', he thought. He carried on as everybody still seemed to be listening. "I was chatting about this with Wendy last night and we both thought Divinity might fancy us as they're targeting renewables."

Emil offered them coffee and pastries. The ones with apple and custard were too tempting to Bob despite his large breakfast. A presentation of the business had been arranged first, before a walk round the factory. Northern, as they called the company, had a bigger rival in California, which they were coy about, and also a couple more in Spain and Germany. The 'big power boys' were moving into the sector, so Northern had to differentiate itself by being quicker on its feet. Their products were lightweight and thus good for buildings not capable of supporting the heavier cells mainly in use at the moment. This was their USP, unique selling point, which no AIM flotation could possibly do without. Bob wondered if it was sufficiently unique, and if he had just coined an oxymoron. Regrettably for the sales figures, he had. Emil was a salesman, full of talk about achieving sales traction and developing channel partners, a broad paraphrase of which was: 'We can't sell the stuff and we haven't found anyone else who can either'.

Production had problems, but no delivery dates had been missed, not surprising since they'd sold bugger all, thought Bob. Solutions were in hand. Research and development were making good progress on the next generation product, capable of fitting together without detailed engineering on site. So, Bob deduced, the present product was a nightmare to install.

George Coulson droned. The revenue growth assumed in the forecasts was racy, despite his tone of voice, and dependent on an order for a series of new schools in a neighbouring state. The capital expenditure to tool up the factory, the working capital to fund the sales expansion, and the investment in the sales team (probably mainly wasted on expense accounts, Bob expected) together meant that they needed fifteen million dollars before they'd be cash positive. They were going to try to raise twenty million.

The shop floor was a mess, tooled up as a jobbing shop and not a process factory. Wayne Robinson, an old-time production director, had sensible plans for solving that. Bob was more comfortable here, giving the guy an evens chance of succeeding. The development team was headed by Christina Perez. She was only twenty-seven and had studied at Caltech, the place where in a few months time Bob was to meet Sheldon and the TV programme he'd discovered expecting something else. When blooded in seeking a solution to the installation problem, she'd found a proprietary answer. Bob was impressed with that. The nuclear engineers he knew would have designed another oxymoron, a bespoke solution. So would Scott Johnson, the guy Christina had replaced. He was the original designer and guy behind the company, who had been pushed to one side.

Back in the Board Room, some sandwiches had been laid on. Without offering anybody else one, Emil took a can from a fridge splattering coke over his cuffs as he opened it, as he asked Bob if a flotation was possible.

"My first impressions are that there is a lot to be done but you guys will get there," Bob cagily replied. "The sales plan needs work, with a detailed analysis of likely customers and where we're at with them. The finances follow from all that. I wouldn't commit on any more capex before the schools order comes in."

Peter sat up from his slouch to complain about the sales team. "We can't decide whether to sell for ourselves or use channels, and that's because we can't make up our minds whether to focus on retail, commercial or industrial. Our USP is for the bigger industrial market, but we keep on trying to sell into retail and commercial." Given that this coincided with Emil's background and that Peter looked straight at him as he said it, the target was clear.

Emil was still dealing with his wet cuffs, so Bob answered for him. "Industrial sales are usually long lead time. Shouldn't we see who wants us first? The product is more or less the same in all markets so it's only sales staff we're spreading thinly."

He needed to be supportive of Emil, even if the miserable bugger hadn't offered him a can, to avoid being seen as Peter's mouthpiece. Wendy added that the listing particulars would benefit from having more than one income stream. This reminded Peter that she was there. He wanted to know more about Divinity, sourly commenting: "They probably won't do it if they're any good. Everyone else seems to turn us down. That's why we ended up with you lot."

Wendy explained that, although Divinity were new, they had good contacts as their founder and only actual partner, Cuthbert Catterall, had made a mint from previous hedge fund incarnations. Also, Bob's friend Richard Shackleton had recently been hired as a Director for this type of investment. Bob then played their joker, suggesting Divinity lead the broking with Black and Robertshaw staying as Nomad, given all the footslogging work they'd already done. Peter was interested enough to ask Wendy if Divinity would accept a part role. She was less of a blagger than Bob and wasn't sure they would unless Richard fancied working with Bob one more time. Bob quickly asked if they would like him to see if he could speak to Richard.

Peter hadn't missed what he was up to. "We haven't decided if we're going to have you as Chairman yet," he protested. But his other directors had already made up their minds. Emil wanted to keep Wendy on the team as he didn't want to go through the education process again. George Coulson picked his moment to praise the relationship Wendy had developed with US attorneys and accountants. They both voted for split advice and for Bob. Peter looked balefully at them, a confederacy of dunces alongside his brimming genius, before agreeing. "OK then, see if you can speak to your guy. It looks like the job's yours if you can persuade him."

It was only two thirty in the afternoon PST, ten thirty in the evening BST. Bob had no idea where Richard would be, if not in bed with that beautiful wife of his. He borrowed Emil's office, paged down his phonebook and found 'Rich Shack'. After four rings he heard Richard's familiar hello, with a babble of noise behind him.

"Bob Swarbrick, Richard. I'm sorry to disturb you at this time of night."

"You're not disturbing me at all. Our PCC meeting is just breaking up and the quicker I get out of this place the better, before I strangle one of them. God is love indeed, bah humbug. There's a bench I can sit on up the path. What can I do for you?"

Bob asked what had happened to loving your neighbour as yourself. Richard understood why Jesus preferred the company of tax collectors and prostitutes if his disciples were like PCC members.

"Not at the same time, I trust," said Bob. "Those girls worked hard enough without rendering a great chunk of their earnings to Caesar. I'm commissioned to offer you a job. I'm in LA at the moment."

"I thought there was a pause each time before you spoke, but then you yokels are pretty slow on the uptake."

Bob explained how there was a chairmanship with Northern Solstice and a whole new image for him at stake. Richard had heard all about the potential flotation on the City grapevine already, saying that Wendy Ballinger was doing it. He guessed what was coming next. "Don't tell me, you want us to come in behind B and R and give them a hand because they haven't got enough clout."

Bob made clear that Richard would lead the broking with Wendy as Nomad. Richard paused for longer than the time lag. He was interested, despite his next comment that it was a recipe for confusion.

"I know that can be difficult at our age. Wendy will help you when you get too confused," Bob replied.

Richard did want to work with friends, not something he often got to do. "I'll get one of the guys checking it out and I'll then talk to Wendy. I'll have to swing Cuthbert, but he owes me one. I'll let you know on Wednesday. Will you still be in LA?"

"No, we're both back into the UK on Wednesday morning. Do your best. DYB, DYB, DYB."

Richard didn't suppose Wendy had been a wolf cub but promised:

"We'll do our best, DOB, DOB, DOB, she'll have been a girl guide.

* * *

Home from Church, Richard went to bed while Helen watched her programme. Forcing his eyes across the pages of a Martin Amis novel, he was trying to stay awake, in case she might feel like making love when she eventually came up. She spent an age in the bathroom. She didn't seem in the mood. He fondled her bottom to check. She wasn't. They both turned on their backs and lay with their legs fully extended alongside each other, his right leg touching her left leg along its length, companionship without movement. Helen was good at stillness. Richard had to imagine anything more. He treated it as practice for eternity.

* * *

Bob went back to the Board Room with the news, upbeat about the prospects of Divinity coming in. He didn't think Richard would let him down. Wendy and Bob had been expecting Peter and Emil to take them out somewhere for dinner, and for more meetings the next day. Peter didn't want to take it any further until Divinity had decided. Emil's wife wasn't well and he asked to take a rain check too. It was only three thirty in the afternoon. Wendy and Bob were on the same flight back at six o'clock the following evening, with check-in two hours before. The logistics of changing to an earlier flight was going to be too much hassle. At least that was Bob's excuse to Wendy, which she didn't challenge. To fill the time, she offered to take him sightseeing. With two bits of days to kill, there wasn't time to go far out of town.

"Out here there's nothing apart from Disney, and you're a bit big for that. Hollywood and going on a tour of the stars' houses could be a bit of fun," she proposed.

He thought that sounded good. "I'm sure Disney's not a patch on Blackpool Pleasure Beach anyway. Why don't we finish off what we need to and then have an early dinner near here? Then back to our respective hotels and I'll get a taxi to your place in the morning to go stargazing. Have you booked a car back to the airport yet?"

She hadn't, so he arranged a car for three o'clock the next afternoon to pick them both up at her hotel. An office was found for them and a booking made at a local Italian restaurant. When they'd closed the door to the office, Wendy gave a wry grin to congratulate Bob, wrinkling her nose in pleasure. He carried on talking shop. "That all finished too quickly. I'm sure Forster's got other plans as well as a flotation. You can't blame him; it's a high risk strategy. At least we'll see Hollywood. How's life treating you?"

His face looked genuinely interested as he asked her, eyes staring deeply into hers. Until then, she hadn't been going to tell him that her husband Frank, fifteen years older than her, had recently been formally diagnosed with early onset Alzheimer's. She carefully described his symptoms which had moved well beyond forgetfulness. "I'd have had to give up work to look after him, if his sister hadn't moved in with us when her husband died. He has the craziest notions, like I'm dealing in cocaine when a parcel arrives from Lakeland. Sometimes he thinks I'm another sister, the black sheep of the family, and he spits bile at me while being sweetness and light with his real sister."

Bob tried to be sympathetic, not a role nature had cut out for him. "Ey, I am sorry. I'm sure that somehow bits of the identity will still be there. The brain's a complicated structure that can replicate things all over the place. Not that it's any comfort but we're all going to end up as ashes or dust. Has this got you in your small corner losing your religion?"

Wendy shook her head, both to the question and at her lack of comprehension. Bob didn't like the idea of anyone losing their identity as this would count against his big idea that the old person we become is in us when we're born. He hoped that he had a spirit with him throughout, a spirit not made of molecules, not dependent on circuitry. He wanted to be the same person in eternity he'd been all his life, not to be spending aeons mindlessly singing the 'Te Deum' from heavenly choir stalls. "Frank will be in there somewhere to the bitter end because he was born, if that makes sense," he asserted.

Wendy shook her head to indicate it was total twaddle. "You've had children," she said. "We haven't passed our genes on."

Bob persevered. "Sometimes now when I do things, I feel as though I'm in my Dad's body, a look, a smile, the way I walk. It's uncanny. I see him in my lad too. You may not have children but you do have parents."

Wendy thought she'd missed out as having children together linked a couple permanently. Bob reassured her: "You've had a good marriage with a good guy and there's not many can say that," while hoping that not to be the case. His intuition was right. Wendy couldn't say it either. "I've got to get this off my chest to someone," she told him. "Frank and I were strangers together before this. It's not been that great a marriage, and he's not been that good a guy. None of us are when we're not where we want to be."

"Or even when we are," Bob's experiences had taught him.

Wendy explained how she'd been Frank's last chance of marriage. He would have preferred to lead a small-town life, immersed in the local cultural scene. It was her fault that they'd married, with her on the rebound after being let down by an absolute shit.

She carried on softly, without a hint of self-pity. "I've bored him rigid, and he has me. That makes what's happening both easier and

50

harder to bear. What might have been never was nor will be. It must be terrible for him to lose himself without having found what he wanted."

Bob told her that she'd masked it all well. She knew she hadn't but chose to agree. "Women can be good actresses and like you I felt that marriage should last forever."

"I've never said that." Bob was surprised at how well she seemed to know him. "I divorced Jane and admittedly never remarried. It wasn't for the want of trying."

Wendy touched his arm. "I see you as an old fashioned character and more than likeable for that. You loved your wife, and probably still do with your quaint theories of time."

Bob changed that subject quickly. "Have you had any affairs? I've maybe had one or two too many, but then I was free to."

"Only once and very discreetly. I nearly left Frank before he developed all these symptoms. Something in my head stopped me. I don't know if it was fear or conscience."

Bob had no doubt. "It was conscience, it was who you are, and you're more than likeable for that."

They worked on until the cab came to take them to the restaurant. By the end of the meal, she wanted Bob with her longer, much longer. Big girl that she was, she wanted to be carried away from her life in his arms.

"We could both stop round here tonight. I assume you've got a large enough bed for both of us," she suggested.

"It could fit three of you in as well. Wow, yes please, ma'am. Are you sure you won't feel guilty?"

She didn't pretend otherwise. "I probably will but that's something I'll live with. I've been lusting after you all day and it seems more honest to go for it. Didn't Jesus say that lust was as bad as adultery?"

"He also said that sex after divorce was adultery. He wouldn't have

51

been saying no to divorce, as Moses had allowed it. I think what he was saying was that monogamy is the ideal, but that divorce is only one of the many ways we break laws we can't keep. I wonder if he did bonk Mary Magdalene in a weak moment."

"I doubt it if he was a good Jew. Is this a weak moment for you then, Bob?"

"We'll see how strong I can be," he joked out of a mix of bravado and worry.

Back at the hotel, they sneaked into the elevator. Bob wanted to be sure that Wendy wasn't having cold feet. She wasn't. "If you find you don't fancy me, we can just be together for the night," she replied.

"I thought my zip was going to burst in the cab. Let's do it at least twice in case I can't contain myself."

"Now you're showing off. At your age, once is a miracle. Don't worry if you flop, I'll only laugh at you."

"Any need for precautions?" he suddenly thought.

She'd been on the pill since her previous affair. "I kept on with it. Until recently Frank would get randy and I'd struggle to keep him off. I didn't want to find that we'd become fertile together."

They were through the door and kissing each other in long embraces. They were soon in bed. She was amazed at how gentle he was. Afterwards, they took turns in giving all-over finger massages, bringing each other out in goose bumps. He called them goosegogs, saying she was good enough to eat.

They slept well, waking at five o'clock, lunch time in the UK. There was a second time, a bit longer than the first. They lay in each other's arms talking about what they found to be beautiful. They both agreed on old houses and country views, and saw each other's point about steam engines and fossils. "And the most beautiful thing is you," he whispered, as he licked her ear. "You're bloody gorgeous, inside and out."

"You say that to all the girls."

"No, not," he lied. And they kissed again, both tongues as active as teenagers on a park bench.

Wendy, dressed in yesterday's clothes, used Bob's toothbrush. Then he checked out, got hold of a cab which she joined outside and they went to her hotel in downtown LA. Bob held his luggage self-consciously, as if the act of carrying a case into another hotel was a clear indication of adultery. They went straight into breakfast there. He waited in reception while she showered and changed. They left their luggage with the concierge and caught the subway to Hollywood. There they had a great time, touring the houses with a party of small town Americans, who Wendy described as coming from Hicksville twinned with St Chad's.

They couldn't arrange a change of seating to sit next to each other on the flight. Bob dozed while Wendy investigated the duty free. He was relaxed, as no longer could anything go wrong with arrangements provided they didn't fall out of the plane or the plane out of the sky. He was intending to sleep through the journey but found himself with high altitude musings as night closed in. The lights on the plane were dimmed. The seats were set horizontally, looking like coffins in a morgue rather than a beauty parlour. 'Nearer my God to thee' was written half a century before Bleriot but it was prophecy. A thin shaft of light from the wing penetrated through a narrow gap by the window blind, diffusing into patterns in his eyes he'd last seen when he was seven years old. Then he'd been walking the long way home from Sunday School, through the park to pick up some conkers, while pondering if he could have got away with putting an old button into the collection bag and using the provided penny to buy ten aniseed balls. A shaft of sunlight had beamed through the branches of the horse chestnut tree like a searchlight, focused on him, only him. He'd carried on squinting into the pale blue sky where to the right of sun an imprint remained for several more seconds. Someone up there hadn't been well pleased with his delinquent thoughts. St Paul had received the full treatment, including voices, on his way to Damascus, but he was having folk stoned to death. Not that much damage could be done chucking conkers, and even less with aniseed balls.

Was this light through the crack, he wondered, a sign that the Lord was unhappy with him again, over Wendy, or to be more accurate, over Frank? He opened the blind in case there was an imprint in the dark Canadian sky. Nothing obviously divine could be seen. He took that absence as a sign that the jury was out in the councils of heaven.

He carried on looking. Cosmologists since the eighties had been talking about the mysterious (at least to him) cosmic inflation, which massively expanded the dimensions of space, just after the Big Bang. Recently, more and more of them thought that there'd been cosmic inflation prior to the Big Bang which created our universe, and this had been going on eternally. That would put the infinity into the Physics rather than with a creator standing outside. In the theory, new universes occurred through all eternity, giving not just the incredibly large number from losing quantum uncertainty but an infinite amount.

To Bob, this was nonsense. His religious beliefs changed his view of science, and his science shaped his religion. He was never with Richard in his view that our minds change nothing. No God with willpower meant no creature with a will either. On the evidence of the life he'd lived, he'd seen a tiny space occasionally filled, or so he hoped. The initial creative act had been a single spoken word no louder than a customer in a cafe saying tea or coffee, the smallest possible perturbation of a skilfully drawn symmetry, a piece of mental geometry breathed into life.

He didn't see how the Big Bang could just be geometry though. It had needed shed loads of dense positive energy curled up in a tinchy ball so tightly that there was an offsetting negative vacuum energy. Prior to reading about cosmic inflation, he'd preferred the thought that there'd been Big Bounces from previous cycles of Big Bangs and Big Crunches in the one universe, with the initial ball getting bigger each time.

Daughter Ruth, who'd read Maths at Warwick, had told him about the theorem showing that any finite system can't contain its own explanation. What Ruth and Bob felt most certain about was that there wouldn't be an infinite regress as the cause of creation. Infinity couldn't exist in the physical world. Somewhere down the line, a will called God had started time and a finite Physics, including as many universes as this God had felt like, up to but not including infinity. The spiritual world was where the infinite resided, outside the system. Bob was halfway to Richard's paradise of ideas.

The taste in his mouth turned from sweet to bitter as he gazed disconsolately. What he could see in his own reflection was that his brief affair with Wendy would last only until her guilt took over. He pulled the blind back down before doing some stretches in the aisle. After that, he lay back on his bed, thinking of the little boy he'd been in his aniseed days, riding his trike up and down the pavement at breakneck speed in St Chad's Square.

"Can't you sleep, Bob? I can't either."

Bob came to with a jolt. Divine appearances come in different forms. Wendy had spotted him do his rehearsal for the danse macabre. He quickly broke the multi-purpose bed into its component parts, offering the larger portion to the Gloucestershire Goddess. This deity did leave a clear imprint where she deposited herself.

"Other way round, boy. My bottom is bigger than yours, but

nothing else is. What were you thinking about? You looked miles away."

She sat on the stool, leaving him to plonk himself down on the chair.

"I was thinking of God judging my sinful past," he replied honestly.

She reached over to kiss him on the forehead while she stroked his hair. Nobody had done that to him since his Mum when he was a little boy. She held his hands and said softly, "Sacred and profane. That's what we are."

He held her hands to his lips. "You're a gift from above."

"You'd not say that if you really knew me," she giggled.

"I would."

She looked at his big hands intently, and spoke in a low monotone. "I wish I'd met you sooner. I can't see my way through these next few years. Say a prayer for me that I'll make sense of it all someday."

"I will, but why not say it yourself?" he asked.

"I do, but I don't get a reply."

Bob was silent for a minute, not sure if the expected brush-off was already happening. "I get no answers now either. God might be almighty outside this bubble he's created, but inside he seems to have about as much clout as us two have, if that much."

"Or are we just too blind to see?" Wendy pondered.

"Perhaps we are. I did once spot him gawping at me through a horse chestnut tree."

She raised her eyebrows. "You did what!? Was he chucking conkers at you?"

He told the tale of the nearly pinched penny. She laughed as she shook her head. "Well, I suppose it's as good a reason for belief as any other."

Without it, Bob said, he would have looked at the useless beauty of the sky and seen only that wretched purposeless inflation. Wendy, having been born during Edward Heath's government, made the obvious comparison. Bob bridled at the mention of the worst prime minister in history, including Lord North and Tony Blair. "Heath decimated Lancashire, the pillock."

Wendy smiled, the lines on her forehead becoming irresistible to Bob's lips. She nuzzled against the nearest ear and whispered: "We had the Avon lady next door to us until we got rid of her. So, you see, God gives us some wiggle room and he has some himself."

Bob felt a tingle down his spine from her breath in his mouth. "The rest of the time we're dancing to the devil's tune, wiggling only when he pulls our strings," he murmured.

She held his hand tight to her breast briefly. "Hey, I'd better get some sleep in," she resolved. "You can't put the Virtues into Maths, Big Man. They've always been there."

If supreme irony is set up in the heavens as a Platonic form, Bob was bound someday to find that he had free will but hadn't the balls to exercise it. "You don't think we needed to live to make the Virtues and not just discover them?" he asked, before desire overwhelmed goodness. "Do you think anyone would notice if I used the right tool to meet the conditions for membership of the five mile high club?"

The trip was to end worryingly with the dangling prospect of a big crunch. "I said virtues, not vices. And that steward's giving us funny looks each time he walks past. I'm going back now."

* * *

The next morning, Richard went to the office as normal, having walked Trotter at the crack of dawn. Matthew caught the same train in as he was meeting his girlfriend in London. Helen delivered the three other children to their schools, returning to Hummills for breakfast.

She cursed as her car wouldn't restart, the battery eventually losing its whimper of protest. She called the surgery and Pierre volunteered to pick her up. As he arrived, she found herself asking him in for a coffee. Few words were said as they climbed the stairs towards the spare bedroom. With the door closed, Pierre slowly undressed her. She held him tight. She couldn't believe that, having been faithful to Richard since she'd met him, she was allowing this to happen so casually, but her body wanted it and her mind couldn't interfere with what had to happen. The dove had grown horns without her even leaving the cage.

Pierre was removing his trousers as the door burst open. Trotter charged in, jumped up and knocked him to the ground. The dog, usually a friendly soul, had been left in the garden and he'd got wind that something untoward was happening, nosed open the latch of the kitchen door and sprinted up the stairs. He stood growling between the pair of them as Pierre floundered, tripping over his half-mast trousers. Helen laughed uncontrollably in relief. She put on her clothes and threw Pierre's shirt over to him. In the car, they agreed that they had been too hasty. They arranged to go for a drink the next week to get to know each other better.

* * *

When Bob woke up over Ireland, he went to see Wendy. She was wide awake watching a movie, hair pinned behind her ears. He kissed her bare neck, and she held him tight to her. Too soon they were waiting at the carousel. Landside, the Virgin drivers were waiting. Wendy's was taking her to Reading Station, Bob's to his London flat.

"A one night stand, Wendy?"

"What do you want, Bob?"

"You, only you," he said. "I'll understand if you don't feel right about it." He was in one of his cruder moments. "I'm giving you lifetime bonking rights over me, although at my age of course I might not be able to get it up much longer."

She didn't take up his offer. "Honestly, I can't see how to make it work and that's a crying shame. If this has to be it, we can still be great friends when we work together, can't we?"

He swallowed in the disappointment and muttered: "This is the best trip I've ever been on".

"That's what California does for you," she sighed softly.

# CHAPTER FIVE

Early on Wednesday afternoon the Virgin car dropped Bob at his flat in Upper Thames Street. He'd a message from Richard saying that Divinity would do the job if terms could be agreed. He returned the call, managing only to inform an answer phone that he was back in the country. Needing company, he then rang his son Robert at his legal firm. This time a live, slightly scouse voice answered. Robert mentioned that Jane was worried about tests that Andrew was having later in the week. She feared stomach cancer.

Bob knew he shouldn't have felt so uplifted by the news. "I wouldn't wish that on my worst enemy and I'm not sure he's that," was truthful while not abounding in charity. "You get on OK with him, don't you?"

"Better than Ruth, but not really," Robert agreed half-heartedly. "He's a bit desiccated, one S two Cs." This was an in-joke started first by Bob's chemistry master half a century before when every write-up of an experiment concluded with, 'Wash and dry in a desiccator, one S, two Cs'. Nobody in the Swarbrick family for two generations has misspelt the word. Ruth's super coconut cake was made with one S and two Cs as ingredients.

Father and son agreed to meet for a jar that evening. "No girlfriend to amuse then?" enquired Bob, hoping there was.

"They never laugh with me, only at me. I'm out with my latest tomorrow."

Bob wasn't sure whether or not to call Jane to find out more about Andrew's tests. He wasn't feeling brave, so he rang Ruth instead. There was no trace of Liverpudlian in her voice and no knowledge of Andrew's problem either. Robert was Jane's favourite. Instead he told Ruth about LA and the trip round the houses of the stars. She joshed him that he wouldn't have known who any of them were as Wallace and Gromit didn't have a place in Beverley Hills. He conceded that reading Hello more regularly might have helped, but that he was more like Gromit, pawing through Electronics for Dogs. She joked that even that would be beyond him, a heavy current man who'd spent his life contending with light current problems. He had to agree with her. She'd bought him an iPod a few years before, choosing the largest model for his fat fingers. He'd made great use of it and, when the battery had finally failed, had railed at Steve Jobs for finding screw holes unpleasing.

"Don't crack on that it was me who told you about Andrew when you speak to Mum," he requested. "I'm seeing Robert for a pint tonight by the way."

Robert was thirty-five and still unmarried, having gone through a cast of suitable and unsuitable partners. Before becoming a lawyer, he'd got a first at Oxford, something Bob still boasted about to anyone who would listen. "Tell him to come up and see us sometime soon," Ruth wanted. "He can bring what's her name, Maria. He's not seen Ben since the christening. Talking of which, I'd best go, Dad, I can hear him stirring. Don't let Robert drink you under the table."

"Maria's gone the way of the others," he told her regretfully.

He made a cup of tea and then braved Tesco as he'd a few meals to eat before he drove back to St Chad's. Real men not using trolleys, he threw his supplies into a basket. He'd a headache coming on so he lobbed in some aspirin. Back at the flat, he felt worse. He thought he'd be better after a wash and brush up but vomited as he got out of the shower. He rang Robert to stand him down. There was no answer. He left a message and went to bed. Within a few minutes he spewed up again, reaching the lavatory with a despairing dive. Then he slept and had a vivid dream about the freeway system of LA, seeing a network solution to all its problems, unfortunately forgotten when he woke up with a head throbbing like a diesel engine. As a consequence, LA still suffers from gridlock. He took more aspirins and puked yet again. As he emerged from the battlefront of the lavatory, Robert rang to ask how bad he was. Bob thought they'd better cancel as he was powfagged, as Robert's Great Granddad would have said. He didn't want Robert catching the bug too.

Bob had never known a headache like this one. He went into a nightmare sleep. He shrank into a multi-dimensional golf ball, his head bound in elastic bands. These spun him round and round until he was giddy. He started to grow so fast that he feared he was about to explode. Tangles of string like maggots in rotting meat formed dense clouds. Nausea was in everything. Time pulsated backward and forward sending the stinking mess around his head in a whirlwind. Then dinosaurs were eating each other, under an atomic mushroom cloud. After vomiting again, his eyes bulging, he sat on the couch with his head in his hands to stop it splitting into many dimensions. He staggered back to bed not caring if he lived or died.

He was stooped over the lavatory again the next morning, certain that the whole of creation was the devil's dance, when he heard the door bang. He could see Robert and the concierge through his legs. He turned to face them, unable to find any words.

Robert spoke for him: "Hell, you look like death. Have you called a doctor?"

Bob found a voice, understated as ever. "I've never had one here. I do feel a bit rough."

He'd been there a quarter of a century and never had a doctor! The concierge turned up the number of a private GP who would come out for £100 for a short visit. Robert found his Dad's credit card and within half an hour the doc was there. Bob described the symptoms, including the dreams. The doctor asked to see his chest. The spots were conclusive. Viral meningitis was the diagnosis, which was not a cause for panic, he said.

"Thank God for that," Bob replied," I thought I was possessed by demons."

The doctor explained that it wasn't a killer like bacterial meningitis. It was a common virus, easily dealt with in the gut, which had got in the fluid round the brain, the outer surface of which had become inflamed. It wasn't contagious and bigger, better painkillers would have him on the road to recovery within a few days. The only surprising thing was that it was much more common in younger people.

"I do still get spots when I eat chocolate," Bob was relieved enough to joke, "brought to you by courtesy of Clearasil."

The doctor was too young ever to have heard 'broadcasting on 208 metres, your station of the stars'. He wasn't a baby boomer, whatever the Office for National Statistics might think. He recommended chicken soup rather than Cadbury's Dairy Milk. Bob asked for poached egg on toast as he had bread and eggs. That was permissible. Business meetings should be cancelled for the next week.

After the Doc had left, Robert took control. He's a handsome guy, shorter than Bob, taking after Jane in looks but more like his Dad in temperament. There was no poacher so he cooked the eggs by twirling the water in a saucepan, making himself some too, as the emergency had meant he'd missed his breakfast. While he was doing this, Bob checked his answer phone. He heard the increasingly desperate calls from Robert, along with messages from Wendy and Richard. Of course he rang Wendy first. She told him quickly that Forster and Emil were coming over next Tuesday to meet Divinity. He needed a while to get his head around that being four days away, deciding that was as good as a week, and that therefore he'd be there. He took so long that she asked him if jet lag got worse in old age. He finally mentioned the viral meningitis.

She found herself stunned into frantic alarm. "Isn't that dangerous? Who's looking after you? Hey, you're going to be OK, aren't you?" The relief when she heard that his son was there and that he'd be fine within a few days had her laughing and crying at the same time. She claimed not to be surprised as only the good die young, but was worried it was a sign that the heavens weren't impressed with their adultery

His stomach was causing him too many qualms for him to be bothered about that as well. He carelessly took the blessing from above for granted. "He'll forgive us," he said. "The bottom's about to fall out of my world, love. Could you let Richard know the state I'm in? I'll ring back tomorrow."

Back in the kitchen, Robert had toasted four slices of bread and managed to poach four eggs with not too many white bits separated out in the pan. Bob emerged hesitantly from the lavatory and viewed the two plates of food, commenting that if a job was worth doing, it was worth doing badly. He kept everything down for an hour. By then Robert had brought the prescription and left with spare keys, promising to come back in the evening. Asleep again, Bob could see all the errors he'd made last night in designing the LA freeway system, what with not being well. Then it was all lost again as the dimensions raced round his brain, photons round spaghetti strings, full of sound and fury. Then a voice of calm from within slowed him down. He woke up at ten o'clock and this time walked rather than ran to the bathroom. Robert was sitting in the living room watching the television. Bob was upset that Robert had postponed his new date by twenty-four hours. They had a cup of tea as they watched the News together. Robert left, saying he'd pop in the next evening briefly before he went out. Bob slept better. His headache wasn't so bad; he wasn't sick again and the onset of diarrhoea was not quite so rapid. His dreaming was more normal until it transmogrified into a tunnel of light. He knew this to be the dream of death and looked to see the face of God. Instead he saw Jane and Wendy knitting a sweater for him. Jane was doing the body, Wendy the sleeves. He didn't get to wear it as they hadn't finished when he woke up.

The next morning he cooked some more poached eggs on toast, and then had a piece of the walnut cake he'd bought. It all stayed down. He rang Wendy, who was concerned he was up and about too soon. She'd fixed a fee sharing arrangement with Richard which had needed the company to agree only slightly higher costs. They had done. She mentioned a guy in her office who'd had viral meningitis and experienced nightmares for months afterwards.

"Maybe I had a light dose. I had shocking dreams at first, but it was back to sex and football last night," he revealed.

Wendy could be as vulgar as Bob. "Did you score at either?"

"The whistle blew before I could shoot. Story of my life,"

She knew that wasn't so. "It wasn't in LA. You're a special bloke, Bob."

He took a deep breath. "That sounds like the Dear John speech I'm expecting."

"It's not. I like you more than's good for me. I'm not letting go that easily."

He hadn't expected that. They said very sweet goodbyes. The Holy Spirit was moving in helpful ways and Richard answered immediately too. Having discussed the fee compromise, with Bob congratulating

Richard for being a big-hearted Arthur, he then asked what the Church meeting problem had been.

"Women bishops, of course, but the less said about that the better. These literal-truth Christians make an idol of the Bible and replace the Holy Spirit with it. Paul was pro-woman and yet some dodgy texts in Timothy are used to keep women out."

"He's said nowadays to be anti-woman and anti-gay," Bob remarked.

Richard wasn't that keen on St Paul. "He did think that being gay was self worship, which is a bit rich with his track record of persecuting folk. And our understanding of things has moved on a bit since then."

Bob was much more liberal than he'd crack on. "It hasn't in those born-again types. We've both grown up happy to live with contradictions but they've not."

"The number of lectures and sermons I've heard explaining why Paul's teaching is consistent with what Jesus said," Richard continued. "Well, it is if you're up for doing double somersaults and landing with your head up your own orifice. He takes the logic miles past what redemption's about. Jesus was a prophet first and foremost telling us to repent."

"Well there's nowt worse than a convert," Bob agreed. "Even our main man got pretty excited for a year or two. I doubt we'd have heard of any of it without Paul though. Anyway, I thought you started with the less said about it the better."

Richard laughed. "You mean you didn't ring me about the meaning of Romans?"

Perverse as ever, Bob had a soft spot for old Paul. "Perhaps I did, as I can't make head nor tail of it. But all lives do stand in need of redemption, even if God made the world so tough we were bound to start out as selfish bastards and end up this screwed-up." The dense prose of Romans, trying to pin down what it was to be redeemed, somehow mirrored his own half-baked attempts to explain creation. He liked the idea that the Holy Spirit had replaced the law, which for him was the vehicle used to keep control both by bonehead dictators through low cunning and by smarmy elites through high skulduggery. He thought the bits when Paul turned from his detailed argument to say sardonically that it was better to marry than to burn, or to tell those insisting on circumcision that he wished they'd go the whole hog and cut their bollocks off too, were both theologically sound and funny.

They at last got down to business. Both Richard and Bob were more intuitive in their approach than suited Wendy. But they could both move up the gears effortlessly when they had to. They were both so determined to prove to themselves that they were brighter than the public school ponces they had to compete with that they would have considered it cheating to put in too much work. None of their womenfolk thought that as they banged their heads against the glass ceiling. Bob warned Richard that he believed Forster might have another option, a trade sale to their local rival instead of flotation, from the sidelong glances when he'd asked about the competition. Western Sun Rising Inc. had heavier product but better retail sales and were privately financed,

Richard thanked him for the tip and asked: "Would you like to come to dinner with us on Tuesday? The Yanks are flying straight out. Helen would be pleased to see you again. I'll invite Wendy as well."

Bob wasn't sure if he was imposing, but he liked Richard and Helen had been good value the one time he'd met her. And he wasn't going to say no to the chance of Wendy. He checked the clock as he put the phone down. It was still only ten o'clock on Friday morning. He decided he'd be well enough to drive back to St Chad's the next day. He rang Robert to let him know and then Ruth to tell her all that had been happening. He agreed not to call in on the way up in case he gave the little ones something. She'd spoken to Jane. Andrew's test results were due in a few hours.

After lunch, he felt up to a stroll over the Millennium Bridge with its fine view of Bankside Power Station, aka the Tate Modern. Ugly looking thing, he thought, should've knocked it down and built flats, probably what they were doing until they got a cold call from a double-glazing salesman just after they'd taken the roof off. He walked up to the National Theatre, whose brutalism he quite liked, though he expected the roof would have leaked less if they'd used thatch like the Globe. He then decided that he'd best stay nearer home with the state of his stomach, and turned back. As he walked through the door of his flat, Wendy rang. "I've spoken to Peter," she said. "He says your pay is only to be seventy thousand dollars, which is at the bottom end. I'll try to make up for it with benefits in kind if you'll let me."

He wasn't sure if he'd heard right. He hadn't realised how upfront Wendy could be. Wanting the unremunerated parts of his package as early as possible, he asked if she was going to be at Richard's, to find that she couldn't go as she had a meeting in Bristol the next morning. He tried to get her to change things, but she said that, with lifetime bonking rights, she could be patient. Once she'd said it, his expression somehow sounded less vulgar. Then she surprised him again.

"I cut you off short in LA when you were about to tell me all about Schrödinger's cat. I forgot to ask you again about it on the trip. Let's hear whatever nonsense Richard came up with."

Bob was pleased she was interested. "I started the discussion off by saying that the observer didn't just see if the cat was dead or alive but actually took the decision. Richard disagreed totally. He's keen on a piece of theology which says that Father, Son and Holy Spirit will only be one at the end of time. He sewed together the few words he knew from physics to prove his point. The Father was pondering the consequences of starting creation by an act of will. In his thoughts, all sorts of entanglement developed, and he could see the hideous horrors of nature if independent life should come about, which his Spirit would be powerless to stop. He was about to abort his big idea when he saw the Son of Man and what he would do. The complete Godhead didn't make the whole story flesh until the end of time. All the uncertainties were collapsed only once, cat in box included, after everything was known, but before anything had happened. The end of time is thus also the beginning and all points in between. Richard reckons the epistle to the Hebrews says more or less the same thing. Christ has saved, and continues to save, everyone from never having existed. An investment banker who'd studied Philosophy at Cambridge described Richard as meta-delusional."

Wendy felt that us making God and God making us had a neat logic to it.

"But where does that circle start? And I can't for the life of me work out why God would single out our awful species," Bob replied. "You don't get up the food chain as far as we have without being selfish bastards. It's all a bit local. Other species, other planets, more worthy than us, need a Messiah too."

"What Richard was probably trying to do is reconcile this hostile world with a good creator," Wendy suggested. "His intentions were good."

Bob snorted. "I'm more with the wild God of Job telling humans not to be so bloody presumptuous. I'd have thought that creation was about making souls, not making God himself. I suppose our choices could be in God's final cut, so maybe we can still live as if we have free will. Something's been added though when things have actually happened, some knowledge of what it felt like, so I guess even God can't end up where he started," he added, more for his own benefit.

"Still, Paul Simon's right. After changes upon changes we are more or less the same. We're all joined in one purpose, whatever it is."

They couldn't take the conversation further as Wendy had to take another call. Soon after, Ruth rang to tell him the news about Andrew. It was stomach cancer and the prognosis was rotten, no more than a year, less if the cancer had spread.

Bob tried to ring Jane's mobile. It wasn't answered.

CHAPTER SIX

That Friday lunchtime was also when Helen and Pierre went to a country pub to get to know each other better. With the surgery covered by just one other vet, they didn't have much time, particularly as both of them still were looking to add carnal knowledge to what they could discover over a drink. They bolted down their Budweisers before moving on in Pierre's Volvo to the secluded car park of a local beauty spot. For reasons she couldn't understand, she made all the running, with Pierre more hesitant. It had become a matter of honour for her to see it through. He nervously glanced out of the window as, banging his head on the roof and scraping his knee on the seat belt buckle, he clambered on top of her. They kissed passionately enough, but that was it. The French cockerel wouldn't crow. She assumed that a fear of the non-existent audience had given him stage fright and was still determined that the fates would not frustrate her will. She agreed to drop in at his cottage, where the curtains could remain closed, on her way to work the next Tuesday morning.

\* \* \*

Bob was wide awake by six thirty on Saturday. He felt well enough to drive to Lancashire in his BMW Z4 Coupé, bought to relive his sports car youth. Thus determined, he cooked a quick breakfast, packed a suitcase and was away not long after seven o'clock. He was approaching

Corley Services at eighty five miles an hour in the middle lane when his phone rang. He moved safely enough on to the slip road, answered with, "Hang on, I'm parking," and drove into the first bay.

Jane did hang on. She wanted to know why he'd rung the previous day. He told her that Ruth had passed on the rotten news about Andrew and asked how he was coping.

"He's being bloody stoical, facing death without hope or pity. I'm remembering what I saw in him."

Before Bob had a chance to say any further false words of consolation, she asked if he was well enough to be driving. Ruth had laid the viral meningitis on with a trowel and told Jane that he was 'poorly sick in bed with a shawl on', yet another of his expressions. He thought Jane was deliberately wrong-footing him for having had something so footling. But then she told him in a whisper that he was in her brain like a maggot. Andrew, sitting downstairs, would be wound up, she added, if he knew who she was talking to. "You gave me kids, Bob and he didn't. They haven't turned out too badly, have they?"

Bob, not knowing where she was heading next, agreed that was a miracle given the sort of parents they'd had. His tone had been light-hearted but she bridled at the judgment. He clarified what he'd meant. "I'm judging myself, not you, and I'm happy others do too. I want the battleaxes of the WI tut-tutting at things, not getting their kit off for a calendar."

Jane could hear Andrew slowly climbing the stairs. She apologised to Bob that she'd have to go. "I know you're not one bit like that. I'll ring you soon, please don't call me."

He went into the services and picked up a chocolate bar in the shop before setting off up the motorway, his head full of Jane. In his mind's eye, she was seventeen and wearing the short maroon velvet dress she'd look perfect in at parties. Another part of his head told him that that wasn't the real Jane; it was a girl who wore a maroon short dress. At the start, she hadn't seemed to be promiscuous, although he did remember his surprise once early on when he found her tongue at the back of his mouth. He knew she'd no super-ego, a good thing to be without, but he'd never known the state of her conscience.

As he crossed the Thelwall viaduct and into Lancashire, whatever the signs might say, he felt his customary antagonism towards Edward Heath. Anyone under sixty would call the region the north-west and, as a final anathema to Bob, that included Jane's Knutsford. He reached the Ribble at the A59. The Fylde, home of the Swarbricks for over a thousand years, beckoned. When he crossed the Mersey he felt he was back with the tribe, over the Ribble he was with family. He took the M55, turned off at Kirkham, and drove into St Chad's past the cemetery where all four grandparents and his parents were buried. His house was down a pleasant side road across from the station. He could see that the grass had grown. He opened the terrace doors and filled the bird feeder with sunflower hearts.

He needed groceries for the weekend. He knocked on old Mrs Metcalfe's door to find out if she wanted anything too, and promised to mow her lawn later. He then set off up the Breck, his stomach opting to eat lunch out at the Tea Rooms first. In Booths supermarket he bought his normal stuff plus a couple of ready-made curries and a blackcurrant tart for his next day's baggin, as he still called it. Mrs Metcalfe also wanted some ready meals and some broccoli.

He mowed the lawns and filled up the bird bath while hosing both gardens. His investigation of the hose coming off the tap had him singing, "Thank you for the sprays." He was soaking wet when Jane rang again. He'd not expected when she'd said she'd ring him that she meant in the next few hours. She'd more test results about Andrew, giving him three months at best.

"Aw hell, that's not a lot. When my Mum died, she wasn't that compos mentis for the last week or two either. Keep him at home with the Macmillan nurses if you can, or a hospice," he recommended.

"I was so sorry when your Mum went, Bob. She was always friendly and never that mother-in-lawish. And your Dad too. I don't suppose they thought that much of me."

"They'd always liked you," he replied honestly. "I think they blamed me and the job."

"I'm sure they didn't."

When he'd recounted his experience of seeing God through a horse-chestnut tree a few weeks after they'd first met, she'd ribbed him about it for weeks. So she held back from telling him that for several months after his Dad had died, she could see his outline standing by the front window in Mossley Hill, listening carefully to her conversations with Andrew. She rang off without mentioning when she'd call again.

Bob plonked himself down onto a garden chair to dry out, chuckling to himself. His incompetence with the hose didn't bother him. He'd never wanted to be an engineer; he'd only changed from Physics for a Generating Board scholarship. He shut his eyes to the sun and thought what a momentous decision, made on the spur of the moment, that had proved to be. Once through Imperial, he'd joined the white-hot heat of the technological revolution in his first job at Shufflers Ferry power station on the Mersey. He'd rented a flat in Knutsford while he worked there.

* * *

Jane had rung Bob from the university where she'd had a weekend seminar. As she drove back to Mossley Hill, he remained in her thoughts. As an upper sixth former, she'd tried out the youth group which met after evensong at her local church. This burly, ungainly guy couldn't take his eyes off her all evening. He was older than everyone else; a few decades later his being there would have provided grounds for a paedophilia charge. She accepted his offer of dinner at the local Indian restaurant only because she'd been teased at school that day by Shirley Glossop for never having gone the whole way.

\* \* \*

Bob was steaming nicely in the sun, looking back with no rancour. He'd been going to the Church for a month, and the curate had persuaded him to try the youth group afterwards. He hadn't seen this girl with shoulder-length dark brown hair and pale, finely drawn features before. She'd given him a furtive, sideward glance from beneath her long eyelashes, almost as if she'd been expecting to see him. He'd never since been able to forget that look, though sometimes he wondered if she was checking her mascara in the mirror behind him. Words of wit and wisdom issued from her nineteen to the dozen. At the restaurant she'd been brilliant and outrageous in equal measure. He was both captivated and captured.

\* \* \*

In Ullet Road, Jane was remembering somewhere much cooler. The idiot had driven her over the Kirkstone Pass in his little Midget in two foot of snow. They'd stopped near the top for a snowball fight. As they'd kissed a truce, he'd told her that he loved her. She didn't know why she'd said she loved him too. She didn't remember the letters she sent him around then telling him that he'd made her feel so warm and happy that she couldn't imagine ever being without him. Then, as winter turned to spring, they'd had a long weekend in London, sleeping in separate hotel rooms. Together they enjoyed the sights and the galleries, with Kew Gardens their special place. The Grinling Gibbons' carvings at Hampton Court were tokens of their shared good taste, but she knew he wouldn't have given them a second glance if she hadn't pointed them out. In Smithdown Road, a wave of sadness reminded her of the little downers she used to get in her late teens. On one of those, she'd finished with him, the pretext being that things were developing too quickly, if not as fast as Shirley Glossop was suggesting. But he'd begged her and she'd relented. They'd bickered on their next trip to London. She'd known she was to blame and kissed him passionately, almost savagely, to make up. This led them to decide to sleep chastely together in their underwear. But she was naturally a sexual creature. All items of clothing had been removed before the sheets were warm, with a deal of assistance from her. A quick coupling took place. She had tight hold of both his buttocks as he climaxed. Shirley would have been proud.

\* \* \*

He was dry enough to go into the house to pour a large scotch. On the way back north from London, he'd made a tactical mistake by asking her to marry him. Once back in Knutsford, parked outside her house, she'd told him that they had to finish for good this time. He'd broken down as she ran into the house forgetting her suitcase, but pulled himself together to knock on the front door, hoping she'd change her mind. Her mother had answered, grabbed the case out of his hands, and said unconvincingly that she was sorry and more convincingly that Jane's mind was made up.

With glass of scotch in hand, he opened the front door, looking for he didn't know what. Three months after the London trip, as he pulled up outside his flat from work, Jane had been waiting in the shadows. When he'd smiled to greet her, she'd returned a sheepish grin. She was pregnant. He held her tight and asked if she was certain that she didn't want to marry him. After a few moments, she'd decided she would. He'd pulled her close to him, whispering the words of a song he'd tried previously in a corny letter to get her back, 'This time, be different, please stay, don't go'.

\* \* \*

She'd reached the Queen's Drive roundabout. Ruth was born in wedlock. They'd rented a flat in Princes Avenue, Liverpool 8, convenient for the bus to university. Robert came along couple of years later, unplanned also. They were in the flat four years. In the bedroom, she'd tease him with something new, coiling herself round him like an octopus. In the living room, things didn't stay good. Those were the only two rooms. Their bickering turned into echoing bawling matches across bare floorboards.

\* \* \*

He moved to an armchair. The sharpness of Jane and Scouse culture had become one and the same thing to him. They'd saved up enough money and he'd managed to persuade her to move to a semi-detached house in Ormskirk. Along came Jason, a friendly Cocker Spaniel, doted on by Ruth and Robert. The schools were good but a carpeted bedroom and double divan bed with dralon-covered headboard didn't bring the magic back. A couple of years later he was given a job at Moresham, forty miles north, where a big nuclear power station was being commissioned. He was rarely home before the children were in bed. After that, he was promoted to a senior management role in Manchester.

* * *

She pulled into the driveway. An anonymous caller had tipped Bob off that she'd been seeing Andrew Clarke. She'd had his suspicions that Andrew arranged for the call. Whatever, Jane was certain that Andrew was good for her and had the better conscience. His wiry muscles and Art Garfunkel hair were the perfect accompaniment to his ruthless pursuit of truth. She'd moved to Mossley Hill, with the two children and dog. She opened the front door into her present life of him waiting to die.

* * *

Bob wriggled in the armchair. He wasn't quite dry yet. She'd conveyed to him, without quite saying it, that Andrew was the better lover. No wonder, he thought, the bastard looked priapic, and with his spiky hair would make a good lavatory brush. He'd done what was considered the noble thing, and moved temporarily to a flat in Manchester. That way he'd said goodbye to Janie Burrows leaving, but as a result he'd never said goodbye to Janie Burrows lost. He'd slunk away hurt. He'd had many girl friends since, but none who'd meant anything like she had. They'd been cell mates, not soul mates. Gorgeous Wendy could be the real thing but she was staring starkly into the future of days caring for Frank. Those lost sacred days of Janie Burrows couldn't be resurrected but nor could they be replaced by endless days with Wendy Ballinger.

Straight after the split, he'd been asked to go to London to join the team coordinating the logistics ahead of the 1984 miners' strike. With his half of the Ormskirk proceeds, he'd bought the flat he still owned in Upper Thames Street. From there he'd viewed London's transformation from a failing city to the booming metropolis that sucked in talent from all parts of the globe, amassing untold wealth in the process by doing things he didn't care about. Still, he had to admit that even the untalented had been made welcome, him included.

The excitement of the strike kept some of the ghosts away. A year later, with the lights still on, the miners went back defeated. The grammar school snots of the Generating Board had wrecked their lives. That evening, he'd gone back to his flat to sign the divorce papers. Then the nationalised industries were sold off one by one, their functionaries sharing in a bonanza not seen since Henry the Eighth dissolved the monasteries. He'd been rewarded for helping see the miners off by being made a director of the public sector nuclear company. A few years later, when the government was foolhardy enough to privatise the more modern nuclear stations, he'd become Chief Executive of this new outfit, Atomic Futures plc. Being privatised was his last break with public sector culture. The CBE came in the post. He went to the palace with his grown up daughter Ruth, son Robert and no wife.

He shook his head sadly, deflated after the excitement of the day. There was nothing to occupy him until Tuesday. He walked round aimlessly from room to room, thinking that he was at least at home. When he eventually sat down, a wild panic set in, the kind of which he hadn't felt since the homesickness of a boyhood wolf cub camp.

He took a deep breath. Then he put one of the curries he'd bought into the oven. He'd spent many other Saturday nights on his own. Gene Pitney wasn't on a juke box but only playing on his iPod as he sprawled across the couch, with no girl standing there with ruby lips and golden hair. He went to check his emails. He'd one telling him he'd a message from Margaret Cornbill on Friends Reunited. He didn't know anyone of that name. He pressed the link with interest. There he found that it was from Margy Barton, his girlfriend from before he'd met Jane. She'd just joined the website after being nagged by her brother, had seen Bob's name and hadn't been able to resist firing off a message. Two kids and two messy divorces on, she survived. In a triumph of hope over expectation, she was on her third husband, Mike Cornbill, a folk singer like herself. For the day job, they were running a fruit growing business near Evesham. She'd remembered that Bob's Grannie was originally from around there too, and mentioned that the last time they'd been back to St Chad's she could swear she'd seen her ghost, thin and stooped like a Lowry figure, with a mischievous grin on her face, pushing her shopping basket up the Breck. She'd love to hear from him, and gave her email address.

He clicked to his Pictures folder, having been vain enough a few years before to upload the one on which Margy had written: "To the loveliest boy in the world with all my love." There she was, a pretty face with golden hair and lips that would have been ruby if folk singers had worn make-up. At the time he'd scarcely paid any attention to the inscription, despite having told her he'd loved her a few weeks before. He cringed at how hurtful he must have been. The other lads were all after her as she drove round in her yellow Mini with her guitar, playing the folk clubs. The Madonna had been his for free. They could have made a good couple if he hadn't wanted just a bit more of he didn't know what. He replied straightaway telling her about his marriage, divorce, his children and grandchildren. The folk music flooded his soul, particularly Margy singing Tom Paxton's 'Every Time'. He'd played Carolyn Hester's version over and over again in his grief when his Dad and then his Mum died, knowing the birds would still sing and the bells of St Chad's would still ring 'when we are gone'. He told Margy that the way she sang the song was so haunting it was like an angel weeping. Bob.Swarbrick@hotshot.com finally thanked her for bringing back the best memories, congratulated her on being happy at last and told her to keep in touch. Margy didn't take long. Within five minutes Bob had an invitation to Skype her straightaway if he knew how. He did.

"Seeing you after all this time's like dying and finding there's life after death," she gushed, with nothing but joy in her eyes.

"You look great, kid. Have you kept that religious stuff with you? The Church was so big in our lives. We bargained for salvation and she gave us a lethal dose."

She said she had, and her daughter was a vicar, before adding: "Great song, that. One of the wonderful things about Dylan is when he's moved on he's honoured his past, his women, his music, the lot."

"You were ready to lend Pete Seeger your axe when he went electric," Bob reminded her.

She ignored the jibe. "Why did your marriage go wrong?" was what she had to know.

"Jane was a great girl, still is. We just weren't quite right for each other. You can't leave stuff behind, and shouldn't try."

She asked if he'd anybody new, and he coyly answered, "Maybe," before asking if she still sang the same stuff. She wasn't going to let Bob easily forget he'd chucked her. She told him how she'd added Dusty's 'Colouring Book' to her repertoire after they'd finished and she'd had to 'colour him gone'. She yelled Mike to come into frame. They sang without any backing the first verse of Don and Phil's finest, 'Let it be me', gazing fondly into each other's eyes, before telling Bob that he was forgiven and promising they'd pop in the next time they were in St Chad's. Then they were gone, leaving him in an empty room. She'd not planned to, but she'd had her revenge, served late rather than cold.

There were so many things that never could be undone, however sorry he was, even assuming Jane was too. He looked through the window and saw nothing but burnt, impassable bridges all the way to Gloucestershire.

# CHAPTER SEVEN

O n Tuesday, Bob stood waiting anxiously for the late arriving first train to Preston. He made the London connection with a minute to spare.

\* \* \*

Two hundred miles to the south-east Helen arrived at Pierre's cottage, out in the country next to a farmhouse. She'd told the lie to Richard that Pierre's car had broken down and she was giving him a lift. Pierre greeted her at the door cautiously, but once it was closed he gently held her in his arms. In his living room, she could see evidence for his sensitive nature on his bookshelves, packed with philosophy intermingled with symbolist poetry, and on his walls, with his preference for prints of English Pre-Raphaelites over French Impressionists. He held her hand as they climbed the stairs. The bed was immaculately made with a smartly-ironed duvet, cool cotton sheets and feather pillows. He wasn't as much of a hunk as she'd thought he was. But they were soon in bed with the foreplay working sufficiently well for both. There was stillness in the air as time waited for the consummation. Then from the farm next door came the clear sound of a cock crowing twice. She sat bolt upright, kicked the quilt off, walked to the chair and put her clothes back on.

Finally, she spoke to a startled Pierre, who was still on the bed, his desire waning. "I'll see you at the surgery, Saint Pierre. It's me who's denied my man thrice, and that's enough." He'd no idea what she was talking about. She couldn't be bothered explaining.

\* \* \*

On his journey, Bob read the documents for the meeting. Wendy's numbers man Paul White and Divinity's analyst Linda Chan had been busy. Wendy had produced a timetable that led to an October listing. The company had already appointed a UK solicitor and she'd made a recommendation for a financial PR company appointment, Imaginative Finance. In his email of support, Richard had commented that it would make an even better name for an auditor. He'd provided no more than a list of institutions and funds who might wish to own the shares.

Bob reached Divinity's offices in Finsbury Square to find that Peter and Emil had already arrived. The newly appointed financial PR team were strutting their stuff to them, while lawyers too numerous to count kept materialising, seemingly out of nothing or by amoeba-like division. Wendy and Paul White, with no Linda Chan so that the facade of her independence was preserved, showed up spot on time. Richard emerged from the lifts to greet them all. On the way to the conference room, Peter complained at the price of their hotel, with the pound overvalued against the dollar making London's outrageous prices even worse. He fulminated against the madness of having to list in the UK. Wendy patiently pointed out that it would cost several hundred thousand dollars annually to do so in New York and that, the stronger the pound, the more dollars they'd get from the flotation.

Richard allowed Wendy to chair the meeting. Her voice deepened as she collected herself. She asked if everyone had managed to read the papers.

"There were enough of them," said Bob. "Once I put them down, I couldn't pick them up."

"I trust that everyone else has read them, unlike poor old Bob who hasn't been well. Not that I suppose he would have if he'd been as fit as a fiddle," she smiled despite having heard his remark many times before. He was still in favour.

Richard joined in. "I always say that the problem of reading the papers before the meeting is that you've nothing to read during it."

Unlike Bob's remark, this was original. He'd let Wendy chair the meeting because he really hadn't read the papers. The Brits laughed and the Yanks looked perplexed. Wendy moved on quickly before Peter said something too tart.

Emil made a good presentation, confident without overselling. They then discussed the timetable over lunch. Wendy handled the discussion well, making a couple of minor concessions to Peter's ego. The meeting was more or less finished by three o'clock.

Bob still had lingering doubts about whether Peter had flotation as his first option. He raised the issue of the local rival, Western Sun Rising, asking how they were getting on and where their money was coming from. Peter didn't dissemble at all, admitting he'd hoped to do something with them, as they weren't far from break-even with better sales channels than Northern. Western would love to buy them, he said, and that way become a quoted company, but their money had come from a bunch of high net worth guys who wouldn't cough up any more. Richard had spoken to an old contact at Grindleton's. He'd done something during the last week after all. Western Sun Rising were actively looking for new private investors rather than their own flotation.

The meeting closed with everyone agreeing that the big thing was finding a market for the shares. They'd all known that before they'd started. Still, they were all off the same hymn-sheet as Wendy had it, to Richard's dismay. The only time confusion arose in his church was when the choirmaster, trying to be relevant, put more modern words on the sheet while the congregation couldn't be bothered finding their glasses and sang the version they knew. They arranged to meet again in London in two weeks, with a Board meeting afterwards. By then Richard would have a better view of the appetite for the shares. If there wasn't any, there was no alternative source of finance for Northern and the sun would go down.

Wendy and Bob met up as soon as the meeting had finished. Frank was top of her mind as she feared he was becoming violent in addition to his deteriorating incontinence. Next door's dog had cowered away from him. The doctors were saying that he really ought to have specialist care. Richard came over as the conversation was ending, and Wendy had to repeat the sad story before dashing off to catch her train. As it was only half past three, Bob suggested meeting up with Richard later. That wasn't in Richard's mind. He was ready for the off.

"Would you like to stop overnight?" he asked. "Helen said I was thoughtless in not asking you."

Bob couldn't say no given that he was carrying his case with him. On the way to Moorgate station, they saw Sir Charles Norman's Daimler with him ensconced in the back seat. On the train Bob told the tale of his dismissal from Atomic Futures. He and Charles had been giving evidence together at the Energy Select Committee chaired by Jonathan Sheldrake, after a couple of minor safety issues. Rebecca Moore had been acting as their minder. Richard knew Sheldrake, a Labour lawyer, who he called a supercilious prat. Bob smiled his acknowledgment as he said: "The tosser discerned a worrying pattern of Atomic Futures not taking safety sufficiently seriously. The engineering issues were beyond their reach, but the other members of the committee could understand that."

Bob saw himself in a yeoman tradition, a self-defined concept, making himself available for service when summoned but otherwise ploughing his own furrow. He listed a little more to starboard than Richard, although he'd never felt comfortable voting for the oily Tories and had usually voted Labour until their sanctimony had made that too gut-wrenching. Richard, from the large town sometimes described as the biggest village in England, still drove slightly to the left of centre. He solemnly explained to Bob that politics is about policy as the superior intelligence so one had to abase oneself on such occasions.

"I tried but I had a bad back that day," Bob chuckled. "I just about managed to keep my cool as Charlie boy agreed with the plonkers before changing the subject. Back outside my office, I let off steam to Rebecca about how a total tosspot such as Sheldrake could think he added any value to the world; how the hell could he eat at his smart restaurants in Hampstead..."

"They're all crap anyway," was Richard's opinion, on the basis of their black puddings.

"...without feeling guilty for not having earned the food on his plate. We didn't know Charlie was listening from behind his door, nor that he'd agreed with Sheldrake to provide him this sound bite in return for no action resulting. That is, we didn't know until he peered out to tell us. We'd had plant breakdowns and umpteen other operational things going wrong. Not even in my dreams was nuclear going to be treated as green for subsidies. Charles elegantly put the boot in. I didn't feel worth the pension I was paid off with but couldn't turn it down."

About three quarters of an hour later, they reached Hummills. Trotter barked wildly as Richard opened the door. Helen was less exuberant. She wasn't expecting them so soon, and she was racked with shame she couldn't share. Amy was at her side, holding the hem of her summer dress nervously. As far as Bob could tell, Helen hadn't offered her cheek to be pecked during the greetings. After an awkward pause, she spoke first, telling Amy to show her new toy to Bob. Amy ran outside while the others went in to the living room. Bob unzipped his bag and gave Helen a bottle of Lanson Black Label Brut. She gave him a very wet kiss on the cheek.

Having misread the social mores of Hertfordshire introductions, Bob over-compensated: "You're looking terrific, Helen. How on earth did an ugly bugger like Richard pull a woman like you? It's not as if he's any good at anything."

Helen couldn't find the expected words of false bonhomie to insult Richard further when she'd done so much recent evil to him in real life. She prayed, really prayed, that he'd never find out. Noticing the gap, Richard answered for her. "I once won second prize in the Sunday School Bible reading competition. The girl who finished first had a lisp."

Before Bob had chance to follow this up with more mistimed banter, Amy arrived with a stuffed cow, Buttercup, who'd been in the garden eating grass all day. Bob noticed the long 'A' in 'grass' and two southern 'U's' in 'Buttercup'. His kids were from north of the funny/fanny line, as Jane called it, a source of the occasional single entendre joke. Richard had travelled further than he had. But Fylde was a dairy farming area and Bob liked cows. "Moo. Can she moo back to me? Moo-ooo."

Amy mooed and mooed. After being told he was ugly, Richard retaliated: "That's the sort of sense Bob's been speaking all day, Helen."

Helen realised that she had to join in, and as perverse as ever, it was on Bob's side. "It was a pretty good impression, and probably makes more sense than the financial gobbledygook you'll have been spouting."

As she spoke, she could hear that she'd jarred against good nature yet again. She showed Bob upstairs to the room he was to occupy. They then all met up in the garden for a drink. Independent schools had started their summer holidays, so both Laura and James were home. Matthew was out with his girlfriend. When Helen and Amy went back in to start the cooking, Richard and Bob played football with the other two. Richard was much fitter and more skilful.

"Don't I remember you saying that you could have had a trial at Bolton?" Bob wheezed.

Richard dribbled past Bob as he answered: "Yeah, but I couldn't beat a tortoise with cramp in a sprint."

Bob pulled up to save himself from further punishment. For the thirds at Imperial, he'd been a centre-half who could trap the ball further than most people could kick it. He asked how much cricket Richard had played.

"Quite a bit, but my Dad was better than me," Richard replied. "I've a press cutting from before the war, when he hit the stumps five balls in a row bowling his medium pacers. You played some decent stuff, didn't you?"

Bob thought of his early years with Jane as he replied: "Palace Shield, and later the Liverpool Competition. I had a couple of games for Lancashire Club and Ground but wasn't anywhere near good enough for anything better. Statham and Higgs were opening for the county then."

"Statham was fantastic. Higgs was pretty good too, when he wasn't looking for his mythical boson in the field."

"You're wrong on two counts, bozo," Bob told him. "Ken calls himself Peter when he's doing his Physics. And some particle has to exist. They hope to find it in that new collider when it gets going. Whether they'll find the super-symmetric weakly interacting massive particles they're looking for too, the superwimps, I've no idea."

"With that acronym, they'll probably be a bit shy to show themselves," Richard predicted.

"In which case, 'Here Be Dragons' will still be written across swathes of the cosmic map."

Once they'd sat down again after the exertions, the talk was of schools, of holidays, the part of life which Bob had missed out on because of the divorce. He knew that he was among friends and yet he felt terrifyingly alone. He shuddered, thinking that someone was walking over his grave too damned often. He didn't know that Helen was thinking something similar.

She'd cooked an excellent dinner, a piece of beef that melted in the mouth followed by a raspberry pavlova good enough to produce more shivers down spines. Although Helen was subdued, the conversation was good, with Amy already in bed and the other children making a decent attempt to be adults. After dinner Laura and James went upstairs to their computers. Richard and Bob sided up (another Bob phrase), washed the pots and pans and filled the dishwasher while Helen set up the coffee. As they settled down in the comfort of the living room, Helen used an event from the day as cover for her downbeat mood. She'd had to put down Barney, the golden Labrador of a family friend whose husband had walked out a few months before.

"That dog has been so important for the kids since their Dad left. I found myself saying that Barney's gone to heaven," she smiled wanly.

Richard's eyes watered up, both at poor old Barney's fate and at Helen's saying something he knew she didn't believe for the sake of the kids. He mentioned an agnostic bit from Ecclesiastes which said that humans have no idea if they've an eternal spirit any more than an animal has. Richard and Bob described their childhood dogs. They were both rooted in the story they told themselves about their lives. They felt they were a bit more than that too, with the part of them that had lived through the story outside the system in Bob's case, and in the mind of God in Richard's idea. Bob thus hoped the whole tale was stored away in the eternal Cloud. The more pessimistic Richard thought it more likely the file would be deleted at death and not to recycle bin. He looked for meaning in life, Bob for purpose. Richard saw events as fickle fate, presently working in his favour, Bob as a catalogue of decisions he'd enjoyed making, with some bad ones currently coming home to roost. Helen reckoned that God had a lot to answer for and it was as well he didn't exist.

"I'll always think he does." Bob said kindly. "Somehow, sad memories add more colour to life than happy ones. We can't know if this place could be any better.

I'm glad I've been here, good times and bad, even if I pop my clogs tomorrow and there's nowt else."

Richard didn't think his life story should fuse bad and good ideas together. The weeds should be composted. His memory was less inclined to be so pragmatic, as evidenced by the time it took before he dropped his first love on to the heap.

Helen felt herself too privileged to dismiss the sufferings of others as glibly as Bob just had, and didn't think a post-war northern upbringing was sufficiently arduous to qualify Richard for sainthood either. Her hands were starting to twitch. Her voice quivered: "What about your bloody God's role as tectonic plate massacrist in the Tsunami? The church bangs on about our need for salvation. The big thing we seem to need saving from is your God killing people in earthquakes, drive-by shootings and the like."

Richard protested that he hadn't seen an old man with a beard in the mugshots on Crimewatch recently. Bob could see too many good things about life to make the problem of pain the ultimate question on every subject. "You win some, you lose some, even if you're God," was his theodicy. He played back to Helen that modern humans came about as a result of tectonic changes in the Rift Valley. She wasn't having any purpose attached to the world's development. She sang word-perfect from the life science songbook that no creature had been designed and that humanity had come from a blind evolutionary process.

Bob's view of God's purpose didn't include any design either, just perhaps an occasional fresh quantum of will. He gave voice, as Helen heckled, to how events since creation could be entangled, how through aeons of random cosmic activity and biological mutations, intelligent beings that can see good and bad, beauty and ugliness had come about. "If you weren't in the universe, but sitting on the outside, you'd judge that as a result. Maybe we can think outside the system, even if we can't go there," was his final flourish.

Richard mentioned his well-rehearsed piece of theology of God still being made too. Helen's eyes fired shards of ice at him. "If you're going to entertain the quaint notion of a God, make him carry the can," she insisted. "A girl from my class at school was knocked down and killed in front of me running across the road to her mother's car. Was she so silly that she deserved to die?"

Richard was adamant that the girl's mother needed to give value to her daughter's life, and the story that God had lost his own Son in horrible circumstances was an attempt at that. "It's not that we're being less feeling and more callous than you," he said.

"You must be," she snapped back. "Look at the jobs you do."

Bob told of another occasion: "Once I thought I'd dropped a heavy table on my daughter's head when she was a toddler. I was damned sure it was going to hit her but it missed by a few millimetres. Just occasionally, the story seems to vary from the inevitable."

Helen wasn't listening to either of them. The tensions of the last few days had taken their toll on her. She was no longer playing devil's advocate, but the devil himself, as she snarled at Richard: "You may have manufactured something that seems beautiful here in Monkey Mead on the back of your ill-gotten gains from being a corporate finance pimp. That's no reality at all, just a gaudy tableau of kitsch that's bound to be blown over in a strong wind. You've made it all yourself. You've never faced heartbreak like that mother did."

This place wasn't that far from crazy sorrow after all. There was a big crack at its core. Neither man could find any words for about a minute. Richard hadn't moved a muscle and Helen was still trembling.

Bob finally had something coherent to say. "If this place is kitsch, then I've lost every bit of taste I ever had. There's nowt wrong with our Richard. You're lucky to have him. Putting poor old Barney down's hurt you more than you know. And where does your sense of justice come from if not by living in this cruel world, and trying to improve on what you find?"

Helen knew it wasn't Barney that was bugging her but was glad of the way out. "I'm sorry, I'm sorry. I married a good guy who right now should hate me. I know that he won't, because he's a lovely man. All we can say, Bob, is that if the world hadn't been this way, we wouldn't have been here to spout our nonsense. There's probably a unifying force we don't know about at work."

Bob was happy enough with Helen thinking that. What he hadn't wanted to hear was that every possibility actually happened. If so, he'd killed Ruth with the table many times. He claimed modern orthodoxy to be motivated by a desire not to commit the heresy of an outcome being willed. Helen logically pointed out that if there were a limitless number of universes producing ever more intelligence, then a supreme being would have evolved and she didn't believe in one of those.

Richard wanted the last word on his specialist subject: "You have to feel God before you believe in him, and he's well hidden." Helen burst out laughing, saying she'd never found his hiding place nor had any message other than that believing in God is a psychological defect, as everybody her age thought.

"There's nothing you know that those of our age don't," Bob snapped back. "Church bells mean freedom to me. Some light refracted through those stained glass windows but God doesn't reveal that much or we wouldn't have to think for ourselves." He then wanted to sue for peace and added: "You met a better class of girl at Church too."

Helen had the devil in her still, telling them their cultural line was extinct apart from the odd new hairy rock band set up as a Lennon tribute act. Richard's favourite building, Bolton Town Hall, might be impressive, she conceded, but it was municipal and from yesterday. She then was more enigmatic, wishing she knew where she was from like that.

"Does it really matter, love?" Richard asked.

She didn't answer, but held his hand. Not knowing what they were talking about, Bob absolved her from any share in his and Richard's sins. "We showed our gratitude by taking the forty pieces of silver and buggering off south. We sold off most of British industry to asset strippers, and the decent start-ups too soon. We've ended up with a stupidly high exchange rate and financial services crowding out everything else, leaving the poor buggers left up there with nowt but state charity, the worst sort."

"I see things from the nuances of the deep south-east, which even Londoners don't get," Helen replied obliquely to Bob. "Richard doesn't enjoy the implied criticism in each vowel lengthening, each change of lip position, which we spent our childhood rehearsing. Whenever we have a row, he bangs on about my style."

"I don't like rows," Richard admitted.

Helen squeezed his hand. "I know. You Lancastrians seemed to be friendly folk with the widest smiles. Then you all changed, producing miserable stuff like The Smiths and The Verve. Every northerner on the News looked downtrodden and glum."

Bob agreed with this more than he wanted to. "They were both pretty good though. But those damned interviews when there's a pathetic, even more overweight than me, middle-aged couple sat unfeasibly close to each other on a sofa telling a doe-eyed, young interviewer their economic woes make me want to throw custard pies at them."

Helen volunteered to give them the treatment poor old Barney got to put them out of their misery. Bob thought a judicious use of the off button was sufficient.

"You've got to be cruel to be kind," Helen smiled. "They're only on again tomorrow that way,"

The other two chose to assume she was joking. She took herself off to bed before she caused more trouble, wishing she could have done more to say sorry, not something that came naturally. Bob and Richard chatted for only a few more minutes before Bob went to his room for the night. Both had been using genealogical records to track down their family histories and they compared notes. Neither had any relatives from south of the funny/fanny boundary but Richard had Yorkshire in him as well as Lancashire, his male line originally from just over the boundary in the Pennine villages beyond Todmorden.

Richard didn't rush to join Helen in bed. The previous night he'd realised that the power base between them had changed. He hadn't had the confidence to wake her to ask necessary questions about the next morning's arrangements. He felt that he was fading out of the picture. Part of his doubts about life after death was not that God would show ill-will towards him but that there would be other, more pressing, things to be done. When he did eventually get in bed, her backside was pushed snugly into his breadbasket. He wasn't sure if she was awake or asleep.

He whispered into the darkness more in hope than expectation: "You've got the sexiest arse in captivity. Can I give it a full assessment?"

"It's my bottom, all mine, and it's never been captured."

Her tone had been friendly enough. He pushed his luck. "How about a shag then?"

"OK, if you're quick."

"I thought I was meant to take my time and indulge you in amusing and sensuous foreplay," he whispered as he nuzzled her ear.

"That was then, this is now."

Richard stood firm in the face of the winds of change. He licked her breasts for a minute or so, savouring both nipples in equal measure. He moved his tongue towards a lower target area. He'd often wanted to do this before, but she'd not let him. She was about to stop him again, before surprising herself by welcoming this day of atonement, this most intimate entry to what lay untainted by any intruder since they'd met. "Does the taste tell you anything different about me?" she asked.

His tongue was otherwise engaged so that he couldn't reply. Her relief from being rescued from mortal sin flooded body and soul. Soixante-neuf was borrowed from French and this debt to Pierre remained forever unpaid. Eventually Richard flipped and they were conjoined. He could speak. "You're delicious, Mrs Gorgeous. I could eat you without any gravy."

"And I couldn't eat you vindalooed, you vulgar pig."

Their flesh was welded together as they climaxed. He wanted to know if the gates of love had budged an inch. Helen was as full of effusive praise as she could manage in the metric age, and conceded they'd moved maybe a centimetre.

He answered the question she'd asked a few minutes earlier. "The taste was delicious. You know the old joke about two cannibals eating a clown. One says to the other, 'Does this taste funny to you?' You don't have an essence. Helen is everything you are, and there's not a bit I'd ever change."

"Sugar and spice and all things nice," she recited. "You're right, that's not me, just my body. I'm as sour as vinegar."

There was no further comment from the mesomorph corner. The next morning, when their train arrived at Moorgate, Richard walked one way to the office and Bob the other to his flat, finishing Ian McEwan off before travelling to St Chad's after lunch. Seeing a married couple row and then make up had almost left him regretting leaving Jane too quickly.

## CHAPTER EIGHT

Following communion on Sunday, Bob felt in need of fresh air. He parked in Great Eccleston and walked over Wyreford Bridge across the fields to the church where his great grandfather was buried alongside his first son. The lad had drowned in the Wyre a hundred and fifty years ago while larking about with his mates. He felt the chill of despair that he'd gone there to feel. On the way back he partook of a spot of lunch at the Wyreford Inn before returning home to not very much.

Early on Monday, Wendy didn't answer. He rang Ruth as consolation. There was lots of news and he was unusually talkative. He learnt that Robert's new girlfriend, Sophie, was from Canada. She was also a lawyer, one of his firm's recent intake. The two of them were visiting Oxford at the weekend, and Ruth was pulling out all the stops for dinner. Bob worried that Sophie sounded too young, since it was time for Robert to settle down. Ruth had the imprint of marital break-up in her soul.

"You're the last person to want him in a relationship that goes wrong. Not that you've ever talked about the break-up," she grumbled, not for the first time.

"Did your Mum?"

"You were never mentioned other than the arrangements for visits."

Bob dealt with Jane's indifference by singing, 'Am I that easy to forget?' Having begged him to shut up, Ruth insisted that he'd been terrific.

"Robert and I used to give Mum a terrible time," she recalled cheerfully. "She did the dastardly deed and we can never unknow that. I'd have a strop most nights, and Robert, well you were his hero. We ignored Andrew. He and Mum were either too mean or too nice in response. They could never get the balance right."

Bob knew that no parent ever could. They did what was most convenient and then repented. "Please do your best for her now, she's going to need you," he pleaded. "We weren't alike but I don't think we were that bad a fit."

Ruth agreed that she could always tell what they'd seen in each other on the times when they did meet. Bob's theory was that one of them turned by a few degrees and they hadn't slotted together after that. He didn't think he was the one who'd moved, evidencing that he'd happily helped her on her first book.

"She told me that was only when your cricket was rained off," Ruth joked.

Bob thrust out his chin and grinned, "It must have had a bad summer. I wasn't the right husband for a feminist academic but that's a cop out. I can't hide behind cause and effect. Some hidden fission force in our characters did its work."

Having such a long conversation was bringing out into the open all the sympathy Ruth felt for Bob, the cool guy chairing an LA company. She considered Jane the backdated one, still playing around in campus politics. Bob thought Jane to be no slave to ideology. She would always be ahead of him in the game. He finished by saying: "Her feminism was fine by me. I'm no apologist for a patriarchal culture".

Ruth's sympathy couldn't extend that far. "You're the embodiment of it, Dad. Just get your own mind straight for when Andrew kicks the bucket. When are you coming to see us again?"

He was chairing a Board meeting for another of his companies, Citel, on Tuesday in London. He jumped at the chance to call in for lunch on his drive down on Monday. He then rang Robert to see if he really was Sophie's choice.

"That movie's about as depressing as it gets," was Robert's answer. Bob repeated his conversation with Ruth, musing if he'd left both children, not just one, to the Nazis if it was that bad in Mossley Hill. Robert picked his words carefully, saying: "Mum did her best, but we missed you too much. You must have known that at the time."

"I thought it was par for the course."

There was a re-awakened pain in Robert's voice as he described it as more like a double bogey, if not a lost ball. Bob apologised for letting them both down before asking

Robert to try to persuade Ruth that Jane was a good woman who was better off without him. Robert couldn't do that because he believed Jane would have been better off with Bob too. In mock despair, Bob told him that he'd become friendly with a lady on the LA assignment. They moved on to cricket and close season football rumours before ringing off. Bob settled down with the newspaper for two minutes before his mobile rang with Wendy's name up in lights.

Bob didn't hide his need to talk to her. "I've had what's usually described as a quiet weekend. I guess wanting to be somewhere else made me realise how lame my life is."

"Where did you want to go then?" she asked.

"Wherever you were."

She called him a big softie. Her voice was as warm and comforting as he'd hoped for. She'd had a weekend best described as difficult. Frank had wandered off for three hours, avoiding all search parties, until he was spotted walking down the main road out of the other end of the village. He'd said that he'd gone to meet his wife at the bus station. Eventually Wendy changed the conversation to business. She needed Bob's help in getting Emil to budge on the financials. Paul White was having no success because old ape-man Foreskin had Emil by the short and curlies. Bob promised to have a bash. He told her his arrangements, hoping she'd be near enough to see after visiting Ruth. She was in Oxford that afternoon. Bob had sometimes taken Robert to the Trout at Godstow in his student days and they arranged to meet there at six o'clock.

"I'm not sure I can live without you for a week but the prospect of our meeting will keep me going," Bob said, in a tone of voice that could have been taken as either serious or mock pathetic.

Wendy wasn't sure which either. "Are you taking the piss?" she asked. "Sadly, I feel the same about you. And I love it when you start flirting. It's like seeing mating rituals from long before I was born."

Bob couldn't tell where Wendy had turned from serious into micturation extraction. "You were born, if very young when I learnt this patter. My daughter told me I wasn't a period piece not an hour ago, and I'm believing her."

Wendy joked that his family was getting in the way even before they'd started. On the spur of the moment, he told her that his ex's husband was terminally ill. He blurted out his fears that his children could become an impediment when Andrew did turn up his toes. "They're planning for Jane and me to become friends again It doesn't matter to them that she'd run a mile and I don't want to," he insisted.

Wendy's voice lost its confidence. "She might run a mile, but you wouldn't. You'd think it the proper thing to happen. It sounds like a big deal to me."

He disagreed as strongly as he could without any feedback that she believed him. Over the next week, he played two rounds of golf and reduced the Northern Solstice estimated sales figure for the next two years, while keeping the third year profit intact so that the valuation wouldn't be too badly hit. Wendy was impressed with him for that. The Northern meeting was firmed up for Wednesday with the Board meeting for dinner with advisers at the Dorchester on Tuesday evening. Bob travelled down to Solihull after another lonely weekend.

Ruth was pleased to see him looking so well. She's an erectly tall, dark-haired girl, interesting-looking if not as pretty as her mother, with a reflective, more forgiving nature. She'd quit working as an actuary when she'd married. Her husband, Harry Jackson, was a production manager in the motor industry, who wouldn't set the world alight but who added much to a happy home. That's what it was that lunchtime. Eldest son Tom went out after lunch with friends. Bob played a game of tig with Charlotte, Rachel and Old English Sheepdog Bess, having fed Baby Ben his dinner with about seventy per cent accuracy. He stayed until half past four without outstaying his welcome.

The M40 was busy, as was the Wolvercote roundabout. He pulled into the Trout car park at five past six, almost performing a handbrake turn to park in one of the few remaining spaces. As he clambered out of the car, a Range Rover screeched into the next space with a similar parking manoeuvre.

"Sorry I'm a few minutes late, Bob. I've had the pants bored off me at this meeting."

"Well if your pants are already off..."

"To the bar before I'm tempted," Wendy instructed.

He asked if she went over for tea at Camilla's in the Range Rover. She called him a boy racer reliving his youth in his coupé, an accident waiting to happen.

"The pair of us both," he said. They kissed full on the lips, and went into the bar holding hands. Both went for non-alcoholic lagers.

They sat outside looking at the fish in the river. Since she knew all his humiliations, he wanted to know about the swine before Frank who'd let her down.

"I studied Archaeology at Reading, I think you know that." Bob nodded and let her carry on. "I was born in Cheltenham, plain Wendy Smith, an only child. There was a boy there that I fell for, a lovely guy in my class called Chris. I was engaged to him. But then I met another guy, Martin, a year ahead of me, reading Economics and, shame on me, I two-timed Chris. He was heartbroken for about a week before he started up with one of my best friends, and he married her instead."

"I bet he still misses you."

"They've been blessed. Martin went into the world of banking, and I followed him as he somehow persuaded Rowland Saul to have me. At that stage they were just about the best merchant bank in London. Into admin at first, but I crossed over to corporate finance within a couple of years. We were going to be married the next month, when he told me it was off."

"Bloody idiot," sympathised Bob.

"He married an heiress instead. He was killed in a skiing accident about five years later. I met and married Frank Ballinger back at home having jacked it in with Rowland Saul when Black and Robertshaw wanted to do corporate finance stuff. We now live in a lovely house in St Kenelm's, just outside Cheltenham. Frank owns an antiques shop in town in partnership with a family friend, Steve. We've been starchy with each other since the day we married."

Janie Burrows was forgotten. Bob held both Wendy's hands tight in his as she spoke in a low monotone. With her career, she hadn't wanted children straightaway When she'd come off the pill, nothing happened. They'd never tested to see if it was him or her. She hadn't felt enough about him to go for IVF. They'd got a cat, Sheba, instead.

Bob thought of the flip comment about trying an experiment with him, but instead remained suitably sombre. She giggled at the caring look of his face, saying it didn't suit him and that she paid him to cheer her up.

"It's not the stuff of comedy," he murmured.

She pulled his hands to her lap. "Send in the clowns."

He finished for her: "Don't bother, they're here. My Grannie was Alice Smith and she was from near Evesham, not that far from you. Maybe we're distant relations. Mind you, there are quite a lot of Granny Smiths in that area."

He went to the bar for two new bottles. Wendy carried on where they'd left off once she'd mopped up the spillage from his over-enthusiastic pouring. Steve, who she thought was a celibate homosexual, had become a good mate and had roped her into volunteering at a charity shop in Evesham.

"Bloody hell, a pooftah antique dealer. There's a surprise. Can't he play front row for Gloucester or at least be out cruising every night on a motor bike, even a moped?"

Wendy lifted his hands up, kissed them and put them on her lap again. "You're so physical, even when you're being kind. You'd like him though. He's taken to going on archaeological digs with me like a duck to water. I'd take you too but tongues would wag."

Bob felt bold enough to offer an alternative venue. "Please come to St Chad's if you can get away. It's an authentic old place, and still got the old stocks and whipping post in the square. The church was mentioned in the Domesday Book and the crocuses are a wonder to behold in the churchyard."

"That's a coincidence! We've still got our stocks and whipping post too. I'd better get to St Chad's before Jane is back on the market. I'll invite you to St Kenelm's once that's possible. We need to know each other better."

"I don't need to know you more to know what you're like, and that's just perfect," was Bob's opinion. "How well do you reckon you know me now?"

She presented Bob with his hands back having kissed them again. "Well enough to know that your past won't leave you. It makes you interesting. You're different from people my age in ways I don't always get. Richard and you are similar in that."

Bob wasn't prepared to share any part of Wendy with his best mate. He was delighted to be a woollyback while Richard wanted to be both hip and traditional. Wendy didn't know what a woollyback was. He explained with maybe a trace of irony that it was what the hip Scousers called other folk from nearby. She could think of nothing less hip than a Scouser. Being the age he was, he couldn't agree. "I liked George Harrison, a Richard kind of bloke. Took religion seriously, keen gardener, President of the George Formby Appreciation Society. He was in a band too."

They chatted animatedly for about an hour more, time racing by before Bob did venture his earlier thought about seeing if he could get her pregnant. She had her answer ready. "I probably can't have children anyway. And, on the off chance an egg was fertilised, Frank could notice. That could put him into unbearable anguish. I'd feel too disloyal, even if he didn't know."

Bob didn't think that all the pathways in Frank's brain would be blocked, with the trillions of possible connections. But he could be too far gone to process new information. Wendy showed impatience, the first time he'd noticed her do that. "You're answering the wrong question. It's not really about Frank understanding which he almost certainly won't. If he were fully compos mentis, I'd not feel guilty. I can't leave him in the state he's in, because he can't retaliate."

Bob more frequently became irritated, including for the first time with Wendy. Nobody would ever know they'd tried if she wasn't fertile or if he was firing blanks. She'd already told him Frank hadn't given her what she'd wanted as a husband. On the off chance it worked, she'd be justified by the outcome of a wanted new life.

That's what he thought. He said: "If he was dead, he couldn't retaliate, so what's the difference?"

"There's a massive difference," she countered. Bob knew that only she could make the decision and hoped her guardian angel was on the case. As Wendy put her arms round his neck to hug him, she saw the time on her watch. "I'll have the devil on my back knowing my luck. Hell, I'll have to be getting back now."

Bob had run away once before and he wasn't born to run. "Can we escape this rap, Wendy? Wrap your legs round my rims in an everlasting kiss."

"You're far too old for Springsteen," she laughed. "I'm not prepared to be rogered by your gear stick at my age."

"I've got a bus pass and I'm prepared to take the chance," he revealed.

"You've got a bus pass! Tramps like us, baby we were born to travel free for our flu jabs."

She did climb into Bob's car. They kissed as if they were parting before a war. Bob's hands were allowed a free rein round her engines. He swore as his mobile rang. But he still answered.

"It's Robert, Dad. Andrew's dead. He's shot himself."

Bob gasped, looking straight at Wendy in horror, "Oh God, no. When did he do it?"

"He was found a few hours ago. The neighbours heard the shot after Mum left for a seminar. The police were called when they couldn't raise a reply. He was lying there in the kitchen. I've spoken to Ruth.

She's going up tonight."

With Wendy next to him, Bob still asked about Jane

"She seemed OK when we spoke," Robert thought. "I don't think it's sunk in yet. Of course the cops and their doctors are all over the place to make sure it's suicide. They've found a note, with this morning's post, which Mum hadn't spotted."

Bob promised to ring him again once back in London. His other hand was still on Wendy's thigh. He left it there as he relayed to her that Jane's husband had ridden the suicide machine to glory. She pressed the hand to her thigh even harder.

"I'll not be able to free myself from Frank. We know that. Go and see if she wants you back," she commanded.

"I want you, Wendy. It's thee I love."

She told him that she loved him too, before adding: "I must see things out with Frank to the bitter end. It will be bits and pieces at best with me."

She clambered out of the car with even less elegance than in LA, climbed into her car and drove off. He rang Ruth to ask how Jane had seemed to her.

"I'm not the one to ask, Dad," she confessed. "We've just had a few words. He's been a cheat all his life, cheated you, cheated us kids, and now thinks he can cheat death too."

Bob refused to think Andrew had cheated anyone. He'd have seen what he did as his duty, and blowing his own brains out certainly wasn't cowardice. He told Ruth at least to show Jane sympathy. Ruth was only prepared to offer her any as long as Jane didn't put on her 'poor Jinny Greenteeth' voice and said that she couldn't honour Andrew under any circumstance. Jinny Greenteeth was a name Bob hadn't invoked for a long time. She was frequently in play in St Chad's fifty years before, invented to stop children playing near water. She lived in a pond,

Barratt's pit, lurking under the duckweed, ready to pull children in. She came from a tale of a woman who'd lost her own family. He'd heard Richard mention her too, so there must have been dangerous ponds in Bolton as well. If anyone was feeling sorry for themselves, his family would say: "Poor Jinny Greenteeth, got no father, got no mother, poor Jinny Greenteeth." He didn't expect Jane to be self-pitying. Ruth thought she would be.

"I'll give her a ring now to see if she 'Jinnies' with me," Bob said.

Jane's mobile was off. Her house phone was busy.

## CHAPTER NINE

A t the same time as Bob was frustrated by the engaged tone, Richard left his office. It was only a few yards to Moorgate station and Pierre had to dash in order to intercept him. The conversation was brief, with Richard making his train.

\* \* \*

Jane was sitting in Andrew's armchair with a cup of tea. The crime scene investigators finished their checks. The police had suggested the good offices of a counsellor, insisted on more like, and a woman was on her way. Her next door neighbour Pete was answering her land-line phone. His wife Gillian was making teas.

Jane had been thinking about how she would cope with Andrew's death since his diagnosis, expecting him to grow frailer and sicklier, before fading into unconsciousness. She'd volunteered to identify him to see him one last time. He'd shot himself through the top of the mouth. Blood, bits of brain and skull were splattered all over the kitchen. The old tea caddy, a saucepan, the kitchen roll holder and a shattered new biscuit barrel were on the floor. Nothing could be cleaned up for forensic reasons. She didn't expect the police would find evidence of time warps.

The investigators had carried out some cleaning up after the body had been removed but she envisaged bits of him in the dustpan and vacuum cleaner for months to come. She'd been horribly sick after she'd seen the body. They'd cleared that up too. When she'd told the police she'd no idea where he'd got the gun from, they'd thought that most likely he'd bought it in a pub. She'd never known him go to the pub alone. The cops had taken the suicide note which she remembered saying something like:

My Dearest Jane,

This will save you and me so much pain. Ever since I've been a teenager, I've expected to end like this, having seen my father die from cancer. It's been a good life together. Savour every moment until you're gone too.
I know your urges are strong. Remarry if you must, but I beg you never to go back to Bob. Remember how sad he made you with his unthinking neglect.
You have been my rock, my human face, and you have made my life worthwhile.
Goodbye Sweetheart,

Andrew

The thought of going back to Bob had never really crossed her mind. She couldn't begin to comprehend why that was at the top of his thoughts. It wasn't guilt or he'd have not been unhappy about the idea; it wasn't triumphant or he wouldn't have been concerned. It was genuine fear that she would. The angst that she'd felt (and caused) in leaving Bob wasn't something to be repeated. That was real pain.

This, as described in her diary, was like the numbness from a dentist's injection.

The language that Andrew had used was constrained. Every word was carefully chosen, all emotions pared down. The Andrew of the last few years had been like that. His passion for causes great and small couldn't survive bodily weakness. All that was left was an impotent plea about his former vanquished enemy.

She cursed herself on his behalf about how she'd massively distressed her children to find it all ended with a hollow centre to her soul; how she was the loser and that was what she deserved; how she could bring no happy memories of Andrew back. Pete interrupted her train of rant to tell her that one of her students, Pratap Dongre from Kolkata, was on the phone.

"I'm so sorry, Professor, I've heard your terrible news on Messenger from another student. Please accept my deepest sympathy."

"I thought we'd done a deal on Jane, Pratap. He was very ill, and he saw this as the best way for both of us. It was only a matter of a few months before he went naturally."

"It must be a fearful shock for you, even so. I gather that you have been married a long time."

"A quarter of a century. I'm ancient. I was married before and have children from that marriage to look after me now," she mentioned, in case he thought he might play a role.

"Meditation might be helpful. I could help you find a route to that. I'm back in Liverpool in a fortnight."

"That's kind, Pratap. I'll bear it in mind…" She could hear herself keep repeating his name. Did she really want to keep him at arm's length? "I wouldn't mind losing myself at the moment. When you're back, you can take me along. And thanks for calling; you're a real friend in need."

The phone was already ringing again as she passed it back to Pete. He told her it was someone called Bob. That would be the one whose life she'd mangled. She shook her head as she took the phone, wishing it could be Andrew's voice she was about to hear. She started sobbing. The next voice Bob heard was Pete's telling him that Jane would prefer to talk tomorrow. "Is she OK, pal?" he asked. Before Pete could answer, Jane had hold of the phone again.

"Give it me Pete. Hi Bob, I need to talk to you. This matters to me at the moment, even if it's the wrong moment. Ruth keeps on telling me how well you've read the social and cultural changes whatever I might think, keeping your religion, doing both public and private sector, being an engineer who makes real things work, having great taste in music, blah, blah, blah... Dad's authentic, she says. That's real praise, I'll concede that. I'll agree you're authentic. You couldn't have kept this up as an act for so long."

"Who says?"

"I've seen you as divvy, compared with my colleagues and of course Andrew. But he blew all their brains out as well as his own, as far as I'm concerned, that's if they ever had any. Why the hell did I leave you?" she wailed. "What with all the pressure to stay together and with my own children never accepting it, I must have wanted to, but why?"

"I'm buggered if I know," he admitted. "The world we lived in forked into two paths and we went down different tracks, real parallel worlds. I don't suppose either of us actually chose the one we went down. You're the real thing, far more authentic than me. I'm a hotchpotch of half-formed notions."

"They're not that fully formulated," said Jane, quick as a flash, tears forgotten.

"Thank you," he answered sarcastically before carrying on being nice. "You write the most fantastic books. You're where it's at still, far more than me. Maybe the few years between us didn't help. I didn't like the seventies much."

A feminist couldn't dismiss that decade so easily. "You tried to make me miss them, at least the twentieth century ones. I don't know why I worry what Ruth thinks. She's even more out of it than you," Jane replied.

Bob had never gone for the glitzy stuff, which he'd deemed tacky, so he'd never liked discos. That made him authentic to Ruth. "She's a serious girl and none the worse for that," he said.

Jane snorted derisively: "Dance music is where it's at for women, except of course St Ruth. Michael Jackson wasn't trying to be a successor to Paul Robeson. You couldn't hack all those good looking black guys and then us women taking over from you white rockers with acne. You were the freaks not getting it. Even your Mum and Dad used to tell me how they danced together to Reggie Dixon at the Tower Ballroom."

Bob felt this was unfair as he would always manage a bop after a couple of drinks, whereas in his memory Jane would stand on the fringes. Helen's recent crack about his cultural line being extinct had struck a dissonant chord with him though and he needed to rationalise his negativity about the seventies. "I've always agreed with all the women's stuff, but everything's been too middle-class and southern ever since, I guess it coincided with grammar schools going."

Jane was unexpectedly candid. "My feminism was probably too much about well-educated women getting the opportunity, particularly me! Even so, women everywhere are better off for it. We're both middle-class, sweetheart and there's still nothing southern about Liverpool," she pointed out, this time fairly. "You're the one who's lived half your life in London."

That was the truth if not the whole truth. "You were always much posher than me," he said before switching back to the time of their break-up. "Remember the rows; they were horrendous, the things I said. Nothing inauthentic about any of that, I was a total shit."

"I'm not sure about that either. Just a partial one," was her razor reply.

Bob was ignoring every gibe thrown his way. "Ruth's wrong about the private sector. It's all a game with stupid money," he confessed. "Don't forget you were never that sure about me, you'd finished with me before you found out you were pregnant. You were dead sure about Andrew. Honour him now. He thought it would be the best way out for both of you."

Jane couldn't see how leaving his brains splattered on the kitchen wall had been a good thing. "It must have gone between us. And, you know you detested him, and he did you."

"I only spoke to him a few times."

"And in one of those conversations you rammed him up against the wall."

Bob shivered at the recollection. "That was when you defended his manhood by telling me he was better at it than me."

Jane smiled at the memory. "For the record, you weren't that bad, if on the hurried side with your hair-trigger cock. That's how Ruth came along."

"A blessing from above. The photon that fired me off wasn't either willed or random. It took a while before I put a time lag into my pre-printed circuits," Bob conceded.

"Maybe you were going off me by then. You'd always manage to put your weight on my arm or jam my hair or something. Are you still the same?"

Bob was thinking that Wendy seemed not to have minded his clumsiness. "They're still not bringing their knitting with them but nobody's complained like you. I haven't trampled anyone to death."

Jane laughed raucously, finding brain circuits somewhere different from those that caused inconsolable grief. "I did like the lifestyle with Andrew though. He related to doing things in groups. You don't."

"I find that hell is other people if I'm in a group setting out to improve the world," Bob admitted. "Is Pete having to listen to all this? It's the strangest of sympathy calls."

"No, I'm in the next room now. You've cheered me up a bit at least. Don't worry that it was, say, a shade unorthodox. I'd better go back next door, I suppose. The police have set up a counsellor who'll be here any minute."

"You'll mourn him soon, Jane, you will, and it will hit hard. You can't stop from being honest with people. Be straight with yourself too. This will hurt for a long time, for the rest of your life. Cry your tears, don't hide them. It's a bugger."

Jane did appreciate those words, verbatim in her diary. "Job's comforter, but thanks for ringing. There's not many would have talked dirty after my husband's shot himself."

He reminded her that there weren't many others she'd been married to, and then asked if he was wanted at the funeral.

"It will be a cremation," she replied. "If you can make it, yes please. Is Andrew burning in hell right now, Bob? The only soul he believed in was one he'd created himself."

"If there's a heaven Andrew will have demanded his rights and walked straight past St Peter. He'll be organising a sit-in over their undemocratic decision-making processes."

The counsellor had arrived. Bob would have been disappointed if she hadn't finished the call favouring Andrew. She did. "Quite right too, and if I get there, I'll expect two women added to the Godhead to even things up, not just one as a token."

At least he had the last word. "Most women only want women

115

bishops. Omniscience replaced by women's intuition. God help us."

Jane went to face the counsellor, a plumpish woman about ten years younger than she was. She asked Jane if she wanted to talk yet or would prefer to leave it a while. After about ten minutes shadow boxing, it became obvious to both that Jane either wasn't ready or wasn't willing to talk about what had happened. The counsellor told her not to worry as there were some people for whom counselling wasn't the right thing. "You're not doing it for my sake," she said. "I'll ring next week to see if you want to do something then." Jane showed her to the front door, thanking her for her understanding, while thinking that a sociolinguistic study of bereavement counselling could be worthwhile.

* * *

As Jane closed the door in Mossley Hill, Richard turned the key in Monkey Mead, unsure what he was going to say to Helen. It wasn't immediately possible to speak to her with the children demanding attention. Helen knew that he'd found something out from his crestfallen face and his inability to make eye contact. She thought she was already as good as on his eternal compost heap whatever she said in defence. She followed him upstairs as he went to change. He spoke first. "Pierre tells me he loves you. He asked me to set you free."

She saw Richard's face fold. He dashed into the bathroom and locked the door. She could hear him sob uncontrollably in convulsions. She tried to console him through the door, telling him that, although she'd been a fool, nothing had happened, that she loved only him. She couldn't believe how she'd been so stupid, so arrogant, to hurt someone she loved so much. Eventually he fell silent. She begged him to come out, scared he might have done something stupid with pills. Of course, he hadn't. What he'd made of himself, although constructed from

116

many things, was a unity. He walked straight past her and down to the children. If they noticed his blotchy face, they said nothing. After that he took Trotter for a long walk. Helen rang Pierre while he was out, begging him to go away. Pierre was too distressed to hear her, still not believing that someone as beautiful as she was had rejected him. She wanted to cut his narcissistic balls off, but had to find out what he'd said. From what she could tell, his vanity hadn't allowed him to tell of the three no-shows. She was desperate to keep it that way, and pleaded with him to say no more.

* * *

The Mossley Hill door next opened at about half past eight, with Ruth arriving and doing her best to avoid the peck on the cheek. Jane was too determined for any evasive action short of turning tail and sprinting down the driveway. Jane then laid down the rules of engagement for the evening, wanting Ruth to emulate her father in going for normal chat and not sympathy. Ruth was pleased Bob had managed to do something right in Jane's eyes, to be told that would be going too far. "It's not so much he's got rough edges as serrated," Jane rasped in imitation of a rusty saw. "Not that you're any better, trying to avoid me kissing you."

Ruth made the mistake of quoting her Dad's view that he'd stick with a handshake and leave the cheek-pecking to tennis club members. The saw's teeth could still bite. Jane knew that 'tennis club members' was code for people from Knutsford, "More socialised than that miserable sod," she said, hiding well the polite etiquette imparted by her refined upbringing. For all his other faults, Ruth had never seen Andrew as strong on the social graces either, and didn't imagine he'd have seen cheek pecking as hastening the revolution. Jane said that

117

being from Southport, an honorary part of Cheshire displaced a bit further north, he could manage the normal courtesies, whereas Bob of course always preferred Blackpool. Ruth couldn't see her Dad walking down the Golden Mile with a kiss-me-quick hat on.

Jane chuckled at the thought. "No. It was one of his inverted snobbery affectations. He'd rather be seen dead than like that."

"Are you sure you're OK, Mum? You've just seen someone dead."

Jane went quiet for a few moments, lost in blackness. She switched her light on again with the hope derived from Bob's comment about Andrew demanding his rights up yonder, but it didn't last long, as she recalled the real Andrew's view that hankering after eternal life was wishful thinking on the back of fear and solipsism. Ruth argued that it wasn't self-centred to hope someone you loved could survive death.

"It is, it's privileging your own circle," Jane said fairly. "I think your Dad only sticks to his faith for his wretched cultural continuity reasons. That's his real religion."

"I find him very modern in picking up the good stuff from all the sources he's heard in his life," Ruth replied, annoyed that without warning Bob's head was back on the block with the saw hacking through his neck.

"Come off it, he's backed the loser. He bangs on about cultural continuity at a time when the country has had a multicultural explosion. His view of the white northern working class being a force for change was outdated before the Beatles released Sergeant Pepper. He thought he could continue to speak low status English in the top jobs he's had and still retain respect. He couldn't."

Jane had finished sawing. She saw the defeat on the severed head she was holding up in triumph and relented just a little. "One of his colleagues told me he was good at clearing the jungle, but useless as the first mayor of the township. Andrew from the start saw that you had to unite to beat the bastards; Bob thought he could do it on his own. His life's been a big ego trip."

Ruth took the chance to give Bob's head a decent burial: "If so, it's been a noble failure. Can I get you something to eat, or a cup of tea, or something?"

Jane had drunk enough tea to sink a battleship. She was feeling hungry and could fancy a Chinese home delivery if that wouldn't look insensitive to the neighbours. Ruth thought they'd be a pair of hypocrites not to order one. Jane disagreed, saying that social sensibilities did matter. Ruth could manage irony without changing expression. In which case, it wouldn't be hypocritical to go and pick it up, she said.

If Jane realised that she was being baited, she didn't show it. "What a good idea!" There's a really good one in Allerton Road. Andrew used to love the crispy duck."

The smile on her face slowly changed shape into an open- mouthed horror which then crumpled into wretched tears, like a clown's face on a child's helium balloon after catching a rose thorn in the garden. Between the tears Ruth caught a few words.

"He's gone. Gone forever as if he was never here. I don't want crispy duck."

Ruth didn't know what to do or where to put herself. She was used to children crying, not an adult pouring out the contents of her soul. Somehow she managed to put her arm round her mother. It was brushed aside. Jane looked at her with tears still streaming down her cheeks, and asked when Robert was coming. The last Ruth had heard was that it could either be that evening or the next day if he couldn't get out of a meeting.

Jane's tears were dry quickly. "Please understand that Andrew was good for me," she continued to argue. "I didn't make a mistake leaving your Dad. I know you don't get it. I'll agree that he's clever and brave, but too different from what I want for us to be close again. I don't know if he's going to expect more, but being friends is the most I can manage and that's on a good day."

Ruth felt she'd pussy-footed around too much. "I don't suppose for one minute that he wants any more either. What A thinks about B, B thinks about A. It may have taken a long time, but I'm damned sure Dad doesn't want to be back with you now."

"You not reckon so? I hope you're right," said a disappointed looking Jane.

Ruth saw her reaction as she asked if it was to be crispy duck or not. Jane went for the set menu without the duck, a reasonable compromise between sensitivity and hunger. Ruth left to collect the food, pleased to leave the conversation, thinking it wasn't possible to understand the previous generation's battles.

\* \* \*

Elsewhere, Richard and Trotter were walking up the lane to home. They heard Helen shouting, "Leave us alone," from the driveway. Young James heard too from his bedroom, and opened the window to see a Volvo car parked, with his mother yelling to a guy he didn't know to get back in and go home. James ran down the stairs. Richard slipped Trotter's lead and they both sprinted full pelt. Trotter won the race easily and by the time Richard caught up was jumping up at Pierre. James emerged from the front door at the same moment. In his lovestruck confusion, Pierre aimed a kick in defence, not the recommended way for a vet to ingratiate himself to dog or owners. Helen, la belle dame sans merci, stepped forward to slap him across the face. Hero Richard squared up to him. Pierre aimed a blow which Richard ducked under, his hands grabbing Pierre's neck. In his red rage, Richard was throttling

Pierre. Helen and James were struck too dumb to say anything. Trotter was very happy to turn a blind eye. Fortunately Richard's conscience acted quickly enough. He let go of Pierre's neck as he slammed him down across the Volvo bonnet in best US cop style. The kick up the arse that followed probably isn't in the good cop manual. The aborted strangulation clearly wasn't, even if prompted by a distant memory of an umbilical cord. Trotter saw the kick as marking the spot where he was to sink his teeth.

* * *

Robert arrived at Mossley Hill. Ruth, just about to leave the restaurant with the grub, received further instructions by mobile from Jane for chicken with cashew nuts or ginger, plus half a dozen cans of beer from the off licence. Ruth suggested she should get some fatted calf and rice as well, to be told that they might have a green-eyed monster chow mein if she'd like one.

* * *

On Paviour Drive, Richard requested nicely that all three of them had a conversation in the Volvo, saying he'd live with the truth better than with a pack of lies. Helen didn't think that would be the case, but could see no alternative. It was wise for Richard to choose his enemy's car with the blood issuing forth from Pierre's nether regions. Richard first led James into the house with an anxious Trotter. By the time he returned, Helen and Pierre were in the front seats. Richard climbed in behind as if the outsider, not knowing that he was sitting where the pair in front a few days before had been under-performing. Helen immediately switched seats to join him, putting her arm around him, clinging to him. She admitted that she'd been temporarily besotted and that only circumstance or divine intervention had prevented them from consummating their brief affair. She told him that he was the only man she'd ever chosen and always the man for her, if he could forgive her.

Pierre heard all this and at last was savvy enough to realise that Helen's beauty was meant for the old contemptible. He'd suffered enough terror and humiliation. Richard knew he had to forgive Helen, though still unsure if she'd really chosen him. He clambered out of the car and held her door open. She leapt out, kissed him, and held his hands as she waltzed him to the front door. James saw them through his window.

* * *

In the House of Horror, the kitchen table was out of bounds, although Jane did seem to relish showing off the residual macabre signs of the shooting. They sat in the dining room in an uncomfortable silence, first broken by Robert. He wanted to know if Sophie and he were still wanted at Ruth's house on the coming Saturday. Jane's ears pricked up at the new name, and had to be told all about her.

"You never told me. You two never did tell me anything," she complained.

Ruth couldn't stop herself from saying in jest, "Poor Jinny Greenteeth. Got no father, got no mother."

Jane was quick on the draw, shooting Ruth down with, "Got no husband either now." Ruth apologised, asking when the funeral was going to be. Jane was aiming for the following Monday or Tuesday at Maywood Crematorium.

Ruth didn't know where the place was but Robert did. "It's down past Calderstones where I had my bike nicked. Do you remember the kerfuffle over that?"

"Only too well," snapped Jane. "Your father wrecked Andrew's chances of making it as your stepfather with that new bike."

Ruth wasn't having her Dad take any more stick. "You were both being mean. Robert was heartbroken and had suffered enough by losing it. Dad realised that and didn't begrudge him a new one."

Robert defended his Dad too. "He didn't make anything of it, Mum. He told me to mind I didn't lose this one and gave me a combination lock."

Jane had seen the sub-plot from an adult perspective. "He didn't need to make anything of it. He was grinning from ear to ear. He knew he'd put one over on us."

Ruth was too far down the path of self-righteousness to spot the note of admiration in Jane's tone. "Anyway, Andrew was finished as far as I was concerned much earlier than that when he tried to stop me going to Church. That's when Dad was angry."

"You forced us to that point by making it clear that you'd come home only when you were ready. And then you told your Dad. The stupid pillock came steaming round like a knight in shining armour to rescue his damsel in distress."

Ruth smiled fondly at that piece of chivalry. "Do you know he drove up from London specially? He told you he was in St Chad's for the weekend but he wasn't."

Jane wasn't surprised in the slightest, saying that when Bob lost his temper he always went manic. Ruth can have an irritatingly knowing smile, but she couldn't be blamed for failing to keep a straight face when she heard that. "Physician, heal thyself!" she smirked. "I decided after that to do double Maths and Physics, rather than English and History, mainly to spite you."

Robert surprisingly joined in more on Ruth's side, accepting that

Jane and Andrew had meant well, but inevitably had been antagonistic to most things Swarbrick, with a string of punishment confiscations after the bike incident, set up in such a way that Bob wouldn't come tearing up the M6.

This pushed Jane from a defence of herself into a vehement critique of her first husband. "You were both doing your best to make our lives a misery. Your Dad punished you in his own way, making you like what he liked, and you fell for it. I'd find him foisting his identity on you like that more difficult to forgive. He's soft in the head, not kind. He'd be in a room with his inane cheerfulness, not noticing that everyone else was scheming. I bet that's how he was shafted by Charles Norman."

Robert defended his father with quiet pride. "You can get away with a lot of softness and still gain respect when you're built like a brick shithouse. And Dad is always great fun to be with."

Jane was in no mood to agree. "I didn't find him much fun. It must be something in the Swarbrick genes that sees his corny views as funny."

Ruth could see nothing corny about her father. "That's because you never get irony," she sweepingly explained. "You can dish out the sarcasm well enough though. You still resent him, despite him having developed into something special, whatever he was like back then."

Robert had never been the soul of discretion, and wanted to change the focus, so revealed that Bob was hitting it off pretty well with a colleague on the LA assignment. Jane immediately wanted to know who she was. Robert didn't know but thought that the fact that Bob had even mentioned her meant she mattered. Jane paused briefly before asking Robert about Sophie. The rest of the evening was conducted at a more amiable and peaceful pace. What the two children had managed, without meaning to, was to put Andrew back in favour.

Ruth went upstairs at around eleven o'clock. She remembered that she had promised to ring her Dad to tell him how things were. He was sitting up in bed waiting for the call. Ruth was worried that she'd picked on Jane a bit too much, opening up some unhealed wounds. "But she was as sharp as ever with her comebacks. You're not her top of the pops tonight."

"I didn't shoot the bugger," Bob protested.

The call finished, he was about to turn his phone off when Jane's name flashed up. She wanted to know about the lady he was cavorting with in LA.

"Bloody Robert's big mouth," he guessed as the source. "I thought lawyers could protect client confidentiality. It's sub judice at the moment. The details are too complicated and confidential for me to explain. It's going nowhere."

"I'm not jealous, Bob."

"How did I know that?"

They spoke for a few minutes longer, more tensely than earlier. She was upset at Ruth and Robert for their criticism of Andrew, saying he was a good man and that they should be able to see the things he did for them, particularly on university entrance.

"I know stepfather is a bloody difficult role," Bob sympathised. "Many animals don't attempt it. They kill the old kids off and have some more! Our two should be grateful that he managed better than that. Should I call again tomorrow?"

"If you must," she said, cheerfully enough to mean yes.

* * *

Down south it was time for bed. Helen offered to sleep in the spare bedroom. Richard felt honour-bound to refuse. She asked if he wanted to kick her arse too. They made love instead. As he lay awake afterwards though, he knew that he'd forgiven her too readily. He'd ridden the roller coaster with his eyes shut. On the other hand, his visceral rage could have ended in tragedy. He shouldn't have been feeling so proud that he wanted it in his story of life, but he was.

## CHAPTER TEN

First thing on Tuesday, Bob had a shower while he gathered his thoughts. He'd a morning of Citel business, where his role was to look distinguished for a couple of hours, and later the dinner at the Dorchester. He flicked through the pack for the next day's Northern Solstice meeting, scrawling pertinent and impertinent questions in the margin. He'd be chairing, apart from when he invited the lawyers to take over. They'd go through their paper page by page, to make sure nobody listened.

He was expecting to find it hard treating Wendy as just another person. He knew plenty about her, much more than before LA. But what he felt had come suddenly, it wasn't knowledge. He'd thought her attractive before the trip and beautiful since. Her face had acquired more dimensions. Her quizzical smile revealed a deep wisdom, the resulting smile lines an inner peace. Rover would sit contentedly by his side as he did his homework. Bob wanted to be with Wendy like that.

With Jane, what she did and what she said was what she was to him. She'd told him time and time again what she thought of him, and not much had been favourable. He guessed that at best forty years ago, he'd been interesting and a possibility. Since then he'd been a verb conjugation for her to practice. He fell short, he falls short, he will fall short.

He pressed Wendy's name in his phone book. She was having a morning at home before catching the train. He asked if he could meet her train and help carry her suitcase. She agreed, telling him to be at Paddington at twenty to three to take her to the Streetley Hotel behind Buckingham Palace.

She lolloped down the platform in tight, cropped beige jeans and a bright orange top, white bra straps visible, suitcase in hand. Physical greetings were deferred until they were in a cab, as she'd known too many people on the train. When the kiss came, it was long and full, worth the wait, taking nearly as long as the taxi ride. Wendy had tried and failed to arrange a pre-meeting with Richard for six o'clock. After she'd booked into the hotel, they strolled around St James's Park, with tourists, ducks and geese for company. Eventually they found a free bench where their lips met again. Richard's PA rang to say that he was out somewhere with his wife and he'd call a bit later.

Bob told Wendy how much he wanted to be with her. She ribbed him that he'd felt the same about Jane for the last quarter of a century. She cut him short as he tried to describe the feeling he had for her that was so intense it had to be real. She said that the only realities she could see were her future with Frank and his past with Jane. He wouldn't accept that, believing that what she was and how he felt were in a harmony that should never stop resonating. She told him that there was no harmony to be had outside the Gates of Eden, and inside it wouldn't matter. He knew then that she wasn't expecting any answers from him or from the Almighty. As she'd used his main man's words, the writing was already on the wall.

"Hey, that's from Bringing It All Back Home. Too early for you," was what he said.

"You're not going to like this. My Dad had it!"

Richard and Helen had finished their business together. Wendy's handbag rang. She rescued her phone in time to hear him say: "I gather you want me to make sure that you two bumpkins don't have straw

128

growing out of your ears tonight".

Bob was surprised to hear Wendy's need to claim her primacy over Richard as she replied: "Watch it, clever clogs. I'm running this show."

Richard told her that she wasn't hard enough, not having eaten the pies and barm cakes. This was countered by Wendy, who argued that the carrots in pasties had helped her see in the dark, a skill she claimed was necessary with the little information Richard gave her. Bob hadn't realised before that the tension between Wendy and Richard was more than banter, nor that her inner beauty wasn't as compelling to others.

Wendy reported to Bob that they had to make their way back to the Streetley as Richard would be there by half past five. They dillied and dallied, reaching the hotel only a couple of minutes before he walked breezily through the door.

"The Three Musketeers are now complete," was his greeting. "Guess what I've been doing today."

"Being far too pleased with yourself, by the look of it," Wendy replied.

Richard let that pass. "Helen and I have been buying out the vet's practice she works at. She's always wanted to be her own boss. It was owned by a chain, and was too small a practice for them to be bothered with after one of the vets moved back to France. There aren't many economies of scale in that trade. And guess what I did this morning?"

"Woke up with that inane grin on your face?" suggested Bob, following Wendy's lead.

Richard ignored that too. "I spoke with the Bishop, who I know quite well socially. He wants me to become a lay reader. There's been trouble brewing for a while at the couple of village churches our vicar also looks after. He's a bit too evangelical for them. They'd like me to run things there."

Bob and Wendy were delighted, regretting having responded

meanly to Richard's enthusiasm. Wendy disclosed that someday she'd like to teach archaeology at the local evening classes. Richard fancied this idea too. "I'll be on the front row if you do. Don't look at me like that, Bob, I'm not in competition." Bob feigned surprise but Richard was bursting to congratulate him. "I know you two are an item. She laughs at your jokes too much. Also it's difficult not to notice a couple walking hand in hand down Buckingham Palace Road, one in a creased suit, the other in her picnic outfit."

"Richard, I feel guilty about you thinking I'm letting my husband down," Wendy scowled. "I could try to explain why it's not like that, but it is."

Richard didn't pick up the vibes coming from her frown. "I've lived enough to know that you two will be legit and I don't need your explanations, which will sound limp."

This crassness in presuming to understand had Wendy seething. "Thanks for that, they would sound limp because that's what they'd be."

Her look of scorn was withering. She was angry with Richard for saying what he had, angry with Bob for no good reason, and angry with herself for not knowing why she was so angry. She turned on both men, fuse triggered. "Bob would have me believe that how your life ends is with you from birth. How can anyone start their life in the total confusion of dementia? And you spout nonsense about us being the story we tell ourselves. What sort of story can Frank possibly be telling himself today?"

Richard at last realised that he'd done his two friends a massive disfavour. "Damn it, I'm sorry. I shouldn't have presumed to understand the hell you're going through, Wendy. But I really like you two guys and I'm bloody sure there's nothing wrong in what you're doing. Your consciences should be clear."

Bob was swallowing hard. Only one outcome was possible; the next stage of Wendy's fury would be to finish with him. Wendy wasn't interested in Richard's apology. She made it clear again to him that it was time to knuckle down if the transaction was to be successful. Bob tried to lighten the mood: "I don't think the Three Musketeers had a leader, love. All for one and one for all".

Wendy's eyes were glowing but not with love. She managed a thin smile before demanding attention to each of the items in the timetable. She instructed Richard to book a cab for twenty past seven, the only thing she did delegate to him. She went to her room when they'd finished, while Richard slipped into the corridor to ring Helen. Bob suddenly remembered that he hadn't honoured his promise to call Jane in that compartment of his life. He did so straightaway and she was chatty. Her sister Mary had separated from her husband on grounds of pomposity. Her brother Roger was being treated for his depression. She was feeling guilty about what she'd said to Bob the last time and would like to meet up for a drink or dinner occasionally, which she said needn't get in the way of his burgeoning relationship with whatever her name was. The funeral was fixed for the following Tuesday at midday. Bob was one of the favoured few to be invited back to the house. It was more a summons, as he'd been assigned the job of looking after Sophie, Robert's new girlfriend, while Robert was accompanying Jane.

Richard returned as he was finishing the call. "Me and my big mouth. Is there any way I can help put things right?" he asked.

Bob felt sure there was nothing Richard or he could do. "Let it run its course. By the way, my ex-wife Jane's husband shot himself yesterday. You know he had terminal cancer. Well he didn't wait for Death's Angel."

Before anything else could be said, the lift doors opened and out walked Wendy, wearing a check trouser suit, and looking most efficient.

Bob would have preferred less make-up, but he guessed for her it was war paint to frighten the foe, him included. She confirmed that thought. "Forster will have some hand grenade he'll lob in tonight. It's in his instruction manual as to how to handle a transaction."

The Dorchester was only a few minutes' cab drive away, during which time they couldn't pinpoint the likely size or direction of the grenade. Peter didn't make them wait long once inside the suite where they were having dinner. Grindleton's were formally advising Western Sun Rising about their fund raise. He'd met their Chairman in LA the day before.

"Not Sir Charles in person!" Richard commiserated. "Have you checked your wallet?"

Bob was still reeling from the early evening blows. Peter narrowed his eyes in his direction. "He didn't seem to like you much, Bob."

Bob admitted to a mutual disrespect. Peter had found Charles a bit of a slimeball as he did most English people. He'd asked one or two others what they thought of Richard and Bob, and found a fair number of fans too. Bob wasn't in a mood to be flattered. "Us slimeballs stick together," he said.

That was Peter's sort of answer. "I'll give you a chance to prove him wrong. You've got balls. Let's hope Richard has too."

Out came Richard's best Johnny Cash impression. "Charlie tried to cut them off, but they're still operational."

Peter set Richard his testicular challenge. "Sir Charles wanted to find out if our flotation was going to happen. Otherwise he was after buying us for nothing. You'd better make sure we get away."

Bob made the reasonable point that Richard couldn't walk on water and that the company needed to beat Western Sun Rising to the schools order. State bureaucracy was still holding up the decision. Richard was adamant that he was only prepared to mention the education sector generically in the flotation documents, unless the contract had been signed.

Bob and Wendy chose to sit on opposite sides of the table, with Richard at ninety degrees. The dinner had finished by a quarter past nine. Bob and Wendy watched the others go, including Richard, while they pretended to chat about something on the timetable. Bob then tried his luck, asking Wendy back to his flat for a nightcap, knowing it to be in vain.

"You can show me tomorrow when we've finished. I'll want to change somewhere before I go home," she said, too confused to lean one way or the other. Two separate cabs were summoned. He felt very alone as he walked through the door of his flat.

Within a few minutes Ruth rang, back home safe and sound. They discussed the funeral arrangements. There weren't enough bedrooms in Mossley Hill to accommodate everyone. As Robert and Sophie were up in the Midlands on Saturday with Ruth, they were going to see if they could take Monday off, and if so Robert was going to ask Bob if he could put them up from Sunday in St Chad's. Bob liked this prospect. Jane's depressed brother Roger couldn't get back from New Zealand but her sister Mary had arrived to stay with her.

Bob thought Mary would be good for Jane: "The two girls always got on pretty well. Mary lets Jane be the boss."

Ruth can say provocative things so innocently. "That's what you should have done."

He poured himself a scotch, and watched the News before going to bed. As he lay awake, his thought dreams were first of Wendy, and them both having a big steak at the pub after walking round Malham, his favourite walk. Then he was with eighteen year old Jane at the Kirkstone Pass pub, him with a pint while she was drinking a brandy and babycham, the drink in vogue back then. As he went into deep sleep, the three of them were round the table at the Wyreford Inn with his parents. He leant back on the chair and it broke, leaving him sprawling on the floor. Rover licked his face. He looked up and he was on his own staring at the sun. Then the film stopped.

In the Streetley Hotel, Wendy was tossing in bed. She couldn't shift the first time she'd met Frank out of her head. He'd been so courteous and charming. If she hadn't accepted his offer of dinner out of a need for company, he'd have met someone who would have made his life a damn sight more fulfilled. It wasn't her fault that he'd succumbed to Alzheimer's, but it was that he hadn't been happy before then. She determined that she must act.

The next morning Bob was the first to arrive and left waiting in reception. Trouser-suited Wendy was the next to get there. She didn't look that refreshed, with puffy eyes. Vast swathes of lawyers and financial PR staff appeared before Richard came down. The two morning sessions were on research and due diligence. Linda Chan had produced a good note and Paul White made a decent job of presenting it. Richard indicated what price he thought would be necessary to get the deal away. Peter thought it too low, while agreeing that a successful transaction was more important than the last few pennies. The lawyers chaired the due diligence session with all due aplomb, which meant that they'd found nothing that mattered. The multitude was fed.

Bob used the afternoon Board to set up a template for future meetings and the reports in the format he liked. The next meeting was set for London on the first Thursday, in September, when final documentation would be agreed, and the price set. In the meantime, most advisers would be in Tuscany. Richard had a week booked in Center Parcs. Wendy and Bob had made no plans.

The three of them saw Peter and Emil off from reception. As their car drew away, Wendy asked both Richard and Bob to sit down in the visitors' chairs. She looked at her shoes as she spoke. "Richard, you learnt something yesterday that I wish you hadn't. Whatever you say, it's not legit. Bob, our brief affair is over, it's not to be, it mustn't be." She looked up at Bob's face. "God doesn't care about us. He doesn't want you and me to be together. He didn't want me to have children. He wanted Frank to lose his mind. There's meaning in life alright."

She fought back her tears as she walked out of the door and down the road. Bob thought of chasing after her but knew he shouldn't. Instead he spoke kindly without looking at Richard: "It's not your fault, pal. She feels guilty. Irrationally, but she feels it. She wouldn't if Frank were well. She's not anti-adultery, just pro-loyalty. She still feels bad about letting the guy before Frank down when she was younger. I'll get over it. I hope she does."

Richard thought that she was pre-programmed for disappointment, the sad-eyed lady of the Cotswolds. Bob had hoped he might have made her happy.

"So you would have done," said Richard. "She was right though, the Gods are causing havoc today. I thought Helen was pleased at me abandoning Mammon. Once she was over the excitement of owning the vets, she started thinking about what being a lay reader's wife would mean for her, and she can't stop bashing my lugholes with it."

"It's your call, not hers," advised Bob.

Richard had to go to his office for a short meeting. Bob started to walk back to his flat unable to think anything coherent for the noise of the traffic inside and outside his head.

# CHAPTER ELEVEN

As he walked down Queen Street, Bob at last managed to re-establish enough circuits to realise that Wendy had consciously attacked his deepest hinterland. The way she'd flipped could only mean that her mind was made up. He felt a strange mix of despair and relief. He'd had an unwarranted fear of the two women fighting over him. Yet what was ahead was more loneliness, with the added piquancy of a new proximity to Jane which he expected would lead nowhere but eventual humiliation. But he couldn't change the movie because it ended badly last time; no price could he pay not to go through these things twice.

It was coming up to rush hour. He'd been assuming that he'd be staying in London overnight, and at the earliest travelling back to St Chad's in the morning. He didn't want an evening in the flat with no means of escape from his thoughts. The smell of the Fylde was what he needed. His soul would be comforted best by gazing bleakly over Fylde fields with, given that he'd no dog, baleful Friesian cows for company, their eyes focused to infinity across the Wyre, Cissie Braithwaites and Ada Shufflebothams chewing the cud over his predicament.

He walked past the flat, onto the Thames path and over the Millennium Bridge, before turning under Blackfriars to sit down on a bench beyond the Oxo building. He didn't need to walk along to Westminster Bridge to judge if he was tired of life. He wasn't. He wasn't doing fine though. He could still feel the crashing but meaningless blow to the pit of his stomach and there was no cowboy angel riding down the line to help.

He felt guilty. Though Richard was the proximate cause of Wendy leaving, he was a good friend whose problems should be soluble. Richard wasn't surprised to get a call so soon after they'd parted; he'd been thinking of calling Bob too. Bob asked if there was anything he could do to soften Helen up.

"I can't believe I fucked up you and Wendy," Richard said. "Thanks for the offer but I don't think Helen will appreciate any outside intervention. I'll make a better job of fucking that up on my own. I'll always hope you two can get it together again."

"Only in dreams, in beautiful dreams, to quote the Big O. Fancy a coffee?"

Richard thought he'd better get home, being father to his children even if he didn't give a tuppenny toss about his wife at that moment. He couldn't have been more angry with Helen for picking a fight so soon after being so badly in the wrong. She was of course recovering her place in the relationship, second fiddle not being for her.

Unaware how much humble pie Richard had eaten, Bob wanted to save Richard from himself. "I don't think that's the language of a prospective lay reader. It's also not what you think about Helen. There's nobody else but her for you and you know it."

Richard knew this to be the case only too well. "I think that toss is just a coin spin, isn't it? I guess though that I'll have to clean up my act a bit."

"I imagine Helen doesn't fancy having to look pi to order either," said Bob, trying to find a peace branch for Richard to offer.

"She'd never have to do that anyway. She's being stubborn on principle, but I'm buggered if I know which principle that is."

"Don't do or say anything you'll regret," Bob almost begged of him. "Since I can't persuade you to pour the contents of your soul into a cup of coffee, I'm going home to the Fylde to mourn with real cows. You go back to Helen and be nice. You'll never get a better offer."

Samaritan deed concluded, Bob dropped off his briefcase in the flat, changed into casual clothes, packed his bags ready for St Chad's and carried them to his car, parked a couple of hundred yards away in the NCP. He intended to take a cool box of food later. Then he watched the News. Feeling hungry, he ambled up to the Burger King on Cannon Street.

As a fortified Bob turned into Garlick Hill on his return, he saw a hoodie snatching the bag off the shoulder of a young professional woman. The brick shithouse charged down the road towards them, bellowing his head off. The terrified thief stumbled, allowing Bob to vent his pent-up frustration by grabbing his collar and thumping him in the solar plexus. The young man squealed and doubled up in agony. Bob gave the lady her bag back.

She had an irritatingly prissy voice. "Did you have to hit him so hard?"

Bob laughed deridingly at the lack of gratitude. "He'll be alright in a minute, won't you sunshine?"

Sunshine was promptly sick. He could only have been sixteen. In agony, he stared beyond Bob, who turned to see another lad, bigger and older, approaching him slowly, the glint of a blade caught by the sun.

"You in fa knifin', man."

There was something about the patois of the street, and its intonation, that didn't appeal to Bob at that instant. And it didn't matter to him if he lived or died. "You sound like a cross between some crap rapper and Kenneth Williams. You need to grow some bollocks before you threaten folk."

He charged towards the young man, feinted right and then piled into his shoulder from the left quickly enough to miss the knife. Carry on vigilante, he thought. The pillock wouldn't have heard of Kenneth Williams, he should have used Lee Evans. He didn't want to be pratfalling right now like Norman Wisdom though. It was silly to suggest the little shite had no balls too, he'd already have fathered three kids. The young man hit the road like a sack of potatoes, the knife falling from his hands. This time Bob kneed him in the stomach, jumping on him from his full height, and punching him square in the face.

"Now you two little pieces of turd, bugger off home before the cops come. And give up thinking you're hard. You're a pair of wusses." His career advice for them was to go and get jobs in social services. He picked up the knife and showed them the way to go. "Faster, or I'll thump you again. I've had that sort of day."

Groaning and bleeding, they left the scene. He watched them off, making sure they were gone. There were security cameras on one of the buildings, but no guards had come rushing out. Prissy Miss wanted to know why he'd let them go. "I didn't feel that way out," he grunted. With that he went back to the flat, putting the wrapped knife into the cool box with his food. With his adrenalin back to normal levels, he walked warily to the car park, looking watchfully to make sure that the boys weren't going to seek revenge with some mates. His hand, where he'd punched the older boy, was hurting badly. He drove too quickly to the Fylde, mainly one-handed, his knuckles throbbing. The knife, washed and wiped, was to be disposed of in thick undergrowth later that weekend. On the journey, he made the decision to sell the London flat; not an act of free will. He'd returned a call from Robert at Watford Gap. They'd be coming to stop with him from Sunday morning until Tuesday. Once home, he had a stiff scotch to numb the pain.

The next morning he went to A and E at Blackpool Victoria with a story that he'd hurt himself making a cup of coffee. He'd broken two metacarpals. His hand was bandaged with an improvised metal splint put over his fingers, which for three weeks he was only allowed take off to sleep and drive.

Robert and Sophie arrived before lunch on Sunday morning. He was surprised; nobody had told him she was mixed-race. Tall too, only an inch or so less than Robert in her trainers, friendly looking with a roundish face and a long neck with soft, downy wisps. Bob had always gone for the pale, like Jane, but then there wasn't much ethnic diversity about when he was young. He thought she was gorgeous. She's still as pretty.

Sleeping arrangements had been clarified. Robert and Sophie shared carnal knowledge. Robert had assessed the banging-the-hand-against-the-mantelpiece-making-a cup-of-coffee routine told to him on the call finalising their visit.

"Come on Dad, who did you thump?"

"I thumped nobody. If ever you see Sir Charles Norman with a black eye, look no further, but otherwise it's peace on earth, goodwill to men."

Robert neither believed the story nor Bob's benign outlook. "Batteries not included. What do you reckon, Sophie? Do you feel safe here with Norman Bates prowling outside the shower room?"

"Is that Psycho?" she asked. "I can look over the top of the shower curtain with my giraffe neck and see him coming. That's what Robert called my neck this morning."

"It looks very elegant to me," Bob said. "His bloody big head comes straight out of his shoulders. The good Lord didn't have a neck handy that could take the weight."

Like all lawyers, Robert was a rational thinker when reason served his argument. "And who do I take after? At least my chins aren't dragging on my chest."

"Give it time," replied Bob. He'd laid out a cold collation of fresh salmon, ham, game pie, a French loaf and salads from Booths, with a choice of lemon roulade or blackcurrant pie and thick cream to follow. There was enough for ten. He'd laid on both Prosecco and Rioja, along with a few cans of Boddies. Sophie picked the fizzy, and so did Robert, saying he was still trying to impress.

"I wouldn't bother," joked Bob. "You've got to hope she finds you interesting. I'm having a beer."

Sophie told tales on poor Robert, letting on that he drank Budweiser straight from the bottle when he was out.

"No wonder pubs are closing down," Bob grumbled. "Anyway, come and attack this food. It needs eating up."

He mentioned that he was planning to take them to the local Italian for dinner. Sophie wouldn't hear of it, saying that there really was far too much food to eat in one sitting. She was a lively girl and Robert was clearly taken with her. On a short walk round the village, Bob found that she was from a Methodist family. She'd recently lost a much-loved grandfather.

"I feel, Bob, that my Grandpa still has to be somewhere. When I looked at his body, he wasn't there, he'd gone."

In honour of Sophie, Bob revealed his hope. "In the war, before I was born and when my Dad was in the navy, the family had a budgie, Tinker, who they'd trained to say 'Where's Sailor Jack?' It's part of our family folklore. My Dad died years ago, but I still ask that question. Just as musical notes play in time but are held timelessly in the memory, maybe all time's encoded on the eternal surface of a hologram, your Grandpa and my Dad included."

Sophie didn't crack on that she didn't fully understand. "It's great when the lyrics in music match the tune. I'd like to think of Grandpa back in his young body. That would really be a Wake, wouldn't it?"

They were walking through the churchyard as she spoke. Lancashire funerals are not joyful affairs, as Bob demonstrated: "Us Swarbricks have no Irish twinkle in our eyes. We expect a boiled ham tea afterwards, while still wearing the shoes made muddy in the cemetery."

Sophie revealed that Grandpa actually was Irish. Her grandmother was of exclusively African descent and had moved up to Canada from California at the time of the gold rush. "Since then we've been mixed-up kids," she said

The Swarbricks of course had been more settled. "Europeans first mixed themselves up by inter-breeding with Neanderthals. That probably explains Robert's absence of neck. Our lot have been lazy buggers since, and haven't moved more than a few miles in the last thousand plus years."

Sophie thought they'd been blessed to stay in one place. Bob agreed with her on that. He liked her idea of Grandpa acquiring a young resurrection body. "Tradition has it that we'll be the same age as Jesus was when he was crucified, thirty-three. I suppose that's nearly young. I'd like mine to have been taken at the moment I first met Robert's Mum. Time somehow stopped for an instant then, as though heaven's portal was open. By the time I was thirty-three, it seemed like an eternity before she'd stop nagging me."

Sophie laughed before having a dig at Robert for not sharing the faith. He'd listened to them with the same benign expression as shown by a psychiatrist to a wannabee Napoleon. They ate leftovers for tea, along with a carrot cake. Robert and Sophie went out on a trip to Blackpool. Bob didn't go, not wishing to cramp Robert's style too much, particularly as they were insisting that he accompanied them on an outing the next day. They were off to Malham.

Bob found himself elated about Sophie. All these years he'd banged on about cultural continuity, and here was a slip of a girl who understood him straightaway. He was still awake when they came back and they all had a cup of tea together before bed. Sophie had been impressed with Blackpool and the way everyone seemed to be having a good time. Bob was honest that it could turn rough when the alcohol kicked in. The place was at its best in the daytime, he said, with three generations of family all having a good time together.

The next morning, Bob was up early. The lovebirds soon joined him. Bob one-handedly cooked a breakfast of bacon and eggs, refusing Sophie's help. She insisted on doing the washing-up with him.

"Tha's a reet good 'un," was his highest praise. "Are your parents professionals or are you the first to break through?"

She was the first, with her Dad as a mechanic and her mother working in an office. He felt that to be much more of a personal achievement than going to grammar school and becoming an electrical engineer. He didn't add that it was a pity it wasn't more useful. In hazy sunshine, the drive to Malham took about an hour and a half. There Bob removed his splint ready for the walk, which was about seven miles if they went all the way up to the Tarn. They had a cup of coffee in the village and bought a few snacks, but not the Kendal mint cake that Robert said Bob might need. Flapjacks and almond slices were more to his taste.

After the hors d'oeuvres of the magical Janet's Foss waterfall and the brutal face of Gordale Scar, Bob and his hand were going well. Having eaten ice creams from a van parked in the middle of nowhere, they decided to walk the whole route, past the Iron Age settlement to the peace of the Tarn. There they ate the cakes before ambling to the Cove with its limestone pavements and vertigo-inducing view. Finally they stumbled down the many steps to the village.

"It's like five totally separate walks in one. The cove is unbelievable. And what about Gordale Scar?" Sophie enthused in the tea shop.

Robert's memory stirred. "I've seen a painting of Gordale

somewhere, either in the National or Tate. It's a bloody big canvas."

Sophie confirmed the details. "I was on Google last night. It's the Tate and by James Ward. Thomas Grey of elegy fame shuddered with awe when he saw the place."

"One gallery merges into another after a while," Robert confessed. "They're all hard on the feet."

Bob agreed: "I find it easier to hike seven miles here than stroll round the Tate. And I find a morning there easier than half an hour in a shopping centre. That's when I need to be homeward plodding my weary way."

They spent the evening preparing to be sombre for the funeral. An early night was the form. Bob didn't expect that the quietude would be rigorously enforced behind the other bedroom door. The next morning, they took two cars so that Robert and Sophie could look round Liverpool later. They arrived at Mossley Hill at about eleven o'clock, within a couple of minutes of each other, men dark-suited and black-tied, women grey-trousered and white-bloused. Ruth opened the front door. Jane was preparing stuff with Auntie Mary in the kitchen. The kitchen where the deed had been foretold and then executed, where Andrew had smashed into the hologram, was also the only place in the house to make sandwiches. Andrew's sister, Shirley, was drinking a cup of tea in the living room. Bob hadn't met her before. She looked burdened by life, with tight, pale skin. Ruth saw Bob assessing her. "Auntie Shirley's definitely one S, two C's, Dad."

He was introduced. Shirley looked both surprised and pleased to see him there. She was in that insecure position of not knowing quite what was going on, and so it was better to have someone her own age to talk to, even from so far behind enemy lines. The forthcoming Southport Flower Show presented itself as the topic. Unlike Andrew, Shirley was a keen gardener, so chrysanthemum experiences could be shared. Ruth chatted with Sophie. In a corner, Harry was feeding baby Ben from a bottle. The other children were playing in the garden. Harry wasn't going to the funeral, being left behind to look after the children, who were considered too young for sadness. Bob didn't agree with this for the older two, but didn't challenge Ruth.

Jane and Mary came out of the kitchen. Jane was clearly bursting to meet Sophie, so much so that she defied the gravity of the occasion. She caught Bob's eye as she rushed across the room, narrowing her smile enough for it to count as subdued.

"You must be Sophie. I'm Jane, Robert's mother. Thank you so much for coming. Robert's looking smart. You must be good for him, Sophie."

"No, she's not at all good for me, Mum. She's a wild woman. I'm good for her," Robert insisted.

He and Ruth were summarily dispatched to provide cups of tea for everybody, while poor Sophie was as good as pushed on to the couch and into conversation by Jane. Bob looked round the room, trying to imagine how his kids had felt when they first moved in. He looked at the furnishings and ornaments. There was nothing familiar, nothing from their joint life. The air was still, the aroma neutral. While doing this, he continued to talk to Shirley, discussing the developments on Southport's Marine Drive. Mary came to join them.

"It's a long time since I saw you, Bob. You're looking good."

"That usually means I've put on weight. You really are looking good, Mary, no weight gain. How's she bearing up?"

"Pretty well. She tells me you've been a big help," Mary said, with a straight face. She was taller and a much less volatile character than her sister, with a less expressive though very similar face.

Bob presumed that Jane was being sarcastic, but that sweet-natured Mary had taken it at face value. "You'd have been proud of me a few days ago. I recommended two young acquaintances that they consider social work as a career," was also taking advantage of Mary's sweetness.

She was called over by Jane to meet Sophie, whether she wanted to or not. As Jane issued her edict, she noticed Bob's hand, bandaged but without the splint. "What on earth have you been doing?" she asked unsympathetically.

"Making a cup of coffee," he replied. "I heard the kettle boil, jumped up and smashed my hand into the fireplace mantelpiece."

Robert came in carrying a tray of cups, saucers, spoons, milk and sugar, with Ruth behind with a pot of tea and some shortbread. They spoke in turn and in character.

"That's what he told us too, Mum. We don't believe him."

"I believe everything my Dad says, even when he's lying. Does it hurt, Dad?"

Bob shrugged: "Only when I talk about it. Then it's agony Ivy."

Jane groaned, whispering to herself about another maggot in the apple. Ruth's eyes shone with pleasure. Teas were drunk and the plenary replaced by bipartisan discussions. Jane sidled up to Bob. She whispered: "Brilliantly avoided, but you've been in a fight. I know when you're telling fibs, Bob Swarbrick."

He promised to tell her later when nobody was listening. The cups were washed up and the two bit players, Bob and Sophie, went off to the crematorium with Mary. Plenty of people were waiting outside, Andrew's former colleagues along with other professional and political cohorts. By the door was the Headmaster of another larger school, Fred Taylor, who was giving the eulogy.

Sophie smiled at Bob as they went in: "This isn't that easy for either of us, is it? I didn't know him and you probably wish you hadn't."

"Nicely put, love. I won't be shedding too many tears."

The hearse arrived. Jane looked distressed, Shirley sad, Robert sombre and Ruth like she meant business. The theme music from The Deer Hunter was played as they arrived. The readings, all secular, didn't fit so directly with the cause of death. The eulogy was an effusive tribute to Andrew's career, Fred Taylor ending with a quotation from Mark Twain: 'I do not fear death. I had been dead for billions and billions of years before I was born, and had not suffered the slightest inconvenience from it'.

Jane thought this too clever by half and grimaced. Bob heard it as an apposite atheistic contribution. She cried as the coffin went to its fiery destination. Ruth made a pretence of comforting her. Jane brushed her aside but then clung on to Robert as she walked out of the chapel, Ruth accompanying a genuinely distraught Shirley. The rest filed out a minute or so later to be greeted at the door by a soon-recovered Jane and a still-upset Shirley. Bob and Sophie made a detour to miss this and joined up with Ruth and Robert, who didn't feel it part of their role to meet and greet.

About three quarters of an hour later, they were back at Mossley Hill. Fred and a couple of other colleagues had also been invited. Mary with Ruth's help produced the food from the kitchen. The party split into two different groups. Robert and Jane were with the work colleagues and Shirley. Ruth, Harry and children were joined by Sophie, Mary and Bob. The first group discussed the funeral, agreeing that it had been a fitting send-off. The second group played I-Spy. After about half an hour, the colleagues left, as did Shirley.

Bob relaxed as the people who remained were those he considered family. Mary qualified by ex-marriage and Sophie because he liked her. Up to this point, he'd regretted being there. Sophie and Robert walked round the garden. Jane and Ruth were jousting about how to pronounce 'harassed'. Ruth emphasised the first syllable, Jane had followed Michael Crawford and the grievance culture into emphasising the second.

As ever, Bob was with Ruth. "Pronounce it your way, Jane, and you get more agitated. It's soothing the old way."

Jane's eyes glinted. "Here we go. I bet you still call Battenberg marzipan square, don't you? You always used to."

"It was considered unpatriotic to use German names. That's why we have the House of Windsor rather than the snappy Saxe-Coburg-Gotha. They must have nicked the name from good old Windsor Woollybacks in St Chad's where my great-aunt worked."

Even Ruth didn't let him get away with that. "I think it might just have had something to do with the castle place, Dad."

"Perhaps. Anyway, I'd prefer our royal family to be named after a cake than either a castle slowly sinking into the slough of despond or a defunct knitted knickers company. Let's call them the House of Marzipan Square."

Ruth liked these word games. Jane did too, provided she was winning. "Having a pudding named after you is the real sign of fame, like a melba or pavlova," she suggested.

Bob looked to finish the game off with a six, "Or maybe a spotted dick." Ruth giggled in delight, Jane snorted in despair.

Mary grinned: "You told me that he was house-trained now."

"He'll always have these little accidents. No wonder Mother thought him unsuitable," Jane recalled.

The afternoon was pleasant until Jane informed Ruth and Robert that Andrew's solicitor was coming round with some legal papers. The will wasn't straightforward, so they'd need a couple of hours. Bob stepped into the breach by showing Sophie the sights of Liverpool, borrowing Robert's car, also a BMW, but an estate with ample room. The two older children, Tom and Charlotte, signed up for the trip, not having had the fun of a cremation to entertain them. So did Mary.

Jane wasn't sure Bob was the right person for the task, given that he used to say he couldn't stand the place, and wanted to know what he was going to show them. He was planning the two cathedrals, St George's Hall, the Cavern, Castle Street, the Pier Head and Liver Bird, and then hopping over on the Ferry and back.

Tom had his own wish list. "Can we go to the football grounds too?"

"If there's time I'll drive up Scottie Road and come back round Queen's Drive."

Jane was still doubtful. "You'll not be back before midnight."

"I'm only going to stop once, near the Pier Head. We'll walk up to the Cavern. I'll drive past the cathedrals and St George's Hall on the way in. I'll show them a bit of the university too. We'll be about two hours."

The trip took a few minutes more, and they missed out on the ferry, but it was a great success. Sophie hadn't realised how much good architecture there would be. "I can tell why people from Liverpool all over the world are proud of their city. I've found them a bit over the top but I can see it now."

Bob knew exactly what she meant. "They're not all maudlin. John Lennon wrote about the places and the people: 'In my life, I love you more.' Do you know it? It's a lovely song."

When they returned, the legal meeting was still going on, with stress showing on every face. The lawyer, Gareth Snodgrass, had arrived late with a weak excuse. Most of the will was straightforward. Robert and Ruth were executors, something they'd agreed to years before. There were no legacies to them. Fair enough, the feeling behind that was mutual. There was a small sum for Shirley. This was fine. The bombshell was the Mossley Hill property. Andrew had changed his will a few days before he shot himself to leave the proceeds of his half to cancer research rather than to Jane. The house had been held by Andrew and

149

Jane as a tenancy-in-common rather than jointly, as when she'd moved in they weren't married and each wanted their own share separately identified. They'd had wills drafted later which left their half to each other. Robert had argued that the changed will must be challengeable on the manifest grounds of mentally impaired capacity as evidenced by the suicide; Snodgrass said that he was satisfied with Andrew's mental state when he had prepared the will. Robert asked if he felt happy with his ability to make this assessment, given that he had signally failed to spot Andrew's suicidal state; Snodgrass was of the view that the suicide was the reasonable act of a rational man.

Jane wanted no part of any challenge. She would automatically get a good pension as his widow. Robert was up for the fight, partly because Snodgrass had the smug assurance of a small-practice lawyer, partly because the ill-mannered wanker had arrived late and mainly because he didn't think Ruth and he should acquiesce in Andrew, the alien from Planet Tightarse, taking Jane's reasonable expectations away having screwed up their lives with his joyless pontificating. Ruth hoped that Satan had stoked the fire up to maximum below the spit he was being turned on, or even better that the coffin was in the crematorium incinerator with him not fully dead.

When Robert saw Bob arrive, he nipped out from the dining room where they were meeting to ask what he should do. "It's your Mum's issue, lad, not yours," Bob cautioned. "I'd suggest to her that she's probably right to let it go, given the good cause it's going to, but it would be best to sleep on it before finally making up her mind. I'd tell Snodgrass you want time to think about it and maybe take separate advice. Take it no further today."

That was exactly what Robert did. Ruth came into the living room white-faced with anger and whispered to Bob, "I hope Andrew rots in hell," while Robert let Snodgrass out of the house.

Jane was flushed but cheerful. "Andrew's given his half of the house to cancer research. I guess it could have been worse. It could have been the cats' home. Then again, he didn't like cats much."

Robert followed her in, saying that he didn't like anyone or anything much, the cold-hearted bastard. Jane didn't seem to mind that being said. Bob wasn't happy with it being left unnoticed, nor that his girl was out of grace with the world in her whispered aside. "No, don't speak ill. He thought it was the right thing to do. You're much nobler than that."

Mary understood the practical implications for her sister quickly, realising that she was going to have to sell the house. "Can't you challenge the will? That's outrageous to force you out of your home. The illness must have affected his judgment."

"I'm allowed a reasonable amount of time to find somewhere else, whatever that might mean," answered Jane as she looked round the room. "It was his money. It was his house. I took my half share only when we sold Ormskirk. His half was his to do whatever he wanted."

Robert was unhappily becoming resigned to her wishes. "I can't help but think that he didn't want the money eventually coming through to Ruth and me. Unfortunately you're the one who's going to suffer first if you don't challenge it."

She'd made up her mind: "This place is far too big. I fancy a flat now, perhaps one of those in Sefton Park."

The party started to break up. Harry and Ruth gathered the Jacksons and possessions together. Robert and Sophie stood to attention. Farewells were said. Sophie was hugged by Jane, while Ruth was only pecked. Bob rattled his keys too to show he thought it was time for him to go, but Jane gestured him not to leave yet. He was in the doorstep party with Mary as the others left. Jane asked him his real opinion of what she should do about the will. He thought she should let it go as she'd be getting a decent widow's pension and wouldn't want to think she was living off money that didn't belong to her. Mary nodded as Jane agreed with him. They were both more interested in who he'd thumped. He told the whole story of Garlick Hill. "I realised that I'd broken bones in my hand more or less straightaway, and got them fixed up here. It was those two that I suggested become social workers, Mary, as my parting shot."

"I wondered what on earth you were on about. They'll re-offend, Bob. You should have had them nicked."

"Then someone from your profession would have encouraged them to think they were interesting," he retorted.

Mary's smile was one of agreement. "They'll remember this escapade more than their others," she said.

Jane didn't show the same admiration. "What a super-hero! Or super-plonker depending on viewpoint. You're just jealous because no-one's ever found you interesting." But she soon showed that wasn't really the case with her. "And how's your affair with your banker friend getting on?" she then asked.

Bob shouldn't have answered but he did. "It's over. Her husband has severe Alzheimer's and she feels she can't be disloyal, although she could happily have been if he was well. I think I get it. I've no choice anyway. We'd just finished for good when I met the muggers."

Jane's sympathy sounded genuine. "Maybe she'll change her mind."

"No, she's adamant. She's set up a brain state that will form whenever it needs to."

Mary had known Bob a long time. "Ever the hard-wiring man. It's been good meeting you again, big fella."

Bob reciprocated by asking about her recent fall in the matrimonial stakes and if there was any chance of a remount. Having sniggered dutifully, she said didn't want one because marriage for life didn't work once women had the choice. In her experience, most men weren't like him; they were arrogant.

"His is an intellectual arrogance," interrupted Jane, before Mary could complete the beatification. "I'm a professor, yet I always feel that he's the academic."

"Bubble burst again. Just when I thought I was in favour," he lamented.

They chatted for another half-hour. Bob said goodbye to Mary in the living room before Jane walked him to his car, reminding him that he'd promised to take her out for dinner now and then. To be fair, Wendy had made him a free agent.

"How soon is decent?" he asked. "I could come over next Saturday evening. Will Mary still be here?"

"No, her daughter's going away and she needs to be back tomorrow to help her pack. Perhaps as well, or she'll be stealing you away. I've a conference next weekend. The Saturday after?"

He promised to give her a buzz a couple of days before to fix the arrangements. She wanted him to ring well before that as she'd got used to his calls.

"I have too," he admitted. "I must be a glutton for punishment."

She put her arms round his neck and gave him a huge kiss. Just before she finished, her tongue quickly entered his mouth. Her hand slipped down and felt his crutch. It was rock-hard. Like so many other things that she shouldn't have written down, the memory lingers on in her diaries.

"I'm glad I still do it for you. See you soon, big boy."

And with that she went back into the doorway. She blew him a kiss. He rolled down the window and blew one back as he drove off.

## CHAPTER TWELVE

The air was still as the wind changed direction. Richard was about to go for a bike ride when Wendy rang to say sorry for being so horrible.

"I deserved it. I loused up something good," he answered.

"It wasn't you, and it wasn't Bob. It's me. Aren't you on holiday this week in Center Parcs?"

Richard sighed: "That's where we are, in ersatz Suffolk. The others are in the horrendously noisy swimming pool."

Wendy told him that the Northern Solstice documentation was ready unless he was about to upset her with something new. He wasn't and didn't. Instead he mentioned that Bob had got dragged into his ex-wife's affairs and told how Jane had to move house. He considerately thought it may be better for Jane as she wouldn't want to stay in a place where her husband had blown his brains out. Wendy wasn't so kind, saying that the kitchen, left untouched, could have won the Turner Prize. She listened patiently to his woes with Helen not attuning to being a lay reader's wife. He said he'd need to sort it out one way or the other before the training began in a few weeks.

"Surely that's your call," she encouraged him.

"Bob's words to the letter. Are you two still in touch by ESP?"

Wendy realised that Bob had used the phrase to her. She felt guilty that Bob was at the top of her mind. Frank had been admitted to a nursing home the day before, and his sister was going home at the

154

weekend.

"I'm glad I told Bob what I had to before Frank went in, or I might have chickened out," she confessed. "Will he get it together with Jane, do you think?"

Richard said he didn't think so. Wendy knew better. "He's a man who only wanted one love in his life. He'll soon be back with her," she declared.

Richard suggested she'd changed his mind about that. Wendy hardened her heart again. "Sort out your own life, before you try to sort out mine. Go and duck Helen in the pool until she gives in or something."

"That's a good idea, apart from I think she'd rather drown than be a lay reader's wife. You see your whole life flash before you in both, only at different speeds."

Wendy laughed: "I must hear you preach one day. Enjoy yourself and make sure you win the knobbly-knees competition."

Richard took mild revenge. "You Cotswolds snob. It's not like a holiday camp here. Well, not much. You look after yourself. Nobody else will."

They both knew she'd kicked out the person who would have done. After she'd rung off, Richard still didn't fancy the swimming pool even with the added attraction of drowning Helen. While riding down one of the narrower paths, he had to brake sharply to avoid a bike going in the other direction. The woman mouthed apologies. He'd once known that face and much of what was below it too. It was his first true love, Emma Greenwood.

"What the bloody hell are you doing here? I'd have thought that your kids were past this phase."

He'd learnt from Christmas cards that she had two children, a boy and a girl, from a liaison which finally did for their friendship. The father was in the Marines so they liked activity holidays, she said. He asked if she'd just come with them. She answered the question he'd really asked. There was no man in tow. Her children's father had a girl in many ports, but had killed himself with the alcohol from the bars he knew by the docksides. She did have a new man in her life who wasn't allowed out on holiday. "My villa's just round the corner if you fancy a coffee," she offered.

Emma's fine bone structure added poignancy to the sadness of the lines sketched faintly on her face. Her legs were still slim and she looked good in shorts. He cocked off his bike behind her.

She noticed his agility. "You don't see people do that anymore, getting off while the bike's still going."

"We all did it when I was a kid. It's a bloody sight easier now than having to lift my leg over the saddle from a stationary position. Who's the lucky guy?"

She giggled: "You never used to have trouble getting your leg over. Nobody's ever lucky to pull me. I'm the black widow spider in human form. I might tell you once I've made the coffee."

As she went over to the kitchen area, his mind was back forty years to when he'd first seen her at an Oxford bus stop, a deadly mix of pale and interesting, petite and dynamic, with dancing, hazel eyes. She lived up in North Oxford then with Somerville don mother and rich father. He'd asked her if she'd been waiting for the bus long, the first thing that came into his mind. She'd told him to use a better chat-up line with her in future. He'd fallen hook, line and sinker for her and so it seemed she for him. In her first year at LMH studying English, she was three years younger than him. They'd had a wonderful Oxford summer together. She'd told him she loved him, only him, because he made her happy. He'd had to work very hard to persuade her to go the whole way. When he eventually did, on the floor of her living room when her parents were out, her fears had turned to groans of abandon. Two days later she'd dropped a note through his door to say that they were finished. He never knew why. She did. She didn't want to need anyone else in order to be happy. The first time he saw her face, he knew that their joy would fill the earth and last till the end of time. It hadn't.

He'd begged her back, to no avail. Over the years, she'd turn up now and then to see how things were with him. She'd tell him about her career as an executive head-hunter, about her new men, her marriage, her divorce. He wouldn't have had it differently. He was out drinking too much of the time, home being where he went to hang his head. He'd report back to her on his latest moves and conquests. She was his twin. Then, nearly twenty years on from when they'd met, they'd spent a few days away together in Florence, making love for the first time since their youthful break up. She wasn't quite as he remembered her, but her magnetic movements still captured most of the minutes they spent together. He'd asked her to marry him in front of Botticelli's Primavera. She'd smiled, her mouth opened, but didn't say yes. Beauty was as ever flawed, spring something they'd both missed in their lives. His memory of the trip wasn't of Botticelli but of Michelangelo's Pièta, the tragic, pitiful, beaten and lost figure he cut on the plane home.

They then hadn't seen each other for six months until out of the blue she asked if she could visit him for the weekend. She'd announced as soon as she arrived that she was pregnant, by someone she couldn't marry, for reasons she wouldn't disclose. He didn't bother to find out if she was angling for him to take pity on her. She'd broken the promise she'd never made. He'd told her she must leave the next morning and for good.

Emma carried in two mugs of coffee and some chocolate digestives on a tray. She studied him carefully before pronouncing, "You look almost eminent. How's your family? You've four children, haven't you?"

"Yes, they're all growing up fast, even little Amy, who was a bit of an afterthought. The afterthought was that I should have put the condom on earlier! She's gorgeous though and keeps me young. Well she would if I wasn't knackered all the time."

"Don't expect any sympathy from me. I've brought two up on my own," Emma complained, as if all her life had been lost in service of others.

Richard had never bothered to show any interest in the mystery of their father before, but for the first time did ask what his name was, if it wasn't a state secret. Emma snapped back that he'd never told her anything about his wife either.

"She's Helen and she's a vet," he said.

"I know that. She's very beautiful too, I'm told. And wears the trousers."

He let that pass by asking if her new man had a name. This became her latest secret, apart from a small clue that he worked in the City. "He's talking about getting a divorce, and marrying me. I'm trying to disabuse him of that notion."

Richard asked why she didn't want a soul mate or even a comfortable companion. She'd get fed up, she said. "They'd only irritate me after a short while. Charles would within..."

"Caught you out. He's Charles," pounced Richard, feigning gleefulness.

"No, he's not. I did that to mislead you. I knew you'd fall for it."

Richard was finding her games no longer fascinated him. "I hadn't realised until now what a complete commitment-phobe you are. I thought it was just with me."

"Love for only one other is the lie I saw through with you."

He didn't care enough to feel too cross. "And won the victor ludorum. The trophy was a crown of thorns to wear through life."

Emma looked straight into his eyes. "And I've worn it proudly. What compromises do you make with your Helen? Is that a match made in heaven, as you tried to say we were? I know you well enough, Richard Shackleton, to expect you'll still be kidding yourself."

Richard wasn't impressed with Emma's knowledge claims. The thought came to mind that if she really did know him well, she couldn't like him much to have treated him the way she had. If she could patronise him, there was nothing to stop him doing the same in reverse. "When we first broke up, the radio was blaring out 'Macarthur Park' as I read your note. Well, I didn't find that recipe again for a long time. I would still be thinking of you and wondering why, if Helen hadn't saved me. But there are no hard feelings now, kid. I've a great family and Helen's as cynical as you but happy to take me as I am."

That was the opposite of the facts on the ground in at least one key respect. The coffees were finished. Richard had a last question; whether or not when she was pregnant she'd have come to live with him if he'd asked that rather telling her to leave.

"I can't remember," she said.

He never did know. He was surprised when she hugged him tight. They kissed long and hard and then he gently pressed his lips against her forehead. This did taste funny to him, musty compared with his younger wife.

Emma looked to the door of her bedroom with a come-on eye for her last question. Richard was a long time in replying. He felt the twitch of approval from down below. He could avenge Helen's Gallic lapse. But his rejection of Emma after she'd got pregnant had been as absolute as anything ever could be. The compost still hadn't mulched down. He let her down kindly. "If we started, I know I wouldn't want just once. We'd better not. Would you like to meet up with Helen and my mob while we're here?"

Emma was philosophical about being snubbed. "We'll stick at exchanging Christmas cards," she decided. "We'll meet again in another twenty years. You don't change that fast that I'll miss much, and I'll avoid all the irritation of thinking how you could be such a good mate if only you were less uptight."

They had one long, final kiss, and then he was on his bike. He still couldn't see this second rejection of her as an act of free will. Yet he felt guilty all over again about being disloyal to her the first time after she'd become pregnant. If he hadn't been, he'd have not had all the happiness his kids had given him. Helen hadn't made it far enough back into his good books to be listed with them. With a broad grin on his face, he met up with the family outside the pancake restaurant as arranged. He held Helen's hand as they went in. As the drinks arrived, she stared over his shoulder at a woman looking at them through the window. "Turn slowly," she instructed.

He did turn very slowly, hoping the face that he once wanted to look at till his eyes went blind would be gone. By the time he'd traversed a semi-circle, Helen confirmed that it had. "She was spying on us and realised that I'd spotted her. Who the hell was she?"

He didn't come clean as he was still in too much turmoil to feel confident in what he'd say. "Perhaps she was an angel, blowing a warm, gentle breeze our way. Give us a kiss, even if I am becoming a lay pillock."

Helen did, only a small peck, but enough for Amy to clap her hands in delight. "Kiss me now, Mummy."

Helen couldn't not do. James summed up the world's response perfectly. "Yuk. I don't want either of you kissing me."

After a healthy lunch of pancakes for main course and for afters, they played badminton. Amy and James were taking on Laura while parents rested. Helen spoke quietly. "I've been thinking more about it, Richard. You're right in becoming a lay reader. It honours your past and you'll be good at it. Just introduce me to your new circle gently, will you?"

His loyalty had been rewarded. The next night was another pleasant one. He was already asleep when she came to bed. He woke up to the surprise of a naked Helen pulling his pyjama bottoms down and stroking him as she gently sucked his ear. The sleep of the just-after was peaceful.

He was back to business on Monday. The Divinity sales team were pretty good but not miracle workers. Markets were poor worldwide. Richard knew that without the schools order it was going to be hard to find buyers of Northern Solstice shares. Yet he couldn't risk putting the prospect into the listing particulars only for Western Sun Rising to announce that they'd won that deal. Emil was confident it was in the bag, but if he didn't hear soon he'd have to delay the flotation. He rang Bob to see what he knew, first asking if he'd had a good funeral.

"Well, he stayed dead," Bob was pleased to say. "There was no banging on the lid. How are you getting on with Helen and the lay reader stuff?"

"Fine, she's even going to come to the odd service. Did you know that Wendy's husband's in a nursing home? He'll not be out again."

Bob didn't know but wouldn't admit it. Richard explained why he had to get news about the schools order soon.

"Even if we win it, we're too expensive in most markets," reckoned Bob. "In logic we ought to merge with Western. We could then sell their product where weight's not the issue, until we get our unit costs down. If we don't win the schools order, we'll have to move to Plan B."

Richard guessed that the B stood for Baldrick. Bob had nothing that cunning to suggest. Fortunately, ten minutes later, Richard learnt from Emil that the fax from the State had arrived. They'd won the schools order. Richard wanted Bob to tell Wendy.

Five minutes later again, Bob was back on to Richard. "It was all very polite. She put on her brave voice about living on her own in that big house. She'll probably move somewhere smaller in a year or two. I could cry for her."

Richard was flippant. "There are three of you living in big houses on your own now. Very inefficient."

"I don't somehow think that a ménage à trois would work with Wendy and Jane."

Richard had always quite fancied the idea, provided he was the un and not one of the deux. Bob was under no such illusion. "You wouldn't after the first time they ganged up on you. Anyway, you're not in this threesome. Leave us in peace to play our games."

"Wendy told me that earlier today."

"Good for her. I always did like that girl."

They arranged to meet for a meal the evening before the September Board meeting. Richard asked if Bob would like Wendy there. Of course he did.

# CHAPTER THIRTEEN

On Saturday evening, with the bandaging removed from his hand, Bob drove down the narrow bit of Queen's Drive south of Allerton Road. He waited in a side street for a few minutes, so that he wasn't early. He couldn't tell if the clouds were coming or going but peering through the grey sky was enough blue to make a sailor's pair of pants. He'd booked the restaurant in Hope Street that Jane had suggested. A minute before the appointed time, he rang the doorbell. She was a while in answering, and when she did come she was wearing a blouse and jeans.

"Bob, oh hell, I'd forgotten you were coming."

Although he'd suffered a fair number of humiliations in his life, none had been so unexpected. He believed it to be a deliberate put-down but resolved to pretend that she'd genuinely forgotten for some reason and to work out how big a grudge to hold later.

"You know how to hurt a guy. I've booked a table at that restaurant for eight. Have you something else planned?" he asked.

She looked at her watch. "No, I'm so busy I forgot all about it. Here's The Guardian. See how the other ninety-nine per cent live while I put something smarter on."

Jane was a quick dresser and a quarter of an hour later they set off for the restaurant, her in a short black cardigan and tailored grey trousers from the funeral, him in a brown sports jacket with light brown britches and brown brogues, wanting to look the country gent. They were in the restaurant only five minutes late.

He looked across at her as she ordered, at the face he'd known from before they'd met. The sudden bursts of energy, the staccato pacing to her speech, the animation that came so readily and yet with such force, were all there on their first date. She could have forgotten he was picking her up then too.

He asked how she was finding life with all the sympathy he could muster. She'd found time to go to a meditation class with one of her post graduates: "The one whose girlfriend beats him up that I told you about. He told me that the freedom of the spirit he achieved from throwing her out of the flat was greater than anything he'd got from meditation."

Bob agreed that people needed to live life as well as contemplating their navels. She'd noticed that his navel needed a bit more contemplating on and a bit less feeding, whereas she described Pratap as a really fit young man. Bob smelt danger ahead and warned her not to go breaking a young man's heart, hoping his fears were off the mark.

Her reply showed they were an outer if not a bull's eye. "Men fall for fluttering eyelids far too easily, you included, and I can't resist fluttering them. But no, this one really is too young."

"Don't lump me in with them," he growled.

"You're worse. After all I've done to you, and still you come round when I flick my fingers."

"If that's the way you feel, I'll bugger off now," he said, turning for the waiter.

She grasped his arm. "Don't go, Bob. Just don't look so much like a panting dog trying to please."

"Mrs Clarke, I'm not trying to please you. I'm doing my duty as a Christian ought."

Jane was debating whether or not to take offence as the main course arrived. The logistics provided the space necessary to catch her breath. When the waiter had gone, she smiled sweetly: "The house will be on the market next week, although I can't sell until we've reached probate. I want to start looking at flats soon. Will you come with me? You'll negotiate better than I can."

He pretended to think before replying: "I'll come on two conditions. One is that you never forget I'm coming again. The other is that I walk behind you if we go up any stairs so that I can watch your arse wiggle."

Jane squeezed his knee under the table. "I could see you liked these trousers at the funeral. I'll give you this, you make me feel noticed. Don't stop, will you? My only condition is that you're helping me out of Christian duty."

"If I can spread love's message as the master taught," the reincarnation of Harry Secombe warbled.

"That's enough. You're hired."

Over the rest of the meal, Bob heard more about her relationship with Ruth. Jane claimed not to care that they didn't get on, as Ruth was a Swarbrick through and through, who'd missed out on the zeitgeist, working with figures for the short time she did deign to work.

"That's reality TV and bleeding emotions nowadays," was Bob's take. "You're as out of it as me on that basis."

"I'm still more interesting though, aren't I?"

Almost speechless, he kept his temper. "What makes you think you ever were?"

"That you were more interested in me than I was in you."

"It was just an act to please you," he lied.

"I didn't even want to please you."

"That's probably true," he said sadly. "Is this evening a bad idea?"

Jane gave him a wicked glance. "Not for me, I'm enjoying myself."

"I suppose I must be then."

It was a great relief to him when the coffees were finished and the bill produced. He paid with no demur from the feminist position. They walked back to the car. He was feeling more deflated than anything else. She slipped her hand into his and scrunged his thumb as hard as she could, something she would do in their courting days when the mood took her. She asked if it still hurt. They'd reached the car. He slipped his hand away without answering, and held the passenger door open for her. He walked round to the driver's side, put the key in and started the car. As his hand moved to the gearstick, she grabbed it, pulling it on to her lap. She threw her arms round his neck, and gave him a long slobbery kiss. He didn't like the taste at first, but manfully saw it through. He still wasn't sure after they'd finished, so he gave her another kiss to check it out. This time she produced her tongue routine. He'd little choice, having succumbed to the return kiss, but to do the same.

"Friends, whatever, Bob."

"Whatever," he mouthed sardonically.

The journey back to Mossley Hill was mercifully quick. He managed to stutter: "Do you want me to come in or rather I didn't?"

"I want to show you some estate agent details. In you come."

They sat down together on the couch with a cup of tea. She was so close that he could smell the tea on her breath. Long ago, in the front room at Knutsford, that smell had thrilled him. He wasn't sure what it did for him now. They studied the details of half a dozen different flats. Only two were actually in the Park, and they were going for quite a bit more than half of what the house would bring. He suggested looking at somewhere a bit cheaper. She countered with: "I can't take it with me. We'll knock them down on price."

"You'll be in a chain while you sell here," he warned. "You might be gazumped."

"It's a chance I can take. We're going round the two in the Park tomorrow. One at eleven, the other at two."

Bob was so surprised that his slight stutter became a full-blown stammer. "Pardon, you're expecting me back tomorrow?" was what he'd tried to say.

She translated correctly. "No, you're staying tonight."

He was on the rota to be sidesman at the Communion service in St Chad's the next morning, but had swapped until next week in case he got lucky. He still wasn't happy at being taken for granted. "Hang on, you didn't remember I was coming, yet you'd lined me up."

"Subconsciously I knew you'd be here," simpered mystic Jane.

"I'm being taken for a bit of a ride. Where am I sleeping?"

"With me. I hope it's more than a bit of a ride."

It was more of a gallop than a canter. He'd paced it better on his last time out with Wendy over the Cheltenham jumps. Jane was happy enough in the enclosure, the final furlong being what really matters on the flat.

There were no action replays the next morning. She found him a new toothbrush and an old electric razor which she promised was Robert's. As they ate toast before they were to set off for Sefton Park, the razor owner rang, as he usually did on Sunday morning. From what Bob could tell, the call was typical of a grown-up son to mother, but he was nervous. He knew Jane and her predilection for saying what was at the top of her mind. This time she was behaving herself. They were at the goodbyes. Then she couldn't resist. "Do you want to say good morning to the guy I've spent the night with? You know him."

He couldn't hear what he guessed were hesitant, confused equivocations. The phone was thrust into his hand. As Bob stumbled over what to say, Robert understood Jane's ability to embarrass too well to do other than laugh. He asked if Ruth had received a similar call.

Bob said that he'd prefer to do that in his own time, a tactical error.

Jane, pinching the phone from him, trilled melodically, "Bye sweetheart, call me soon," and rang off. She speed-dialled Ruth, greeting her with: "Your Dad and I have spent the night together but he doesn't want you to know." After the reply, Jane's next words were an angry, "I don't play games with people."

After a few more exchanges, Jane said her goodbyes, with no exhortation to be called soon. She passed the phone to Bob for him to have a word with his 'wretched daughter'. The Jacksons were about to go to Church. Ruth hoped Bob knew what he was doing. He'd no idea, he said, so could she say a prayer for them?

Jane shouted: "Don't say one for me, unless it's to the devil. That's who you seem to think I am."

The first flat they saw was not to Jane's liking, with no view of the Park, being on the ground floor, with an old kitchen and drab, discoloured wallpaper. Bob suggested that she shouldn't rule out places where she didn't like the decor, as she'd redecorate anyway.

"Good advice, my little chickadee," she agreed. "When it comes to everyday common sense, you're always on the ball."

Back at the house, Bob mowed the lawn, his specialism, while Jane made the lunch. They sat on foldaway picnic chairs with salmon and cream cheese bagels and a glass of Chablis. Jane was relaxed and started asking him more about his jobs, offering to be his bag-carrier on the next trip to LA, if that wouldn't that cramp his style with Wendy Ballinger. He asked how she knew Wendy's name. She didn't reply, wanting to know instead if Wendy was nicer than her. Although Bob was thinking, "Of course she bloody is," he was content to say: "Easier, certainly. Nice wouldn't be the first word I'd use for either of you."

The afternoon property was on the second-floor and was much better. As the owner was away, they were shown round by the estate agent, Tomasz Nowak, a young guy on the Sunday shift. The place was immaculately decorated throughout, the kitchen classy, the bathroom even better. The views were of pleasant trees with grass beyond. The fitted carpets were Axminster, in boldly patterned reds and greens, which would fit in well enough with Jane's rather plain furniture.

Jane discussed family with Tomasz as if she and Bob were a pair. Bob wanted to come clean, but was worried that the wrong tone would sound petty. He'd forgotten how indecisive she could be on procurement decisions, from hats to houses. After she had exhausted all possible questions and several others besides, he cut to the chase. Tomasz tried to pretend that he had a cash offer close to the asking price and without a chain. Bob successfully called that bluff. Jane and he then slipped into the kitchen for a private chat. She was rather coy about the value of her savings and Bob spelt out that he needed to know so that he could gauge what she could afford. "I can add up too, Dimbo," was her reply.

He took that to mean that she wasn't sure if she had enough. After much bargaining, Tomasz reluctantly agreed to put a low offer to his client, unacceptable as it was. They all left the flat together, Tomasz to his Polo and the two throwbacks to the BMW, not quite the right car to plead poverty from. Despite her years, Jane climbed in more elegantly than Wendy.

"I could lend you some money if you need," he offered.

"Look, I don't know what I want to do about you, and from the look on your face when I mention Wendy Ballynuisance, you'd be no pushover to get back. But I'm enjoying you and money would spoil it. Have I told you that you're taking Pratap and me to Communion at the local church tonight? I promised I'd reciprocate his meditation session."

"I'm in yesterday's shirt and underpants, and was thinking I was about to escape," he confessed. "I'd say no if I knew how."

"You're going home tomorrow," she told him. "Get your stuff off when we get back and I'll wash them before Pratap arrives."

"Dry them too, could you?"

So he spent the rest of the afternoon in Andrew's dressing gown reading The Observer while Jane flitted in and out doing chores. She said he looked like Noel Coward. She was right on one thing; he wasn't at all sure what to do if she wanted him back. He longed for Wendy, but she wasn't on. It was Jane who had just pecked him on the lips. They had an early tea of bacon and eggs followed by a slice of Madeira cake. His clothes were dry enough to wear. She changed into a shortish black skirt and white jumper. She introduced her other guest as her friend Bob when Pratap arrived on cue at six. He was greeted by Jane with an unprofessional hug and a long cheek peck. She put on her coat, a green suede waist-length affair. Bob could remember another suede coat. "I hope that doesn't moult on my jacket like that brown one used to way back when."

Pratap looked puzzled. He was a careful listener. The service was a mix of evensong and communion, using the 1662 prayer book. Pratap stayed in the pew while they took the bread and wine. Jane went forward without guilt. She felt in a state of grace, making love at the moment as she was only to the one husband she'd married in church. Jane explained to Pratap how the prayer book had come about from the reformation and how Anglicanism had developed as a broad church with all three of its wings, evangelical, liberal and anglo-catholic, believing that they had captured the true Christian spirit. Pratap listened to her every word as if she were speaking the gospel truth. Back at the house, Jane opened a bottle of mid-priced Cabernet Sauvignon. Pratap was bold enough to discuss the similarities and differences between Christianity and Hinduism. The three-fold aspect of God, the richness of the scriptures and the generosity of spirit towards others were the items in his first category; if and how the soul survives were in the second, with Hinduism seeing the individual subsumed into the one true Self as the final goal. Bob wanted to meet Jesus in a heavenly pub, have a game of dominoes with him, everybody get merry and JC himself join in with 'What a friend we have in Jesus', Mary Magdalene on the harmonium in a low-cut dress. Jane protected her student by touching his arm, apologising for Bob's coarseness and asking if Hinduism would describe that view of personality as an illusion.

"We would, professor..." Pratap hesitantly started to reply.

She interrupted him: "Jane, or are you killing my individuality before I'm dead?"

He looked at her intently through his clear, brown eyes. "Sorry Jane. In a sense I am. We call the illusion Maya."

Bob's next contribution was more refined. "My good friend Richard's a great Christian apologist. I don't think he's that different from you, but he does see individual personality as the end game. For him, ideas are fundamental with physical things ideas we all have. I guess he sees matter as Maya."

Pratap tried to explain how Maya causes the physical to be seen, so it was true but compared with Brahman, the one true self, it was untrue. That was clear as mud to Bob, who needed to understand the mechanism uniting all ideas, which he'd happily call God. "But I can't see us humans as only ideas," he said. "What we feel while we're here is powerful stuff and it seems a denial to call it an illusion."

Jane and Pratap spent the next few minutes discussing his time in Kolkata while Bob poured more wine. Pratap took a second glass, plucking up enough courage to ask his burning question: "You two seem to know each other well. Have you been friends long?"

Maya was what Pratap wanted to feel his crush on Jane to be; for

Bob Maya was what he suspected Jane's feelings for him to be. He didn't know if they'd ever been friends until this weekend, and then only since lunch today. Jane was less reticent. "Bob's my first husband and the father of my two children. And now a good friend at a time of need."

Pratap left with more pecking. Jane, deeming the evening a great success, asked if she could meet up with Bob's guru, Richard. Bob liked the inclusivity she was showing.

"I'll see what I can do," he promised. "He lives near London. You know I'm thinking of selling my London place. Maybe we could do a weekend there before it's gone."

"I'd be in the bed where you conquered Wendy Balletshoes," her eyes flashed wickedly.

"That was LA. There have been a few conquests in that bed, most of them pyrrhic victories. Love's not some kind of victory march..."

"No, it's a cold and a very broken Hallelujah," she finished for him. "You won't be cold tonight either, big boy. Or broken. Apart from your ribs, it's my turn on top."

He drove off the next morning feeling the collywobbles as he looked back at the house, Jane still waving. Experience told him that the good feeling wouldn't last. He felt guilty towards Wendy too. She'd only been a one-night stand; she'd no doubt say she was pleased for him; she'd encouraged this to happen. Yet it had happened too easily. He still wanted her.

Once inside, Jane wailed out loud, "What have I done?' while at the same time smiling into the mirror. She hadn't been able to save herself from the old routine of pretending she'd forgotten their date. In fact she was late getting ready and wasn't sure she wanted to go out. Then she'd thought that he deserved better and had conjured up his apparently planned involvement with the flat-buying and Pratap.

She'd started enjoying the warmth of it all, so different from the last few years. Bob had handled it, avoiding being wound up at the start or making avowals of eternal love at the end. It was right that he both preceded and succeeded Andrew to mark his place as her most loyal friend. Yet she'd broken up with him before and she knew why. He took her over with his idiosyncrasies that bordered on self-parody. He thought that everyone given the choice would want to be like him.

## CHAPTER FOURTEEN

On the morning of the first Wednesday in September, and at the start of an Indian summer, Bob walked into Lime Street station smelling of another long weekend spent in Mossley Hill. A price had been agreed for Jane to buy the Sefton Park flat and her house was on the market.

Jane had dropped him off at the station. He'd booked to come back from London on the Friday evening, their new liaison predictable enough for advance booking rates. His car had been left in the drive, the equivalent to his slippers being under the bed.

He looked out of the window. It had been a long time since he'd travelled out of Lime Street. The train sped over the Mersey to Weaver Junction and on to familiar territory. He'd only Northern Solstice business during the trip, starting with the dinner that evening. Before then, he was instructing estate agents to sell his flat. And surprise, surprise, Wendy had accepted Richard's invitation to the smart Italian in Walton Street.

He went to his flat to dump his suitcase before a quick visit to Tesco Express. The estate agent arrived at three o'clock. She was a glamorous, smartly dressed and, by her accent, privately educated girl who sounded the part until asked a question. Property prices were buoyant and he was amazed at how much he could expect.

He put on his brown sports jacket uniform for the dinner on the basis that eventually it had worked with Jane. He took the tube to South

Kensington. Five minutes early, he was being taken to the table when Wendy arrived. Richard had rung the restaurant to say he was running a few minutes late.

"I bet he did that deliberately, so we could say hello first," she said. "How are you, big man?"

"I'm fine, it's all these others. And how are you, gorgeous girl? I gather Frank's in. Is it a bit lonely?"

"It's made things better. I'm still visiting him most days, but I can see my parents and girl friends more. Steve's been attentive too."

"What, you got it wrong, or does he bat for both sides?" Bob fretted.

"Probably opens for the gays and eleven for the straights, but he's a lovely, sympathetic guy."

Bob was still concerned. "That's what women always say. You want to be careful of last-wicket stands. Number elevens can be difficult to prise out once they're in."

"I hope that was still metaphor. Don't worry, he's not going to get to bat. Knowing you, I thought you were going to tell me what I might catch off him."

"That was coming next," he said, although it wasn't.

She wanted to know how he was getting on with Jane, and whether they'd batted together yet since she owed him a big innings.

"Bloody hell, Wendy, you're getting as vulgar as me." He didn't want to say that they'd shared a few breezy partnerships together. He was about to say things were still developing when she answered for him: "I can see from your face that you have."

He looked soulfully at her. She laughed at him, knowing it was bound to happen. "If it lasts, I'll be really happy for you. If it doesn't, you'll know the truth." She squeezed his knee under the table.

"She's making all the running, either away from me or towards me," he tamely told her. "This next bit is not bull. I wish it were you."

Unfortunately, before Wendy had the chance to be tempted by this little piece of bait Bob had cast, Richard breezed in, apologising for being late and asking if he was in for a walking-on-eggshells evening.

Wendy spoke for both of them, "No, Bob and I have rhinoceros skin on. We're cool with each other. How about you and Helen? Is she reconciled to your official sanctification as a reader yet?"

Richard pulled a face. "She has been for a while, but I'm not sure I'm going through with it. I had to go to a prayer meeting this week, with folk showing off their religiosity, like the scribes saying their prayers out loud from the best seats in the synagogue. The thought of having to take a prayer meeting is hard to contemplate."

Bob pointed up that, only the previous year, Richard could have beheld something bigger than a mote in his own eye when he'd made public the bonus he'd refused.

Richard agreed that he was a hypocrite as was everyone who got on their hind legs in a Church, pretending to be God's representative on earth, whether they sacrificed on the altar or preached from the pulpit. "They can sort out their consciences as they please," he said. "I can't handle mine that way. That's why I didn't become a clergyman the first time round."

Wendy was having enough doubts herself to hear of anyone else's. "No, you mustn't back out now. You'll be super at it, and you'll find a way to make something good out of all the stupid things you have to do, so just override your conscience. Go and have some of the action you missed out on and stop making feeble excuses."

Bob should have heard that she was wavering over Frank. She'd have been in his arms that night if he had. He didn't nibble at her bait just as she hadn't at his. The one good thing was that Richard heard. "I needed someone to tell me that, Wendy. I thought you were hacked off with the Almighty though."

This was the only time Wendy made a remark that sounded to Bob like one of Jane's. "I might forgive him yet. But I'm off men, and he insists on being one of those."

The waiter came to take their order. Once that was done, Wendy determinedly took the conversation to business. Everything was in place, the pre-market had been primed, and she'd squared Peter Forster on price at sixty-five pence a share. Richard was miffed that she'd trespassed into his territory by fixing the price.

"He still doesn't know if I've got balls with you settling it."

Bob rushed to her defence: "She did better than you would have, because he knew she hasn't any of those appendages. You'd told me sixty-six pence was your top figure. Have you definitely got buyers at the price?"

Richard had. "Including all the stuff Forster's chums, our stuff and a bit from Wendy's mob, if markets stay where they are, we'll reach twenty million dollars, the top end of our range. That values the existing shares, mainly Forster and his mates of course, at about sixty million dollars."

Wendy asserted: "Quite a bit from my mob. They weren't the slouches you said they were."

Richard claimed never to have said that.

"Admit it, you had your doubts," was Bob's attempt at peacemaking.

It wasn't necessary. Wendy came clean. "In which case, he was right, we couldn't have done it. You're back in my book of heroes, Richard, provided you become a lay reader."

"Please, Miss, can Bob go back in there too?"

The door was shut for today. "Definitely not, I know him too well."

Bob accepted his lowly status.

Richard revealed a bit of breaking financial news. Sir Charles

Norman had resigned from Grindleton's to become Chairman of National Bank. Charlie had played every card, outmanoeuvring the senior non-executive director Bill Robinson, who'd thought he was a shoe-in. "Western Sun Rising's fund-raise is up the scatological, paddle-less creek unless Charlie thinks they're worthwhile. If so, they'll be a National client within a few weeks."

Wendy had liked Charles to begin with when she'd met him at a function. He'd heard of her and her work at Black and Robertshaw, and had been complimentary. Then she heard him go to the next conversation and say the same things.

Bob had similar memories. "He does his smooze homework well. He starts writing his Christmas cards in September, so that they all have something tailored to the recipient on them. He's a convoluted character, a bit needy even."

Richard didn't show any charity either. "I won't be feeling sorry for him, however much he missed his mother at school. Or was it nanny?"

Wendy was back on the side of fair play. "Come on; rise above the formulaic, however bitter you feel. Writing personal cards is considerate. Give him that."

Richard wouldn't give Charles anything, since he'd only grab more. The dinner didn't come alive. The restaurant could have done with a cribbage set. There was no teleology. Perhaps the Lord had aeons like these while the stars formed, while dinosaurs roamed the earth. On the next day, the Board meeting was also unexciting. The flotation was going to happen. Making the company successful was on the back burner until the money was in. Bob and Wendy were not going to be heavily involved in the roadshows for investors, unlike Richard, who had two weeks of taxis, airports and hotels. He produced the tightest itinerary he could. He knew it would wreck him physically and he'd have piles again. All the other advisers were preparing their fee notes, their money easily earned.

Bob and Wendy said goodbye with wan smiles. Their next meeting was to be the formal completion meeting in three weeks time. He returned to Liverpool, intending to spend one night there with Jane before needing to be back in St Chad's. He spent two and was also needed for the following weekends. Probate had been granted, so selling Mossley Hill started in earnest.

The completion meeting came and went in low key also. A few days later on the Friday morning they all congregated at the Stock Exchange in Paternoster Square to see trading in The Northern Solstice start and to munch canapés. The Americans came with wives, parents, grandparents to see the great event, conducted by the PR department of the exchange with the same ruthless efficiency and attention to timekeeping that crematorium managers demonstrate. Farewells were said in the foyer. Wendy cleared quickly, touching Bob's sleeve while he was talking to someone else.

The November Board meeting was to be in London late in the month, to agree the interim results statement. The next LA trip was scheduled for February when the following year's budget would be approved. The Americans summoned taxis to take them west to their hotel. They were all going to the theatre in the evening. Bob and Richard were the last to leave.

Bob remembered his promise to Jane. "Hey, Jane would love to meet you two and we're down next weekend. If you could get a baby sitter, maybe we could drive up to a restaurant near you on the Saturday."

Richard liked the idea. "There's a decent Italian in Potters Bar. The older ones could look after Amy who'd be in bed before we came out. I'll let you know tomorrow."

"We'd pick you up, so you could have a glass or two. Oh no, you don't drink. Still we'd come to you first so that Jane can have a nose round your house. Do us a favour. Don't tell Wendy," he requested.

They went their separate ways. In the afternoon Bob was meant to be showing three prospective purchasers of his flat round the premises. He'd given the estate agent the keys and a quick phone call was all it took to clear his involvement. Within half an hour he'd packed his bag and was fighting his way up to the M1. He was past Birmingham before rush hour and into St Chad's in time for some tea. He rang Jane to tell her he was home.

She was cheerful. "Can you stay till Monday? Judy's looking forward to meeting you tomorrow at her party. They think you're a new man in my life. I've not told them you're my ex. By the way, I've had an offer on the house today, but it's quite a bit less than the asking price." He advised her to reject it. He then begged her to tell her friends who he was before the party.

She surprised him by agreeing: "You're right. It isn't fair on you, much as I was looking forward to the dénouement. What time are you coming?"

That was a first. Jane had backed off on one of her games. "I'm playing golf in the morning. I'll give Blackpool's game against Plymouth a miss. I can't fit too much excitement into one day. I can be there whenever you want from about five o'clock."

He sat down and watched the News while he ate a microwave lasagne, and then started a new novel, On Chesil Beach.

# CHAPTER FIFTEEN

That Saturday afternoon, Richard's great niece Olivia was married at a parish church in Norfolk. He was scheduled to start his lay reader course the next week but hadn't finally made up his mind to go through with it. The Shackleton clan were out in force for the wedding with only Trotter missing. He was spending the day with a friend, a beagle who lived up the road.

They'd all visited Richard's mother in the nursing home before the ceremony. Catharine was bed-bound and unable to attend the nuptials, indeed had no idea who Olivia was. She didn't seem to know who Helen or the kids were either. But her eyes had lit up as she'd seen Richard and she'd greeted him with a, "Hello, love," before falling asleep a few minutes later. He didn't know if she thought he was her son or her husband.

Sister Carol, grandmother to the bride, had prevailed on Richard to read 1 Corinthians 13. The tinkling of the cymbal stirred in him and he made up his mind while on his hind legs that he would become a reader, despite not understanding how Paul could have written the convoluted Romans within a few months of this wonderful prose. From the sounding brass of her past, echoes reverberated in Helen's head as she heard Richard's deep voice say, "And now abideth faith, hope and charity, these three; but the greatest of these is charity."

\* \* \*

At about five minutes to five that day, Bob left Queen's Drive into the avenues of Mossley Hill, listening to the scores on Five Live. Blackpool had drawn none each, not a bad game to miss. Jane opened the door before he'd rung the bell, saying he was like clockwork. She gave him a shiny gold yale key and a longer mortice one. She'd had them cut that morning. This was one up from being allowed to park on the drive. She'd received a final offer on the house, quite a bit higher than the one she'd rejected. Bob offered to help with seeing how much her investments were worth, the crucial bit of information he'd needed for weeks. She wasn't too keen on the arithmetic but the filing was good. Bob knew a web site where the prices could be updated. Half an hour later, he was close enough to knowing.

"After Shirley's dosh is taken off, you'll have just a few thousand to spend as you move in," he'd computed. "I'd accept, as you've got all the ducks in a row, but make sure that you charge all the fees to the estate before you give the money to cancer research."

Jane needed help in selling the investments. Bob explained that she'd have to talk to each of the funds but wrote down all the phone numbers, account references, units held and amounts for her to do on Monday. She then asked how his golf had been that morning.

"Not too bad. It was stroke play so the seven on the first par three was a bit expensive. I'm having problems with my fingers when I play now, arthritis I guess."

Jane picked up his hand and kissed each finger separately. "That didn't mean much to me. Andrew didn't play and neither did you when we were married."

"I'm still not that keen," he said. "I'd rather walk a dog."

"Good, I'd hate to be a golf widow."

"You'd have to become a golf wife first," he informed her.

She went to make the tea, while he did the paperwork. She'd showered and changed for the evening by the time he was finished, about a quarter of an hour before they were due to leave for the party. She sat on his knee. "I know I shouldn't say what I'm about to, Bob."

"Don't then," he said, and couldn't have meant it more.

"I've got to. You deserve to hear it. I'm in love with you again."

He'd thought that was what was coming. "And will the feeling last?"

"How can I know? I'll love you until I die. I can't guarantee always fancying you or liking you."

He felt happier when he heard that. Nothing irrevocable was at stake. On that basis, he loved her too. They went off to the party. That was when he found that Jane hadn't made any contact and Judy didn't know who he was. To make up for this, Jane called the whole gathering to silence to announce Bob as her first husband and present lover. Such an unorthodox arrangement was inconceivable to some in this audience for whom a divorced husband had to be boring, or abusive, or obsessive, and had never been a match in the first place. He would have understood this, without it all being said by a red-headed woman.

He did his best to be sociable, as to be fair so did most of the other guests. Jane didn't let him down. She held his hand as she wheeled him round early on. She came back to him from time to time. Red Head was Louise Buchanan. He found himself in a corner with her, and with Geoff Parkinson, Jane's old psychological beau. Louise reminded him of the parties of his youth, where there usually would be a girl wearing a long dress and no shoes who could float between groups seamlessly. She was a psychologist too and asked questions, staring intently into his eyes as he talked. After a while, having decided on his category, she glided away, without any need for an explanatory word or shoe removal.

Geoff remained. Bob wanted to move on, but didn't know how to glide and had to face Geoff's laboured inquisition. "She's quite a girl, your Jane."

"You could say that, I suppose," Bob cautiously accepted. "I think the possessive adjective would be a bit presumptuous."

"Remind me, how long were you married?"

Bob noticed the first two words of that sentence. He tried to play for laughs. "Nearly sixteen years. I could have murdered her on the first night and been out before we divorced."

"She has these mood swings, doesn't she? She led Andrew a merry dance, and he didn't enjoy it. She'll never accept that she's got bipolar tendencies. She blames her underactive thyroid," Geoff disclosed.

All this was news to Bob. "She has many ordinary moments too. She's no freak. If she's got two poles, entangled together they still make our Jane. Her Dad was a depressive but then after years in Japanese prison of war camp, who wouldn't have been? There's nothing else underactive about her. As you say, she's quite a girl."

This was meant to be dismissive, but Geoff persisted: "That she is, quite the most interesting woman I know. She does well to sit on that seething volcano beneath."

Bob looked at him more carefully. He'd need to recognise this fat bloke with a round face, bulging eyes and permanent grin on his face if they were to meet again, Still, he'd been friendly. Jane arrived to drag Bob off to the group Louise had moved to in the corner.

"Louise and Reginald are falling out over what's fair. Come and help Reggie boy out. It's a one-way contest so far."

Reginald was in full flow as they arrived. He was a flowery-looking guy with a dapper moustache and a mandatory bow tie. Jane introduced Bob to him.

"I'm Reginald, a historian and a high Tory. I'm tolerated here only provided I continue to amuse," he admitted.

Louise agreed that his views were laughable. She then smirked as she addressed her remarks to Jane. "I've introduced myself to Bob already. I've seen the car he's driving, and someone's just told me the exploitative jobs he's done. He's a rich white male with nothing interesting to say."

Jane did nothing to defend Bob. Maybe, he reckoned, that was what she thought about him too. Perhaps it was a fair summation of the value of his parallel universe. So, despite the rising hackles, he tried to be agreeable. "Yes, I'm comfortably off and for that I'm eternally grateful. And I hope nobody nicks my car while I'm here."

Louise didn't do light banter. "I hope they do. I might go out and scratch it later on."

Bob knew that Jane was testing him out, so he had a swipe at her as well as Louise. "You academics represent normal folk no more than I do. You know nothing about me, and if you did, as you say, you wouldn't be remotely interested."

Jane hadn't actually expected quite such a full frontal from Louise and pulled Bob away. But nobody was allowed to confront Louise. Her rules didn't permit it. Her face reminded Bob of Rebecca Moore's postmodern disdain. She followed them, no longer floating. "You can't take criticism, can't you? Power's always been seized by alpha males like yourself. You don't like it now because we've got you caged."

With that, she stomped off, Reginald behind her, like a cleaner fish with his predator client. Bob hadn't detected much of his self-proclaimed amusing side. He wondered if the bow-tie rotated at great speed or squirted water like Charlie Cairoli's did at the Tower Circus. He'd been a very white male apart from his red nose.

Bob turned to Jane, not knowing whose side she was on. "You women won't need men once cloning's possible. The debate will be whether to exterminate us, or to allow us to co-exist like the proles in 1984 and die out gradually."

"Orwell didn't get his linguistics right, so let's hope he was wrong on everything else. I wouldn't want to inflict the world with more of me. Louise just has these convoluted theories about what's fair."

"Being fair to men isn't one of them," he said bitterly.

"Come on, she gave you an alpha for machismo. I'd have you at beta double minus. She's always having a go at me too because I use ordinary language rather than her theories to decide what's going on. To me one word seems to shout louder."

Bob knew what the answer would be but still had to ask. "What happens if we don't agree which word shouts loudest?"

Jane squeezed Bob's hand and smiled. "We take my word for it."

The party lasted for another two hours. The dividing line became between those who were drinking and those who were driving. Neither group had much useful to say. Jane ended the evening with Geoff Parkinson, before she came to tell Bob it was time to go. She was a bit tipsy.

"You did pretty well after Louise," she effused. "What did you make of our Geoffrey?"

"I quite liked the guy. He seemed to know you pretty well."

She looked sheepish as she told him that Geoff had got to know her a bit too well about three years into her marriage to Andrew. "He seems to get me somehow," she reckoned. "His ex-wife's officially bipolar. So I must be too."

"He told me. I said that, if so, the poles seemed to fit together without a join."

She leant over and kissed him on the cheek. "Don't worry. I'm not. He still carries a torch and it's his entry point for staying interested."

When they arrived back, she asked him to make coffee while she got out of her heels, the first time he'd been welcome in the kitchen for more than the washing up. He struggled to find the coffee in the recesses of the fridge and then had to confront a cafetière lurking on the draining board. A fully catered tray including biscuits was set out on the coffee table when she came down in shorts, T-shirt and slippers. She'd only expected a couple of mugs of instant.

"Now you tell me! You look dead sexy. You know how to keep a man entertained," he said, ogling her legs,

"You're laughing at me."

"I'm lost in wonder, love and praise," he intoned. "Geoff Parkinson was speaking through his arse."

She fought the thought that, even though they were on different sides, they were moving inexorably towards living together. "You said I had no constancy, so I didn't exist, in our worst argument."

"It wasn't what I really thought. I was sorely provoked. Are there many more like Geoff carrying a torch?"

She confessed to a few where the torch had gone out. "Tonight, I only have eyes for you, the most grown-up man I've known," she flirted. "I'm comfortable and at home."

He couldn't go that far. "You're not comfortable; that's the last thing I'd say about you. Have I turned into an old pair of slippers?"

She reassured him that he was surprisingly venturesome with less predictable ideas of morality than Andrew. He'd been conscientious; Bob wasn't, she said, however much he thought he was. "You'll do what's expedient, though staying loyal to your past. You change in line with the facts, something Andrew couldn't do."

He was a bit shaken by that. He always took seriously her view of him; she was the one he'd always trusted to see the invisible line he'd overstepped. "Would I really have said that it was expedient for one man to die for his people?"

"No, because you like to stand against the crowd. But, believe me, Bob, you walk too much on your own. Now tell me all about this Wendy

Balihai. Is she conscientious?"

Bob answered with a clear yes, illustrated by the loyalty she was showing her husband. To overcome his own feelings of disloyalty, he described the impact she'd had on him, so much so that he'd granted her the hideously-named lifetime bonking rights. Jane said that she'd be happy for him to honour his promise, as she preferred to live in the present. She yanked him on to the hearth rug, a naff mock sheepskin. "Show me why it's called shag pile," she said. "Pretend I'm your favourite sheep." Her eyes were glinting with mischief. His feelings for Wendy were a futile exercise of will set against fate. However sheepishly, a ram could tup.

As they continued to lie on the rug afterwards, she asked for the same bonking rights. He didn't quite grant them. In that first anxious look she'd given him, he said, he'd seen eternity in her eyes, so why stop the rights at death? She'd heard about the mystery of her first look before. "I was only sizing up what was gawping at me. The other girls thought you were the bee's knees and you were staring at little me. It was unexpected and intimidating."

He laughed that she hadn't stayed intimidated for long. They both dressed and had another drink, a gin and tonic for her and a scotch for him. He asked what she'd planned for the rest of the weekend.

"Well, maybe we could give the kitchen table a go, like in The Postman Always Rings Twice, to excise Andrew's ghost," she teased. "Or did you mean go out somewhere?"

He wasn't too keen on that location or the thought behind it. He stuck to his original question, "Do you fancy a day out? I packed some walking stuff in the car. We could maybe have a walk around Hardcastle Crags. Richard and Helen are on for dinner next Saturday evening by the way. He has ancestors buried in Heptonstall Churchyard."

"Good idea! Andrew and I stayed round there when we walked the

Pennine Way. It's an eerie place, as well as where Ted Hughes did his worst."

She was in the bathroom first and asleep by the time he joined. He had a bad night's sleep, troubled by Louise's personal vendetta. A rich white male indeed, from his humble origins! He'd shared in the greatest flowering of white, working class culture, the late fifties and early sixties, with not only the music but the novelists, the artists, the edgy actors and much more. Was it too masculine? Whatever, Louise didn't give a damn for any of it a few decades later. He didn't expect that she'd ever had a crap in a freezing cold outside lavatory with bits of cut-up newspaper to wipe her arse on as a kid either. Still, those years had been worth it for the number of times he'd been able to use that line since. And if she'd been to a public school, the lavatories wouldn't have been much better, the food worse.

He didn't know anyone from the underclass, or anyone from a high-rise flat. All the Asians and blacks he knew were from the cricket club, or well-educated and in business. Being caring wasn't his bag. Friendly, yes: considerate, maybe: caring, no. Wendy did some voluntary work, but he couldn't go visiting the fatherless and the widows in their affliction without an introduction. Still, he'd done his Christian duty with Jane. And he did mow Mrs Metcalfe's lawn.

\* \* \*

That night Richard and Helen slept in each other's arms. At six in the morning, there was a phone call from Carol. Catharine had suffered a massive stroke overnight and was close to death. Richard was on the road back to Norfolk within quarter of an hour.

\* \* \*

The postman didn't ring before Jane and Bob set off for Yorkshire. In the old Heptonstall graveyard they found Richard's Shackleton graves, as well as Sylvia Plath's resting place in the newer part. Jane said that Bob was a perfect match for Dick Straightup, an early poem by Ted Hughes about a guy of almost supernatural strength who could hold his beer. Straight up, Bob suggested one of the local pubs for lunch; Yorkshire pudding filled with beef, roast potatoes and vegetables. The Dick Straightup in the poem wasn't driving and so didn't have to drink non-alcoholic lager.

Bob outlined the rest of the programme for the weekend: "If we set off after lunch on Thursday, we could visit the Jacksons on our way down. We bifurcate on Friday. I'm working while you have the day to yourself. That evening, it's the National to see Pinter's The Hot House. Saturday we're together, going to the Shackletons in the evening up in Potters Bar. Robert and Sophie are coming round to the flat for one of my famous cold collations on Sunday lunchtime."

Jane was happy that they saw the Jacksons on the way down. Bob rang before she had second thoughts. "That would be really nice, Dad," Ruth answered. "I'll get a turkey and we'll have a roast dinner. The kids will love it. They've never known the two of you as a couple."

He passed the phone to Jane. "Hi Ruth, it's the scarlet lady," she said. "I've not broken his heart yet."

Bob yelled in protest: "She never did. I was glad to be rid of her last time."

Jane preferred this Bob to the younger version. "Did you hear that, Ruth? And the tears I cried too."

"I can't wait to find out how it feels seeing you two together," Ruth gushed. "I'd given up on the thought years ago."

Jane said that Bob had surprised her. "He's only about nine tenths as bad as I remember him. The other tenth is far worse. It'll never work!"

Ruth was jumping up and down in delight as she told Jane: "Make sure it lasts until next Thursday. I'm not buying a turkey for nothing." Jane and Bob drove on to Hardcastle Crags. The walk was easy, taking only a couple of hours. They looked out along a stream over the peaceful late summer vista.

"It doesn't tell the story though," said Jane. "That's in the undergrowth, in the bushes, in the detail of small animals rearing their young."

"While other animals try and eat them. It's the valley of the shadow of death we're looking down. As we came out of the trees, we had to hit the savannah running before we were eaten too. 'After you chum,' isn't an easy thing to say in those circumstances."

"Not for you stone-age men but some of us have moved on a bit."

"Not a lot," answered Bob. "The Fylde's cow fields are my Garden of Eden. Hardcastle Crags are quite civilised too."

"A bit like you," she quipped. "Semi house-trained."

They drove back without saying much. She slept on the M62, waking up to order as they reached Queen's Drive. They went to bed early and made love more for the record than anything else. Bob returned to St Chad's as Jane left for the university on Monday morning.

* * *

Catharine died on the Wednesday morning without regaining consciousness.

## CHAPTER SIXTEEN

The Indian summer was over, though the rain was easing off as Jane and Bob arrived at Solihull. With Ruth beaming, Rachel opened the door. "Hello Granddad, hello Grandma. Mummy says that you're friends again."

Bob picked her up. "We always were, love. But we can see each other a bit more now."

"Gruncle Andrew shot himself, but Tom says you must have done it."

"Did he now?" laughed Bob. "I'd have missed. Gruncle Andrew was an even worse shot than me, and managed to hit himself. Maybe we'll have time for Hide and Seek before tea."

That had already been planned for when Tom and Charlotte arrived back from school. Jane was strangely quiet at seeing Bob so at home. She'd not realised how in favour he'd be with the grandchildren.

Ruth prodded her into life. "You're both looking well, Mum. I gather you've been doing all sorts of things together."

"Yes, and we've been going out as well. We're Darby and Joan, who used to be Jack and Jill."

"You missed too many years out to win the Darby and Joan competition," Ruth giggled. "The kettle's on. My spy watched you park."

Ben was beginning to crawl, under the watchful eye of Bess the dog. Tom and Charlotte returned. A big, home-baked lemon cake took pride of place on the coffee table in the living room. Tom cut himself a ginormous piece.

Charlotte, as proper as her mother, scolded him: "You should have given Grandma and Granddad some first. How big a piece would you like, Grandma?"

"About half the size of Tom's."

"And you Granddad?"

"It looks a cracking cake. If Tom can manage that big bit, so can I."

Ruth smiled her appreciation. "Harry's coming home early, about five. We'll eat at six if that's alright. The turkey's cooking nicely."

They chatted for about fifteen minutes, drinking their tea, by which time Hide and Seek could wait no longer. Jane resisted the repeated requests for her to join in, saying that she would help with the vegetables. From the kitchen, she could hear shrieks from outside. It wasn't a big garden and so some hideouts were inside too. Bob was told off for making the floor muddy.

While they were alone, Ruth tackled Jane with, "Is it going to last?"

"I've no idea," she replied honestly. "He's been great, but he's not like my circle. Last week at a party, he knew just as much as the academics there, yet managed to sound reactionary and authoritarian to them, though not to me. He needs an army to lead or something, and that was taken from him."

"He's the most open-minded man in the world. It's your chums who are in the time-warp," Ruth insisted.

"I'm now beginning to think you're right, which is why I'm enjoying it so much, but it's a damned big time-warp with me in the middle of it."

Hide and Seek came in again, without shoes. The outside aspects of the game had been abandoned. Bob found an old dishcloth and wiped the mud from the tiles. The children were all pleased to see

Harry when he arrived. Dinner was eaten a lot more quickly than it took to cook, despite the choice of three puddings. Afterwards, Bob washed up with Ruth while Jane talked to the children in the living room. Harry had gone upstairs to take a call. Ruth inevitably started probing Bob's feelings.

"I don't know, love, so don't press me," he pleaded. "It's more like when we first met than when we separated. On that basis, she'll finish with me at Christmas, make up again on New Year's Eve and break up finally at Easter. Unless I get her pregnant, but I think she's through the menopause."

"Why do you do it when you expect that?" she said, trying to understand.

"With your football team, it's the hope when they win a couple of games that ends up killing you. She fascinates me, and so I start thinking that it might work. It won't. I'm a rich white male to her chums. We'll be eating the Easter turkey without her."

Harry brought more dirty glasses. He said something rather different. "I've never seen you guys together before, you and Jane. You're made for each other."

They left with everyone waving ferociously. Ruth wasn't as positive as Harry in her whispered valediction. "It's exciting, if nothing else."

By eleven, Bob and Jane were sitting in his London flat with scotch or gin in hand.

"Tired, love?" he yawned.

"Not at all, Bob. I feel good. This is a masculine place. Very stylish and modern for you."

She made him chat inconsequentially for two hours more, high on the way the day had gone. In bed she was still talking after the lovemaking while he was trying to sleep.

The next day had to start early as Bob was due at Citel at nine o'clock. Jane hadn't brought a dressing gown with her, and he enjoyed her walking back from the shower to the bedroom with the too small towel he'd left out for her. She walked up to him and let the towel slip away. He planted his hands firmly on her bare, not fully dry bottom. Her wet hair soaked his face as they kissed. He moved to carry her to the bed.

"Not now," she said. "I'm clean. I don't want your stinkiness all over me again."

"Charming. I'll have you know I've already showered this morning."

"In which case, you don't need to get all sweaty again."

They went their separate ways for the day. The play was disturbing that evening. Liberal left and considerate right could both appreciate the problems with institutional bureaucracy. Jane was tired and again asleep before he was in bed.

The next morning Bob went to the nearest Waitrose to buy the cold collation while Jane had a lie-in. His mobile rang while he shopped, Richard telling the news of the death of his mother but insisting that they still come, as the funeral wasn't for several more days. Jane and Bob trogged round Kew Gardens after lunch. She rushed up to a tree every so often, and demanded Bob's attention as to what it was. To him this seemed a random process that she could equally well have done with the next tree, but he humoured her as he had done way back when. She could have been a botanist as much as a sociolinguist. They were engulfed in planes of light as they passed a beautiful cedar without receiving a divine message. Having dallied too long, they had to change quickly into smart clothes for the trip to Monkey Mead, driving up the carriage drive more or less on time. Bob walked over the pressure-hosed, moss-free paviours and knocked while Jane waited in the car.

Richard opened the door. "Amy's just gone to bed, so we'll stay out of the house until we get back, if you don't mind. You can nose around then."

Jane rolled the window down and shouted: "Hi Richard, I'm Jane. Bob sees you as his spiritual guru."

As she came through the door Helen yelled: "What, that pillock! He'll have you on the road to hell. The last time Bob was here, they both spoke crap, Bob in that nicer accent from north of the Ribble."

Jane got out of the car to meet her. "Looks like it should be a disastrous evening. I'm from south of the Ribble too, but also from south of the Mersey in Cheshire. Bob thinks I'm refined, but you won't."

"I'm from Sussex or Upper Normandy as Richard calls it," Helen revealed. "Cheshire's more my taste than these riff-raff. They should have been kept down the mines or in the fields. Richard looks far more at home in overalls."

"And Bob makes a great scarecrow," Jane added.

They clambered into the car and set off. Richard was in the front next to Bob, who expressed his condolences.

"It was a merciful release," Richard said softly. "Her time was done, and wherever she is or isn't, it's better than what she's suffered this last couple of years. You guys have a good day?"

Jane was the guy to answer. "We had a walk down memory lane in Kew Gardens. It was spring when we last went and the autumn of our years today. I wish we came up as good as new again like flowers do."

Helen surprised everyone. "Maybe something does abide beyond death. Some of Richard is finally beginning to wash off on me."

Richard didn't know if she was just being considerate to him in his grief. Jane chose to be flip. "Bob took the religious stuff seriously at youth club too. He didn't see it as a phase he was going through or the opportunity to pull a nice girl like me."

Helen behaved herself all evening, so that Jane had to follow suit.

196

She was exhilarated on the drive back to London. "I was scared that all your friends would turn out to be golf club types; rich, white and male in your new best chum Louise's words. Helen is stunning and Richard's not bad. And wow is he bright? Brave too, as he was obviously mourning his mother."

Bob agreed that too many of his circle were Farmer Steadyturds, as he was. They were both relaxed when they reached the flat. A gentle coupling took place as they lay and then slept in each other's arms.

Bob had a lie-in the next morning which meant it was quarter to eight before he got up. Jane was an hour later, by which time he'd been out for the Sunday papers. They read those together, Jane frequently interrupting his 'News Review' with something from the 'Culture'. Then he opened up the table and laid everything out that didn't need to stay in the fridge.

"How many more sorts of pickle can you want?" Jane wanted to know. "Who's all this pork pie stuff for? Why did you need the beef as well?"

"To go with the horseradish sauce I'd bought."

She'd expected just some quiche and tomatoes. He brought those out on his next visit to the fridge. The courting couple arrived spot on time.

Robert looked at the table as they walked in. "Where are the peaches? When Ruth and I used to come and see you, there'd always be a bowl of tinned peaches to have with the pork pie."

Jane shuddered at the thought. "I wouldn't have let them come if I'd known. The pair of them are so coarse, Sophie. Can't you find someone better? My mother has just done a somersault in her grave."

The door wasn't even shut yet. Sophie opened her mouth but didn't get any words out before Bob added his voice to the babble, "Put wood in t'hole, Robert. Grandma Burrows was a lady of pronounced tastes,

197

Sophie. That's pronounced with a superior expression in her voice."

Jane had to have right of reply to that. "You're jealous because you don't know how to sound superior. My mother did things properly. Admittedly, on her definitions, nobody else did."

Sophie hadn't managed to say hello. At last, as Bob started taking coats and asking about drinks, she flashed the ring in front of them. "Robert and I have some news to tell you. We're getting married next May."

Jane rushed to hug her. Bob punched the air in delight. "You've only known each other five minutes, but I thought you were made for him up in St Chad's. I hoped you'd think so too."

"Most of my friends don't intend to marry for years, if at all," she admitted. "But now I've met Robert, it seems to make sense. I mean, I wouldn't want to end up looking as hangdog as he did before I met him, would I?"

Jane looked at Sophie with apparent approval, but Bob could detect the first undertones of animosity. That was a shrewd remark, something Jane didn't do at that age. Or her present one for that matter.

"Do your family know, Sophie?" he asked quickly.

"Yes, I rang them last night. Robert's going to meet them at Christmas when we'll go over. We wanted to tell you personally today."

They were already living together in Robert's flat, with plans to find a house in Richmond. Soliciting paid well. They were going to marry in Canada, at the Victoria church where Sophie had been christened.

"It's all off if you two guys won't come," she blackmailed.

Jane was in no doubt. "We'll be there, won't we, Bob?"

"Of course. Can't you make it sooner in case you change your mind?"

As the day developed, Bob and Sophie hit it off well again, with Jane and Robert naturally close. Bob worried that Sophie and Robert would be like Jane and him, not quite compatible. Still, he couldn't have been happier that Robert was down off that shelf. Jane and Bob were less of a pair than they had been at Ruth's. He put this down to her still assessing Sophie. He could already feel his ear being bashed later and he wasn't disappointed.

"She's a very self-contained young woman, isn't she?" said Jane as soon they'd left. "I hope Robert has thought it all through. It's rather quick for them to know each other. She'll probably drag him off to Canada at the first opportunity and our grandchildren will speak in that dreary, flat accent."

"I like flat accents. Stop chunnering, love They're going to settle in Richmond. She's a grand girl and our Robert's fallen on his feet."

Jane reserved judgment on the basis that she'd married Bob in too big a hurry and that had ended badly.

"That's still not ended anywhere yet," he laughed. "We don't know if we'll land in clover or cow shit."

Jane seemed to come round. "I'll give her the benefit of the doubt. The last bit's easy. Sefton Park is clover, St Chad's cow shit."

Bob accepted that St Chad's might be cow-shit but expected Sefton Park to be more dog shit. Jane thought that the refined middle-class residents would all pick it up in their little black sacks and put it into the shiny red bins. Bob believed there'd more chance of the dogs doing that themselves, perhaps even the cows. Jane put her arms round his neck. He'd nearly won a word play. He was expecting a sloppy kiss of congratulations. She pulled him hard against her and whispered fiercely in his ear.

"And don't forget, clever clogs, you don't own me. You don't own Robert, you don't own your precious Ruth. Not everyone loves Bob, and nobody does all the time."

She kissed him so hard that he could feel the blood. He showed no reaction but quietly said: "Let's get this lot cleared away. Do you need to be back to Liverpool tonight?"

"Yes, I'm lecturing tomorrow. Are you driving on to St Chad's?"

He said he'd been hoping for another night of passion in Mossley Hill, but it was up to her. She grabbed hold of him again, by the arm. "You still haven't got it, have you?" She pushed him away, giving his bollocks a hatefully hard squeeze as she did. He still felt sick from it as they set off for the car quarter of an hour later. Jane slept most of the way back to Liverpool.

He pulled into the drive in a silent fury he'd maintained for the length of the journey. He took her case from the boot as she woke up blinking, leaving his own where it was. She asked what he was doing since he'd wanted to stay.

"You made it abundantly clear in word and deed that you didn't want me too," he retorted, to be told to come in and stop playing his face. Reluctantly, he did, still without his case.

Her face softened a smidgeon. "Put the kettle on, sulky pants. Then go back and get your case, or I'll really give you something to sulk about."

"And what's that?" he snapped grumpily.

She threw her arms round his neck again, and gave him a long kiss, ending up with her tongue down to his throat. Her breath smelt of her sleep, but he was learning to love that taste again. Eventually he went out for his case. As he drank coffee, still glowering, she clicked on Match of the Day 2 for him to watch. After a few minutes, she sidled up next to him and started to undo his shirt. She tickled his nipples. She unzipped his trousers. She went down on him. In vain, he did his best to focus on the football. He pulled her up quickly before she bit, and rolled her on to the shag pile. She pulled him on top of her. He made the most aggressive penetration of his life while her fingernails dug deep into the flesh of his backside. The savage grin on her face came straight from a movie trailer of a female vampire with the blood of a virgin rival dripping down her chin.

"I love you; I hate you, Bob Swarbrick. That's the way it will stay."

Until it doesn't, Bob thought.

As he drove back to St Chad's the next morning, he was wondering what the hell it was he'd met all those years ago. He'd thought then she was impish, not a fully-fledged she-devil.

\* \* \*

A week later, the Shackletons had a much sadder trip to Norfolk than the one just over a fortnight before. The funeral had been delayed to allow Olivia to finish her honeymoon. In the meantime, Richard had started the lay reading course. Catharine had spelt out what she wanted at her funeral service several years before, and Richard again found himself at the lectern, two chapters later in 1 Corinthians. This time his deep voice cracked and a tear rolled down his face, but he kept going.

"If in this life only we have hope in Christ, we are of all men most miserable." Johnny Cash took over. "But now is Christ risen from the dead, the first fruits of them that slept."

Helen could not have been prouder of her man as he walked back from the lectern. Not only did she love him, she found that she was hoping for what he'd just read. That evening, he sat alone in his study. He'd need to believe in what he'd read too, to believe in what he'd be preaching. Nell, Dad and Mum had gone. Carol, born before him by the length of the war, was looking old. He wondered if that once happy family could come together again in death. Except for old Trotter, he'd be gone much earlier than the rest of his present, much happier, home. He imagined Helen and the kids round his graveside lobbing in the bits of soil.

There were things he'd have to preach about where he believed the theology had swayed biblical reportage. But the events had given rise to a story for him more fundamental in its meaning than a history could ever be. As many do, he projected himself into how he saw Christ, compassionate, intelligent, humorous and sometimes tetchy, a likeable guy. Even if Christ was nothing like that, Richard saw in the gospel accounts a historical Jesus who was a real man with human foibles and with a simple, Jewish faith in the one God. During his healing and preaching ministry, the idea of the value of the ultimate self-sacrifice had developed. Jesus wasn't shown to be perfect, only that he knew what to do about not being so. There were two big issues where Richard would have to tread carefully, the virgin birth and the resurrection. He couldn't see the need for a virgin birth but he'd need to keep that to himself. He did find the different resurrection accounts in the bible achingly honest. This was the one place where he felt that there must have been at least a spiritual miracle, the place where God decided to have people live out the tales written for them.

"He is risen indeed. Alleluia," Richard said to himself, believing that it was Christ's resurrection body that had appeared on earth before being taken up.

Like Bob, he didn't want his resurrection body from when he was the same age as Jesus. At thirty-three, he was drifting in no direction. A memory suddenly struck the back of his head like a cosh. A friend had driven him to Bolton after his first term at Oxford, back home to see Nell. He'd been transfixed by a feeling of utter stillness as he looked across the North Oxfordshire countryside. Time had been suspended for a few seconds: the car didn't move. Could that have been when a simulacrum was taken, he asked himself, nineteen years old, fit as a fiddle, just about an adult but still a virgin, before he'd rejected the ministry, before he'd been torn apart by Emma, and most of all, a few weeks before Nell died? If that body could be linked with his memories and with his conscience, then he thought the result would be a complete Richard Shackleton, not the Rich Shack presently on display. He couldn't decide if this was too good, or too good not, to be true.

His thoughts returned to what had been his stumbling block over becoming a clergyman in the first place. He'd no quarrel with the need for lives to be redeemed. Everybody should want to be a better person, if that was an option. The Christian message that Christ, and by extension God, suffered with us could help us get through life. But to condemn someone, his Dad included, for not declaring this belief still struck Richard's conscience as wrong. The wonderful author of Hebrews could see true faith not needing that formality.

He didn't accept either what he'd read at the funeral service, that if he'd believed just for this life, he was the most miserable man. He didn't think he would earn salvation for a next life by his belief or through his good works. He was sure that, if at all, it could only be by the grace of God. For him, the passion showed humans how to live and the resurrection gave the hope that eternal life was possible. He didn't want to start bible classes in the villages under his tender care. He intended coffee mornings and home visits to be the focus.

In bed, he asked Helen how far he should go into things.

"You've got a kind face," she said. "Smile and say the platitudes. You'll do more good that way."

CHAPTER SEVENTEEN

The November Board meeting of Northern Solstice, with Richard and Wendy present, was in full flow at Divinity's offices. Sales of solar gear were going just a little better than expected after a couple of orders had come in on the back of the schools contract. Production was as a result behind schedule. Any further new sales wins, however welcome, would be difficult to fulfil for another three months. Before the lunch break, Bob asked if there was any other business.

Peter was champing at the bit. "I met Sir Charles Norman for breakfast this morning. He'd like to see Western Sun Rising and Northern Solstice together at some stage..."

"He could go to Stonehenge with the hippies on the twenty-first next month and, if he faced the wrong way, his life could be complete," punned Richard with impeccable anti-timing.

Peter carried on regardless: "He says it's inevitable and we ought to start co-operating now. National may well act for them and he kinda dangled their cheque book in front of me."

Emil wanted to co-operate on marketing and sales as soon as possible so that he could begin to populate a decent prospects list. The debate went on for at least ten minutes before Bob spoke. The Americans were clearly keen to do something and, Bob guessed, knew more than they were cracking on. Wendy and Richard were both sceptical and untrusting.

"If I'm honest, I think we have to co-operate on sales," Bob concluded. "Otherwise we won't acquire critical mass. Eventually we ought to share production facilities too, perhaps even merge. Let's try and negotiate a joint marketing approach on a fifty-fifty basis, and tackle the rest later. What would he do with his cheque book, Peter? Make an offer for us, or have us buy them?"

Peter was pleasantly surprised that Bob had seen it this way. He thought that Western wanted to buy Northern for cash. Bob realised that a game plan was being worked up already. He decided to explore what price Peter hoped to get by flying the kite of shareholders always being happy if they'd doubled their money. Peter doubted they'd get anything like that much. Bob deduced that a price range had already been discussed too. Peter and his cronies were already lining up mooring for their boats at Newport Beach.

Richard was puzzled as to how a cash deal had suddenly materialised. "I bet there's another angle to this," he surmised. "National recently launched a green fund and also advise on others. I reckon they're taking more money in than they can find investments for and they're going to move this into one or more of the funds. Charles needs something to put other people's money into. What that could mean is that price may not be his first concern."

For the first time, Peter appreciated Richard and wanted him to find out if he was right. Richard knew where to look. His old chums at Grindleton's would be sick if they were losing the Western Sun Rising account. They had a green fund too, and Charlie was probably tapping them up to take a stake as he wouldn't be allowed to put more than half into his fund. After the meeting, the three of them waved goodbye to the rest and then held the post-match inquest in reception.

Bob knew the score. "There's a bit to play for still, but the rest's been decided. All we can do is make sure the price is high enough for the shareholders. You'll both earn some more fees and I'll make a bit on my flotation options."

Wendy smiled thinly. "Another good start-up sold out for a fast buck. It's not a glorious end, is it?"

Bob touched her hand before he remembered that they were off limits. "I guess not. Everyone but poor Scott Johnson is making sordid millions out of his invention, us included. Still, he'll have a job and more green electricity will be generated than the friction we've dissipated. It's probably the best thing all round."

Wendy liked the touch. She praised both of them for cottoning on to what Peter and Charles were up to. She'd felt second division, she said. After a few more pleasantries, Wendy and Bob left the building together. She was walking to Moorgate tube. She finally asked the question she had to. "How's it going with Jane?"

"OK, I guess," Bob faintly praised. "She's forever dragging me off to parties, exhibitions or functions. They're beginning to drag. How are you managing on your own?"

"Like you, OK, no better than that. I'm going back to an empty house, Sheba aside."

They reached the station. Bob risked seeing if she fancied a coffee. She did, being booked on a later train from Paddington. He ventured further. Since he was completing on his flat next month, this was her last chance to go there. He reassured her it would only be for a cup of coffee.

Wendy couldn't resist teasing him: "What if I insist on my lifetime bonking rights? I'm now calling them LIBOR."

"A gentleman's word is his bond," he said, not in jest. "LIBOR mustn't be manipulated."

"I bet it is, but don't worry. You're Jane's again. Let's go and see this den of iniquity."

They walked briskly down Queen Street to the flat. Wendy found it very masculine. Bob told her that Jane had told him that too, before commenting on everything individually, being more a cataloguer than a theorist. Wendy miaowed in reply. Neither of them had a template as to how to behave. They stayed at the flat about an hour, the time flying by. They tried to figure out why sex had reared its ugly head too often in their pasts, as both felt that the purpose of life was to become the person you were meant to be, the person you were born as, according to Bob.

They were both searching for a soul mate. They didn't want to be to be subsumed into each other; they wanted to know and like each other so much they could honestly say they loved each other. But she still found it impossible to give him the full come-on. Similarly, he couldn't find the trigger to dismiss his past. At least neither need have felt guilty. Bob had the good grace to sound pathetic when he said that he'd hoped their relationship would be so good it would leave him in the right state to meet his maker, which it would if only the Good Lord would allow it.

"I'm not up there with Jane, and you know it," insisted Wendy.

"Only because of the history. Otherwise you'd be miles past her."

He walked with her to Mansion House tube. He went round the Circle Line to Paddington with her. He walked to the platform. She kissed him lightly on the lips and whispered, "Have a good Christmas, Bob."

"Is it time we were saying that? And you, gorgeous girl. See you on the flight to LA in February, if not before."

And that was that. It was winter, cheerless and grey. The window had been open, but neither had climbed through. It would have only taken a quantum of will. He went back to the flat, hating himself for his cowardice. He'd already lied to Jane and told her he had a dinner that evening, to avoid having to dash back for a concert. He drove home to the solitude of St Chad's.

He was at Jane's for the weekend though, going to the theatre and a party. The weeks passed by quickly up until Christmas, with both of them completing their property sales. With Sophie and Robert off to Canada, Ruth invited both parents to spend four days of Christmas with them. Bob was keen but Jane didn't want to go as it would mark her decline into grandmotherhood.

"Robert came to me for Christmas Day last year, and Ruth for Boxing Day. I was Mother Hen, Andrew gruff uncle," she wailed.

"I'm more used to being guest. It saves a lot of work but you have to do the washing up. Why don't we just go for the main two days?"

"OK, provided Ruth promises not to be sweetness and light the whole time. Tell her I'm only coming on the express condition that we have a blazing row on Boxing Day afternoon."

"Fair enough," agreed Bob. "I'll probably go for a walk and let you get on with it."

Jane felt her temper going several times in the weeks up to Christmas, with Bob, with colleagues, with shop assistants, with herself. She couldn't find time to co-ordinate presents with him, and they decided to do their own thing. She knew that she was going to be out-bought. She kept him away from her party season. Her friends didn't want him there.

She missed Andrew. She saw him as far more like Christ than Bob was. He'd crucified himself. He didn't believe in God, but she could interpret Christ himself as starting that line of thinking. She wrote in her diary that it wasn't a big intellectual step from a human becoming the Son of God to creation being its own cause.

Bob didn't stay with her on Christmas Eve. He'd been to midnight communion in St Chad's. He arrived, car stacked with presents, at Sefton Park at ten o'clock as planned. He had his front door keys, which was as well. Jane was in bed asleep. She woke with a fright, and spoke in a deep voice, full of cold, like a diamond bit drilling into marble.

"Oh shit, it's not that time, is it? I drank far too much last night. I've got this awful sore throat. Tell Ruth I'm not coming. I mean it, Bob."

"I hope you don't. Come on love, the turkey will be in the oven, the kids will be excited. Harry will have that fire roaring. You'll feel better once you've got up."

She saw Bob's face, nearly angry, nearly disdainful, trying to look compassionate. She knew he'd always lived his life on a 'let your yea be yea" basis and wouldn't even cancel something insignificant. He was right; she had to go. She kissed him quickly, and went into the bathroom, shouting through the door.

"With any luck, I'll have given you my germs. Milky tea, please, I'm not up for your stuff you can stand a spoon up in. And burnt toast to absorb the alcohol."

Though the crisis had passed quickly, Bob saw it as irritatingly repetitive, with the same motifs recurring. He said little as they drove.

"Don't be so disapproving of me, Bob," she said brightly. "I had a good night last night. Geoff asked me to marry him."

Bob gulped. He wasn't ready to lose her again, though a moment ago he'd wanted to strangle her. He couldn't understand why she told him these things. He acted tough and asked what she'd replied. She didn't answer. He asked instead how she'd had a good night with Geoff. She told him he wouldn't want to know.

"I live with the truth nowadays," he claimed with minimal justification. She explained that Geoff and she had lain on his couch in front of a rom-com and eventually had fallen asleep. This was the truth, the truth she couldn't understand herself. She'd been thinking about Andrew in the run-up to Christmas. Not with grief, not with longing, but with the affection that produces little smiles of recognition. She didn't know why she'd been happy for Geoff to be with her when she'd wanted Bob out of the way.

Bob had said that he could live with the truth and thus didn't move a facial muscle as he said: "We'll be sharing a bed tonight at Ruth's. Are you up for that?"

"Yes, and I expect some action. Geoff's strictly a sleeping partner."

"Do you still need others as well as me?" he asked, a stupid thing to say with the chaos that was his mind.

The riposte was inevitable. "What about you and Wendy Ballykissangel then?"

But then, out of the blue, she smiled and he didn't have to lie. "We haven't given each other Christmas presents yet? Or haven't you bought me one?"

"I picked up a box of chocolates at the petrol station on the way over," he told her. "They're in the sack for the Jacksons."

"I at least went out to a shop to buy yours. The Oxfam shop."

He said that was where he got his wardrobe from. She wasn't having that. "I've looked at your suit labels, and none of them are cheap. You never quite make it all the way to smart..."

"Er, Ruth tells me that," he said, apparently having trouble remembering his daughter's name. Wendy told him that too, and he'd changed the name an instant before he'd said it.

"I was going to add that it's one of your many endearing characteristics," said Jane, agreeing with her two foes. "You've plenty to be proud about too. I'm sorry I was a pest this morning."

Jane had apologised. It was Christmas. They were met at the Jacksons by excited dog, grandchildren, daughter and husband as they staggered in with cases and parcels.

"I've got an awful throat, Ruth, so you'd better not give me a peck,"

Jane said. "You'll be pleased about that."

"I'd braced myself too. Shut the door, Dad, it's cold over Bill's mother's."

Jane grimaced at the apple maggot. Bob grinned before revealing that Jane had deliberately kissed him to give him the cold and then breathed fire over him to be sure. Ruth asked Jane how Robert was in the far west and if he was snowed in. Robert had sent an email to Jane for Bob to read too but the second part of the action hadn't yet been fulfilled. He was having a terrific time without any snow.

Then they had to examine all the children's presents, one by one. Tom's were mainly computer games of course. Both grandparents were preparing their excuses so that when approached they could avoid playing them. There was something called a Wii which was new. Charlotte had lots of books, Rachel and Ben mainly toys. Bob stroked Bess the dog while having a conversation with a new teddy bear of Rachel's. She asked if he had a teddy when he was little.

"Yeah, we used to call him Jo Stalin," he recalled. "I still have him in a cupboard somewhere."

"When Grandma lived with Gruncle Andrew, did you used to take him to bed with you? Mummy says that Teddy can come to bed with me. I'm going to call him Jo thingy after yours."

"Maybe we'll just call him Uncle Joe," Ruth suggested

Rachel wasn't having that. "He's Jo Stalin. See, I can say it. What was your favourite dolly called, when you were little?" she asked Grandma as she picked up her new doll, capable of crying real tears.

"That would be Rosebud," Jane said.

"That's a nice name. This is Rosebud."

Jane looked pleased to be counted in too. Bob laughed: "That's a terrific pair of names we've landed you with, Harry, if Rosebud represented more than the sled in Citizen Kane. Still it is a lovely name."

Only Jane was old enough to know what he was talking about. Lunch was a proper Christmas dinner. Harry jovially announced that, "Lancheon is sarved." The washing up had to be finished before the presents were exchanged. Jane and Bob had both spoken to Ruth to find out what the children wanted, and had their lists. Bob had been to Manchester to Kendal's, sadly re-named the House of Fraser, Jane into Liverpool to John Lewis, regrettably no longer George Henry Lee's nor even in the same place. Both of them had spent far too much on games, toys, clothes and the rest, not to be outdone. Harry had a wonderful new power tool and a smart Peter England shirt, Ruth a solid silver cross with a chain and a Fossil handbag. Jane and Bob were laden with loads of good things on return, too many of them fattening. Finally it was the turn of Grandma and Granddad to open their presents from each other. Jane had bought Bob a stylish black leather shoulder bag for his long flights. Bob had seen that Jane had no decent watch and had bought her a gold Lacroix.

They all went for a long walk, Harry pushing Ben in his buggy. As they walked along, Jane held Bob's hand. As she scrunged his thumb gently, she chided him: "You spent too much. But thank you. It really is gorgeous."

"And I've been meaning to get myself a decent shoulder bag for ages. You must be telepathic," he replied.

"Of course, I am. You know that."

The two days passed in no time, with no rows at all. Ruth grinned as she said goodbye to Bob. "You said that you two would break up at Christmas and make up on New Year's Eve." He warned her not to hold her breath beyond Easter. They were back to Liverpool late. Jane asked Bob to stop the night in her flat. Not only that, Christmas had gone so well that she wanted more of Bob and asked if she could stay with him in St Chad's until Geoff's get-together the following Monday.

Bob's fixed line in St Chad's rang on the Thursday morning as Jane was planning their next outing, a walk round Chipping. There was no screen to forewarn him that it was Wendy, ringing from Keele services. She was driving Steve to visit his mother in Keswick as he'd picked up a disqualification for dangerous driving. Wendy asked if he was free for them to pop in on their way.

Bob had a reckless urge. "Jane's alongside me making a right mess of the OS map, but that walk could wait till tomorrow. Come and have lunch here on your way up. I'd better just consult the oracle."

Wendy didn't want to come between Jane and Bob and explained to the telephone that she didn't know Jane went to St Chad's or she wouldn't have rung. Bob heard none of what she said because he'd pressed the mute button and was telling Jane what was planned. Anybody who knew Jane well would have known she would find the idea irresistible, and Bob did know Jane.

Wendy was surprised that Bob appeared to have been cut off and was about to hang up when she heard his voice. "That's fine. We're off to the supermarket to get some grub. You should be here in about an hour and a quarter. How come you're happy to leave Frank behind?"

Wendy put it down to a need for respite. In Booth's supermarket, Jane manically took over. She played rock to him, Wendy ballad. His head had both genres blaring at the same time in a cacophony. As she hurriedly laid out the more refined cold collation she'd chosen on the dining table, she could scarcely contain her excitement about the ballyhoo over Wendy Ballyhoo.

"You should have come up with that one before some of the others," Bob thought. "Pretty impressive that you've still not repeated yourself though. I've not got beyond Geoff Parkinslice."

"Is Wendy full of oats and treacle too?"

"That's more you, rough and smooth," Bob answered honestly.

Wendy and Steve arrived bang on time. She was wearing a pair of jeans with a lumber jacket and boots. By then, Jane had changed into a short dress, looking sweet and fooling no-one. Steve was smartly dressed in wardrobe-department tight casuals. Bob was modelling something from the previous year's M&S Autograph Collection.

The two women pecked while barely making contact. "I've heard too much about you already; all said with a starry look on his face," said Jane. "He idealises his women, that's his problem. I bet we're both a pair of cows."

Steve made a mooing noise, a camp mooing noise, very heiferish. It wasn't that long ago that Bob had been mooing to Helen and Amy. Fireworks happened that evening before peace broke out. Bob nodded to Steve: "They'll either get on like a house on fire or they'll set fire to the house. Either way, enjoy it."

Steve's eyes lit up at the thought of them scratching each other's eyes out. Wendy put her arm round his shoulder. "Stop trying to wind things up, or I'll put you back in the car," she ordered.

Not to be outdone, Jane made a remark too far offside to be allowed for United at Old Trafford. "I wouldn't, Wendy. He'll only need the loo within a few minutes. Bob has to get up every night. He'll need a pot under the bed soon. He'll no doubt call it a po."

Bob covered his embarrassment by taking coats and serving drinks. By the time he'd finished that, Steve had taken the stage and the other two were enjoying his anecdotes about events older than the furniture he sold. Jane's barbs were the right side of amusing from that point on. Bob was subdued, feeling more with Wendy in the jockeying for position. The lunch worked well enough, despite a lack of peaches.

When Jane went to the kitchen, Wendy interrupted a conversation about the grandfather clock in the hall in order to tell Bob why she needed respite. Her never-loving Frank had fathered a son to a woman in Gloucester and had been paying her maintenance for the last ten years. He'd been using money from the business. Steve had only found out the previous week when he'd been investigating the direct debit payments. Wendy and Steve had been to see the woman who'd told everything. She'd known all about Frank's illness and yet hadn't bothered to see him for a couple of years. They'd seen the boy and there was no need for a DNA test. Frank had shown no reaction when the matter had been delicately mentioned in his presence.

In the afternoon, they all went for a little walk around St Chad's, taking in the church, his schools, and the off licence where the family ironmongers used to be. He told Wendy about the lilac tree in the backyard where he'd lain in his pram gazing at the changing Lancashire sky, shafts of light coming through foliage, preparing for an epiphany.

It was too soon time for Wendy and Steve to go. At the door, Wendy stood five inches taller than Jane, and looked the fifteen years younger that she was. Her bosom was the shelter where Bob would have liked to rest his throbbing head.

Then they were gone with only the usual, insincere words of meeting up again. The ménage à trois was not the way ahead. As the car turned the corner, Jane took the fixed grin off her face to say: "She might be younger, but she behaves like an old frump. What on earth can you see in her, apart from the obvious? I saw you ogling her tits. You couldn't take your eyes off them."

"She's not an old frump, Jane; she's from a different background, Western rather than northern maybe. You're entitled not to like her, but she's a lovely lady. Criticise her, you criticise me. She's normal; it's the Louise Buchanans who are freaks."

Jane scowled at him. She put her hand down to his penis, saying she'd better keep tight hold to prevent Wendy Ballsnicker from running off with it. "Wendy might pander to your ego, but Louise got right under your rich, white, male skin."

Her squeeze was gentle this time. Bob spoke thoughtfully, wrinkling his nose and cocking his head slowly, but he was cross. "I'm buggered if I'm playing this last part of my life off the back foot. I don't flash my ill-gotten gains around that much. I'm not going to start hating myself for being white; I'm proud of where I'm from. And yes, I have a prick. Am I meant to apologise for that too?"

Jane liked this righteous anger which reminded her of Andrew. "Only for where you stick it," she said. "And then only to your maker, not to me, even if it does pleasure Wendy Ballpond again, which one day it no doubt will."

She let go. He said no more. During the rest of the week, she became friends and on first name terms with Mrs Metcalfe, Ethel. She baked a date and walnut cake for her. Geoff's eyes popped at the amount of cleavage she showed at his party. In Bob's eyes, there wasn't much to see. He joined in with 'Auld Lang Syne' half-heartedly.

At around twelve thirty, he couldn't see Jane anywhere. Geoff was still in the room doing the ludicrous dance he'd been performing for much of the evening, so he wasn't the reason. Bob half-needed to go to the lavatory and sought her out on the way. When he passed a bedroom, he heard loud sobs. Jane was there alone. When he gently asked what was up, she tearfully told him they weren't in the year Andrew died any longer. He held her hand. She wanted him to drive her home. As they reached the flat, she asked him to stay in the car as she had something to say. He knew what it was. He sat motionless as she faced him, the teenage Jane outside her home in Knutsford. Then he saw a friendly smile. The ghost flew away.

"I'll always love you, Bob. You're worth ten of all that lot," she murmured. He relaxed for a moment. Then she spoke louder. The ghost hadn't gone far. "No, that's not what I was going to say. We've moved too fast and I miss Andrew too much. And as Geoff said, you looked like a gorilla at the chimps' tea party tonight. I'll tell Robert and Ruth we're over again."

Bob laughed as he pleaded: "This time, be different, please go, don't stay." She opened the car door and ran into the flat. He sat thinking for a minute or so. He started the car engine and then remembered her case in the boot. He took it out, and rang the bell. She answered on the intercom.

"You forgot your case. I'll leave it down here. I'm on my way home. Home."

He drove off before she was down. He was wrong when he told Ruth that they would finally break up at Easter. This was New Year's morning, both too early and too late to ring Wendy in Keswick.

Back home, he finished off On Chesil Beach, wondering how unusual his carefree childhood had been. He was pleased that Ruth's children were enjoying something similar.

CHAPTER EIGHTEEN

On New Year's Day morning, Bob rang Wendy in Keswick, to see if they could start something going again. There was no answer and he didn't leave a message. Two minutes later his mobile rang. He expected to read Wendy Ballinger on the screen, but it was Jane Clarke. She wanted to change her mind. She couldn't face losing him as well as Andrew. Two minutes before, he'd been about to declare his undying love for Wendy. Instead there was Jane, mother of his children, and undying love is not necessarily exclusive.

"Jane, please don't play with me," he beseeched her. "You said you needed time to yourself. That meant more than twelve hours. Create the bloody circuits in your head that stop you chopping and changing, will you?"

"I can't stop myself sometimes," she whimpered. Her whims could seem random, but once acted upon they were followed with great determination. Her voice hardened. "I need you, Bob."

He felt powerless. "I'll come over tonight after watching the Blackpool game. Then I'll decide what I think. After all, you keeping the same thought until this evening would be a bloody miracle. No point me bothering before then."

She told him that she was out that evening.

"If you've arranged to see Geoff Apeshit, the acclaimed zoologist, the answer's no right now," he bellowed down the phone.

She promised to be there, and asked if he was keeping her in suspense. He remembered that he'd been sad as hell on New Year's Eve of each of the years his parents had died. "Don't miss the part when I fold up," he'd said before ringing off. Almost immediately, Wendy rang, not knowing what she'd missed out on. She'd popped out for a short walk. Having been turned upside down on this last roller coaster only to end up at the start, Bob was in despair. He pretended he'd rung to talk about what her awful husband had done. She was certain that the infertility was her problem. Bob tried to reassure her, although he believed that to be the case as well.

Children were on her mind. Jane had said three times to her how happy Ruth and Robert were that she was back with Bob. Bob told her he was sure that, if he wasn't happy, the kids would want them separated. Wendy had found Jane hard work, but could understand why Bob must have been attracted by her delicate features, and still was. With Jane's dynamic personality, there wouldn't be many dull moments. Bob readily agreed to that, saying Jane would be the death of him.

Wendy finished with: "Keep on with her until you really know what you want."

"We'll stay together until after Robert's wedding in May," Bob reckoned." She'll bugger off after that."

Blackpool beat Burnley three-none. He was relaxed as he arrived at Jane's flat, with the outcome not a worry. She met him at the door to ask if here was where their story was to end.

"You tell me," he replied. "When we first met, you were everything I ever wanted in a girl. I'm always having to stop myself from thinking I have the same impact on you."

Jane didn't want things to finish. "What makes you think you don't?"

"Andrew. Even Geoff. I know there are other girls who could have captivated the callow me, but it was you who did. So even if I'd met another who did it for me, it was too late. Until Wendy."

He'd said it. And Jane heard only too well, which meant that she'd make damn sure he'd stay with her. "At last I've heard you say I'm nothing special. That's good. Pity it's when I'm realising that you are. I promised forever to you before and that failed. I promised for life to Andrew and he shot himself. I'm making no promises as to for how long, but please stay."

"You know I'm going to, to see where it's all going to end," he said, before murmuring, "And when."

Jane ordered a takeaway Chinese. After the meal, they curled up on the sofa, not rolling off for an hour. The Axminster carpet in the flat was less confusing than the shag pile. He wasn't up for it again when they went to bed.

"'Night, Cheshire kitten."

"Sweet dreams, limpy Lanky."

They spent the next morning together, but he had to be back to St Chad's by evening for a meeting of the Church Hall refurbishment committee. Mrs Metcalfe opened her door and called to him to come round as he got home. She wanted to know who Jane was exactly. He couldn't think of a way not to tell her. The whole neighbourhood knew by the weekend.

He Skyped Emil Fares to see how things were going. The Board meeting would take place on the last Tuesday in February, with a dinner afterwards. Bob had not yet met the local shareholders and Emil asked if he would do that the day before. Agreement with Western on joint marketing was close.

Bob let both Richard and Wendy know the Board dates. Richard was irritated at having to stop until Wednesday. Neither felt they needed to see the local shareholders, Wendy because broking wasn't her show and Richard because he was preaching on the Sunday. Richard chatted for a while and said how much Helen had enjoyed the evening. They'd both liked Jane.

"Your friendly neighbourhood Nomad doesn't fully share our views," admitted Richard. "I did tell her that to describe someone as an exhibitionist gadfly was not showing charity. They didn't come to blows, did they?"

"Nice as pie to each other, but there was menace in every breath. That ménage à trois would be like a hissing snake pit."

When he'd called Wendy, she hadn't hissed too much. They'd mainly discussed Frank. The mother of his child had started to visit him as well his sister. Wendy was going to knock her visits down to twice a week to see if he noticed or cared. "I have to go though, I must be dutiful," she said. "His anger has all gone, and he's a shell. He'll never be Frank again."

"That will leave a lot of time to yourself."

"Don't you start feeling sorry for me."

After the call was over, Bob sat in dismay with his head in his hands. No prayer would come. On Saturday, Jane and he went to an Ann Frank Exhibition at Liverpool Cathedral, where they met up with a couple of Jane's colleagues. On Sunday, they read the newspapers together and walked around the park holding hands. In the evening, Jane asked more about the trip to LA. He went through the arrangements. She wasn't asking out of polite interest. She wanted to go with him to prevent him climbing into Wendy's bed and fulfilling his longstanding contractual commitments.

"I could get out of my lectures for a couple of days. I've a good colleague there, Doreen Grabowski, who co-operated on a book," she said in too matter-of-fact a way.

"You're sure you don't mean your sociobiologist chum," he asked, suspecting she was going for the double whammy of snookering him

221

before potting the balls herself.

She wouldn't mind meeting him again, she said, as he was very handsome and younger than her, a year below at university. Bob reminded her she was married to him at that point. Jane didn't blush as she recalled Tue Brook. "And nothing untoward happened then. I've seen him a few times over the years and we've both behaved ourselves."

"There's a record!" he thought to himself before saying out loud: "I'd be expecting to travel Upper Class as Virgin call it. I don't suppose your funds run to that."

"I don't think funds run to anything. I'll travel cattle class and you can pass me back a petit four."

Bob volunteered to travel economy, using the air miles from his last trip to get money off the tickets. To make more of a trip of it, he thought they should fly out on the Saturday. Jane agreed to the timetable but refused to have the air miles offset against her ticket. She was beyond reproach with money. "What does Northern Solstice make again?" she asked.

"Solar power systems. It would be even better if we could sell them."

She spent an hour or so sending and receiving emails to the US to make sure she'd get time with Doreen and her colleagues. Bob checked the availability of tickets on the Virgin website. Jane dug out the sociolinguistics department address, which was on the main campus, north of the airport close to the Interstate 405, from the Northern Solstice building an hour's drive away as places usually seemed to be in LA. This time Wendy was using the Stonehaven. Richard was too. Bob asked Jane if she'd prefer to stay in a hotel near the campus, but she wanted to be able to gloat over Wendy in Anaheim. To be certain of that delight, she asked him to book everything there and then, saying that she'd fix up her leave when term started. He booked the flights, the hotel and a hire car, a Chevrolet Avro, naming both of them on the insurance.

Early February saw the formal merger of the two marketing departments under one BIPV roof, that of Western, who had appointed National Bank as their advisers to replace Grindleton's. The order books of both designs were gaining momentum, with another large order coming for Northern for completion in the winter. They needed factory space as well as sales collaboration and the full merger of the companies was becoming essential. Bob talked to Wendy and Richard, who would be happy to recommend any sale if the price was half as much again as at flotation.

Richard and Wendy had lunch with the miffed Grindleton's team, who confirmed that a takeover was on Western's agenda. Richard rehearsed with them why he thought National were prepared to provide the cash. They wouldn't say too much, but did say that Sir Charles was treating the project as a bit of a hobby. Bob rang Forster with the news. Peter only wanted to know if he'd get more if they hung on another six months.

"You're taking on several risks at once then, Peter; production risks with us; trading risks in both companies; AIM market risks not in our hands at all. And umpteen more that I haven't thought of. If they'll pay a 50% premium I'd take it. Remember Rothschild's view as to how he'd made his money. Selling too early."

Bob had stumbled on the figure they'd been talking about in California. "That sounds about right to me too," said Peter.

Bob was a bit concerned that Peter was agreeing too easily and that they were leaving too much on the table. "Maybe we can get a bit more if National are anxious. Richard thinks his theory about wanting to put the company into green funds is right. He'll have to be happy the deal is best for shareholders too."

223

"Pain in the arse, being quoted," Peter grunted. "I'll talk to Richard myself. He's done fine on thinking it all out."

A few days later, an indicative offer at a 40% premium was received in a draft letter of intent. This offer was described as substantially too low in the reply drafted by Richard and signed by Bob, requesting a face to face meeting. This was arranged for the Monday before the Board in LA. In the meantime, due and undue diligence took place.

Richard and Wendy would have to go over on the Sunday, Richard's parishioners thus missing his sermon that day. He'd said he'd write his next sermon about Sabbath rest, the biblical promise of heaven, which was not a ten hour Virgin flight.

"Jane and I are flying economy."

"That's hell on earth, or maybe in the sky," Richard reckoned.

"And I thought you'd liked Jane," said Bob.

"I was thinking of what she'd have to suffer sitting next to you."

Bob and Jane were down to only one day alone in LA. She stayed at St Chad's on the Friday night so that she could give Ethel a couple of tops she'd bought her. They set off early for Heathrow on Saturday morning. He'd told Jane that it was better to stay awake until it was time to go to bed LA time. She had no problem with this; he fell asleep on the plane. They landed on time but, slower off the plane in Economy, they spent more than an hour clearing immigration.

The car hire company was Alamo, named after the battle to find the way out of the airport. They both woke early the next morning and were drinking coffee by 5am PST. Jane was showing a great deal of interest in Bob's movements on Monday, wanting to know if he'd be free that evening as, if not, she'd make arrangements to go out with a few of Doreen's colleagues.

Bob knew the answer before he asked the question as to whether a sociobiologist was on the list. Jane knew she'd be rumbled but thought the game was worth it. She said she'd behave herself with John Westwood if he did with Wendy. She then kissed him with coffee lips before any troth had been plighted thereto. That day they went to the Queen Mary at Long Beach, feeling like a pair of thirties film stars. They ate at a fish restaurant and drove back to Anaheim.

As they went through the hotel lobby, Wendy came out of the restaurant while Richard was signing the bill. She visibly hesitated before greeting them. "Had a good day?"

Bob left it to Jane to reply as he didn't want to be presumptuous. "Very good, thank you. He didn't take me to the stars' houses as he'd already done that with you, so we've been to the Queen Mary. Who got the better deal? Thinking about it, I seem to have him back. Who got the better deal there, do you think?"

Wendy was unprepared but recovered quickly. "I don't know, I give in, who did?"

Fortunately Richard arrived before the claws were extended further, asking if anyone wanted a nightcap. Jane wanted to continue to enjoy herself at Wendy's expense and voted in favour. Wendy was unready for a cat fight and declared for sleep. Bob smiled reassuringly at her and arranged for everyone to meet in the restaurant for breakfast.

"We'll all be wide awake anyway as it's the middle of the afternoon our time."

Richard still wanted to keep the mood light. "Back in London, I try to sleep in my office in the afternoon. Perk of the job."

Wendy smiled wanly and said goodnight. Bob would have loved to put his arm around her. Instead he was off to the bar with a Jane into her second wind, and Richard wanting intellectual conversation. Neither the problems of the world below nor the heavens above were solved.

That night, Jane was unable to get comfortable in bed, kicking out in all directions. Bob knew that the next day must be important for her. He was only selling a company. It took an hour before the two sweat-sodden bodies were quiet. She was kneeing him in the back at three o'clock and out of bed by six.

Not surprisingly, Wendy and Richard were in better shape at breakfast. Even so, Jane was full of her day, dressed in a swishy cream skirt and blue blouse, with a white cotton jacket. She ate her breakfast quickly and left before the others had finished. "If I'm late back, don't wait up for me. Don't look after him too well, Wendy."

With that she was away, flouncy skirt flouncing off on a flouncy adventure. Bob didn't reveal that he didn't know if she was off to consummate an old crush. He set off an hour earlier than the other two to shake hands with the local shareholders. This had to be rushed as Emil and George had major issues. Bob called Richard and Wendy for them to come quickly.

The executives had been discussing job titles with their counterparts. Since Western was buying Northern, the presumption was that they would take the top roles. Emil and George had expected to have to work a level down to Alfredo Alvarez and Bill Connors respectively, with Chuck Walters, the Western Chairman, chairing the new outfit. That wasn't the view back in London. The only senior people National wished to stay from Northern were those with expertise, Wayne, Christina and Scott. They wanted to pay off Emil and George immediately with only three months' salary. And they'd upset Chuck too by insisting as the largest shareholder on appointing a new designate UK Chairman, former Select Committee Chairman, Sir Jonathan Sheldrake. The knighthood had been acquired on loss of seat in the 2005 General election.

Richard intended discussing the deal first but Wendy realised that there were a couple there who'd contribute better to that if they knew their future. She took control. "The people things are more likely to be a real problem. How do you two guys feel about it all?"

George spoke first: "We should be given at least a year's contract to give us a chance to find new jobs. I'm only making eighty thousand dollars on share options."

Emil broadly agreed: "I'm on about a hundred thousand. Our negotiating position should be a two year contract. George will get another job quickly, but I'll have to change sector, never easy for a CEO."

Wendy then asked Peter how Chuck was feeling about it all. Peter was bristling with indignation about what he called typically bitchy British interference, which had left Chuck losing his company. Wendy sympathised and then suggested that lifetime President might satisfy him, if Charles could be made to agree. Peter thought Chuck would want rights of attendance at the Board. Wendy showed a touch of Bob's expedience. "That will be more difficult with National. They should just have chucked Chuck after the deal."

They went off to the Western Sun Rising office in three different cars. Bob whispered to Wendy: "If you'd had any sense, you wouldn't have chucked me until later either."

"If you'd had any sense, you'd never have gone back to Jane Trollop."

Along with the many lawyers, they were greeted by Chuck, Alfredo, Bill, and Alastair Johnstone, who was finishing a phone call as they trooped in. He'd been speaking to Sir Charles, who was about to leave the office for home. He'd sent his regards to everyone.

Richard grinned: "Big deal! You'll have to get this one right, Alastair, with the boss's hand up your arse."

"So coarse, Richard. Too damned accurate too. He's going through a messy divorce at the moment," Alastair revealed.

Richard laughed loudly. "He's not pensioning off Lady Angela, is he? It will be open warfare between them, no prisoners taken. They deserved each other, those two, but they did have the decency not to spoil another couple."

"Someone else has spoilt them, another woman. We're calling her Lady Emma, after Lady Hamilton. She's a headhunter with Frank Stewart."

The blow hit Richard like a sack of potatoes in the stomach. He realised why Charles was taking such an interest in this titchy deal. Last summer, in Center Parcs, Emma had been playing a deeper game with him, teasing him at two levels. He didn't double up into agony. He was after all only losing a bit of compost from his garden. Their affair had started while Charlie was looking for his successor at Grindleton's. Emma couldn't resist pitching when she read about Richard's departure. Charles had loved the feeling of seducing a rival's girl, the ultimate expression of power. But Genghis Khan would have balked at taking on the Ladies Angela and Emma at the same time. Richard hoped that Charles would not be concentrating fully on the transaction.

The meeting did start with the people problems. Alastair had no delegation on the issue, so Bob suggested that Alastair with Wendy made a conference call to Charles, who had reached his home in the Chelsea war zone. The two went into a side office while the others tucked into some sticky buns.

Charles was cheerful. He flattered her with: "Ah, the fragrant Ms Ballinger. I'm glad that it's you and not the other two ruffians."

"I'm the soft one sent to beguile you, Sir Charles."

"I guessed so." Charles hadn't got where he had by believing in his own sales pitch. "But what a lovely lilt to your voice, even from half a world away!"

"We're a bit puzzled why you faced up Chuck Walters before the

228

deal had been done. If you'd not said anything, it could have been easily accomplished afterwards. Have we missed something and if not can we recover it now?"

"Alastair, the lady's right," he realised. "Why did you let me?"

"Er, I don't remember being asked."

"Sort it now," barked Charles.

Wendy had worked up her scheme. "I'd give him lifetime President with rights of attendance at the Board for a year. Tell him that was always your intention. If he asks for longer, then you start the blackmail by saying you've been honest with him by fronting it up before the deal rather than firing him afterwards."

Alastair was told to let Wendy do it. She thought she might be on a roll, and raised Emil and George's concerns. "If you kept them on for a year, they'd be out of your hair much quicker than that. The CEO's a good salesman and you could let him lead on some major contracts. It's always worth keeping the CFO around for a while. He'll have a new job within six months, for sure."

Charles didn't think for long before agreeing. Emma was with him and he was on a promise. He'd a fresh debt he had to repay to the ubiquitous Jonathan Sheldrake that was bothering him more. "I hope they're happy with Jonathan as Chairman," he probed.

"Of course," Wendy sweetly answered. "Bob Swarbrick told them what a splendid fellow he is."

"You're teasing me, Wendy."

She moved to the serious business. "How delegated is Alastair as the day progresses?" she asked. "You're going to be in the land of Nod by the time we'll be finishing."

Emma had only made one promise. Charles was happy to be disturbed. "He knows his parameters. Wake me up when you're ready."

Wendy couldn't do the other stuff on her own. "Alongside my

lilting voice will be those two coarse Lancastrians and an even more vulgar South African, Peter Forster. Can you cope with that as you wake up?"

He thought that a big ask, and wanted to know how well she liked Swarbrick and Shackleton. "Very much," she replied. "It's been a pleasure to work with them."

"Not quite my view, particularly not the hairy-arsed engineer. Chacun à son goût."

Wendy didn't rise to the bait. Sugary farewells were said. She went back and asked for a personal word with Chuck. He accepted the new position after she did the latter stage blackmail with a sympathetic smile on her face. She told Emil and George that they would get twelve months provided National were happy with the rest of the deal. That battle commenced. Both parties wanted an outright purchase for cash, supporting Richard's thesis. Alastair admitted privately over lunch that he had it spot on.

The afternoon started with a presentation by Emil and George on the business, ostensibly using only public information where material. Fairly loose definitions were used by way of compliance there. After a further half an hour of boxing round the subject, Chuck made the first increase in offer, a 45% premium. This was quickly moved up to 50% after the hoots of derision from Peter. It edged up to 55%. Richard could see Peter weakening as he imagined navigating his yacht across the water, drink in hand, and sharply said that this was nothing like enough for him to recommend to the shareholders he'd brought in on the flotation. Both sides then needed a side meeting.

Peter was almost begging: "Don't lose this deal, Richard, over the last few per cent."

Bob agreed. "I'm not sure they'll go any further, Richard. They looked spent."

"Leave it with me for quarter of an hour," said Richard. "You can disown me if this doesn't work."

He had a one-to-one with Alastair. "Forget what the old owners will settle for, it's the public shareholders who will have to vote it through. They won't settle lower than a 60% premium. I won't let them."

Alastair had to check back with Charles, who took the call politely, pleased there was no Bob. "Good to hear from you, Richard. All going well with Divinity? Give my regards to Cuthbert."

"I will do," promised Richard, not that he would. "I'll cut to the chase. 60% premium or I can't recommend. The story on our own is too good. And let's be honest, you need somewhere to put all that money you're raising."

Emma had tired Charles out. He audibly sighed: "I want to get some sleep. OK, I'll agree 60%. I'd like to know how you knew that's what I'd pay."

They said civil farewells. The Western team weren't that happy at the price but knew where the money was coming from. Hands were shaken and bottles of champagne produced. Peter sidled up as Richard sipped his orange juice, interested in how he'd known what Charles would go to. Richard tapped the side of his nose and said nothing. Bob asked him the same thing a few minutes later. Richard still wouldn't say. Wendy came over a few minutes after that. "Some disaffected National guy told your old chums at Grindleton's?" she guessed.

"As if," Richard replied. "What's good about today is that us two did it, not Peter and Bob."

Wendy's mind had already moved away from the transaction. "I think Bob was a bit worried about what Jane was up to today. There was something wrong when she left this morning."

Richard told her not to worry as Bob was big enough and daft enough to look after himself. That's why she was worried, scared that things were getting to him more than he was cracking on.

There were then detailed sessions finalising what was necessary by way of notifications and consents. The two Boards would formally approve the deal in the morning so that the Announcement could be with the Stock Exchange for opening of trade on Wednesday, along with the date of the necessary Northern Solstice EGM.

Back in the hotel late, they ordered coffee. While Richard and Bob were in the Men's Room, Bob's mobile rang and Wendy answered. It was Jane, somewhat worse for wear.

"Have you tied him to the bed so that he can't answer the phone?" she slurred.

"No, perhaps that's more to your taste," Wendy suggested. "He's in the Gents. We're ordering coffee after hitting the champagne big time. Will you be joining us?"

She wouldn't. She'd hit something big time too and was stopping over at John Westwood's house. She'd see Bob tomorrow morning.

"I'll get him to ring you back," Wendy promised.

Jane still had some of her wits about her. "Does the champagne mean you've sold the business? That's a swizz. I won't be able to come here again. The good bit is that Bob won't be able to come here with you exercising your rights."

"How the hell do you know... Bob's back now, Jane, speak to the grantor."

A very red and angry Wendy held her hand over the phone while telling Bob what was going on. "It's Jane. She's stopping at a John Westwood's overnight as she's pissed. Not so pissed that she can't recite the details of a joint rights agreement between you and me. You know the one. You can explain how she knew about that in a minute."

Richard made an excuse that it was morning in the UK and he needed five minutes out to give Helen a ring. Bob grabbed the phone.

"Jane, when will you learn to keep your big gob shut? You don't care who you hurt or what chaos you cause."

"Never could stop myself," she chuckled." It looks like I can't stop myself with John Westwood either, doesn't it? I am a naughty girl."

"For fuck's sake, how much do you want to humiliate me? You're the most pathetic human being I've known. You're...."

The coffee arrived. Jane rang off. Wendy just shrugged her shoulders. "How could you tell her that? There wasn't anything we shared that was private, was there Bob?"

"It was to let her know how much I cared for you."

"You could have said you loved me," she said with a catch in her voice. "Richard's coming back. I'll think as we drink our coffee. I'll either exercise those wretched rights tonight or cut your balls off, I'm not sure which. Maybe both, to do you a favour." She smiled at Richard as he hovered. "It's been our day and not Bob's. No need to feel sorry for him. He looks as if he's feeling sorry enough for himself."

Richard stuttered, "Look, I'll go. Helen sends her best..."

She told him to stay while she built up the defence mechanisms to stop her from castrating Bob. "And if Jane's body is washed up at Long Beach, the cops need look no further. Bob, you weren't needed today. Good for you to know that other people can do things. You need some humility and I'm giving you a dose."

"Fair enough, but don't forget Jane's just given me an overdose."

She took compassion. "Right, that's enough. I won't kick a man when he's down. At least not anymore."

Bob was still standing. Wendy stood up, pulled him down on to the couch next to her, and kissed him full on the lips. "It's a good job I like you or you'd be a goner."

Richard was still standing too. "Sit down this side of me," Wendy commanded.

He did as he was told, as otherwise he'd no idea what to do. It was a large couch. She put her arm round him too and pecked him on the cheek. "All for one and one for all," she smiled.

Richard was totally flummoxed. "We're the Three Stooges, not the Musketeers." They toasted each other with coffee. There was then a silence before Richard said: "I've no idea what's just happened. Can we have an action replay? Starting from the top."

Bob didn't fancy that, unless they could find a hole for him to be swallowed up in first. As usual, Wendy took the other two back to business, wanting the Board to be adjourned the next morning to give time for the announcements and resolutions to be drafted and then reconvened in the afternoon to authorise everything. "While we're drafting away, you and Jane will have a bit of talking to do," she expected.

"She might still be indulging in sociobiology," he replied.

"She'll be back, and you'll take her back."

Richard drained his cup. "Look, I'm going to bed. See you at breakfast. You two stay up until you've sorted yourselves out."

They watched him go. Wendy started the sorting. "When's your son's wedding?"

"Late May, in Canada."

"When she comes back, Bob, stay with her until then to see if you really want her still. Make up your mind, your own mind. Not because of me, we're gone. Not because of some stupid view that you belong together even if you hate every minute apart from when you're screwing her. If she makes you unhappy, just tell her and go."

"It won't work out like that," he muttered forlornly.

"Make it. Now, we're going to my bedroom. It's my best revenge for what she's said to me, and most of all for what Frank's done to me. Promise you'll go straight afterwards or you're not getting this."

He promised and followed her meekly for a moment deservedly stolen from Jane. They undressed quickly. After all the schmozzle and all the alcohol, he wasn't sure if he'd perform. The feel of Wendy's contours, the taste of her lips, her fingers on his back were enough to lift his spirits, racked with guilt and fear as he was. Western took over Northern. Once they'd finished and had a ten minute laying together, Wendy leapt up. "There's nothing more to be said. Back to your bedroom. Back to Jane, your best dream, your worst nightmare. Clothes on now."

She pushed him out of the door. Bob had a shower once in his own room, to recover a sense of being. As he was towelling down, he heard the door open, with Jane's frightened face peering round. "How the hell have you got back?" he asked. He saw her eyes. "You're stoned, as well as tipsy, aren't you? Very west coast, only forty years too late."

"John booked me a taxi. I insisted. Bob, I'm sorry. What have I done, what did I do? I know it's awful," she wailed.

"You told Wendy that you knew about the lifetime bonking rights. You told me that I was being cuckolded. My friends heard it all."

"I don't think I did bonk John." She looked puzzled as if trying to remember. "If I did, it wasn't that memorable. What about you and Wendy?"

"I'm not fucking telling you anything ever again."

Jane's eyes became even bigger as she pleaded, "Bob, it's not going that wrong. Please don't spoil Robert's wedding. Let's go as a couple."

He obeyed step one of Wendy's instructions. "We'll go the wedding together for Robert's sake, but nowt bloody else. Turn the lights off when you're finished."

The next morning, Jane didn't want to face Wendy and Richard. Bob insisted that she said sorry to them, for spoiling what should have been a good day. She complied and went to breakfast full of sweetness

235

and light. Richard accepted it at face value, but not Wendy, who said nothing.

Bob went to rescue the car in the late morning. At the Board dinner, Jane and Bob sat apart. Wendy asked him what Jane's present surname was. The next day as they said goodbye at Heathrow Airport, Bob found out why. "Goodbye, Mrs Clarke. Look after our Bob. We'll not meet again."

The fates decide things like that, not human wills. In the car on the way back north, Jane felt the coldness of Bob's seething anger. He hadn't spoken to her except when the others were present since they'd taken off back from LA. She asked if he could forgive her.

In reply, he was still so angry that he forgot to remember that they had to stay together until after the wedding. "You stripped every bit of what little pride I had left in front of my two best friends. All for some typical piece of incontinence, and an inability to keep your mouth shut. You can't change the end of a story however often you read it. Everything I've felt for you over the last forty years must have been self deception."

She forgot to remember too. "It's nothing to do with John Westwood. It's because I was guilty of the breach of your precious bonking rights' confidence. You stand around with a hangdog look on your face for forty years, taking all the stuff I've thrown at you, and then some trivial wind-up of Wendy Balloon-Burst causes you to go ballistic. Or the other way round. Whichever, you're just weird. I was right to leave you each time I did, and wrong to come back."

"That takes the biscuit, a professor calling an engineer weird. Language has lost all meaning."

"Get real, that's what it means, sweetheart, whatever we say it does."

They drove on in silence to St Chad's, where Jane had left some of her clothes. It was early evening by the time they were back. Neither knew what they were going to say next. As Bob opened the boot, he saw that the milk was still outside Ethel's door. He climbed over the wall and rang the bell. There was no answer. On his key ring was her front door key. He opened up and shouted. There was still no answer. By then Jane had come in too. The stair lift was at the top of the stairs. Ethel was lying on the floor in her bedroom, half-dressed in a pile of her own excrement. She looked wild-eyed as she saw them and started crying.

"What's happened, Ethel?" Bob asked. She said nothing. Jane spoke next, "We'd better ring for an ambulance."

At that, Mrs Metcalfe managed to find her voice. "Don't do that. I don't want to go to hospital. They'll never let me out again."

Bob spoke soothingly, the way he'd done with his pets and his children when he was a younger man. "Tell us all about it, eh."

Ethel had worked out what had happened as she'd lain on the floor all those hours. "My knees can't push me up, they're both replacements. I must have fainted going to the toilet in the middle of the night. They changed my blood pressure pills last week."

They managed to pick her up and sit her on the side of her bed. Jane cleaned her up while Bob stoically faced cleaning the mess on the floor. Ethel had bashed the side of her face on the bedside table and had a bad gash. But it hadn't been a cold night and there were no other ill effects. Ethel asked Jane to move the pillow so she could see her better. She seemed quite perky. "We'll have you good as new in no time. We'd better call the doctor and see if you really need to go to hospital," Jane told her.

Bob went downstairs to find her book of telephone numbers. He called Dr Craig's surgery and then Ethel's son, Fred, who lived over in Accrington. He came back with a cup of tea for her. "You're as hard as nails, Ethel," he said. "It'll take more than this to see you off. Fred's on his way."

Dr Craig checked her over a couple of hours later. He said that she'd have to go in unless someone stopped with her full time. Jane volunteered to sleep in the chair beside her. Fred arrived on cue.

Bob, Jane and Fred took turns to be with Ethel for five days, when she made it clear she could cope on her own. There was little affection shared between Bob and Jane until that evening. They slept together as if John Westwood had never existed. Wendy Ballinger wasn't so easily forgotten by either of them.

## CHAPTER NINETEEN

On the third Saturday in May, the thirteenth anniversary of his father's death, Richard went to watch his son James play for his school's Under 13 side away at Highwood. The game was petering out as a draw and, as James picked up the ball to bowl the last over of the day, Highwood still needed twenty to win with five wickets remaining. For his age, James was quite a quick bowler but hadn't bowled particularly well in his previous two spells. This time, his first ball hit middle stump as the batter swung across the line in a bid for glory. The second ball came back to clip the top of off stump. James focused hard on the hat-trick ball. So did Richard. This was a yorker hitting leg stump, accompanied by youthful whoops of delight from team mates. The next ball, a middle stump yorker, was far too good for a number ten. Suddenly it dawned on Richard that James could emulate what Michael had done seventy years before, clean-bowling five in five. The last-man for Highwood shuffled to the wicket nervously, pads hastily donned with the straps flapping. The fielders crowded round the bat. James bowled a good length straight ball which kept a bit low. Never had Richard heard a sweeter sound than the clunk as the ball hit middle stump. His cheer could be heard in the heavens. As the boys shook hands after the game, Richard looked upwards in vain for his father. The cricket master had the ball mounted and presented to James in the next week's assembly.

* * *

Bob picked Jane up at Sefton Park on the following Thursday afternoon. They were cutting it fine for a Saturday wedding the far side of Canada but Jane had already taken too much time off. They stayed with the Jacksons in Solihull on the way down to Heathrow. Since Ethel's recovery, Jane had taken to sitting on his knee again so they could read the newspaper together. She was a featherweight and even if she was a bollock squeezer she wasn't a balls crusher. He didn't tell her that or it would have become a new epithet for Wendy.

The Northern Solstice transaction had been finalised, general meetings held, cheques banked. At the final dinner, Wendy had asked Bob not to keep in touch.

"We'll meet again someday on the avenue," he'd replied.

She said maybe so, but in the meantime she didn't want to spend the rest of her life tangled up in blue. There would possibly be a spot of business that she'd be in touch about in a month or two. When Wendy dug her heels in, the entire Gloucester pack couldn't move her. He decided to comply until returning from the wedding, when he'd no doubt find another reason to do nothing.

Ruth sent them on their way with a photo of the present she'd bought for the bride and groom, a bread-maker, which was being delivered straight to Richmond. Bob asked if it sliced the bread too and put it in a wrapper.

The journey to Victoria was complicated. They'd had to be awake by four in the morning for the drive to Heathrow, reaching Vancouver by lunchtime on the same day despite the nine hour flight. Bob had wanted to include a seaplane landing in Victoria to the itinerary to give a feel of Pleasure Beach but there hadn't been time. He sensed that 'you will get wet, you may get soaked' could be an apt motto for the trip.

Sophie's parents, Jackie and Malcolm Fry, had come to meet them at Victoria Airport, along with Robert and Sophie. They'd three other children back home; disappointingly, there was no log cabin but a largish terraced house in a town suburb.

Jackie's eyes shone with pride as she introduced her children, all of whom were doing well at school or college. Sophie was the oldest. Malcolm took Bob to one side for a man chat while Robert had to stay with Sophie and the others. Also in that group was Rupert, Robert's friend from his Oxford days who was to be best man. Malcolm and Bob liked each other well enough, despite having no sport in common to talk about. Also Malcolm was fifteen years younger than Bob and didn't prefer Ray Charles to Michael Jackson. He was too young for Bob's usual routine of, "I could listen to him if he stood still and if his voice were to break." In the end they had no choice but to rejoin the main group for coffee and cookies.

Sophie gently ribbed Bob. "I bet you'd have preferred a sausage roll."

"When in Rome, Sophie... I'll have another one to show you how cosmopolitan I can be."

Jane of course couldn't leave that unchallenged. "He's the least cosmopolitan person in the world. He'll soon be the fattest though."

This didn't quite work seeing that Malcolm was carrying two stone too much compared with Bob's stone. Sophie grinned ruefully, "Sorry, Bob. I set you up for that."

"Water off a duck's back," he said truthfully.

Jane wasn't letting him off the hook. "Fat off your belly's what I'm looking for. Don't you take his side, Sophie. I'm nagging him to lose some weight."

Jackie was trying to get Malcolm to do the same. He ate far too much, she said. "A man after my own heart," said Bob.

"Your cholesterol infested organ, more like," Jane suggested.

The Canadians smiled. Sophie had told them of the tortured history between Jane and Bob. The impending nuptials were looming large with Robert, who said little, too worried about what Jane might do or say next. The two sets of parents had an evening meal with bride, groom and best man at the hotel where the Swarbricks were staying and where the reception would take place. Jane was still assessing Sophie for suitability and Jackie was doing something similar with Robert. Jane was most interested in the property they were buying, a four-bedroomed house in a lane on the edge of Richmond Park, wondering why they wanted anywhere so big. Robert replied that it wouldn't seem that big if they had a family.

"You can't take that for granted," Jane told him. "How soon do you intend to start on that? Sophie mustn't miss out on her career."

Malcolm agreed with the first sentiment at least. "The Lord decides on the children, not us."

Sophie was capable of speaking for herself and did. "I'd like to gain two years more experience and then go for it. Robert had a lot of money in investments and it made sense to buy a bigger place. We didn't want to spend a fortune on a serviced high-priced apartment. It's time he became a gardener anyway, and found his roots."

Bob grimaced: "What, in Richmond? You did mean Surrey, didn't you, not Yorkshire? The only roots you'll find there will be some must-have, new-age vegetable sold in the bijou greengrocer's."

Malcolm laughed. "We kinda hoped it was Richmond, BC. That's British Columbia for you Brits, south of Vancouver. Lots of wealthy Asians there and pretty smart."

Jane confronted her biggest concern. "Do you plan to stay in the UK, Sophie or would you like to come back to Canada some day?"

The silence around the table showed that everyone was waiting for the answer to this, including Robert. "Who can say?" Sophie answered carefully. "I've, we've no current plans and I think I'd like any kids to feel English if they start out that way. My career's behind Robert's by fifteen years and I guess for a long time his job will determine where we live."

Jackie and Malcolm looked down. It was as they feared. Bob said that if so, they must make damned sure they came to Canada regularly as her Mum and Dad would miss her loads

Jackie looked up at her daughter. "We do already, but they've got to fly the nest. We plan some great vacations in England. We want to see Blackpool after Sophie told us all about it."

Jane thought that Jackie must be the first person to say that for fifty years and they ought to see Liverpool instead. Bob claimed that nobody in human history had ever said they wanted to see Liverpool, not even a Scouse soldier on jankers in Afghanistan.

Sophie explained to her parents: "As well as Robert having the two most dysfunctional parents you can imagine, they also have this local rivalry taking place between them. That's not what he said when he showed me round Liverpool."

Jackie frowned: "You can't say that about folk."

Jane and Bob spoke as one, "She can."

Sophie's eyes flashed appreciatively. "Liverpool's a great city and Blackpool's the only seaside resort I know that hasn't given up on being fun. Get Bob to take you to Malham for a great country walk too."

Jane showed that she was still planning a future with Bob. "I'll be there as well."

Bob groaned: "In which case you'll also find out the botanical name of some obscure plant in every hedgerow we pass."

Jane knew Bob as well as he knew her. "And with this great oaf, the beer served in every pub."

Malcolm liked the sound of that. The party broke up early so that

243

everyone was refreshed for the big day. Bob and Jane had lasted very well given their thirty odd hour day. Jane was too tired for anything that night, and Bob wasn't sorry.

At lunch the next day, they sat behind Robert and Rupert in church, the men in morning dress. Bob had hired his from a shop in Blackpool. Sophie's two sisters were bridesmaids. Grandma was also there, a wizened old lady with a frame.

Sophie had a long white satin dress which looked like it had cost a bomb. She came up the aisle to Wagner. The bridesmaids had been made to wear pink. Quite right too, thought Bob, as Jane whispered in his ear about how they looked too frilly. Jane was in a blue suit with white shoes. Sophie gave a nervous smile to her parents and blew a small kiss to Robert.

After an eternity of photographs, they reached the reception. The guests were either Fry family or friends of Sophie, apart from the four from England, and numbered about sixty in all. Malcolm's speech was full of pride for his girl. Rupert had some good gags a bit too near the knuckle. Robert was brief and quietly witty. The audience urged Sophie to speak, Jane saying that women must stand up too on these occasions. Sophie caught Bob's eye, followed by Grandma's, and decided to oblige by saying how she wished Grandpa had been here to see it all, not the sort of contribution Jane had in mind.

Sophie and Robert departed in the late afternoon for their honeymoon in Australia. Bob and Jane were flying back the next day to Heathrow with Rupert. By now both were dog-tired, but had to stay and party for a few more hours. Bob went to the bar for some drinks. As he returned, Jane, who had been talking to Jackie, quickly changed the subject, looking flustered. Bob heard only the last few words, "Never been the man for me." He expected that she was referring to him, but couldn't be absolutely sure. He buried the grudge a level down. After the drinks, Jackie suggested that they both could use a rest. She urged them to go for a nap and come back for the evening. Bob agreed that it would be a good idea with Jane less certain. As soon as they shut their room door, she turned on him.

"Why did you want to leave?" she complained. "I was enjoying myself. You took the decision without asking what I wanted."

"Oh hell, not again. I don't want to know, love. I'm knackered. Go back on your own if you want to. I'm having an hour's sleep, that's all."

He started setting the alarm on his phone. She knocked it out of his hands in a fury, yelling at the top of her voice "I can't go back now without looking an idiot. You think you should take all the decisions. You don't remember anything I tell you, because you don't listen."

His anger was icy for once. "What's that about? Either you're having a go because I didn't ask you, or because I didn't listen to your answer, but you can't do both at the same time."

"I'm talking about the rest of the trip," she muttered beneath her breath

"Look, I'm not up for this right now," he said in a conciliatory voice. "If you want to carry on when I wake up, I'll put the gloves on then."

"No, you won't. You'll try to be sickly sweet."

"There's nowt wrong with that," he said, thinking she was calming down. "Blessed are the peacemakers."

She wasn't. Her voice trembled out of control: "Don't make me laugh. You a peacemaker! Trouble follows you wherever you go because you're an offensive, arrogant pig. I'm going back to the party."

She slammed the door. He finished setting the alarm and had his sleep. Jane didn't go back but went outside for some air. Poor old Geoffrey was woken up back in Liverpool in the middle of the night. Bob was sitting on the edge of the bed feeling a bit sick at being wakened by the insistently shrill alarm when the lock turned. Jane walked in. Her bottom lip was further out than her top one, the usual bad sign. Her voice was deep, not the alarm clock imitation tone he was expecting. "I've just rung Geoff to tell him you and I are no longer a couple," she revealed. "This row has finished me. I've hoped we could work it out, but we can't."

He still didn't know if he'd correctly heard what she'd said to Jackie earlier on. If he had, she wasn't being strictly truthful about the argument being the cause. The grudge became a howling beast. "You've known for sure damn near every time you've finished with me. There's one difference this time. I know for sure too. I'm not the man for you. Let's go and party to celebrate our mutual repulsion." Bob put his shoes and jacket on.

She looked incredulous. "You mean you aren't going to have a wash, you foul pig?"

He reckoned he smelt fine the way he was: "Essence of arrogant male, worn specially for you, because you're worth it." He went back to the party. Jane didn't follow. Jackie was on the dance floor to Stevie Wonder. Malcolm was at the bar. They drank beers together. With the song finished Jackie joined them at the moment Jane's face appeared at the door.

Jackie whispered quickly: "Is she alright, Bob? She was a bit uptight with you earlier."

Bob knew then that he'd heard more or less correctly. But he also knew that Jane didn't always mean what she said. Jane walked up to the group with a huge smile on her face. "Bob and I might be dog-tired but we can still dance."

She took hold of Bob's arm and, strangely for her, started dragging him to the dance floor. He turned to Jackie and Malcolm. "Don't believe her, I never could dance."

They did, to Bob Marley's 'Redemption Song', a singer from well after Bob's golden age and far from his hinterland. He started thinking of how Sophie had saved Robert, and the words pierced his soul. Mental slavery was what he had to overcome. He couldn't stop time and Wendy was slipping away in it. There was no book of life he had to fulfil because he'd once been married to Jane.

She was holding him tight as they smooched around the dance floor, feeling nothing but affection for this man in her arms she'd once again wronged. It was all smiles as they left for the journey home with Rupert. They landed at Heathrow mid-morning both knowing that something would be said in the car outside Jane's flat. They were there by late afternoon.

Jane took control. "You see, we can row and make up. I don't want us to be over. I like being with you. But I'm going to see you less. I've been ignoring my girl friends and Geoff too much. Can you come over next weekend, not this coming one?"

Bob had been thinking about this moment all the way over on the plane. He'd been expecting the brush-off and planning his reaction. This wasn't the sequence he'd reckoned on. He thought for a couple of seconds and was happy that he still wanted to say what he felt. "No, Jane. I'm not coming this weekend or next. We'll meet at family events but nothing else. We're not good for each other. You're happier with people of Geoff's ilk. I made the decision to idolise you and only I can make the decision to stop. I'll carry your case upstairs and then it's a quick goodbye."

This was a vital act of will that changed a lifetime. This wasn't in him when he was born. And there was no parallel universe where he and Jane would ride off to a golden sunset. Of that he was sure. Jane tried to change his mind. "Hey, you know that John and I didn't make love that night in LA. I remember now making an excuse to him when

I realised what I was doing."

He shook his head. "That's not the reason. It's time for me to go."

She realised the game was over. Never before in her life had she offered an olive branch that big and it not be taken. She looked at him with her eyes wide open, anger and disbelief fused together. "This is the way you take being dumped, for your future reference. Open the boot and I'll take my own case. See you at the next wedding, or christening, or funeral. Unless it's yours or mine."

He watched for two seconds as her bottom wiggled to her door, and was back in the car before she turned. They waved to each other as he drove off.

There was an accident on Queen's Drive. There were roadworks on the M6. The junction to the M55 was closed. There were temporary traffic lights at Singleton and a queue to join the New Road. As his head pounded, Bob didn't know if he regretted what he'd done. This time she wouldn't be waiting outside in a few weeks to tell him she was pregnant. Symmetry couldn't do its work. As he finally reached home in the early evening, Ethel Metcalfe was pushing her trolley along the road.

"Have a good time, Bob? Jane not with you?" she asked.

"It went very well. I'm afraid Jane and I have decided not to get together again."

"Well, I'll go to our house. You were getting on so well. You two were good with me and with each other. There's nowt as queer as folk."

When Ethel used sayings from the past, they were still the present for her. When Bob did, he was consciously going back. "There is Ethel. Folk's wives," he said.

Ethel had seen Bob at close quarters since he'd moved back and thought he'd be lonely again. He wondered if he should get a dog. Coincidence or entanglement was at work. Ethel knew of a five year old little Lancashire Heeler, Hattie, in need of a good home. Mrs Leadbetter in the Old Road had died the previous week and her daughter Eileen couldn't take her as she lived in a council flat. Although Bob would have naturally gone for something male and a lot bigger, it was time for something new. Ethel arranged for Eileen to bring Hattie round while Bob unpacked. That evening, he had the company of a far easier going female companion than the one he'd gone to bed with two evenings previously. It had been love at first sight by both parties. Hattie looked as bemused as anyone would who'd lost her lifelong partner and was being smuggled in and out of a council flat. Bob looked as forlorn as anyone would who'd abandoned his lifetime dream. Once Ethel and Eileen had left, with the promise that Eileen could visit Hattie whenever she wanted, man and dog went for a stroll round the streets.

Hattie was fastidiously clean and he'd already found preferred to do her stuff in grass, having obliged down a grassy ginnel. He'd never had a bitch before. She didn't cock her leg at a lamp-post. It was like not being able to use a urinal. At last he'd found something where men had an evolutionary edge.

As he went through the door, Robert was ringing from Australia. "I've just spoken to Mum. I thought you'd be there too." Hoping not to burden the newly-weds, Bob told him that he hadn't stayed over. Robert knew, as Jane had told him why in some detail.

"Enjoy yourselves and forget about us," Bob requested. "I hope our row didn't take any shine off the day for Sophie's folk. We didn't burden them with it."

"I know, Dad," answered Robert, "but Sophie's cross with Mum for something she said to her Mum. She won't tell me what it was."

Bob knew. "Jane told the truth. We're not meant for each other."

Robert didn't want to hear that. He liked them both too much. "Don't say that, you'll finish up together. You know you will. You love each other."

Bob let Robert down gently. "We won't, lad. I love her, I've adored her. But we can't live together. Put Sophie on and I'll try to explain to her."

There as a lengthy pause as the phone handover took place. Sophie's voice sounded small as she spoke. "Hi Bob. What you don't know is that I've had a blazing row with Jane on the phone. It finished with her saying that I was another independent-minded Swarbrick by nature and now by name. With one or two expletives added."

Bob chuckled appreciatively: "That's Jane to a tee. We bring out the worst in each other. She was right in what she said to your Mum. I'm not the man for her and what's better is at last I know she's not the woman for me. But we like each other. You'll like her too if you give her a chance."

"I'll do my best, but don't expect too much. By the way, Grandma said that she loved meeting a real English gentleman, as she called you."

"Canadians have a well-developed sense of irony," Bob said. "The one thing you must understand is that I'm not ever going back to Jane. Robert's assuming I will. Let him know I won't. I've had a dog bequeathed to me instead and that's going to need much less maintenance."

Hattie then became the remaining item of conversation with Sophie and then with Robert as the phone was passed back. Towards the end of the call, the little beeps told him someone else was calling. Within thirty seconds of him putting the phone down it rang again. It had to be Ruth.

She hadn't been surprised by the outcome. "I wanted you to be together, of course I did, but I knew it a long shot. Harry's the one who doesn't understand. First love is best, he says. He thought you were great together."

Bob agreed that most of the time they were, but when they weren't, it was bad and he didn't need any more bad. He told her all about Hattie. Finally Ruth was allowed the space to ask her most important question, whether or not he'd be back with Wendy.

"The heavens are against it," he said

"They can change their mind."

Bob was pleased that Ruth had taken the news well. Before they rang off, he promised that he'd take Hattie to see them soon. He settled down again and turned the News on. The headlines hadn't finished before the phone rang yet again.

It was Wendy, apologising for calling so late. She'd tried earlier and he'd not been there. It was about the spot of business she'd mentioned at the Northern Solstice final dinner.

"I only got back this evening from my son's wedding," he reminded her.

"I wasn't sure when you'd be back," she said cagily. "Did Jane behave herself?"

"Funny you should ask that. I've finished with her forever a few hours ago. I've traded her in for a dog."

The tale was told again. Wendy surprisingly focused on the dog rather than on Jane's demise, asking how Hattie was with cats.

"Apparently she's not bad, as her owner had one who died last year," Bob replied, somewhat mystified.

"Good. She can visit Sheba at some stage then. Let's get down to the business. Are you sitting comfortably? Then I'll begin. Ever heard of combined infertility?"

He hadn't and was analysing the two words for relevance, penny poised to drop while she described the problem. "My eggs were too fussy to have anything to do with Frank's sperm. For some strange reason, my February egg wasn't as fussy about your sperm. I'm pregnant, boy. By you. I thought I might be but I didn't want to say anything until I was more certain."

Chemicals flooded Bob's brain until everything was still and he was changed. All theories were Maya, the truth but not the whole truth. He'd travelled half way across the world, lost his woman, taken over a new dog, and found he was going to become a father again in his sixties. The only thing he'd consciously willed was to break up with Jane, driven by events. The candidates for who could have done the rest flashed before his mind's eye. Wendy's love for him? Their unborn child? His parents or his Grannie up yonder? The Holy Spirit? All of them in cahoots?

"That's fantastic. Bloody fantastic. Hey, you are pleased, aren't you?" he suddenly worried.

"I'm pleased, Bob, I'm pleased."

She was aware that at her age quite a bit could still go wrong and didn't want to count her chickens. She'd shown quite a bit of blood early on. A second scan that morning had confirmed that all systems were go. It was thirteen weeks since LA which made her just under fifteen weeks pregnant in medical jargon. The due date was around the twentieth of November.

"Did you find out what sex?" Bob wanted to know.

"Not officially. The lovely Irish scan operator told me it was against policy to tell me. She then said with a broad grin that that I might find a daughter a great help around the house in later years. Now tell me more about finishing with Queen Jane."

"A girl, ey, two new girls in my life in one day. The wedding in Victoria had a sour note, although not as bad as LA. I was expecting Jane to finish things once we were back home and had prepared a line for ensuring I wasn't humiliated by that. When she started her set piece outside her flat, she was plain arrogant in stating her conditions for us to stay together, assuming I was always going to be her poodle. The neuron, photon or whatever fired and I finished it."

"Why this time when not before?" she asked.

"I'd had enough."

Wendy needed no further explanation, being pleased that he hadn't mentioned her as the reason. He said that her conscience could be clear as he honestly wasn't thinking of her as he did it. "One of the few times when I wasn't, mind. Can Hattie and I come down to see you this weekend?"

She was even happy for him to stay at the house. "But I don't want you thinking we're going to start living together or anything. I want a bit, in fact I want a lot, of courting from you, Bob Swarbrick. That's condition one and if that terminator neuron fires again, so be it."

"You're the boss. I expressly agree to condition one."

"Condition two is that LIBOR is suspended for the duration of the pregnancy. I know it's meant to be safe, but I'm a very old mother to be and I don't want to wreck everything."

He consented to condition two. He was knackered after Jane anyway.

Wendy hadn't finished: "And if you think this is what I was expecting when I rang you, you couldn't be more wrong. I was expecting a guilty Bob agonising over how to tell his precious Jane about the baby, and me telling you not to bother, that the news was only for information."

He told her she was a special woman to be so good with him after all the stuff with Jane. "I'm going to make you suffer yet," she promised. "I'll throw it all back at you whenever I'm losing an argument."

"That's alright; you've not lost one yet," he said.

Wendy wanted to know how his family would react when they found out he was going to be a father again. "The kids will be fine with it," he reckoned. "Maybe after a few weeks courting I could introduce you to Ruth. Solihull's not that far away from you."

"Let's do it this weekend, when you're down. I'm warming to this. She'll want to meet Hattie anyway, if not me. I'll arrange for you to meet my parents too."

Bob smiled at the thought, at his age, of being an anxious boyfriend meeting the girl's parents to discuss her pregnancy and his role in it. He remembered doing that once before. He asked Wendy all about them and how they were going to be about it. She was sure they'd be fine, they being Audrey and Walter, only a few years older than Bob. Both retired, Audrey had been a teacher and Walter an aeronautical engineer.

They said lengthy farewells. Bob and Hattie then went for a last turn around the garden. He made a bed for her in the kitchen with some old blankets. She settled down happily. When he woke up the next morning, he went straight to the kitchen to be met by a cheeky grin and wagging tail. He escorted her round the garden. She didn't do the needful there. She happily ate her kibbles and then drank some water. They went for a walk down the Breck and on to a field. There he let her off the lead and she quickly obliged in the long grass. Bob reminded himself to buy some poo bags. They walked across the golf course and down the path towards the creek. She wouldn't go more than a few yards away from him and happily went on the lead as they crossed over the main road before setting off past the yacht club. He used to do this walk with Rover when he was a lad. His parents would point out the boat that had joined in at Dunkirk. It must have taken a hell of a long time to reach France, he thought. Still someone had to pick up the stragglers. Wendy had done that for him.

He breathed in sadness from the waters of the Wyre. There'd been so many good things gone. He looked to the green fields beyond the mud banks of the river, as sharp a dividing line as between life and death. His mobile rang. "Bob, it's Jane."

254

"I do recognise your voice after forty years," he warily answered.

"Look, I've not been straight with you. I knew it would all end in tears after the wedding..."

No, you didn't, he thought, you were planning to carry on playing the game. On this he was only half right. Her diaries revealed how relieved she'd been when he'd finished it all.

"...and I've become much closer to Geoff. We're going to marry within the next few weeks. He's moving in with me today."

Bob guessed that, last night, she'd been frightened at the thought of having to live by herself, had put on her little-girl-lost voice and the lovestruck dupe had fallen for it. But no words came out. Something in him was mourning yet he still felt pleased. The airwaves were only temporarily jammed.

"Bob, say something," she urged.

He managed one word, "Congratulations."

"Now you sound all hurt."

His determined voice kicked in. "No. I'm really pleased for you. You'll be good for each other, not star-crossed as we made ourselves out to be. I had a new arrival into my life last night too, and news of another one. I've inherited a dog whose owner died. Her name's Hattie. And Wendy Ballinger rang. She's three months pregnant after that evening in LA. I'm going to be a father again."

Contrary brain states at the other end of the line caused a deep silence. Then there was a click. She'd rung off. Bob didn't ring back. He was putting Hattie on the lead ready for the main road when Jane called again. He answered as he looked along the Wyre and the scene of the drowning all those years ago. Inside a bit of him was drowning too, but no tears came. He leant against a post. Hattie sat down.

"Sorry, Bob. It was too much to take in. You've upstaged me yet again," she said, with no bitterness. "That's why we didn't make it, you know, I couldn't live in your shadow. I thought that the one thing special between us was the children. Now you'll have done that with someone else too."

"Nothing can take away Ruth, Robert or any of our memories together. Where Baby Ballinger will fit into those we can't know yet, but she will."

"It's where Bossy Boots Mother Hen Ballinger fits in that upsets me," she spat out. "You remember our conversation on the sheep shag night. You said I could have some of you in eternity. I'm going to hold you to that."

Bob felt at peace with the world. "I've known you since before we were born which was after we were dead. I'm looking across the Wyre and Paradise is just beyond the horizon. We'll be together there, kid. We've a bit more life to live first. Thee and me will always be tangled together, as you will be with Andrew, and I will with Wendy. What we've done with each other and to each other was for real."

"Thee and me. Bob. I like that now."

"You've made my life what it's been and it's been great," he said, reading every word etched into his brain. "I'd have just been another engineer without you."

Jane showed she really was hurting. "And I'd have been another feminist academic. There's a sick, heavy feeling at the bottom of my stomach..."

"I feel the same way. It's a wrench."

"You're telling me," said Jane." It's au revoir then, big boy."

He wished Geoff and her all the best.

"Good luck to you, Wendy and Bump," she replied, less at peace with herself than he was. "She's probably a lovely girl and I was being jealous. She won't be able to step into my shoes anyway with that size feet. I'm ringing up Robert next to tell him about marrying Geoff, and then Ruth. Do they know about the baby yet?"

"No, I only found out late last night and I was going to tell them later on today."

They fixed up that Jane would ring first but not mention Bob's news. She wouldn't invite him to her wedding as she didn't want Geoff upstaged. Bob was going to keep Jane and Wendy apart at Bump's christening too. They'd next meet at one of the kids' places at Christmas some year or other.

"It's sad, Jane, I know," said Bob by way of farewell. "I'm hurting."

"So am I. So long, Swarbrick bonce."

Hattie made a great fuss of him as he stroked her. He felt more upset than he'd expected. The next job was going to be to ring Ruth. That didn't feel like an easy call. He'd half an hour to kill before he was allowed to ring on the timetable. Jane at last occupied a good place in his mind. He didn't have to hold Wendy up in opposition to her. Though a ménage à trois couldn't work, thoughts didn't have to result from synthesis and antithesis. His experience of disputation was of the Holy Dove flying rapidly out of the window, bringing everything into disharmony.

Ruth was upset when he rang: "Mum's just told me something dreadful. She's going to marry someone called Geoff Parkinson. Do you know him?"

"Yes, he's the Head of Psychology at Mum's university. He's a decent bloke and will be good for her."

"It's all on the rebound from you though. That's crazy," she said.

"It's a reprise not a rebound..."

"I thought she'd have had one too many of those with you."

"...she had an affair with him when she was with Andrew." His voice slowed down. "There's something else I need to tell you. When Mum and I went to LA, she badly offended Wendy and then stopped

257

out somewhere she shouldn't have. Wendy and I comforted each other over our joint affront and the upshot is that she's pregnant. She's delighted and in truth so am I apart from any impact it might have on you and Robert."

Ruth gave him a volley: "Dad, how could you? That's why you finished with Mum, and set this ball rolling."

He had no choice but to defend himself. "I only found out last night that Wendy was pregnant. She'd kept it from me until she was sure. Mum and I had broken up by then. She knows what happened and will vouch for me."

Ruth believed him but was still livid. "No need for that. As Mum says, you're too arrogant to tell lies."

Bob took in his stride. Nothing was going to upset him. "When she said something similar to me, it was because I was too stupid."

"You're both of them," snapped Ruth. "Are you going to marry Wendy?"

He outlined Wendy's marriage to Frank, his Alzheimer's, that it hadn't been a good marriage and that they hadn't been capable of having children together, none of which got him off Ruth's hook. She called it all a right bugger's muddle before asking if he was going to live with Wendy. He told her how Wendy wanted courting and that he was coming down to see her on Friday in Gloucestershire. He wanted to drop in on the way down to explain things better. He'd been beaten to the punch. Jane and Geoff had already arranged to stop with the Jacksons on Friday evening, going back Saturday tea time.

"Super competitive, our Jane, while pretending not to be," he commented. "Could I persuade you to meet Wendy on Sunday?"

It was the 'our' before 'Jane' that stopped Ruth's salvo. From this point Bob only had to look out for the odd sniper bullet. "Come on round here," she offered. "Let's see how unsuitable she is. It's going to be an interesting weekend for the kids making sense of the antics of the late middle-aged. Or actuarially speaking, the neo-elderly."

Bob was pleased the attack was over. As much as his, Ruth was her mother's daughter. Her barbs could sting just as much too. But Jane wouldn't have relented as quickly. He told Ruth that Jane had never developed a super ego to stop herself. "Geoff Parkinson acts as that for her and that's why she's retreated to him."

"Mum doesn't do retreat, tactical or strategic," laughed Ruth, full of admiration. "The poor guy won't know what's hit him in a few months. What's he look like?"

"He's a big, shambling guy with eyes that pop out of his head, a cross between Bluto and Popeye. He was banging on about thyroid problems, and I guess his is overactive. To be safe, I wouldn't feed him any spinach. What time should Wendy and I arrive?"

"You don't usually ask and you still don't need to, even if you are in my bad books," she said. "I'll cook a roast for about one o'clock. Any time in the previous hour will do, once we're back from church."

Bob closed down the conversation while he wasn't losing. "I haven't spoken to Robert yet; I'll do that now."

"He'll be less disapproving," Ruth knew. "That doesn't mean that I don't understand. I've seen you cop it from Mum too often not to. I'm sure I'll get on with Wendy Ballyhoo eventually."

"Mum's called her that and worse already," were his parting words. He'd been well and truly told off. Sophie answered when he called Robert. "Hi Bob. He's just coming out of the shower. Are you ringing about Jane's latest bombshell?"

He said he'd one of his own which had better wait until Robert was out. He asked if they were having a good time.

"It's been wonderful," she enthused. "I'm more watery than Bob and enjoy the diving and snorkelling. He's not very good at it, but he's a good sport."

Robert came out of the shower. "Don't you know we're on our honeymoon? We're meant to be left undisturbed, two birds of paradise."

"Chrissie Hynde, one of my favourites. I think this is going to be too rock 'n' roll for you. I found out last night that my good friend Wendy Ballinger is going to have a baby, and I'm the father. The deadly deed happened on the night of a big row with Mum in LA when she went off with someone else too."

"Bloody hell, Dad. What a pair!" hooted Robert. "Sophie thought she was marrying into genteel respectability. Hang on while I tell her."

Bob could hear explanatory voices followed by giggles, followed by raucous laughter. Then Sophie was on the phone again, "I knew there was life in the old dog yet. We were both thinking how down in the dumps you'd be feeling, and you've come up with this. That's trumped Jane magnificently."

Bob wanted to say that wasn't the most important thing but didn't need any more jarring notes. He told of how he couldn't marry Wendy and that the courtship was about to start in earnest. "Back to front, I know, but why does time have to go only one way."

After happy farewells, he informed Wendy that lunch for Sunday was arranged, and that a trip to Richmond could also be safely accomplished. Wendy asked him to be down to St Kenelm's for Friday evening, as she'd arranged for her parents to come round. It was as well he hadn't arranged to see the Jacksons. He arrived at seven o'clock. The house was a big, rambling, turn of the century cottage, well maintained and elegant. Wendy was better off than Jane with no need to embrace the modern.

Sheba was a beautiful slinky tortoiseshell. She hissed at Hattie, who didn't react. They gave each other a wide berth but did sit in the same room. Sheba sat on Bob's knee as Wendy stroked Hattie. This reciprocity was accepted by the animals and they reached an accommodation that was to be permanent.

Audrey and Walter arrived on the dot at eight. Bob was clearly welcome in their lives as a provider of a grandchild and a new partner for their sad-eyed daughter. They left three hours later with their lives freshened up.

Prudently, cat and dog were separated for the night with Hattie put in her basket in the Utility Room, or wash-house as Bob called it. He felt strange in someone else's home, but he didn't once he was in Wendy's arms.

The next morning, it wasn't possible for them to explore the village together, as Wendy didn't want too many tongues wagging. He took Hattie for a walk by himself and then they drove into Gloucester where Wendy dragged him round a few shops. He was just as bad as she'd expected. "You're not a patch on Steve at this. I might as well be leading a Herefordshire bull round the town on a rope. I'll not risk any china shops."

"Mission accomplished," he grinned, "You'll not ask me again. How about a drink and some lunch? That pub looks as if it will oblige."

"We've still to go shopping at Tesco's on the way out of town. I want to see if you can push a trolley."

"I'll have non-alcoholic if they have it," he promised. "I can't be drunk in charge of a shopping trolley..."

"Nor in charge of a high-powered sports car."

He kissed her lips and carried on. "Do you know what they say about a non-executive director with a shopping trolley?"

She did. "Yes, the trolley has a mind of its own but you can fit more food and drink into the non-exec." Jane, Ruth and Wendy all could best him. It was time for him to give up the jokes.

The supermarket was negotiated with only minor collisions. Hattie was pleased to see them back. If Sheba was, she didn't show it. Bob put Hattie on her lead, ready for a walk. Wendy was fed up of being discreet. "To hell with the tongue waggers. I'm coming with you."

"So be it," agreed a happy Bob. "Tats, Hatts."

They bumped into most members of the St Kenelm's jungle telegraph service. Wendy's abandon was controlled, but not massively. Bob was introduced as a business colleague, a good friend or the father of Bump depending on how well she liked the person. Of course, about half of those they met were more interested in Hattie anyway, including a couple who knew her breed.

The next day, Wendy and Bob arrived at Solihull at a quarter to twelve, sitting in the car outside the house until the Jacksons came round the corner. Tom, Charlotte and Bess the dog formed the advance party.

Bob yelled out as they ran up. "How are you two kids? Anything new?"

Charlotte giggled: "Only Grandma's antics, and yours. There was no need for you to have shot Gruncle Andrew if you're not marrying Grandma again. Is this Wendy?"

Wendy introduced herself when the others caught up. Harry stood in the background. Bess and Hattie sniffed bottoms. Charlotte immediately became Hattie's best friend for the rest of the day. Rachel gave Bob a big hug. Ben was watching everything from his pushchair. Ruth bided her time while she patted Hattie. She then carefully paced her words to the children. "Inside Wendy's tummy is a new brother or sister for me, and an Uncle or Auntie for you. You'll be older than your Uncle or Auntie. Isn't that wonderful?"

Wendy stood listening with her habitual interested, puzzled expression on her face. Ruth looked stern but with a hint of a smile she couldn't quite suppress. She walked up to Wendy and hugged her. "He's been split in two this last nine months. This is the right answer, even if I wanted the other one. Stories sometimes end back at the beginning, but not usually. Look after the old bugger."

"I can tell it's been hard for you too," Wendy said gently. "I know how much he cares about you. And your Mum. I'm pretty sure it's a girl, a sister, from the scan. If it is, we'll call her Alice Smith after your Great Grannie from Worcestershire, your Dad's favourite. My maiden name was Smith."

Ruth thought the idea was lovely. "She's the one who used to make him jelly when he went round." Bob's eyes filled up: "Wendy, you didn't tell me about Bump being Alice Smith. That's beautiful."

They all trooped inside. Wendy found that Rachel wanted to be with her so much that she couldn't shake her off to help in the kitchen. Bob played cricket with Tom, Charlotte and Hattie, showing them the different finger and wrist positions for an inswinger and an away swinger. Hattie didn't take much interest in this as she was in the team for her fielding. Bess was watching from the boundary.

On the way back in through the kitchen, Tom deliberately raised his voice loud enough that his Mum could hear him tell his Granddad about the club cricket match next Sunday. "Mum's not sure she'll let me play. She says I'll miss Church. All we do at Sunday School is stupid cut and stick."

Bob lingered behind to talk to Ruth after the children had taken their shoes off and gone to the living room so that he could ask how'd she'd found Popeye the sailor man. Ruth wasn't positive, seeing him a crutch for her Mum, who really didn't need one.

Bob felt no remorse at all when he learnt that they were marrying in as soon as four weeks. The Jacksons were going but Jane had said she wasn't inviting Bob. Jane had told him that already but he still said, "For this relief, much thanks." He then took up Tom's cause, asking if there

263

wasn't a bible class he could go to in the afternoon so that he could play his matches. Ruth said that it wasn't so easy in this pagan world with even the damned Crusaders having transmogrified into the Urban Saints and only meeting every fortnight. Bob bemoaned sports clubs for having done as much as anyone to wreck Christianity by playing Sundays and certainly didn't want Tom belonging to anything urban. But Ruth knew he was getting too old for Sunday School.

"I don't suppose he's quite ready for discussing if God should be a woman, as your Mum wants him to be, but he needs more than colouring things in," Bob agreed.

"He'll not get anything that unbiblical at Urban Saints, Dad. God isn't either. Gender comes from nature and doesn't start until billions of years after creation."

"I could have done with you whenever I had a debate with Jane," Bob reckoned. "If Tom gets too literal, we'll just have to tell him that it ain't necessarily so."

Their joint doubts about an evangelical bible class were thus cast aside and the Urban Saints acquired a new member. They joined the others to tell Tom the good news. Bob added that it had been like drawing teeth from a crocodile, an injudicious remark to a boy still developing his sense of humour. He then asked Ruth if he could do anything to help with lunch.

"After that you can. You can lay the table, then you can carve the beef. And you can do all the washing up on your own," he was told. Wendy finally escaped Rachel's clutches and asked if she could help. Bob didn't have to think before saying, "Yes, Ruth's just asked when you're going to shift your arse and do something useful. She'd like you to lay the table, then carve the beef. Then do all the washing up after the meal for not volunteering earlier."

Wendy looked nonplussed. Ruth explained: "I did say all of that, apart from I said it to that lazy lummox. Don't give him any help whatsoever."

"He's been helpful so far at my house," Wendy admitted. "Has he just been trying to impress me?"

"No. we're joshing each other," Ruth answered." He's good really."

Wendy and Bob laid the table together. Bob had no intention of discussing Jane's visit with the children. No doubt Wendy, Ruth and Harry had a similar lack of intention. But children have their own agendas, particularly if they have recently started at school.

Rachel had been quiet for a long time before she plucked up the courage to speak. "Wendy, when you met Grandma, why did you remind her of Mummy? You don't look anything like her."

Wendy realised that it was important to answer the question seriously not only for Rachel's sake but also for Ruth's, and for Bob's. "People have different qualities. Your Grandma is very clever and thinks quickly, darting from one thing to the next. I prefer to be more methodical, only changing my mind when I'm sure. I've only just met your Mummy, but that could have been what your Grandma was meaning."

Ruth accepted that analysis, much as she didn't want to. Tom also agreed. "Yes, Mum wouldn't change her mind about me playing cricket on Sunday morning until Granddad told her to."

Bob had to speak quickly before his chances of the Nobel Peace Prize were ruined. "Your Mum decided to let you play cricket, not me. The rest was a joke. And I'd like you to take church things seriously. They're your birthright."

Rachel continued probing: "Grandma said that you're hexpedient or something, Granddad. What does that mean?"

"I suspect it means that your Mummy was giving Grandma a hard time and she thought it was time someone else took the flak."

Wendy scowled at Bob. "It doesn't mean that at all. It means,

Rachel, that your Granddad prefers to find an answer that works to a problem rather than spending a long time discussing it. It's one of the reasons why I like him."

Ruth added her two penn'orth, "Granddad and Wendy are both right. Granddad answered the question as to why Grandma said it when she did, Wendy why Grandma thought it in the first place."

Life can always be explained two ways or not at all. As they left, Ruth whispered in Bob's ear, "She's passed, with distinction."

Harry hardly said a word that lunchtime. A couple of weekends later, Wendy and Bob made it to the Richmond mansion. As they left, Robert confided to Bob that Geoff was, "Not our sort of guy." Bob considered the possibility that he could be Jane's sort. Robert was doubtful of that and was looking forward to the divorce party. Bob suggested that they could combine it with the wedding.

In the car on the way back, Wendy sprung a surprise on Bob. She'd had enough courting and was ready to ready to take him off probation. She'd found a pretty, three-bedroomed cottage to rent by the river in Nether Piddle. With the power of attorney she had for Frank, she could let St Kenelm's out. She finished with: "But I know you've only recently moved back to St Chad's and I'll understand if you want to stay there."

In his life, he loved her more. "Nether Piddle. Well, I'll be living with four women who'll all piddle sitting down. You're on, provided I can still stand up when I pee."

"It's a deal," she agreed. "Lift the seat first though."

She wasn't going to make up her mind about returning to work until after maternity leave. He assumed that meant he was still on a sort of probation, confirmed by her wanting him to keep St Chad's for the odd trip north. He preferred to do that anyway, as Ethel Metcalfe might be disappointed if he disappeared altogether. Once back home,

Wendy lay on the couch with Sheba between her breasts. Bob sat on an armchair with Hattie perched on the arm with her head on his knee. The grandmother clock ticked slowly in the corner. Peace at last had come to his life, peace at last.

# CHAPTER TWENTY

The first Saturday in July was Founder's Day at Letchmore School. Laura had won the Year 11 History Prize and the proud parents were there for the morning prize giving. Matthew was arriving at lunch in his own car, bringing Trotter along for the picnic, before taking part in the traditional cricket match between the school and the Old Letchers. The school band would play during the tea interval, with Laura tootling her flute and James blowing his trumpet.

The morning speeches mirrored the previous eight occasions the Shackletons had attended. The Headmaster listed the capital projects that were being deferred in the present economic climate. Some years capital expenditure was going ahead to safeguard the future of the school and some years being deferred for the same reason. Either way, fee increases would be necessary. The High Sheriff of the county gave the keynote speech worthily, meeting triumph and disaster and treating those two impostors both the same when his microphone ceased to function, and the head boy attempted a slightly risqué joke which didn't go down well apart from with Year Nine.

The dress code clearly specified on the mailings was lounge suit. Three quarters of fathers adhered to this while the rest preserved their individuality by choosing to wear similarly scruffy T-shirts and baggy jeans. Introduced to wearing much tighter jeans in the fifties in imitation of James Dean, and having pushed the boundaries at his school with drainpipes and winklepickers, Richard saw these middle-aged fat blokes as born too late to be rebels without a cause. None of his children were with him on this, not appreciating that you couldn't be hip if you were under sixty or born south of the Mersey.

They spotted the pink banner of the Evans House tent at the other side of the ground. Richard carried the chairs, hamper and cool box over while Helen laid out enough food to feed a medium-sized regiment. When Trotter and Matthew rolled up a few minutes later, they took an age to cross the field to reach the rest of the Shackleton clan as various teachers asked how university was going. Laura was elsewhere with friends having eaten one smoked salmon with cream cheese sandwich. She returned to ask Trotter about his morning. James enlisted two boys in Year Eight from Hong Kong to help eat the food. Teetotal Richard wasn't allowed the Pimms provided from the House budget. Helen had thoughtfully bought some bottles of traditional Dandelion and Burdock for him.

"Great. Have you made any sandwich spread sandwiches as well? Or potted paste?" he asked.

"Shut up and eat the pork pies I bought you. Nobody else will."

Trotter made it abundantly clear that Helen was misinformed in that judgment. Nearly all the food was eaten. The two boys from Hong Kong welcomed any change from school food with open mouths.

The cricket match started, with Matthew opening the bowling for the Old Letchers. Despite being overloaded with Pimms, sandwiches, sausage rolls and cake, he was too good for the school side. He was taken off having taken two wickets in his first three overs after a shorter ball hit a third batsman in the box. This had caused great merriment around the ground if not with the young man's parents. The Old Letchers' captain explained to Matthew that the idea was for the game to last through the afternoon with a majority of players still possessing their vital parts. Richard heard one older boy explain that Matthew's ferociousness was caused by his father being a barbarian northerner. That was the default position of his southern life; nearly but not quite accepted, and this was just as he wanted

While Matthew was fielding, Richard and Helen were able to watch James play in the house football. James showed good skill but was not that strong in the tackle. He was to be a terrier a few years later when his barbarian instincts and the testosterone kicked in. They then watched Laura in the girl's tug of war, an event where she was clearly making up the numbers. Trotter moved happily between venues, a snapper-up of food dropped from picnics, including a half-eaten unconsidered strawberry trifle. All the while, he would look to make sure Amy was still in the pack. She was his special charge. During the tea break between innings, the band duly played while scones with strawberries and cream were scoffed. As they queued for tea, a correctly-suited but braying male blatantly pushed in a few places in front of them.

Helen bridled and was clearly about to be rude to him. "Them's gentry manners," Richard murmured under his breath. She smiled instead, realising she'd been a pushy bum too much herself in life. A replete and happy dog listened to the music with a benign smile on his face, enjoying the power of the blockbuster film theme music, sharing in the sadness of the big ballads, his eyes glazing over in ecstasy at the soaring cadences of popular opera sung by a sixth form girl. He missed out on the irony of the band playing 'Fanfare for the Common Man', living the life of Riley as he was, contemplating the unsurpassed, unsurpassable genius behind putting flaky pastry round a sausage. A woman in a flowery dress gave him some of her scone as he looked longingly. Laura and James had hit the right notes, and mainly in the right order, as far as their parents could tell. The irony of the Fanfare hadn't been lost on Richard. As he laughed about it, Helen pulled him up quickly. "We're off to Goodwood next. You're gentry now. Anyway, you've always stood apart from the common man."

Richard wasn't so sure Helen was right about either proposition, but knew he was too far through his life of privilege to argue. They packed everything away in the car apart from the chairs, from where they watched the rest of the game. Matthew was batting at number eight. When he went in, the Old Letchers only needed another twenty. He finished with a six over long off into the pavilion. He was much stronger than Richard. Helen, tongue-in-cheek, gave a convincing explanation. "Those must be my genes."

"If you sought out your real parents, we could find out," Richard said.

"I'm going to. I'll discuss it with Mum and Dad at the racing."

\* \* \*

That same day, Jane and Geoffrey married in a registry office, a raucous affair with colleagues enjoying so much merriment that the registrar threatened to stop the ceremony. The Jacksons were there, as were Sophie and Robert. At the reception, Louise Buchanan smiled condescendingly at Ruth when she discovered who she was. Later Ruth overheard her congratulate Jane for rejecting the boorish Bob. Harry heard too and reacted: "You stupid woman. It was for both of them their first love, their true love and it lasted all those years. This is a pantomime."

Louise floated away happy. While Robert made light of the incident with Jane, Ruth pulled Harry to one side. "What came over you?" she asked. "Don't let an awful woman like that get to you."

"You can't hold back what you feel," he replied before turning away to talk to Sophie.

Jane and Geoff flew out for their honeymoon in Sri Lanka the next day after a wedding night at the Manchester Airport Premier Inn. Geoff hadn't heard the encounter. Jane couldn't stop thinking about why Harry, of all people, had taken this so much to heart. Her mind was elsewhere as Geoff made his portly love to her. As he lay beside her afterwards, she looked at his features in the dim light, thinking he was rather like the picture in the holiday brochure of the reclining Buddha in Polonnaruwa. She wrote that she'd made him happy.

* * *

Richard had invited fourteen people, including Wendy and Bob, to Divinity's corporate hospitality box for the Wednesday of Glorious Goodwood. Right by the finishing line, it had cost the company a pretty penny. Two of his corporate guests had dropped out and Helen had suggested that it would make a pleasant treat for her nearby parents if he could find nobody else. Cuthbert Catterall had been happy when Richard mentioned it to him. As it was a sunny day, Helen wore a short dress with no tights. She had to take Richard's left hand from advancing up the bare flesh above her right knee several times on the long drive down from Monkey Mead, letting him go a little further each time. He gently reached the forbidden area in the car park. She let him linger, as he did have a VIP permit. Her hat was in the back seat, created with the same affection that a good confectioner gives to a strawberry tart. Richard was wearing a lightweight tan suit, with blue shirt, tie and brown shoes. His ten year old Panama was keeping the strawberry tart company.

Wendy and Bob drove over in Bob's sports car. She was five months pregnant and looking matronly in a floral cotton dress. Jane would have called her frumpy. To Bob she was radiant. He'd given up on county set and was in a blazer with grey flannels, white shirt, yellow tie and black, shiny shoes. By the time they reached the box, two pairs of guests were already there drinking champagne with the Shackletons, who were on coffee.

Helen's parents hadn't arrived. They'd rung to say they were about twenty minutes away having taken a wrong turning around Chichester. While Richard greeted the new arrivals, Helen made Wendy sit down, saying how nice it was to put a face to a voice. "Richard makes you into a saint. I hate you already. He'd like me to be as relaxed in a crisis as you are."

"Bob's told me loads of good things about you too," Wendy replied. "He's the one for the crisis. I get flustered..."

Bob was listening from the edge of another conversation. He jumped ships to say: "No, she doesn't. She's sweet reasonableness personified, while I go ethnic and hard-faced. It's not a bad double act. It would be even better if either of us knew what we were doing."

Helen looked him over. "You're very smart today. Tall and dignified. Unlike that pseudo-liberal I've the misfortune to be married to over there. Were you in the Guards?"

"I was a Wolf Cub and we did march on St George's Day. Is that close enough?"

"Not quite," said Helen, "You might look more like a regular guy, but you're like Richard underneath, undermining anything which smacks of authority."

"That's probably why Charlie Norman and I didn't hit it off. Wendy had him eating out of her hand. She must have reminded him of his nanny and real smacks of authority."

Wendy remembered the successful phone call. "He said I was fragrant..."

Bob inevitably interrupted: "Those in-bred upper class twits could never say their consonants, like the Chinese."

Wendy would have preferred that. "He made me sound like the latest Jo Malone product. Don't you make me out to be authoritarian, Bob Swarbrick, or I'll make you stand in the corner with your hands on your head."

Helen had liked Charles and his charm at first, too, while having real problems with his wife. She'd set herself up as Queen Bee, there being no females in the Directors' team, and hadn't been able to accept that Helen wouldn't join her hive. Bob told that they were going through a divorce. "There's to be a new Lady Norman. I can't believe Angela will take that lying down."

Helen joined Richard with other guests. Bob parked himself next to Wendy, who could see why Richard didn't have things all his own way.

"They're good together though," Bob said. "It's a wonderful meeting of opposites. They're ionically bonded, whereas I like to think we're covalent. We share bits of each other. Did you do that in Chemistry?"

Wendy's Chemistry was long forgotten, and she asked which bond was the stronger.

"Ionic bonds break down in water, but are hard to pull apart in a vacuum," he said. "Maybe that's why Helen and Richard argue in public but are rock solid at home."

The Durells arrived at last, looking flustered. Bernard's shirt was hanging out of his lightweight suit, which would have benefited from a dry clean. Elizabeth's floral dress was almost as creased as Bernard's suit. Richard saw the need to put them at their ease. "Terrible road system round Chichester. I've been lost there. It's a miracle you didn't end up in Portsmouth. What'd you like to drink? Something fizzy or a hot drink?"

Liz went for champagne. Bernard still had to drive home and

didn't want to see Portsmouth that evening, so had a cup of tea. While Richard arranged the drinks, Helen introduced the couple to the other guests. Elizabeth noticed Wendy's bump and commented how late in life women were having children. Bob was wondering how old the Durells were. He guessed they were probably about fifteen years older than he was. He couldn't see which parent had given Helen her looks. Elizabeth answered this thought. "Unfortunately, Bernard and I found out early that we couldn't have children. We adopted Helen when she was a baby."

Bob remembered Helen saying something about not knowing well where she was from. He hadn't thought that she was being so direct as she seemed the epitome of smart Sussex girl. He noticed her give a small shudder.

Bernard did too. "That bit wasn't unfortunate, dear. We couldn't have been more blessed."

Richard was his usual self. "Well, she's certainly a blessed nuisance."

Bernard chuckled to order. Elizabeth didn't seem as keen. Wendy thought of empathising by mentioning her difficulties in becoming pregnant but decided not to be so bold. "Yes, I'm going to be an old mother. I didn't meet anyone like Bob earlier. I'm not sure if that was fortunate or unfortunate for him."

Bob jumped into the conversation: "Fortunate, I was a hopeless case. Hi you two. I'm Bob Swarbrick, Richard's accomplice on one or two transactions."

Bernard smiled broadly, "And another from the north."

"I'm the same county, Lancashire, but further up and nearer the coast. St Chad's. Richard's a southerner to me."

Bernard had visited St Chad's. "I did some sketches of the old Church and the stocks in the square outside. Lovely place, apart from that appalling Slashed Sozzlers shop sign across from the stocks."

"That used to be the ironmongers run by my parents. We're not that good at Heritage with a capital 'H'. But there's the whipping post there too. Could be useful if we can find the culprit."

Bob chatted to Richard about Helen's adoption as they went for a postprandial pee. Until recently, she'd preferred not to know the name of the girl who as a gymslip mother had put her up for adoption. Richard explained Bob's part role in her change of heart. "She says that we're grounded in a way she isn't."

"I thought she was of the view that we were a couple of old farts from pre-history."

"She can think two things at once."

As they walked along the corridor, the door of another box opened. Emerging in front of them were Emma Greenwood and Charles Norman. Eye contact was unavoidable. The grounded Richard spoke first: "Hiya, Emma. I thought we weren't scheduled to see each other for another twenty years. You're looking good; the high life suits you. Hello, Charles."

Charles mumbled greetings. Richard felt almost buoyant. "The grapevine hasn't passed me by so I'm not shocked to see you two together. Mind you, bumping into each other today wasn't mentioned. Someone up there's having a laugh. Emma, this is my good friend Bob Swarbrick, ex Atomic Futures CEO inter alia. Bob, this is my very old friend Emma Greenwood."

The penny dropped with Bob as to exactly who Emma was. Richard hadn't cracked on. She recognised Bob too. "Didn't you and Charles have a bit of a public disagreement?" she asked.

"That's what the newspapers seemed to think, but I couldn't comment under the terms of my termination agreement," he said, with a deadpan face. "How's the world of solar power, Charles?"

"What was that disgusting expression you used to use when we played Liar Dice at management conferences? Ever been had, that was it."

Bob was pretty sure that he'd never aspirated the 'had'. Charles was still indignant from having twice overpaid when buying businesses from him and he knew why this second time. "Shackleton ingratiated himself with my team to gain access into confidential thinking," he drawled, before revealing: "Northern Solstice is a success compared with most of the stuff I'm sitting on."

Richard grinned. "Feeling a bit sub-prime, are we? How bad is it?"

"I've no idea," Charles admitted. "I'm only the Chairman."

Emma had been quiet long enough and asked if Helen was with Richard as she'd like to meet her. The facts to date were plainly contrary to this. When offered the opportunity at Center Parcs, she'd declined. With Bob present though, Richard didn't feel he had any choice but to acquiesce. After all, he'd witnessed the cage fights to the death between Wendy and Jane, and if he let Charles' and Emma's stories back into his own, he could reduce the size of the compost heap.

"Yes, she's here," he replied. "Do you two fancy a glass of something in our box?"

"Come on, Charles," urged Emma. "Our lot are pretty boring and we won't be missed for a few minutes."

Charles wasn't sure but couldn't deny Emma. "I suppose it will make a change from talking shop. I'll be jumping under a racehorse like a suffragette in despair soon. These two might be planning to murder me in there though."

"Bags I put the knife in first, Bob."

"I'm using a submachine gun, Richard"

The four trooped into the Divinity box. Helen was with her parents to one side of the room. She only needed to take one look at Emma to recognise the woman watching the family in the pancake place. Emma introduced herself as Richard's long time ago girlfriend. "I knew you'd seen me. I just had to have a peek. I'm sorry I didn't have the courage to introduce myself."

Helen had already moved on to the next lamb for slaughter. "And if it isn't Charlie Norman. I use newspapers with your picture in them under the litter trays at my vets. He treated you even worse, didn't he Bob?"

"It's time that was behind me. Big hearted Richard's asked him in for a drink."

Helen wasn't yet prepared to be gracious. "You should both imagine his balls on your tee on the par five the next time you play each other, cut off with a blunt Stanley knife. I imagine Angela would be happy to do that part of the operation for you."

Charles languidly commented that Angela had been doing just that for the last thirty years.

Wendy took compassion on him. "That's perhaps enough entertainment, Helen. This is called a hospitality box."

Richard explained his act of forgiveness. "Emma wanted to meet you, love, and I thought let's see what happens with Charles. Bob and I shouldn't be stuck in a victimhood groove."

Helen still needed a bit longer to adjust. "I don't know much about you, Emma, apart from that you don't spend much on your Christmas cards. When did you go out together?"

Elizabeth tugged Helen's sleeve and whispered for her to calm down a bit. Richard made sure that drinks were produced noisily. Charles sought refuge by inquiring of Wendy as to how the pregnancy was going. Again the grapevine had done its work and he knew all about it. Bob chose to join that conversation which soon turned affable with such pleasant subject matter.

Emma replied to Helen with only Bernard and Elizabeth listening,

"It's forty years ago now and it was for less than a year, when we were at Oxford. We met from time to time afterwards, and I've not seen him at all since you and he got together, apart from that day in Center Parcs. He was a special boyfriend. I wouldn't be standing here if he hadn't been. In the end he saw through me, and I've always respected him for that."

As Richard arrived back with the drinks, Helen turned the inquisition on to him. "Why haven't you introduced me to this woman sooner?"

He was pleased to hear a positive tone. "We've not been in touch since you and I met, apart from the Christmas cards."

Emma didn't let him down by telling Helen that they'd met, and kissed, at Center Parcs. The story of her two children and death of the alcoholic marine was told. Helen perceptively spotted that Emma seemed to prefer driven and self-centred men, so she wasn't too surprised that winsome Richard hadn't made the final cut. Her final judgment needed one more bit of information: had she pinched Charles from Angela or had they already parted?

"I guess I've pinched him," confessed Emma. "I didn't mean to. I'm a recruitment headhunter and when Richard was fired I couldn't resist pitching to find his replacement so that I could meet the guy as evil as me who'd stuffed him. It's turned into a bit of a circus with Angela behaving outrageously."

Despite all the heartache, Richard still couldn't let Helen form her opinion of Emma without hearing his character reference. "You're worth a million Charlie Normans, Emma. You're only frightened of commitment." He then supported Helen. "But Angela has every right to feel aggrieved. They were a couple, both being equally grasping. Knowing her, I'm surprised she's not coming through the door right now with a horsewhip."

Emma didn't care about their joint condemnation. "She'll get tens of millions pay off. She's been thoroughly unpleasant and she's now started talking to the press. There's going to be a big piece in one of the Sundays about it all, fat cat banker and gold digger mistress."

Richard didn't give up on dissuading her, saying that with the Northern Rock scandal, top bankers were sitting ducks, and did she really want all that? Helen came back into the conversation to say it depended if she loved him or not.

Emma did. "I have a terrible fascination watching him. He's so single minded, so driven. He's my opposite in that, but a soul mate in not liking niceness for too long."

Helen couldn't get that. "I'm not always easy. You saw that by the reception I gave Charles, but that doesn't mean I like badness in others. Surely it's not a turn-on?"

Emma hadn't come in harbouring doubts about Charles. There was laughter coming from the other side of the room. She glanced across to watch him charming Bob and Wendy. Charles spotted her look and walked over to them. "We'd better return to our guests, darling. Thank you for the drink. It's been good to see you all."

Bob ended on a friendly note too. "You know one end of a horse from the other, Charles. Give us a tip for the big race."

"Henrythenavigator's not really worth betting on being so heavily odds on. You like football. Go for Mick Channon's horse in the Veuve Cliquot."

Richard pecked Emma's proffered cheek. She looked good in an elegant blue dress fitting tightly with no visible panty line, which she smoothed unnecessarily as she walked away. He didn't think there could be much special about what was inside that dress if she'd allowed both Charles and him to share it. Helen watched Richard's eyes stare at the expensively tailored bottom. She saw his eyes move away with a look of dismissal on his face.

The rest of the day was what all the guests hoped for, with some good racing. Richard and Helen walked past Charles and Emma on a few occasions when visiting the paddock or the Tote window. They nodded in acknowledgment each time.

Richard told Bob of the mind-blowing event from the early summer. "Our James is bowling for the school under thirteens, Bob. Last over and the other mob need twenty more with five wickets left. He clean bowls all five in the next five balls. What's more spooky is that the game is on the thirteenth anniversary of my Dad dying. Before the war he bowled five in five off the last over to win a game."

"'There are more things in heaven and earth, Horatio...' You think your Dad influenced things from the great beyond then?"

"I'm not taking the wickets off James, but I hope so," Richard said. "It's like comedy; if you ask why it's funny, it isn't."

Bob felt that too many things re-emerged later in life to be explicable by the laws of probability, or as patterns reforming out of chaos. He reckoned the sequence in which entangled events emerged was what was fundamental. "If we could look at similar events from outside the system, outside time, we'd see each layer to be the next in the sequence. Chaos is when non-entangled stuff gets in the way, and is the illusion of time."

Richard still thought that everything was entangled and it was up to us to separate the wheat from the chaff.

Henrythenavigator left a gap behind him to come home first. Orizaba, trained by Mick Channon, won his race. Richard and Bob celebrated their wads of dosh by essaying Mick's arm-wheeling celebration, and were both soundly berated by their partners. Towards the end of the afternoon, tea and scones were of course served.

Elizabeth had made friends with several of the other guests, while

Bernard stayed more with Helen. "Mum and I really won't mind," he said, "if you want to find out about your natural parents. But don't forget that you might not like what you find."

Helen had made up her mind that she needed to know. He told her that the Salvation Army were the adoption agency, and her mother was a Jill Wilson from Streatham. The racing came to its conclusion. Bob and Wendy were the last guests to leave.

Helen and Richard had a quiet snog in the box when everyone had gone. "That was a great day, Richard. It would have been even more fun if Angela had come with the horsewhip to smooth out the creases from Emma's dress."

They walked out hand in hand and watched as a chauffeur opened the doors of the Daimler for Emma, and then Charles. He looked more than a little worse for wear. Emma waved, and they both raised their hands in acknowledgement. Helen muttered out of the side of her mouth, "And not waving but drowning."

Richard took up her theme. "She's been too far out to sea all her life. She's had an idyllic upbringing and everything she's wanted on a plate. But she doesn't seem to have any free will attaching to her."

He didn't use to believe in any such thing attaching to himself either. Helen didn't use to need salvation. She was changing. "Those two need to be saved from each other."

\* \* \*

Bob drove carefully back to St Kenelm's. He mulled over the day with Wendy. She hadn't derived the same pleasure from the day that Helen had. She praised the way Richard had handled it, and Bob for not losing his temper.

"That's because Helen did all the hard work for us," he said.

"Wasn't she magnificent?"

"Yes, but she reminded me a bit too much of Jane."

"Don't you believe it! Jane would have been egging me on, but not on the front line herself. Helen's a woman who does things for herself. So do you, but more quietly, thank God."

Wendy was visiting the nursing home to see Frank the next day, on the way to her parents. Bob was off to St Chad's to collect a few things before they moved into Nether Piddle in the middle of the week. Goodwood had made him realise how far up the class structure he'd moved. He could go back, but not all the way. Life had changed him, even if a seed had always been there.

The move to Nether Piddle went smoothly. Frank didn't seem to notice Bump as she grew, or any longer seem to know who Wendy was. The twice-weekly visits were a small price for her to pay for an otherwise happy existence. Not for her the adventures that Jane and Emma needed. Not for her the need to assert herself as Helen liked to do. She could manage this man called Bob in her own style.

August passed slowly. Both Wendy and Bob were putting their business into a lower key. He divested himself of all but one directorship, Citel, where he was wanted to lead a trade sale process in a year or so. Wendy was running down her portfolio for maternity leave, scheduled to start in the middle of September.

They spent long evenings together at Nether Piddle, in the garden and by the river when they could. The house was called Cruck Cottage. Although originally thatched, it had a tiled roof which presented less of a fire hazard. Bob enjoyed lighting the log fire each morning, having riddled the ashes through the grate. He then would carry out the more modern activity of emptying the dish washer.

They visited her parents every weekend. Bob liked them. He sorted through old family photos to include the best in a two hundred page rewrite of his family history, including anecdotes. He learnt to cook, baking pies becoming his forte. Wendy started distance learning for the certificate in further education teaching, necessary if she was to teach archaeology with the WEA.

They became friendly with Margy and Mike Cornbill. When they went round to the Cornbills for a meal, with Hattie invited too, the guitars came out afterwards. Margy started with 'Annie's going to sing her song', always one of Bob's favourites. At the end, he whispered to Wendy that he'd quoted from the lyrics to Jane only a few weeks before. Margy was puzzled, as she'd understood him to have been divorced twenty years. Wendy outlined the events of the last year. Margy wasn't surprised, as Bob's life not running smoothly had always been in his face. To commemorate their difficulty in finding the right partner, she and Mike sang a triumphal version of 'It Ain't Me, Babe' with them all, Hattie too, joining in the chorus, spluttering with laughter. Margy then sang 'Every Time', the song where she made angels weep.

Wendy's music tastes were later of course, and her faith had been more tested. She felt a shiver she couldn't ignore. "If we're lost or we're forgiven, the birds will still be singing," she quoted, to be mightily impressed that Bob knew it was from The Juliet Letters by Elvis Costello . She invited Margy and Mike for the return fixture, telling them to practice an Annie Lennox song for her. Margy said that her voice wasn't up for the diva stuff. Bob liked Annie Lennox but felt that Dusty judged a song perfectly and let it speak for itself. Wendy tossed her head back. "Are we going to squabble over music," she laughed.

"Probably," Bob said. "Just look at Helen and Richard. They'd argue over anything. They still love each other. And you're a damned sight easier going than she is."

Wendy explained that these were two married friends of Bob's, Helen being from Sussex, Richard from Bolton.

"It's a shame the Boltonian had to marry beneath himself," said Margy to hoots of derision from Mike and Wendy.

* * *

Rumours abounded about National Bank being in dire straits at the same time as Emma and Charles suffered the hatchet job in the press. As the bank was effectively nationalised in October, Sir Charles was fired ignominiously. He and Emma sensibly disappeared for a few months before he was hauled back in front of a Select Committee to explain his misconduct. By then they'd reinvented themselves from their almost stately pile as charity workers helping the homeless in Oxford, which was more dignified if less honest than appearing on I'm a Celebrity. Emma rang Richard at his office when everything first went belly up to say she was sticking with Charles.

* * *

With a minimum of fuss, Helen found and met her natural mother, Jill Wilson, using the Salvation Army Tracing Service. She chose not to involve Richard. Helen icily listened as Jill in her South London accent outlined the mundane facts of the adoption, typical for 1960. She'd been in the sixth form at the local state grammar school when she'd become pregnant by another sixth former from the Catholic school. Both sets of putative grandparents had felt that their children could continue better with their lives without this mistake holding them back, particularly with the difference in religious denomination. Helen spoke in a deliberate voice, sounding like a headmistress interviewing a truant who'd just been caught, asking what Jill would like to discuss next, the father, or what she thought about it all.

Jill stuck with facts. "He was called Christopher Corbishley. You're the spitting image of him, Helen. I've never been in touch with him since, but I know he's a cancer doctor up in Manchester. He was far cleverer than me, too handsome for his own good."

"How did it feel to give me up? Was I taken from you as soon as I was born?"

"About six weeks later. I was in a home with you to that point. Up until now, I've blotted it all out of my mind as best I could. I've not always been able to keep it up."

There was a catch in her voice as she finished. Helen's eyes were turning to anger before she heard the last bit. Instead she burst into tears, torrents of tears. The patterns in her ice-cold brain, her sense of self, dissolved and waves cascaded over the edge of the rocks. Jill held her tight, stroking her hair, and they both howled together. It was more than a minute before their brains re-connected, Helen saying: "It must have been hell for you. You were so young."

"What about you, brought up without knowing who you were? When did they tell you?"

"When I started school. Both of them have been wonderful. I couldn't have been more fortunate."

"And now you're a vet," Jill gushed. "That's lovely. Did you have lots of animals down in Sussex?"

Helen sounded like a schoolgirl with her new best friend. "Loads and loads! My husband likes animals too. He's Richard. We've four children."

Jill cried all over again, this time with joy. "I've four new grandchildren? Can I meet them?"

"Of course you can. Have I any half brothers and sisters?"

Helen found that she had two. Arrangements were made for Jill and husband Barry to come to Monkey Mead the next Sunday. By the end of the afternoon, Helen felt as if she'd always known Jill. The children were a bit mystified by another grandmother but took it in their stride. It could mean more Christmas presents. Helen's reserve was inherited from her mother, and Jill played it all low key. Before all the leaves had fallen from the trees in November, Helen had met her siblings at a return fixture in Purley.

She certainly harboured no doubts as to paternity when Christopher Corbishley strolled into the Manchester Midland Hotel. He was on his third marriage with a daughter from the first, a son from the second. She could see from the way he talked to the waitress that he was still up for flirting. She asked him curtly if he'd ever regretted what had happened. He confessed to not having thought about it as much as he should have done, and that she should see him as well beyond the pale. His wanderlust had always driven him the wrong way with the only good he did being in his work, and that was mainly for the glory. She shouldn't be fooled into thinking he cared because he was a doctor, as most of his patients ended up dead from the cancer they came to him with, after painful, intrusive treatment.

His arrogance in setting himself up as unreachable didn't go down well with Helen, nor did the humility about the purpose behind his work, which sounded too rehearsed to be fresh. "Stop sounding so damned pathetic. You're a doctor, a real master of the universe and clearly an arrogant bastard too. I'm a vet, so that crap cuts no ice with me. At least have the grace to say sorry properly to those you've hurt. Jill knew that's what it would take all along and meeting me has given her that chance."

Christopher winced. "Is that cold burning fire in your belly from me or your mother? I didn't really ever get to know Jill that well."

"All from you," Helen answered. "I liked Jill. I bet you took advantage of her."

"It takes two to tango," was his honest but self-serving reply. "She did ask me to stop and tried to push me away at the fateful moment. Honestly I would have done if she'd asked a few seconds sooner."

Helen couldn't prevent a tear from rolling down her cheek at being unwanted at the point of conception. Christopher's years of giving bad news meant that his sorrowful but distant expression kicked in. Helen knew the look straight away from her similar experiences with her customers. She hugged him only briefly. As she reflected on her meeting that evening, she felt she understood him quite well. She felt similarly about herself. Without outside help, she would have added promiscuity and unfaithfulness to her list of faults. She also thought that she could see herself as Richard must see her. She wasn't sure that she liked that much, but he seemed to, at least most of the time.

CHAPTER TWENTY– ONE

While these events were changing the boundaries of the Shackletons' world, Wendy and Bob were living contentedly in Nether Piddle waiting for their big event. But the change from major to minor was only temporary. On the Saturday after bonfire night, while they were comforting the cat and dog as the village fireworks display closed with the 1812 overture, the phone rang. It was a very disconcerted Ruth to the sound of bells and cannons. "Dad, thank God you're there. Dad, I don't know how to tell you. Harry's lost his job and now he's left me."

"He's done what? Why, what's happened?"

Ruth managed to pull herself together enough to tell him that he'd gone off with his first girlfriend, Karen Henderson, the one who'd mattered most before they'd married. She'd got divorced last year and sought Harry out by working in the office at his factory. They'd both been fired last week when they were found at it in a storeroom. He'd gone to live with her in Coleshill.

Bob wanted to know if she was alright on her own, offering to come and stay overnight. That wasn't what Ruth wanted. "Your place is with Wendy right now. He went about two hours ago, but I've known all week. I just wondered if you'd tell Mum and Robert for me. Robert's so happy with Sophie, and Mum would somehow blame me for being a fool."

"I'm sure she wouldn't, she's never been mean," he said. "We need to come over. Hang on."

He told Wendy what had happened. "We'll go now," she insisted. "Those children will be taking it badly, particularly the older two. It's their lives being torn apart too."

He picked up the phone again. "I'll make those calls you wanted, pack a few clothes and then we'll both be on our way. Wendy's already calling her friend Steve for him to feed Sheba. Hattie will be with us if that's OK. Make up the spare double bed."

With no further protestations permitted, Bob rang off. He retrieved a large suitcase from the loft, and threw in a few clothes. Wendy more carefully folded them and added her own as Bob went downstairs to make his calls. He rang Jane on her mobile as he'd no great desire to speak to Geoff, who of course then answered. Bob half heard, "What on earth does he want?" before Jane came on. "The last person I expected. What's up?"

"Ruth. Harry's left her for another woman," he said tersely, "his first girlfriend, Karen Henderson. They're shacking up in Coleshill."

"When they were courting, I remember something about that girl. Ruth was on the rebound too from that Freddie Corbett she was crazy about. Harry was never any great shakes."

Bob had missed out on all this. "Up to ten minutes ago, I liked the guy," he admitted. "Worse, he's lost his job having been caught in flagrante delicto with Karen in the storeroom. There are going to be real financial problems. Wendy and I are driving over to see if we can help."

"I'll have rung her while you're on the way, though she preferred to tell you of course. Isn't Wendy almost due now?"

"A couple more weeks."

"Good luck with that."

Bob then rang Robert who also remembered Freddie Corbett. The car journey to Solihull was taken steadily in Wendy's Range Rover. Ruth had the door open before they were up the drive. Tom and Charlotte were still up, with the other two in bed.

Charlotte asked Bob: "Are you going to bring Daddy back? He's being silly."

Before he could answer, Tom contradicted her. "He's being selfish, not silly."

Ruth looked wanly at them both. "He's following his dream. We'll have to realise that."

Wendy put her arm round Charlotte. "Let's sit down to talk about things. Your Mum needs you to be strong for her." Ruth led them in to the living room and then went into the kitchen to put the kettle on. Bob followed her to find how she was really feeling.

"I don't know, Dad," she answered. "You didn't need to come, you know. I feel rejected but that's pride. I can't wish I'd never met him or married him with four children, all his, can I? I can't forget him."

"Would you have him back if he changed his mind?"

"I don't think so. If he can do this after all these years, he can't like me much. He says that all us Swarbricks look down on him as a little man, while his precious Karen makes him feel tall. He's obsessed with her, his brain's addled."

The tea was ready. They carried the tray back into the living room, Ruth still talking: "I told you he was worked up when you and Mum split up again. He said then that first love is the best. It wasn't you two he was thinking of."

The kids were told to get some coca cola for themselves. Wendy was pleased to be relieved from looking after them. "Charlotte's a bit tearful and Tom is very cross. Are you either of those, Ruth?"

"Neither, you're here under false pretences. Go home tomorrow. But I'm glad you're about tonight. Harry's coming round to take some of his things."

Bob offered pragmatic advice. "Make sure he only takes his things. Anything joint's yours, that's your start point. And end point unless you want to get rid of something. He's the one who's buggered off."

Headlights could be seen through the curtains. Harry had hired a van. He wasn't only coming for his toothbrush. He wasn't alone either. There was another guy about the same age that Ruth didn't know climbing down from the passenger side. She was expecting problems but couldn't send the children to bed as they'd just poured their drinks. Bob girded his loins and answered the door. He opened it wide, standing square in the middle of the frame, with a dog either side of him.

"Hello, Harry. I was told you were coming for a few things. I wasn't warned that you were bringing a pantechnicon. Before you come in, I'd like to know want that you're proposing to take. I'd hate there to be any misunderstandings in front of the children."

"What the hell are the kids still doing up? We're taking half the furniture. My money paid for it while Saint Ruth sat on her fanny."

Given that all the women and the two children were in the hall, some of this could be viewed as a shade provocative. Bob only managed to keep his temper as the children were there. His heart was pumping as he guessed what would most likely happen next. "The courts will decide that if you don't come to your senses. You've come spoiling for a fight, and that's in nobody's interests. Who's this guy you've brought with you?"

"It's Neil, Karen's brother. He's going to help me carry the stuff. Get out of the bloody way, old man."

Jane had kept the secret of the Battle of Garlick Hill from the Jacksons. Harry tried to brush past the geriatric, and also past Bess who was hoping to be stroked. Instead, he found himself on his backside a few yards outside the door, doubled up in agony, after a punch in the stomach followed by a hefty shove. Bess barked, setting Hattie off too and Neil looked alarmed. He wasn't the next contender. Bob was pleased about that as he felt a sharp pain in his chest. "You get back in your van, Neil and I'll let Harry in."

Neil was only too pleased to oblige. Bob walked out, picked Harry up and more or less dragged him into the living room. "I might be an old man, pre industrial revolution even, but you'd be fitter if you worked in cow fields and not in a factory being ordinary."

Heroes often fail. Bob felt sharper chest pains as he dumped Harry on the couch. And then he clasped his chest and keeled over. The cows that ate the grass in those fields contributed to the quantity of cholesterol in human arteries. Bob's moments of physical triumph in these latter days didn't last long, before broken metacarpals or acute myocardial infarction took away the gloss. He sank to the floor clutching his chest.

Ruth and Wendy both rushed to him. "I don't think he's breathing," Wendy gasped. "Get me the phone, Tom." Charlotte was begging for Granddad to get up. Ruth snarled at a slowly recovering Harry that he'd killed him. Tom brought the phone for Wendy to ring 999.

A groaning Harry ignored Ruth and took some sort of charge. "I've done a bit of first aid on heart attacks." He placed his hand on Bob's chest and checked the pulse by his Adam's apple. "I think he's breathing and he definitely has a pulse. Let's roll him on to his side into the recovery position."

Bob's breathing had become a little stronger by the time the ambulance arrived, pulling up alongside a bemused Neil in the van. Harry whispered to a distraught Ruth that he'd call her to find out how Bob was and shuffled back to the van, still holding his stomach. The paramedics came in as he opened the door to leave. "It looks like you need us too, mate," quipped one.

They did their stuff and a semi-conscious Bob was taken to the ambulance. The senior officer had a quick word with Wendy. "He's survived the first bit, but it's not over yet. I think he'll need emergency angioplasty."

Wendy went with Bob in the ambulance, with Ruth staying to look after the children. It was some time before they drove off while the paramedics attached equipment and took measurements. Bob was taken straight to the Cardiology Department at Heartlands Hospital, where the angioplasty was to be started almost immediately. Wendy was informed that the worst of the danger had passed, that he'd regained full consciousness and in her condition it would be better if she went home while he was in surgery. She could call about half past midnight to find how that had gone, and see him in the afternoon if all was OK. She said that's what she'd do. She was allowed to see him briefly. He smiled painfully and said: "I'm not leaving you and our Alice for all the tea in China."

Tears streamed down Wendy's cheeks. "I thought you were dead. I love you, boy. I love you."

"I love you too, girl. You're one hell of a woman. Let's give Alice a little rub before you go."

Wendy took a taxi back to Ruth's house. Ruth was still up with the children, who were sent to bed after hearing the news. The two women hugged each other.

"He's what's meant by a Dad," Ruth sobbed. Wendy was certain there was nothing he liked being called more. Ruth had something else to tell her once she'd steadied herself. "Mum and Geoff are speeding down the M6 as we speak. Can you face them or do you want to go to bed?"

"I'm ringing at half past midnight to see how the surgery's gone. If he's come through that, I'll be up for it. I've not met Geoffrey

Parkinslice, as your Dad calls him. Hadn't I better move out of the double bed for them?"

"I'll move out of my bedroom. In your condition, you don't want to be perched on a titchy camp bed."

"You're as bad as your Dad," Wendy said. "He's always taking the proverbial out of the size of my bottom. It's his stomach size we'll have to be doing something about if he pulls through. He's been learning to bake cakes and pies too. I can't see him steaming fish with the same relish."

Ruth had some of her Dad's earthiness. "He won't be allowed any relish either."

So did Wendy. "He'll have to be at some stage. I'd like a brother for Alice."

Ruth smiled bleakly. Wendy squeezed her hand before asking if she'd told Robert and Sophie. They were coming up the next morning. Auntie Joan from Totnes would drive up later in the week.

At exactly half past twelve, Wendy phoned the hospital. Eventually she found out that all was well. Within five minutes, headlights could be seen through the curtains. Bess and Hattie pricked their ears up, and barked as the doorbell rang. Fortunately the children were heavy sleepers. Ruth opened the door accompanied by the dogs while Wendy stayed seated in the living room. She heard Jane's voice first. "How is he? Any more news yet?"

That was real concern she could hear. She had to accept that she shared her man with his ex-wife, as well as his children and his ancestors.

"Good news so far," Ruth told her Mum. "He's had angioplasty with no ill effects. We can visit him tomorrow afternoon. Hiya Geoff. Thanks for coming."

Jane noticed Hattie. "Have you got a new dog? She's a sweet little thing. She is a girl, isn't she?"

"Yes. She's Dad's, and Wendy's."

Wendy stood to greet them. Jane was pleasant as she spoke. "The last time we met, you said you wouldn't see me again. Pax, Wendy?"

"Definitely pax, Jane. It was a good war, and now we need a good peace."

The two women actually embraced, holding each other tightly. Jane hoped the shock wouldn't cause problems for the baby.

"Alice is fine so far," Wendy replied. "That's what we're calling her, after his Grannie."

"He'll not be able to eat any more of her green jelly with bananas now. It will be steamed fish," said Jane.

They all smiled at their shared inside knowledge. Wendy was introduced to Geoff. He pecked her proffered cheek. With Bob not there, she'd thought it safe to do so. Ruth's eyes watered and gleamed at the same time. "Dad would be saying yuk right now."

Jane put on a Fylde accent, "He would that, he would that."

Geoff liked Bob too. "There's no more sincere expression of affection than to be mimicked."

Jane bit her tongue. She'd been about to say that Bob did enough of that himself in self-parody. The sleeping arrangements were explained as they drank a cup of tea. It was half past one before they were all in bed. Ruth shivered in her camp bed on her own. What made it worse was that Geoffrey Parkinslice was in her bed with her mother. She wondered if they'd be up to anything.

The answer was available next door, though not to Ruth. Jane had requested that the sex be very occasional and she intended the next occasion to be long delayed. Geoff lay on his back snoring as Jane dug him in the ribs to shut him up. They were already in separate beds at home and Jane would have preferred two camp beds here. She'd married him for his daytime company. There was a delicious irony that both Jane and Bob, who'd been at it like rabbits, had moved on to almost celibate existences with their replacement partners.

The news from the hospital the next morning was positive. He could have visitors late morning and mid afternoon. With four children active and a trip for food necessary, Ruth couldn't go to hospital in the first party. Geoff understandably didn't think Bob would want him there. Robert and Sophie had encountered traffic and were an hour away. There was nothing for it, Wendy and Jane had to go together.

"Sisters under the skin, Wendy."

Rudyard Kipling was an 'A' level staple in Wendy's sixth form days. "Colonel's lady or Judy O'Grady for you, Jane?"

"Judy sounds more me, I think, but I don't really mind."

"Colonel's lady for me then, more fitting for a City woman."

Jane wondered if they should take some flowers with them. Wendy thought he'd prefer a pork pie.

"Or maybe a slice of parkin," suggested Jane. "I understand from Ruth that he now calls me Jane Parkinslice."

"He baked some parkin the other day," Wendy revealed. "In fact, he hasn't eaten it yet. He was most disappointed when he found that he should keep it in the tin for a week to moisten up. He tempered his disappointment with a shop-bought éclair."

Jane had taken to her new nickname. "I'll be round to help you eat it since he won't be able to now." Wendy said that both of them were always welcome. "I do mean that."

"I doubt if you do but you're a decent woman, Wendy Ballynice," Jane replied. Wendy revealed that she was trading as plain Wendy Smith, her maiden name, and that Alice would be Alice Smith, his Grannie's name in full.

Jane had never known Bob's Grannie. "She'd died just before I met him. He'd say a long prayer at the end of a church service. I asked him what he was praying about. It was for Grannie and his dog Rover who'd also just gone. I remember thinking that was so sweet for such a big, clumsy oaf."

Jane had to stop speaking as she could feel herself about to lose it. She saw Wendy's eyes welling up too. They both managed to pull themselves together as Wendy asked what his parents were like. "They were lovely people, very nice to me. I feel I let them down more than I did Bob. They didn't see as much of Ruth and Robert after we split up."

"Maybe they'll be able to catch up in heaven someday."

Jane was understandably unsure of her place in Bob's affections. "If you and I were to die before him, would he want both of us there waiting for him, or just you?"

"Both of us, Jane. The pair of us are in his heart, poor bust thing that it is." Then she giggled, "He'd probably say 'how do' to Rover first."

They reached the hospital, paid the parking fee, walked through endless corridors and endured the lift stopping at every floor. Finally, they found the side room he was in. "We've found your hiding place at last," Wendy announced. "It's the Kipling Sisters."

He squinted towards them. "What are you on about? It's me who bakes the exceedingly good cakes."

Jane was only just behind. "The writer, philistine. We're sisters under the skin."

"The sisterhood was deeply subcutaneous last time you were with each other. Hell, both of you together. It could give any man a heart attack."

Bob rubbed his chest gingerly. Jane went outside to find another chair as Wendy sat down.

"How's our Alice? Is she OK?" he asked.

"She's fine. You worry about getting yourself better. I want another one after her."

"We'll do our best," he said. "I made a right prat of myself, didn't I?"

Wendy didn't think so at all. All he'd done was defend his own, carrying on even after the heart attack started. She'd been watching his face and known something was up. He was still more concerned about Ruth, saying that what he'd done wasn't going to help her any. "What did Harry do when it all happened?"

"He was a big help with first aid when you were unconscious," Wendy revealed. "And he took no furniture so you achieved that objective. Perhaps there could have been easier ways!"

Jane came back in with a chair. Bob quizzed her straight away. "Ey, what've you got out of Ruth this morning? There must be something strange happened to make Harry turn up like that."

"Reading between the lines, he really has something for this girl Karen. He's not coming back in a hurry. The place where they're living in Coleshill is an unfurnished rented flat. He'd asked for some furniture when he left Ruth and she'd refused him any. You and I stayed more civilised."

"There are a few differences," Bob recalled. "Andrew had a place with armchairs for you to live, and we had jobs."

Wendy thought a change of subject would be better for Bob's stress levels and recounted how his chum Charlie boy had been on the Sunday holier-than-thou slot on the box talking about atoning for his mistakes. Bob asked if Emma was on too. "Yes, in their stately pile with a beatific smile on her face, surrounded by disadvantaged children, feeding pigs," Wendy answered.

"Dogs look up to you, cats look down on you, pigs is your equals," he recited. "I wonder if Richard and Helen saw it."

Wendy was going to let Richard know what had happened later in the day and she'd ask him then. Jane was prompted to remember the last time she'd seen Richard. "He had a ringside seat in LA. I probably ought to apologise for that personally."

Wendy laughed as she vividly remembered the evening. "There's no need for that. Those of us in the ringside seats were hit by flying gumshields and cascades of spurting blood, but it wasn't ours. Leave the public atonement to phonies like Charles. Alice is going to be the tangible result of that night, and that's a truly wonderful outcome."

It was time to go. Jane said her farewells, followed by Wendy. Jane kissed his cheek, Wendy his forehead. He kissed her lips. As they drove back, the women were quiet. It wasn't unfriendly, but they were both conscious of who it was they were with, and both preferred for things between them to be left at about the point they'd reached.

They arrived back to the smell of hot chicken, which Ruth had hastily procured from Waitrose along with salads. Wendy was conscious that she was walking into a Swarbrick home, one where she was a visitor and Jane had half proprietorship. She was warmly received by Sophie though, and Ruth asked her how Bob was while Jane caught up with Robert's news. After lunch, Robert and Ruth had a heart-to-heart about Harry leaving. They'd shared another marriage break up together many years ago. Wendy listened from a distance. She'd known Bob just a short while, yet she was starting to belong to this family, his family, as she had never done with Frank or with Martin when she was head over heels in love. Please God, keep Bob and Alice safe, she prayed.

Bob was asleep when Ruth, Robert and Sophie arrived. He woke and stared at them bog-eyed for a second or two. "You three aren't dead yet, so I guess I can't be either. Good to see you all."

Robert and Sophie went in search of more chairs while Ruth had a quick word. She made it abundantly clear that she blamed Harry for Bob's heart attack. He disagreed, saying it would have happened soon enough anyway and he might not have survived in the wrong place. "We haven't much time to talk about what's gone wrong between you. You said last night that you didn't think you'd have him back if he asked. Are you sure about that?"

"I'm relieved he's gone. I was bored with him, you know. I haven't made enough of my life other than the family stuff. I'd really like to discuss what I can do by way of a job."

Robert and Sophie came in. When asked how he was, he told them that he was still aiming to go to the maternity ward with Wendy. He'd missed that when Ruth and Robert were born, when fathers stayed outside pacing the corridor, smoking a fag.

"You mean you weren't down the pub?" asked Robert.

"Your mum would have said I was at the power station! No, I was in the waiting room outside for both of you. This time I intend to be there. Wendy will tell me to bugger off if she doesn't like it."

Ruth recalled that Harry had been to all her births. "I wish I'd told the useless pillock to bugger off then."

There were at least three occasions when the conversation ended similarly. Bob winked at Sophie on the last occasion, and Ruth saw him. "You think I protest too much. You'll see."

Bob thought it time for Sophie to get a word in, so he asked how life was in beautiful downtown Richmond.

"Not bad," she replied. "Commuting's a pain though. Perhaps I'll change my mind about waiting two years to get pregnant. In fact, I have changed my mind. We weren't going to tell you until after the scan, but according to the tests and the doctor I'm expecting."

This great news brought a huge grin to Bob's pale, drawn face. "Wowee, terrific, superlative, fan-bloody-tastic." All four had inadvertent, inane smiles on their faces. Robert had no idea that Sophie was going to mention it, since she was still to tell her own parents, and

Jane.

"I'll ring my parents once we're back home," Sophie said. "Telling Jane wasn't an early priority."

When Bob heard Sophie's tone of voice, he mentioned how Wendy and Jane had made friends despite all that had happened between them. He asked her if she could do the same for his sake, and Robert's. She again promised to try, but she never really succeeded.

Harry's head peered round the door within a couple of minutes of them all leaving. He said how sorry he was about Bob's heart attack. Bob told him it was his own daft fault for not spotting the signs and acting his age. But Jane had it right when she'd worked out there wasn't going to be a reconciliation with Ruth. Harry had no doubts. "When I met Karen again, the last fifteen years were wiped out. My door at the factory has a pane of glass at the bottom. I could only see her turn of ankle above her high heels as she filed stuff away. I didn't need see anything else to know that I wanted to spend the rest of my life with her."

Bob looked at Harry's creased trousers and scruffy shoes, and asked if she felt the same. "She does, Bob. She regrets finishing when we were young."

They chatted a bit longer, Bob learning that Karen had no children, and few possessions. Her ex-husband had a bad drugs problem. Harry was hoping that Ruth would come to terms with him going, as Bob and Jane had managed.

"Jane was the one who found someone else, not me," Bob replied. "Maybe it was my fault, I don't know, but I didn't see the kids anything like as much as I would have liked. Hell hath no fury and all that. Ruth could go back to the north-west."

This thought disturbed Harry. "Won't she stay here? You're near in Nether Piddle."

Bob reminded him that Jane was in Liverpool and that Ruth had spent her youth in and around there. He also pointed out that he'd have to find work, as would Ruth, and that wouldn't be easy if he restricted himself to the West Midlands. Harry was horrified at the thought of moving. "I'll not leave the Birmingham area, it's my home. I never had that sort of ambition."

"I guess you didn't. You're not wrong on that. Anyway, I'm feeling knackered, lad. It was good of you to come. And thanks for the first aid before the ambulance arrived. Good luck with the rest of your life."

Harry stood up and walked to the door. He opened it with his back to Bob and then turned to face him. "There's no turning back."

Bob laughed. "You just have. See you later, God knows when."

"He's not here. I'll be glad to be rid of him."

Harry walked out of the door without looking back again. Bob drifted off to sleep feeling sorry for Ruth, thinking how well it was going for Robert after being the other way round for a long time. The blue brick railway wall by St Chad's station was in front of him. He was suddenly standing on top of it. Then he fell. His heart jolted and he woke up in a cold sweat. He was pleased he was still in hospital and not in hell. But if he could withstand that jolt, his heart couldn't be too bad. He hoped that, mixing his religions, his astral body hadn't at that instant been carted off to the everlasting pit. St Paul had salvation open until the very end of life, by one existential decision of belief, one vital act of will. Bob had believed for as long as he could remember. He saw all the events of his life as going to mould his character. He was what he'd chosen. But he'd follow the Lord's call to repent yet again, in case Richard's ideas of universal salvation were wrong; conscience and good cheer without any expediency was what was needed from this point on, along with heavier drops into the charity bucket.

Wendy had to go back to Nether Piddle to feed Sheba. She went to visit Frank that Monday having missed her normal Sunday slot. His sister was also visiting and was sniffy at the pregnancy. "So much for loyalty when you're down," she'd said.

"After what he did to me with his child, it seems fair revenge."

As Wendy passed the residents' lounge she saw faces, not vacant but with stories behind them that could no longer be told. She'd wronged Frank by marrying him. She'd always believed that you should try to redeem things yourself before seeking forgiveness, but with Frank that wasn't available. Someone else would have to do that job. The only way she could atone was to make the best of the rest of her life, without expecting the guilt to be taken away.

For the next week, she dropped in on Ruth every day on her way from Nether Piddle to the hospital, looking after the smaller children while Ruth visited her Dad. Bob was then well enough to go home. Once out of hospital, he started his charitable donations by giving the profits from the Northern Solstice share options to a mightily surprised Scott Johnson.

He'd only been out for three days when Wendy went into labour. As he was to say later, she'd have had her first child on the living room floor left to her own devices. She was still unsure if anything was happening when Bob's experience told him that it was, and he rang the maternity unit, passing the receiver to her as the call was answered. Wendy was already seven centimetres dilated on arrival at the unit.

Unusually for a first baby, Alice didn't hang about. With one last push from Wendy's pelvis, out she came like a ball flying off the slip cradle at cricket practice. The midwife took the catch over her shoulder, with Bob's hands ready to cover any fumble.

All was well and mother and baby were home after two days, despite Wendy's advanced years. She was able to breast-feed, a great boon for Bob's sleeping routine. He did change nappies. On the odd occasion when he was left trying to comfort Alice's crying, he'd walk up and down singing hymns. Out of tune.

The christening was in mid-January at St Chad's, held in the middle of the morning service. Steve and Margy were the godparents. Wendy insisted that Jane and Geoff came. Ruth cut a forlorn figure coping with four children and dog on her own. To save some money, they stayed with Wendy and Bob at his old house for the weekend. Robert and a slowly expanding Sophie were in a hotel by the Wyre, along with Grandma and Granddad Smith. Ethel Metcalfe was at the service, saying how much she missed having Bob next door and making an equal fuss of Wendy and Jane. Richard and Helen made the day part of a Lancashire weekend. There was a sandwich and pork pie reception afterwards in the upstairs room at the pub across the road from the church. A careful Bob made do with two sandwiches. Ruth took him to one side and whispered in his ear.

"Don't tell anyone, but I've an interview at Lytham St Annes next week for an actuary's job at HFS, the insurance conglomerate. And they've a crèche. I don't suppose I'll get it, but if I do I think I'd like to live in your St Chad's house. It's such a coincidence that it's my only interview offer."

"Fingers crossed then. I assume Wendy isn't on the list of people I'm not to tell."

She meant Robert particularly and Jane secondly, as she didn't want them to see her fail. Her confidence was low. An honoured few were invited back to the house after the pub. Helen was impressed by the friendliness of the day and confronted Bob with it.

"You told me being a grammar school boy had divided you from others. You made out that you and Richard were stateless people. You look like you belong in this world well enough to me, Bob Swarbrick, in St Chad's or Goodwood."

Alice started to cry. Wendy picked her up from the carrycot and cuddled her tenderly. Bob picked up the conversation in similarly gentle mood. "You're right to put that back to me. Everyone here belongs in this world, my world, your world. I've nothing but affection for all you shower."

Jane gave Bob a smile. Wendy sat in the nursing chair in the corner feeding Alice.

## CHAPTER TWENTY– TWO

Two and a half years later in September 2011, the same people assembled in St Chad's for the christening of Alice's brother, named after proud godparent Richard Shackleton. Sophie was the other godparent. The baby was blissfully unaware of the economy going down the pan.

The fifty year curse had cleared. A home-grown Lancashire side, given no chance as the season started and playing their home games in the dry of Liverpool while Old Trafford was being refurbished, won the county championship right at the death, Blackpudlian and Boltonian batting as the last runs were hit. Guys in white, with warm grins, crinkled eyes and broad accents, from state schools and apart from the glottal stops the same as yesteryear, were smiling out from a glossy cricket magazine on the coffee table. And poor old Yorkshire had been relegated. Bob hadn't known a year this good since 1485. Richard, with a Y for Yorkie chromosome in his Lancastrian heritage, was more conciliatory. "We found a Welshman, Henry Tudor, called him a Lanky and got him to marry Elizabeth of York to bind us together."

"I can't think why that didn't work for me," Bob laughed. "Now is the winter of our discontent made glorious summer by these sons of Lancs."

"You'll jinx us again just as the curse is over. We'll go down next season while the Yorkies get promoted."

The moment when old things became new again didn't last long.

That's what happened. Helen was in a mellow mood, but couldn't fail to mention the chaos caused in Fukushima by another tsunami. She wisely walked away without waiting for a reply. Richard suggested to Bob that the case for nuclear power had been wrecked.

"It wasn't the greatest design but the place has stood up pretty well," Bob reckoned. "I've told you before, proliferation's the bigger issue. We'll have to start using thorium rather than uranium."

"Never heard of it."

"Named after Thora Hird and found exclusively in Moresham Bay."

"Another leak from up the coast at Sellafield then," joked Richard. "You lot should have built a barrage, not a nuclear power station."

Bob agreed: "You could be right there. With it, we could build a road to Furness, on condition they come back into Lancashire."

"You wouldn't need to bribe us Boltonians," Richard growled. "I like the place but nobody's ever going to make a Manc out of me. It's the towns that make the north what it is."

"Counties unite people, cities divide them," Bob asserted, forgetting his five-hundred year war with the Yorkies. "Anyway, we've found all this shale gas under St Chad's, the epicentre of the universe and of an earthquake after the last fracking trial. It's not that green but it's Lancastrian. Let's hope they can extract the bloody stuff without knocking St Chad's Church and Blackpool Tower over."

Apart from Little Richard, usually called Richie, Patrick Swarbrick had also been added to the cast list, the first born to Robert and Sophie. Ruth had taken over Bob's house in St Chad's having sold the Solihull property. Harry and Karen Jackson had visited Blackpool a couple of times on strained visits. Wendy and Bob had acquired a larger place in Nether Piddle, following her sale of St Kenelm's. She'd left Frank's half of the proceeds in a fund to pay for his nursing and his son's upbringing. She found time to visit him regularly while giving lectures at three local WEA archaeology courses.

Sophie was expecting again. Fed up with the commercial world, she'd completed a post-graduate course in human rights law since the latter stages of pregnancy with Patrick. Amazingly, Bob agreed with her choice, whereas before he'd met her he'd have said that folk needed jobs, not rights. Jane's marriage to Geoff was working well. She was at peace with the world and he was where he wanted to be, Big Buddha watching what she did next.

Audrey and Walter were the first to leave the party for their long drive back to Cheltenham. Steve went with them, with the Cornbills following behind. Jane hugged Robert. Sophie said cheerio and moved off. Geoff came over to shake hands with both Wendy and Bob. Jane and Bob waved to each other as she exited stage right. She lingered long enough to blow him a kiss once she was sure Wendy was looking. Wendy pretended to shoot her with a two-fingered gun.

Sophie pecked Bob's cheek and hugged Wendy. Robert said see you soon as he carefully carried baby Patrick. Dogs barked, car doors slammed, engines stuttered into life. The adults left were Ruth, Helen, Richard, Wendy and Bob, who was driving the Shackletons to Preston in an hour or so for their train back to London. Ruth still had more to do in the kitchen, having placed a large pot of tea on the table. Bob acted as mother. Then he picked up a tetchy Alice and walked round the room. She was tired after being the life and soul of the party earlier.

Wendy asked Richard how Northern Solstice was getting on as she fed Richie. He'd heard they were doing quite well as green energy had been insulated from the carnage elsewhere.

Bob joined in with glee: "Just like you bankers have, despite being the cause. Are you in for another mega bonus this year?"

"Middling," admitted Richard, remembering to be forgetful of his previous bonus refusal. "Better than last year, and I hope worse than next."

Bob was even more jaundiced by bankers than he had been in his golden days, believing that public school pillocks were better than smart-arsed maths graduates devising instruments to be the playthings of testosterone-charged traders. Richard's take was that the winners from the zero sum derivatives game were grabbing huge bonuses and the losers merely large ones.

Bob carried this from the city to the world in a pontifical diatribe. "Money's the unit of account for everything else and can't be left to these chancers. It's damn near as bad outside banking. My salary was grotesque enough, but the average chief exec's pay today is embezzlement. What sticks in my craw is that these megapillocks think they're worth it. Can't they see that the market's been rigged in their favour? All our generation who rose with the meritocracy have taken far more than we've put in. Pity the poor bloody infantry. We can't give it all back, not all the gigajoules of energy we've wasted, the food we've scoffed, the drink we've necked, the people we've used, the society we've loused up. None of us ever earned the food on our plates. Our debts to the poor sods we left behind can't be repaid so we owe it to them to look like we've enjoyed it."

Helen walked over to pour herself another tea. Ruth returned from the kitchen to ask if they'd like a fresh pot. There were no takers. Helen sat down and talked of her real parents, the mother she liked and the father she was like. "I've a brain full of wriggling worms, sometimes hissing snakes," she confessed, "yet Richard and my adoptive parents have chosen to love me. I've realised I must somehow make sense this way and that's made me accept my father."

Ruth, standing with an empty teapot in her hand, wasn't as ready to forgive. She still couldn't feel any warmth when she thought of Harry and wanted to forget all about him. Bob stood up too, and walked to the window, carrying Alice. He talked directly to Ruth: "The whole sordid business will weave into the tapestry of your life at some stage, in ways you can't see yet."

Richard didn't agree with that of course, thinking that minds should be free of wriggling worms, not be made up of them. He saw his storylines as a battle between a good and bad author, and when the good lost out, the weeds should be wheeled to the compost heap. Bob knew too well from his stop-start life that the story wasn't warm all the time. "It might not have been authored, but it's all been written down and published. It exists, it happens and it hits you with echoes from the past and future."

Wendy paused briefly from feeding to agree. "Frank's Alzheimer's no sense at all, but when it's so blindingly obvious that something does stack up, I'm not going to deny it. Some things are clearly intended, seen through a glass darkly, like the way Bob and I finally got together."

There was 1 Corinthians again. Richard still wasn't a total fan. "Paul picked a fight with himself and everyone else about where our salvation comes from," he said uncertainly. "In the end he realised that there was still a gap and filled it with the grace of God. That's all he ever needed to have said."

Bob recognised the 'Paul' in himself in wanting to understand the mind of God. "You can't blame him for being inquisitive. Even if we can't change our lives, they can be redeemed, the bad bits too."

He slipped upstairs to put Alice in her cot while contemplating if Jane either time round was a horror story to be put in the discontinued section. No way would he have her there. The men who'd jumped into Jinny Greenteeth's pond to try to get to know her had got more than they bargained for, but they hadn't been short-changed. It wasn't love's illusions he was recalling, it was the real thing. Jane wasn't Maya; she never deceived anyone about who or what she was, and she'd made him into the guy he was, the guy who loved Wendy, the guy Wendy loved.

Downstairs, there was a long silence. Richard was deep in thought. He didn't like Ruth agreeing with him; he didn't want her unhappy. He could have got over Emma quickly, and it was his own daft fault that he hadn't. If she'd become pregnant forty years before, she'd have stayed in his life and his head. He'd rejected her at the one time she might have needed him. He'd not been there for Nell either. Those were two important truths he knew he shouldn't deny.

"Like Ruth, there are some things I'd prefer not to have to carry with me," he said. "But I guess that's not my shout..."

Wendy interrupted him: "We make our choices and wait for what happens. Meaning comes from being, knowing and doing somehow melding together. You and Bob worked it out between you; three become one in the whole story."

There was a slightly awkward pause as the others tried to understand. Then Helen spoke. "I did, Richard, I chose you. The best decision I've ever made."

Richard couldn't believe her when she said this with Pierre and Trotter in close attendance. He did this time with his friends present as witnesses. He was hearing what he'd needed to know since he was nearly strangled at birth, since his family broke up, since Emma first finished with him. He was wanted. He was perceived. He remembered how his father had apologised on his death bed. His mother, in her final hours and though she no longer knew who he was, had enough spirit for her face to light up as if she had a choice. He hoped she thought he was Michael.

He turned from Helen to Ruth. "They're right. We've got to accept history and not delude ourselves in the devil's hall of mirrors." Ruth took a deep breath as she said it could take a long time before she found her way out.

Richard looked back at Helen. He chose her, both because of and despite Emma. The storyline needed Emma and also needed him to have turned her away. It was time for her to be raked into the flower bed where the forget-me-nots grew. He stared at Helen and could see the outline of Emma's face cheekily pulling her tongue out at him. He told Ruth that ideas don't have to be perfect to be good.

Bob could hear the conversation upstairs. He walked back in. "Praise the Lord, Alleluia. The best is the enemy of the good in this life. Nothing's perfect. Light can only get in through a crack. Is the good old Church of England about to split into its different wings, Richard?"

Richard answered that maybe someday they'll be welcomed into the bosom of the Catholic Church.

"I prefer Wendy's bosom," Bob said. "Richie seems to as well."

The next day, Monday, neither Bob nor Wendy were working. After a leisurely breakfast, they drove home to Nether Piddle with Alice, Richie and Hattie. They stopped at Cornbill's on the way to buy a Christmas tree and some new decorations including a handsome carved crib scene. 'God with us' was inscribed above the stable door.

They spent the afternoon putting up the tree and decorations. In the evening Alice sent two notes up the chimney to Father Christmas, one for Richie. Eventually, tired out, she went to sleep. Bob lay her down in her cot, whispering: "The hopes and fears of all the years are met in thee tonight, my little bobby dazzler."

* * *

The following afternoon Jane and Geoff arrived back in the Sefton Park flat after a boozy lunchtime with colleagues. Jane made two cups of tea as Geoff plonked himself down. She put biscuits from the new

313

biscuit barrel onto a plate. On an impulse, she dropped the lid to hear the sound as it shattered. Geoff came in to see what was going on. He swept the pieces into the dustpan, picked up the two cups and the plate of biscuits and carried them to the living room as Jane darted off to the spare room to Skype one of her collaborators at next week's conference in Stockholm. She shut the door. The computer was already turned on. Her call was answered straightaway in Kolkata.

"Sorry I didn't call on Sunday," she said. "By the time Geoff and I were back here you'd have been in bed. Caste differences will make a pleasant change."

Pratap replied in an almost inaudibly low voice that he wasn't going to be able to stay on long and that he'd email the latest draft the next morning. He'd not be able to go sightseeing with her on the free day. "My wife is jealous," he whispered more fiercely. "She says that she doesn't know if you're an enchantress or a devil, and has asked me to catch the early flight home. I've told her that she's being stupid and that nothing untoward has occurred. That made things worse."

Jane was both pleased and horrified. "I'm both. I'll see Stockholm with Doreen. It can only be from you that your wife has any idea what I'm like. Does she know how old I am and that she's being silly?"

"I don't think she's being silly and you're right, she must have got the idea from me. I'll have to ring off."

Jane sat at her desk for a few moments and then wrote in her diary: "Am I reduced to this? Being falsely maligned? Pratap adds a bit of noise to my life, the opposite of what he'd want to do. What's worse is that I feel happy that I can still cause trouble. Save me, Geoff, save me."

Jane distanced herself from Pratap from that point. She danced down the stairs to find Geoff asleep in the armchair. She kissed his forehead. He woke up, smiled and said: "You'll always come to love like a refugee." Jane recognised that to be Leonard Cohen.

"Bob liked him too," she remembered. "Tuneful he wasn't."

* * *

A hundred miles away, Bob shuddered, but not because he was out of tune with Jane. He was showing old family photos to Wendy. There was one of his Dad, Sailor Jack, in his navy uniform.

* * *

Wendy and Bob were never to have a cross word with each other or with their children. The only shadows to be cast were the deaths in old age of Hattie and Sheba. Then, in the year 2019, an hour before daylight on what should never have become a bright summer's day, Wendy went off to a local dig with Steve. Bob was looking after Alice and Richie. Although Steve didn't have a Harley-Davidson to go out cruising on, he did have a high-powered sports car. They zoomed off from the house in Nether Piddle. Only thirty seconds later there was a great bang. Bob told Alice to look after Richie as he chased out of the door. Some joker had pinched the lamp from the front of a rubbish skip. Steve was killed instantly. Wendy died a few minutes later, carried away from life in Bob's arms. He insisted to the police on telling Alice and Richie personally, the waters of the River Wyre engulfing him as his voice struggled through the dreadful words. He then bravely rang Audrey and Walter, before returning to the scene to see Wendy off to the mortuary, the sad-eyed lady of the Cotswolds never able to make him happy again. A neighbour stayed until Bob returned to the children, sobbing their hearts out for their lovely Mum. He told them she was the sassiest, kindest, gentlest soul ever to walk this planet before himself breaking down. The tears stripped everything from his soul but what mattered, which would never leave him, or Alice, or Richie. After ten precious years, ten beautiful years, the Great Author of all had decided to wreck the rest of Bob's life, Audrey's life, Walter's life. He'd resolved that Alice and Richie would never know their Mum as grown-ups. She didn't see what they made of themselves. And they never knew why. Bob pondered if this was the only way the stories would entangle. He could see many other ways. Must all happiness pay? Sometimes it felt like divine retribution, and sometimes a price God had paid to the devil. Bob shook his head as he told the children that the Lord giveth and the Lord taketh away.

In accordance with her wishes, Wendy was cremated for her ashes to be buried with Bob at a later date. It was a time for deaths. Frank died a week later in the Nursing Home as a result, Bob liked to think, of Wendy persuading the Author that it was time he was put out of his misery. Ethel Metcalfe lay down her weary head for the last time in January. Bob bought her house in St Chad's and in spring he and the two children moved in next door to Ruth and family. By autumn, as the leaves fell, Audrey and Walter left Cheltenham to go to live with them too, the only family they had left.

They all had to learn to put the horror to one side and carry on with the business of living, Bob sometimes with the aid of a large Scotch. He took up helping with teaching physics at the local academy school. Some six years later, with Alice and Richie teenagers, Audrey and Walter died within a few months of each other. The following Christmas, Ruth organised a Christmas day for the family, held in Bob's house as he had the bigger dining room. On the sideboard was the crib scene from when God was with them. Sophie, Robert and mob came up from Richmond. Jane and Geoff drove over from Liverpool. Lunch was good fun. Before the scheduled present giving, Bob picked up the crib, smiled at Alice and said: "This must always be yours, my little bobby dazzler." Then his face started to crumple. He was looking at Jane. She gave him a frightened, sideward glance as he fell. He was dead before he hit the floor. His broken heart could beat no longer.

In early January, along with Wendy's ashes, he was buried under the green, green grass of St Chad's cemetery, with a bare lilac tree in the field alongside. There was a power cut during the service, the veil rent in twain as his life had been, until he'd cross-stitched the exposed threads together again. Harry Jackson sent Ruth a deeply religious sympathy card. Ruth and Robert clung on to each other as tightly as they did during those first days in Mossley Hill. Alice and Richie followed suit. They didn't know what had hit them. In his eulogy, Richard, hoping against hope that he'd meet his great chums again, reasoned that Bob had always known where he was from and that's where he'd gone, back with Wendy. Jane buried her head deep into Geoff's overcoat as Mary lent her an already tear-stained handkerchief. There was a pretty ring-collared dove hopping near to the grave. Richard imagined that down below the Son was saying to Satan, "These are mine now."

In the pub afterwards, with the defeat of death not seeming quite as heavy, Ruth and Jane were together smiling at the thought of Bob being reunited with all his ancestors. Sophie whispered to Robert that if he'd found Sailor Jack, maybe he'd met her Grandparents. Wendy's death didn't feel so bad to Alice and Richie once they were orphans. In their minds, their parents were back together, either nowhere or somewhere. They went to live next door with Ruth, Rachel and Ben. Tom and Charlotte had moved away by then. Ruth was brilliant, tailor-made for the role of pulling them through.

Helen and Richard inevitably had their share of family problems as their children made their way in life. They handled these well enough that they would say the years had been kind to them. The occasional fear of death could be put hastily to one side. In the early summer of

317

2034, Richard shuffled off his mortal coil. Godson Richie, with Alice keeping him company, walked out of a country church in Hertfordshire some distance behind the Shackleton family. A distraught Helen was in front accompanied by all her children and grandchildren. Richard's coffin was lowered into the clay earth of the grass graveyard, ready for the sod to be laid o'er him. The drum didn't beat slowly but at Helen's request their son James played 'O mein Papa', Eddie Calvert style, on his trumpet at the graveside, not missing a note despite the tears streaming down his cheeks. The main party started to move off. Alice and Richie were in no hurry as they'd been invited both to the refreshments in the church hall and then on to Hummills with close family. As they paid their last respects at the graveside, a small, elderly woman, previously seated head-bowed at the back of the church, walked up and gently dropped a red rose onto the coffin.

Helen doubled back a good twenty yards to talk to her. "Richard would have been delighted that you've come, Emma."

"I couldn't stop myself. Charles died a few months ago, you know."

"I read the obituaries."

Emma picked up some earth and tossed that in too. "It's bleak, stuck at the end of that street of hope I never dared go down. Knowing this guy isn't around any longer is unbearable. I shouldn't say this to you but I wish I'd had a child by him when we were young."

"I'm pleased you didn't, but it's brave that you admit it. Will you come back to the house?"

"Thank you, that's kind, really kind, but I'd better go home to feed the pigs."

On that note, Emma walked away. She smoothed her black skirt as she climbed into the waiting limousine.

Richie was carrying in his pocket the prayer book godfather Richard had given him on his confirmation. On his desk at home was the Bible brought on his christening day, placed next to the birthday card sent a few months ago, with its message in shaky handwriting: 'I'm jiggered, cocker. I've had to give up the preaching stuff. Soon I'll either be finding out that I was right or I'll just be gone. Ask my Helen if ever you or Alice need any help.'

Helen introduced Alice and Richie to the trumpeter, James Shackleton, unmarried in his late thirties like his Dad. James told them that, as he was playing, he could hear Richard singing the words as if to his own Dad, Michael. Helen looked cynical, but did say that her one consolation was that someday she'd be with them in nowhere land. Back at Hummills, James asked Alice out for dinner. A year later, she moved down for a museum curator job in London and to live with him.

# RECESSIONAL

Richie, with Ruth the last still to be based in St Chad's, is a physicist at the nuclear research place near Warrington. At last there's a new man in Ruth's life. Richie feels awkward and knows it's time for him to move out. It's going to be a wrench to leave St Chad's for the flat he's bought in Knutsford. In the mirror, he looks as big and bold as his Dad. In his head he feels small and lost.

He's recently finished his early, big love affair. Alice has been his big sister through everything. He visits her and James in London one weekend. Helen comes for Sunday lunch and reminisces happily about the days leading up to his birth. Those days made her, she says. Richie promises to rewrite his Dad's Swarbrick family history to include it all. To help, James gives him a copy of the Shackleton one written by Richard. Back in St Chad's, Ruth lends him Jane's intimate and unexpurgated diaries to make him blush, bequeathed to her on Jane's death a few months ago.

The years when his Mum was with him are a golden age that can't return. He listens to his Dad's music spanning eighty years, recovered from an old computer. Although sometimes the words hang from his head like jewels and binoculars on a gauche tourist, he can feel how they were written in his Dad's soul.

His research is in using accelerators for medical applications. His nephew Patrick, eerily a year older than him, is an environmentalist. Brought up in Richmond by wealthy parents, he's inherited the earth and a bag to put it in. Richie has one foot stuck in the mud of the past, trapped in the unrealisable promise of 1963.

It's early June. Alice is pregnant and she's marrying James next month. The baby's birth is contingent on two guys managing to scrounge some Christmas leave in the last year of the war. The wedding in a couple of weeks will be in St Chad's. The birds will be singing their songs but they do that for everybody. The bells will ring out joyously for both families, and only for them, eternally entangled.

Richie walks one last time through his personal wilderness, the footpaths of the Fylde. They're anything but sparse. The cow parsley, recently out in wondrous profusion along the verges, with the May blossom filling the hedges above, is dying back. The field over the hedge has grasses growing tall, with thistles and wild flowers of all descriptions poking their heads through in a beauty that nobody could describe as chaos. Feeling humbled that he knows the names of so few, he ponders why there's so much, why there are so many. As he looks in all directions, everything he sees can be numbered, however big the number is. No-one can count to infinity. It's outside the system, beyond physics, beyond maths. How is it then that he's surrounded by universal, or should that be multiversal, scepticism?

Today his soul dares to dream that the spirits of his parents and his godfather are with their ancestors. He feels the spark of his own being as being in that realm too, with the part of him born in time about to be happy again. In his mind's eye, he can see his Mum and Dad sauntering across green meadows rich with daisies and buttercups, their dogs swishing through the long grass, Richard a little behind carrying the picnic basket. Wendy tries to blow the seeds off a dandelion and fails. Their faces crack into everlasting smiles.

Richie sings the lyrics of 'Where the blue of the night meets the gold of the day' gently to himself and when he's finished he can still hear Bing's cheerful whistle. That crackly old song is from well before his Dad's time. It must have meant something for it to be in his music library. Richie knows that his Dad could hear Sailor Jack doing the whistling.

Richie's hope isn't sure and certain. Viewed from outside the system, the lives of his parents and godfather could stand on their own without the need for more. Although tinged with and singed by disappointment, they'd won more battles than they'd lost. Bob and Richard were lucky to be part of the one generation of lower class provincials in England ever to get a real shout. Bewildered by the inevitable loss of meaning, as much the last Victorians as the first baby boomers, they'd been protected by their innocence as they'd clung on tightly to their optimism. The one piece of luck his brilliant Mum had in her adult life was in finding herself by helping them do that. She'd been the lone soldier on the cross. But even she couldn't win the final war on her own. He prays they've all been spoken for.

He looks to the sky for a sign. He can't see any epiphany or hologram. He's a decent quick bowler but, unlike James and his five uncanny wickets, he still hasn't even a hat-trick to his name. Is the real purpose of the universe to produce meaning, he thinks? And is that meaning the thing that demonstrates a will behind it all? Or is he simply one bounce further down the path than his parents, two on from Sailor Jack, and three from the original Alice Smith?

It's the people themselves and not only their story that he wants to live again. The best and worst that can be said about that is it ain't necessarily so. He goes home to load up the car for Knutsford with an unknowing smile on his face.

11268626R00189

Printed in Great Britain
by Amazon.co.uk, Ltd.,
Marston Gate.